WITHIN
THE HEART OF
WICKED
CREATURES

WITHIN THE HEART OF WICKED CREATURES

Rima Orie

Translated by Laura Watkinson

INK ROAD

First published in the UK in 2024 by Ink Road

INK ROAD is an imprint and trade mark of Black & White Publishing Ltd
Nautical House, 104 Commercial Street, Edinburgh EH6 6NF

A division of Bonnier Books UK
4th Floor, Victoria House, Bloomsbury Square, London, WC1B 4DA
Owned by Bonnier Books, Sveavägen 56, Stockholm, Sweden

Originally published by Uitgeverij Moon, part of
Overamstel Uitgevers – Amsterdam, The Netherlands
Published by agreement with agentur literatur Gudrun Hebel, Berlin.

The publisher gratefully acknowledges the support of the
Dutch Foundation for Literature.

Nederlands
letterenfonds
dutch foundation
for literature

A CIP catalogue record for this book is available from the British Library.

ISBN: 978 1 78530 495 8

1 3 5 7 9 10 8 6 4 2

Typeset by Data Connection
Printed and bound in Great Britain by Clays Ltd, Elcograf S.p.A.

For my parents
For my grandparents
For my ancestors
They fought
so that I
can live this life

AUTHOR'S NOTE

Within the Heart of Wicked Creatures is a story about survival, belonging and a history that isn't known by most of the world. The country Awaran in the novel is based on the history of Suriname, a small country in South America, and the home country of my parents. For almost three centuries it was colonised by the Dutch, who shipped people from West-Africa, Indonesia, China and India to Suriname to work for them on plantations. This is why Suriname is such a colorful mix of different cultures.

I've woven the different cultures of Suriname, which I grew up with, and the brutal history of Dutch colonisation into this dark fantasy. But none of the characters, incidents and/or backstories are based on real people and events.

Since Awaran is colonised, like Suriname once was, topics such as slavery, racism, bodily harm, violence and warfare are addressed and/ or mentioned in the book.

· I ·

WHEN THE MOON BLEEDS, GUARD YOUR SOUL

1

'THOSE WHO ARRIVE DURING the blood moon are cursed for all eternity.'

It was a saying that Priya Chkadhari had grown up hearing.

Before the red moon was high in the sky, the inhabitants of Disin retreated to their homes, the korjalen, dugout canoes, were pulled to the riverbank, and the sandy paths, usually well trodden, were deserted.

The dark clouds above their heads were all that separated them from the starry sky. From the moon, which might turn blood red any moment now. They didn't know exactly what would happen if they didn't reach home in time. The village elders told them just enough to feed their imagination: primeval creatures, blood children, vengeful spirits, lost souls that roamed the paths. Would they kill them? Eat them up? Possess them? They were not told. The story always ended just before that point, with a warning that they should never be outside when the moon changed colour.

And this time they were late. They were very late.

Their feet rhythmically hit the path, which was slippery from the big raindrops and black with mud. Priya, the eldest, carried the largest basket on her head as they ran home. She was deliberately holding back, so that she could stay behind her sister and brother and keep an eye on them.

Panting, his face twisted in pain, Umed stopped to massage his shoulder. The full bags on his back swung back and forth with the movement.

'Come on! Hurry up!' shouted Ishani. The basket she was carrying looked far too heavy for her tall, slender figure and lay at a crooked angle on her black curls. A flash of light lit up her brown skin. 'We're already late because of your dawdling.'

'*My* dawdling? We set off late because you insisted on studying for that "oh so important" test,' replied Umed. 'Anyway, it's raining so hard that the moon's hidden. And look, we're already at the strangled tree.' He wiped one hand over his wet cheek and pointed at a huge tree covered with clinging vines. 'We're almost there.'

'Yes, almost,' said Priya, peering up from under her basket. She blinked as the raindrops fell into her eyes. Concealed behind the clouds, the moon was indeed almost invisible. Even so, an ominous feeling settled in the pit of her stomach. 'But as soon as the blood moon shines, the clouds will disappear. They won't protect us anymore.'

Not that Priya actually needed their protection, but she was worried about her brother and sister.

'And what then?' Resting his hands on his thighs, Umed looked up. He was still breathing heavily. A flash of lightning illuminated his face. His eyes had their usual dreamy look, as if his spirit were wandering through other worlds than their own. 'What will actually happen then? Will the Bakru come to get us?'

'Umed,' Ishani whispered angrily when she heard the name of the evil dwarf spirit.

'What? No one will tell us the whole story. I'm just curious,' Umed muttered back at her. The dreamy look had gone from his eyes. He hitched the bags up onto his shoulders and walked past her. The two girls followed him.

The stars above their heads seemed to be going out one by one, making it darker and darker. Priya felt her stomach clench. What little time they had left was slipping away. She was starting to wonder if they were going to make it home.

'Come on! Hurry!' she said, trying not to sound panicked. Ishani started running faster. Priya grabbed Umed's arm, pulling him along as she chased after Ishani.

The dirt path was bumpy and strewn with stones. On a sharp bend, the wicker basket wobbled precariously on Ishani's head before she regained her balance.

The large raindrops turned into a fine drizzle. With every step she took, Priya's heart pounded louder, harder, faster. Still holding Umed's arm in an iron grip, she pulled her brother along so fast that his feet were almost dragging over the ground. His cries of protest had long since died away. He was just doing his best to keep up with her.

In the distance, their house emerged from the trees and bushes – a crooked wooden hut with closed shutters on the windows and built on high stilts so that it wouldn't float away when the river, the Cotari, burst its banks.

A faint light shone out through the cracks of the shutters. On the wooden front door, as with every other house in Disin, there was a circle drawn in charcoal, with three linked circles inside. It was the sign that the villagers used to ward off the creatures that roamed the night during the blood moon.

Umed stumbled. Priya felt him fall. Felt his arm slipping from her fingers. He landed on the ground, followed by the basket on her head, which crashed down beside him.

Startled, Ishani turned to look back at them, but then her gaze was drawn to the sky.

'Keep running,' Priya shouted after her. She didn't need to look up to know they were already too late. Ishani's face said it all. 'Get inside!'

Ishani hesitated.

'Go!' screamed Priya.

Ishani did as she was told.

Priya crouched beside Umed. As she grabbed hold of him, she couldn't help glancing up. The clouds drifted away, and she caught a first glimpse of the red moon.

The crickets fell silent. The birds stopped singing. The screeching of the monkeys stopped abruptly.

Everything was hushed.

'Pri . . .' Umed just managed to grab hold of her salwar before his eyes rolled back in his head. His hand dropped to the ground.

'Umed. Umed!' She gave him a good shake. When he didn't react, she lifted up his limp body, draped his arm around her shoulders and stood up. The hairs on her skin were standing on end. As more of the moon appeared, everything around them grew quieter and quieter. Unnaturally quiet.

Priya started running again, dragging Umed along with her. Her eyes were fixed on the front door, which Ishani had reached just in time. The edge of the roof had shielded her from the light of the blood moon. The door opened a crack. A hand pulled Priya's sister inside. Then the door slammed shut.

Priya could hear the river flowing in the background, but now other, strange sounds began to fill the stillness. A rhythmic chattering. A hissing sound. Snarling.

The wind rose, blowing Priya's hair into her wet face. Umed's skin glowed red in the light of the moon.

Priya felt something approaching.

'Please . . .' she mumbled, trying to run faster. Umed almost slipped again. She clamped her fingers around his arm, pulling him up and lifting him onto her back, her heart pounding like crazy.

There was a thunderous clap behind them. Then another. The ground shook beneath Priya's feet.

They'd reached their house, but they still needed to climb the stairs. Her hands shaking, Priya tried to keep hold of Umed as she climbed. They were too slow; he was too heavy, too limp.

'No,' she croaked. It couldn't end like this.

In desperation, she focused on her curse, which was shifting restlessly within her, a ball of energy. She clumsily tried to get a grip on Umed's body with her curse, so she could force him to move by himself. It didn't work. She had no idea what she was doing. Normally she held her curse in, keeping it hidden from everyone.

'Come on,' she growled, biting her bottom lip as she tried to ignore her nagging headache.

As all of her focus was on Umed, her foot slipped, and she went crashing to the ground. Umed dropped from her shoulders, falling beside her. A stabbing pain shot through her shoulder. All she could hear was her own heart hammering inside her chest.

She couldn't think.

In blind panic, she scrambled to her feet. She only just managed to stop herself from glancing over her shoulder at the creature that was coming for her little brother.

Not for her, of course. The stories of the village elders, of her mother, of the men and women who guarded their village, echoed in her mind. During the blood moon, the darkest of creatures clawed a way into their world. Forgotten and evil spirits came to call on them. And the cursed ones were born.

Like Priya.

No, it was Umed who was in danger. Priya had heard enough stories about the monsters of the blood moon to know that normal people were not safe from them. But Priya was not normal.

She pulled Umed to her, shielding him with her body. The pounding footsteps had almost reached them. It would be impossible to reach their front door in time. Priya braced herself.

'Sorry, Umed,' she whispered.

Before she could look up and stare the monster in the face, a movement attracted her attention. In the distance, on the smooth river, there was a korjaal, bathed in the red light of the blood moon. A solitary figure stood upright in the middle of the boat.

Priya's eyes grew wider. It was not a spirit or a monster. So, it must be a human. But not a normal human – they didn't go outside during the blood moon. It must be a blood child. Like her.

Priya's breath caught in her throat.

The pounding footsteps stopped, and the wind died down.

Something had changed. Priya stood up and quickly hoisted Umed onto her back. Pain shot through her shoulder, but she didn't let go. With one hand clutching both his wrists so that he wouldn't fall, she carried him up the stairs.

Breathing hard, she reached the porch. The door flew open and their mother, her face and hands covered with cloths, stepped forward to catch hold of Umed. She said nothing, but her dark eyes, just visible between the layers of protective fabric, bored into Priya's. Priya saw anger there. Disappointment. Fear. Together, they pulled Umed to his feet and took him inside.

As soon as the door slammed shut behind them, Priya knew she was in serious trouble.

2

'WHAT *WAS* THAT?'

Priya had landed on all fours. Every muscle in her body felt tense and sore, and she couldn't stop shivering. Umed lay on the wooden floor with his legs and arms outspread, and their mother had taken charge of the situation. His face was wet from the rain, and there were twigs and leaves in his black hair.

Outside, they heard a loud thump. The house shook on its foundations. Somewhere behind them in the house, something fell rattling to the ground.

Priya crawled over to Umed and held him tightly. 'What's wrong with him? Why is he unconscious? Is it because of the blood moon? Has he been possessed by a primeval creature?'

The stories that Master Haripersad had told her echoed in her mind. She tried to remember what she knew about primeval monsters, as if identifying where she'd gone wrong might help.

Primeval monsters were attracted to violence on a large scale, so it seemed unlikely to have been that kind of creature. The people of Disin would never risk that. Violence happened, of course, but they always took care not to escalate conflicts. Unlike the warrior villages on the edge of the rainforest, Disin didn't have the means to distract or to stop a primeval monster. But anyway, Priya had never heard that primeval monsters could harm humans from a distance. On the other hand, only monsters could make the earth move that way. So, if it wasn't a monster, what was it? Not for the first time, Priya was frustrated that so little was known about the monsters that appeared during the blood moon.

Another heavy thump made the house shake again, sending their mother crashing into the doorframe.

She didn't respond to Priya's questions, just staggered over and sank to her knees beside Umed. Reaching out to her son, she pushed Priya away with her shoulder, her narrow, oval face tense and her lips pale. She touched his cheek, her hand trembling.

'Umed? Open your eyes, sweetheart.'

He lay there motionless.

Her mouth turned into a hard line. 'Help me carry your brother.'

Priya grabbed Umed under his armpits, ignoring the pain in her shoulder. The noise outside increased as they carried Umed into the room.

The shutters on the windows rattled in the wind. In the centre of the room, the kokolampoe, casting its faint light, bounced up and down with every thud. Ishani was rummaging through the pots and pans in the cupboard. There was an empty gourd beside her feet.

Priya and her mother carefully laid Umed on the rug. Their mother stroked Umed's clammy cheek with the back of her hand. He shook uncontrollably, his eyes darting around behind his half-open lids.

'What can I do to help?' Priya asked more urgently. 'What's wrong with him? And what *was* that outside? I've never seen or heard anything like that before, and I've often been outside during the blood moon. Mother?'

Priya reached out to touch Umed's face, but her mother knocked her hand away. 'You exposed him to the red moon,' she hissed. '*That* is what happened.'

Another thud shook them back and forth.

'Yes,' said Priya, withdrawing her hand. She tried not to let it show how much the rejection hurt. Her mother's reaction didn't come as a surprise. Priya had been expecting it ever since she saw the blood moon appear and her brother stumbled. Even so, the pain in her heart seemed to have a will of its own. She desperately tried to contain the feelings of guilt – and anger, hurt and frustration – that came rolling in like heavy rainclouds. It was her fault, she knew that. She swallowed. 'I'll fetch some blue water and cloths,' she said, standing up.

'No need,' Ishani said, walking over with some clean, white cloths and the gourd, which was now filled to the brim with blue water.

'I didn't mean for us to be out so long,' Priya blurted, wringing her hands. 'I . . . I . . .'

'You knew what the dangers were. You knew Umed and Ishani wouldn't be safe out there, but still you . . .'

'Here you go, Mama,' said Ishani. Priya watched, frozen, as her sister crouched down, dipped the cloth in the blue water and handed it to their mother. Even after what they'd just been through, Ishani looked calm and collected. The image of a perfect daughter. Only her shoulders, which were slightly raised, revealed that she was tense.

Their mother took the cloths and dabbed Umed's damp face. With her other hand, she took some herbs from among the folds of her yellow sari and mumbled something as she sprinkled them into the blue water. Again she dipped the cloths into the water and patted Umed's skin to draw the negative energy out of his body.

'Take off his clothes,' their mother commanded.

Priya jerked into motion but stopped when she saw that Ishani was already obeying their mother's instruction. Priya was the one who was cursed, the one who could play people as if they were musical instruments, and yet she'd never been able to refuse an order from her mother.

Priya had made a mistake. An unforgivable one. Every fibre in her body screamed that she should have been faster, that she should have dragged Umed along with her sooner, that she should have done whatever it took to prevent Umed lying there like that.

She hadn't done it on purpose, but that didn't matter.

As the eldest daughter, it had been her job to protect Umed and Ishani. Her mother had been counting on her. She had looked straight at Priya when she said they shouldn't be outside when night fell. That Priya of all people should know why. And Priya had failed.

The blue herbal water didn't wake Umed up, but the shivering eased and he seemed to calm down. The unhealthy yellow sheen didn't leave his skin though.

'Is he going to wake up soon?' asked Ishani. She had lit some incense, and the pungent smell was stinging Priya's nose.

'I don't know,' their mother replied. The frown line between her eyebrows had grown deeper. 'Victims of the blood moon react unpredictably. I'll have to call in a healer from one of the other villages if he doesn't wake up by tomorrow. Hopefully they'll be able to tell us more. The best thing would be to send for a healer from Kuwatta, but we can't afford that.'

'Maybe . . .' said Priya hesitantly, leaning over Umed. 'Could I force him to wake up?'

It came out tentatively, but she was serious. There had to be something she could do to help, didn't there? She rarely used her curse, and she certainly never did it deliberately. Mostly because it would mean putting herself and her family in danger, but also because she didn't really know how. No one who was aware of her curse – and that was only her family – understood exactly how it worked. All they knew for certain was that she could force other people to do things.

But right now, Priya was desperate and prepared to do whatever was necessary. Not only to save her brother's life, but also to put right her own mistake.

'What?' Ishani looked up at her, shocked. 'No! You know how dangerous it is.'

'As long as I don't give an order that hurts him, it should be alright,' said Priya. 'It's worth a try. I'll be careful.'

'No.' Their mother's voice felt like a lash from a whip. 'You've already come close to killing him with your curse.'

Priya clenched her teeth, more to stop her tears than to hold back her words. She didn't want to give the world her tears. She'd cried all throughout her childhood because she was a daughter of the blood moon. All those years, she had prayed to the Suryan gods for a different life. But nothing had changed.

Quite the opposite: her emotions only made things worse.

Priya was good at holding back her curse now. It was a matter of controlling her emotions. But when she was younger and still exploring the world, she reacted instinctively to her surroundings, as all children do. Of course, her parents had told her from a young age that she must never use her curse. But she was a child. And children don't always understand the weight of words.

The dark memories, carefully hidden in a small room that she usually kept tightly shut, had come clawing their way out one day when she was three years old and her stomach was aching with hunger. Two children, just a little older than she was, had walked past with some dry bread and a banana. She'd had no idea what was happening, was consumed only by her own hunger and longing, but then they gave her all their food.

Or that time, a year later, when she was playing with some other children by a stream. One of the boys had been bothering her for a while. She couldn't remember exactly what he'd said, just that she was angry with him. And then he jumped into the stream.

She tried to push the memories away, but every time, another one took its place. A year later, when they had just come to live in Disin. Without Father. Their mother had her hands full with Priya, Ishani and Umed. Priya, who already received little enough attention, was ignored even more from then on. After all, she was already five years old and could feed herself, wash herself and do chores around the house. Umed, though, spent most of his time crying and constantly demanded their mother's attention. It got so bad that Priya couldn't stand the shrill sound of his screeching anymore. She just wanted him to be quiet, but instead she'd made him stop breathing. If their mother hadn't come in . . . She'd taken one look at Umed and Priya and given Priya such a shaking that something inside her – she didn't know what – had shifted and she'd lost her grip on her brother. If she hadn't, Umed might not have survived.

Priya felt her breath racing. But that was the past. She wasn't the same person anymore. She'd learned how to keep her emotions and her curse under control, so that she couldn't hurt anyone.

'That wasn't the same. I was young and I didn't know what I was doing,' Priya said, with as much control as she could manage. It was precisely because of what had happened in the past that she wanted to do *more* to help this time. She would be careful and not take any risks. All she wanted Umed to do was to wake up. She couldn't hurt him that way. Could she?

The terrible thing was that she couldn't even say that for sure.

'And you know what you're doing now, do you?' her mother asked, eyebrows raised. When Priya didn't reply, she added, 'You are not touching him. If you want to help Umed, you should have done it before he ended up in this state.'

'It wasn't her fault we were late,' said Ishani, brushing a lock of Umed's hair from his forehead. 'She warned us many times. Umed didn't want to come.'

Priya looked up in surprise. Although Ishani didn't treat Priya the same way their mother did, she had grown up in Disin and, like the rest of Disin – of all of Awaran – she loathed blood children. Her disapproval of Priya took the form of cold disinterest. She tried to ignore the curse, and that meant she often ended up ignoring Priya herself. When there were conflicts between Priya and their mother, she never spoke up. Until today.

'He was distracted, as usual. Said he saw a tigri kati, and he wanted to follow it to make sure. I told him to hurry up too,' Ishani said. 'We were already late when we got to the cassava field.'

'You were late? Why?' asked their mother sharply. 'I told Priya to hurry and pick the cassavas with you two and come straight home.'

Ishani realised her mistake. 'Well, I mean, we would have made it if we were faster. Priya . . .'

Their mother's attention shifted, as Ishani had intended, towards Priya. 'Why didn't you hurry? You had plenty of time. You could have sent them home ahead of you, couldn't you? I've told you so many times that you have to keep them safe.'

'I . . .' The truth was that she couldn't bring all the cassavas home without help, and her mother wouldn't have been happy if she delayed the chore to the following day. She truly had believed they'd make it in time, though. It was a miscalculation on her part. But Priya knew her mother wouldn't want to hear her excuses.

'That's enough,' their mother said. 'I don't want to hear another word from you.'

Priya bit hard on her bottom lip to keep herself from speaking. They weren't late because of *her* but still their mother blamed Priya. Everything within her wanted to keep fighting, but there was no point. The only thing Priya's family ever wanted from her was her silence.

Umed was treated with more blue water while Priya watched without saying a word. She wasn't allowed to touch him. Murmuring, their mother ran the damp cloth all over his body. Her face was marked by deep lines of worry. A solitary tear escaped from the corner of her eye, sliding down her cheek. Priya stared at it, digging her nails into the palms of her hands. Inside, she could feel her curse swirling restlessly.

'Priya,' their mother said.

She looked up.

'Did anyone see you?'

A thud, quieter than before, made the dishes in the cupboards rattle.

'I . . . I don't know.' Priya didn't feel like telling her mother about the person in the korjaal. She knew it would only lead to more questions and accusations. 'I was just thinking about Umed.'

Her mother pursed her lips. 'And what about the cassavas? Where are they?'

'I dropped them.'

'Go and fetch them.'

Priya didn't react immediately, too startled by what her mother had said.

'Now?'

'When else? After the birds and the monkeys have eaten them all up? Of course I mean now.'

'But the blood moon . . . The creature outside . . .' Priya closed her eyes for a moment. 'Do you really want me to go outside now? While those monsters are still wandering around?'

'The blood moon has never hurt you. And it never will. Make sure no one sees you and bring those cassavas home. Our supplies are too low for us to waste good food. Do you understand?'

'Yes, Mother,' she replied. 'As long as there's nothing for me to fear outside.'

Her mother looked straight at her. Her dark eyes glinted. 'You know very well what's out there,' she said.

+++

Priya closed the door behind her and leaned against it.

It had stopped raining, but the air still smelled damp. The moon was high in the sky, turning the deserted paths a shade of red. Priya couldn't see any monsters. Or vengeful spirits. Or people. Nothing. Even the thuds had faded to a soft rumbling in the distance. Slowly, she breathed out.

You know very well what's out there.

Monsters like her. Wasn't that what her mother meant? Well, she wasn't wrong. The blood moon brought monsters with it. They'd always been there, deep in the rainforest, but they usually kept their distance from large groups of people. That all changed in the light of the red moon, though.

Priya suspected that the people of Disin didn't even know about some of the monsters out there. But the monsters they did know could be divided into three categories. Primeval monsters, forces of nature that destroyed all forms of life and had greater strength than any living creatures. Vengeful spirits, which devoured people until nothing of their souls remained, leaving them as dry husks. And blood children, who could play with humans' souls until their will was broken.

Priya shuddered at the thought of the monster that had just chased them. She couldn't say for certain what category it fell into, but it was most likely a primeval monster.

Her gaze swept over the other houses. The villagers didn't normally dare even to look out of their windows during the blood moon, but you could never tell. Priya didn't want anyone to see her. The thought of them watching her as she walked through the glow of the blood moon without being harmed gave her the chills. They might kill her on the spot.

She wasn't the only blood child around here, though. She knew there were others like her, and this time she'd seen the proof. The korjaal on the river. The lone traveller.

Priya gasped. She'd just realised that the other person had seen her too. But they couldn't know for sure what Priya really was. She was being chased by a monster. The stories said that blood children were left alone by vengeful spirits and primeval monsters. From that distance, there was no way the traveller could tell that the creature was probably pursuing only her brother and sister.

Besides, she realised as she headed down the steps from their porch, the person in the korjaal had also been unharmed by the blood moon. And they must have helped her. Why else did that monster suddenly disappear?

Her eyes moved back to the river. The korjaal was no longer on the Cotari.

She was alone.

'Those who arrive during the blood moon are cursed for all eternity,' she murmured – the mantra that every village child in Disin had grown up with.

Two monsters had set eyes on each other in the presence of a third monster.

There was no way she was going to tell her mother about it.

Right in front of their house, she saw some deep grooves in the soil, about the size of human hands. They couldn't have been made by the same monster that had produced those thunderous steps.

Priya gulped. She'd never encountered a primeval monster or a vengeful spirit before, so she'd always thought the stories were exaggerated, that the village elders were just trying to frighten children with gruesome stories so that they'd pay attention.

She bit her bottom lip hard. Now that she knew there was more truth to the stories than she'd thought, she didn't know what to think about herself. Deep inside, she was afraid that the monsters saw her as one of their own. Just like the villagers whispered to each other about blood children.

Cautiously, she walked along the dirt track, hiding under low-hanging branches whenever she could. Nearly all of the wooden houses on high stilts that she walked past were built in the same way as her own. Made from woven palm leaves, wood, clay and reed, with shutters on the windows and with most of the boards painted white, they were a combination of the colonial architecture on the coast and the style that the native and refugee population groups in Disin had developed themselves. On every front door, the villagers had drawn the circle symbol in charcoal.

Priya didn't know exactly where the symbol came from. Probably from the sacred writings of Suryan, the country that everyone in Disin originally came from.

That included Priya's mother. And her father.

The Suryans from the low castes had been a vulnerable group, with few prospects. The Freelanders had seen their chance and taken them, under false pretences and with empty promises, to distant Awaran, a colony of Freeland.

The Suryans believed a better life awaited them there. However, nothing could have been further from the truth; they found themselves in a different nightmare – one that meant working day and night on plantations, under dictators who considered them inferior.

Protests and uprisings against their bosses, the colonists, cost them their lives. That was what had happened to Priya's father. She could no longer remember what kind of person he had been, as he'd died when she was still young. Her only memories of him were vague and confusing fragments. A smile. His voice as he said her name. And his broken body, motionless on the ground, among the grass and the plants.

But he had protested against injustice. He had fought against a system that belittled and oppressed him. Her father was everything that Priya wanted to be. Brave and principled.

Priya reached the basket she'd dropped and bent down. With more force than necessary, she put the fallen cassavas into the basket.

She could understand why her mother had grown bitter. After Priya's father was killed, her mother fled into the rainforest with three young children. Her life had been a succession of disappointments and defeats.

Priya tried to let go of the thoughts of her mother and to focus on her task. It wasn't only the basket that had fallen to the ground. Umed's bags had also gone flying when he fell. She cautiously made her way along the path and stooped to pick up Umed's belongings.

She paused.

Beside the bags, there was a dark puddle.

Slowly, she squatted down. It was some kind of grey slime. She held out a finger and traced around the sand at the edge of the puddle. Her touch made the dark substance ripple. It stank of rotting meat. She clasped a hand over her nose and mouth and moved closer to take a better look.

In the middle of the puddle, there was a human tooth.

Priya jerked her head back.

She didn't have time to investigate or to think too hard about it. The moon was growing darker, and the blood moon would soon be gone. As soon as the moon regained its even, yellow-white colour, the villagers would leave their homes, at which point Priya needed to be back inside.

Priya hung the bags over her shoulder and picked up her basket. She carried it on her head, using the shadows to stay out of sight and keeping a close eye on the houses she passed.

When she reached home, she stored the basket and bags in the shed. Gradually, faces appeared at windows, and doors opened. Priya waited a couple of minutes before emerging and swiftly clambering up the wooden stairs.

The moon above her was white again.

3

THE SWELTERING NIGHT PASSED slowly and restlessly.

'He's drinking.' Their mother held up a small gourd to Umed's lips. This was the first time he'd accepted it. Umed drank with small sips. His eyes remained shut.

Ishani kneeled down beside him. She started dabbing Umed's forehead with a cloth again. He groaned quietly. 'That's good news,' she said, studying his face. 'Maybe it won't be long before he wakes up,' she added hopefully.

With her other hand, she turned a page of the book that was open beside her. No matter where she was, Ishani was already reading, always studying.

Priya stood in the doorway with a fresh bowl of water to which she was about to add some lumps of blue remedy. Just as she put down the heavy bowl, Umed started to choke. Spluttering, he knocked away the gourd. Their mother tried to get him to sit up a little, so that she could rub his back. His arms thrashed around.

Then he started screaming.

Everyone shrank away.

'What's wrong with him?' said Ishani, falling over backwards as Umed's elbow hit her in the face.

Umed screamed even louder. The raw sound hurt Priya's ears.

She rushed over to him. Together with her mother, she tried to hold Umed's arms to his sides.

'Hold him more tightly!' her mother shrieked.

He trembled at their touch. For a moment, they struggled to gain control of him. Then he seemed to lose his energy and collapsed against their mother. His screaming subsided. Foam appeared at the corners of his mouth, and his head slumped.

'Village elder Remasar's daughter was once exposed to the blood moon too,' said Priya. Umed's body felt unnaturally hot. 'Did she react in the same way?' Priya looked at Ishani, who was friends with the girl.

Ishani slowly shook her head. Her face had turned pale. 'I can't remember her ever . . . I know she didn't leave the house for a few days.' Her gaze was fixed on Umed. 'When I saw her again, she looked normal. I could ask her how she recovered.'

That sounded promising. Priya slowly breathed out and relaxed a little.

'That was different,' said their mother. She pulled Umed, who had gone limp again, bringing him closer to her, and he slipped from Priya's hold. His breathing was irregular. 'She was exposed to the blood moon for just a short time. A few seconds, no more.'

Priya's hope faded. Umed had been outside for a lot longer than that.

'The light of the blood moon must contain something toxic,' said Ishani.

A toxin that it seemed only monsters could tolerate, Priya thought bitterly. Then something occurred to her. 'You were exposed to it as well.'

Ishani was silent for a moment. 'Not really. I was already standing under the edge of the roof.' She looked away. 'Maybe it will help if we bathe him.'

Priya felt her curse writhing inside her again. She pressed her hand to her stomach in an attempt to push the strange sensation away. For the first time, she was afraid. What if Umed never woke up again? What if he stayed in this drowsy, semi-conscious state for ever?

'What are you doing?' Her mother's voice cut straight through Priya's thoughts. 'Don't just sit there. Make more blue water.'

+++

'I can see you.'

Master Haripersad's voice came from somewhere behind the thin wall of reeds and bamboo. His small hut was on the edge of the village, and it was one of the few not built on stilts, so there was always some doubt as to whether it would hold up if the river burst its banks. Everyone seemed to think it was a problem – everyone except Master Haripersad himself.

'There's no one else around,' he added in an amused voice. 'You can come in.'

Priya looked around one more time. The path to his hut was indeed deserted. She stepped forward, pushing aside some reeds and palm wood. A few weeks earlier, part of the roof had collapsed, and no one had cleared away the mess in the meantime.

It was dark in the hut, in comparison to the sun-drenched world outside. The sun was high in the sky, and Priya's skin gleamed with sweat. The cool interior did her burning eyes some good. She hadn't slept the night before.

Master Haripersad was sitting in his usual spot in the middle of the room, at the desk that one of the village elders had given him. Behind him, on rickety bookshelves and every flat surface, there were piles and more piles of books and loose sheets of parchment. The dank and musty smell in the room suggested that something was going mouldy.

And yet this was the only place in Disin that Priya liked to spend time.

'Where are your students?' Priya asked cautiously. 'Shouldn't they be studying?'

Master Haripersad gave a disapproving sniff. 'Not today. Right after a blood moon, they often don't show up. They think the lethal

· 23 ·

influence is still lingering in the air. It's stupid superstition, nothing more.'

His words didn't entirely ease Priya's anxiety. Her mother's lifelong warnings had made her instinctively avoid people. Particularly large groups of them. She couldn't stand out too much. If she did, people would start paying attention to her. And if they did that, there was more chance of them finding out Priya was a blood child. She didn't know what exactly that might mean, as she'd suppressed her curse, that strange, electric ball of energy inside her, all her life. But still she couldn't bring herself to spend much time around the other villagers. She'd grown used to being alone.

Master Haripersad turned a page, still making disapproving tut-tut-tut noises. He was one of the few teachers in Disin, and also the only one who would take anyone who knocked on his door under his wing.

The teachers who gave private lessons to the village elders' children generally didn't take him too seriously. They didn't believe that everyone in Disin deserved to be taught. But that didn't bother Master Haripersad. To annoy the other teachers even more, he'd started to refer to himself as a 'master', a title normally reserved for the instructors at Kuwatta, the largest military fortress in Awaran. Whenever he used the title in front of other teachers, Priya saw his eyes twinkling.

At her mother's request, Priya often took him food or other small necessities in exchange for the lessons he gave Ishani. So she knew the old man well, even though she hadn't studied with him for long.

Master Haripersad put down his book. It was held together by a fraying piece of string, which looked like it might give way at any moment. 'It's a mystery to me how they expect to cope at Kuwatta with that mentality. Have you eaten yet?'

'Yes,' Priya reacted automatically. She walked past him and started searching for books about the blood moon.

'Ha!' cried Master Haripersad. He struggled to his feet. Every time she saw the old man stand up, slowly and jerkily as if his joints were taking some time to start working, she imagined each of his vertebrae protesting as they stacked themselves back up. 'No need to answer that question. There's some food in the back for you.'

'There's no need.'

'Good food is always necessary, Priya. As I've told you so many times.' Muttering to himself, he disappeared into the back room.

Priya found a section about the blood moon in a book with an orange cover and a faded title. It was written in Awuran, the common language of the peoples of Awaran, which was a mixture of the different languages spoken throughout the country. Priya couldn't speak or read it very well. But she'd had a number of lessons with Master Haripersad, so with some puzzling she could figure it out.

Since time immemorial, the blood moon has appeared once every few lunar cycles in Awaran. Historians and astronomers have been able to ascertain that the blood moon appears only during a full moon. The night before a blood moon, the moon has a red rim, known as the ring of death. Care should also be taken on this night . . .

Priya leafed impatiently through the book. There. *Primeval monsters, vengeful spirits and blood children are immune to its dark light.*

'The blood moon?' Master Haripersad suddenly asked over her shoulder.

Startled, Priya dropped the book. 'The light,' she said, as soon as she could speak again. 'What exactly does it do to people?'

'Hm,' said Master Haripersad, handing her two sukru bakba. 'It won't kill you right away, but it's certainly harmful. Some people can handle it better than others. When the blood moon appears, there's something in the air.'

'And if someone's exposed to it, can they recover?'

He took the bananas from Priya's hands and peeled them. Then he held one up to her mouth. 'Eat.'

She wasn't hungry, but she still took a bite.

'Your sister came to ask me the same question. Is everything alright at home, beti?'

Priya was about to nod, to pretend nothing was wrong, but she felt herself shaking her head. 'It's Umed,' she whispered almost inaudibly. 'He was exposed to the blood moon and we don't know how to help him.'

Blood children were the real monsters, according to the villagers, but they were also a little wary of the victims of the blood moon. Anyone who had been outside during the blood moon might have been possessed by a vengeful spirit. Or maybe even by a primeval monster. Priya had never met anyone who had experienced anything like that, but stories didn't always have to be true to be believed. That was why people often kept it to themselves and sought help in secret if a loved one had fallen victim to the blood moon.

'Ah.' Master Haripersad's face clouded over. He nodded sympathetically.

'There must be something we can do,' said Priya, furiously leafing through a book. 'Umed can't be the first person to end up like that. And he won't be the last.'

'I'm sorry, beti.' Master Haripersad laid one hand on her shoulder. 'I've read every book in this room. They have plenty to say about possible treatments.' He sadly shook his head. 'But none of those treatments has actually worked on victims of the blood moon.'

Priya felt panic bubbling up within her. 'The daughter of one of the village elders recovered. So how did that happen?'

'By itself. Naturally. Not because of any medicine.'

'But there's no medicine at all that will work? How is that possible?'

'If only we knew,' said Master Haripersad with a sigh. 'Ultimately it seems to be the blood moon itself that decides whether someone survives or not.' He paused. 'The healers at Kuwatta probably know more. But Kuwatta never reveals its secrets. Maybe if your sister wins the contest . . .'

The contest. That subject was constantly coming up in combination with Ishani's name. Priya was sick of hearing about it.

The contest was how the general of Kuwatta, the leader of the rebel army, selected potential scholars. Once every few years he sent out a scholar with a number of soldiers to visit various settlements and oversee the contest. Winning this contest was the only way for an ordinary citizen to be admitted to the military fortress. Ishani was one of the people who studied day and night, desperately hoping to achieve this goal. The contest was the reason why teachers like Master Haripersad existed.

When Priya was younger and more naïve, she'd often dreamed about winning the contest herself.

The last time it had taken place in Disin, she'd been ten years old. In theory, it was possible to participate at that age. Everyone who wanted to, regardless of age, was eligible for the contest. But Priya hadn't been able to get away from her mother for long enough. It was also unlikely that she'd have stood a chance at that age. Probably not. Still, she'd watched with envy when a son of one of the village elders had been named as the winner.

'Yes, maybe,' said Priya. Her thoughts returned to Umed. If Kuwatta was really the only place with an answer, what were the chances that her brother would be cured?

+++

Feeling defeated, Priya headed home. The sun had long since disappeared behind the horizon and the moon had hidden somewhere among the clouds. But she didn't need any light; her feet knew the way. Even so, when she came to a crossing where traders and soldiers from the nearest warrior villages regularly passed, she made sure to stay out of sight. She didn't want them to notice her, a girl on her own.

A little further on, she passed the wooden sign with the name of their village on it. It had fallen to one side. Priya walked past swiftly, listening out for footsteps.

As she climbed the steps to their house, the front door burst open. Ishani stood panting in the doorway. Her brown eyes glistening in the darkness.

'What is it?' asked Priya. For one horrible moment, she thought Umed hadn't made it.

'No, no, it's not Umed,' Ishani said quickly when she saw the panic in Priya's eyes. 'There are korjalen coming this way. They're still a long way off, but I saw a flag waving. I think ... It's got to be ... The scholar from Kuwatta's about to arrive in Disin!'

Priya looked past her. In the distance, she saw the dark lines of the korjalen sailing down the river.

It could mean only one thing. This was what Ishani lived for. What the whole family lived for. Their only chance to make a difference, to work for a free Awaran. And to save Umed.

'The contest,' Priya gasped. Her heart skipped a beat. For a moment she thought only about herself and she was ten years old again, dreaming of Kuwatta. Then she roughly dismissed her own longing, pushing it away.

'Yes! It's the moment we've been waiting for. Oh, Pri ... I might be going to Kuwatta.'

4

A SLIVER OF CASSAVA fell to the floor.

Priya sat cross-legged, holding a knife and the vegetable in her hands. Between her legs, on her blue salwar, was a wooden bowl to catch the peeled chunks of cassava.

The kokolampoe in the middle of the room flickered.

Umed lay in the corner, across the room from her. He was under a window and the curtain fluttered lightly in the warm, damp breeze. A red wasp buzzed around the beams of the ceiling, where the first signs of a nest could be seen.

'It's a surprise, them suddenly turning up like this, but that doesn't matter. It's what we've been waiting for,' said Priya's mother. She was standing with her back to Priya. 'Do you know when they're going to make the announcement?'

Priya's grip on the knife tightened. All she really wanted to do was run outside to see the scholar. Just to catch a glimpse of him or her – that was all she was asking right now. But that meant risking a huge argument. Head bowed, she stayed where she was.

In the daylight, winning a place at Kuwatta was Ishani's dream, and it was supported by the whole family. But the nights were the time for Priya's own secret longing for the famed military fortress, and she didn't dare to share them with anyone.

Priya's gaze shifted to Umed, who wasn't moving. Why did the scholar have to arrive now of all times?

'No, I haven't spoken to anyone. The korjalen haven't moored yet,' replied Ishani. Her cheeks were pale pink and her dark eyes sparkled. 'We'll probably find out more tomorrow morning.'

'I'm sure they'll make the announcement about the contest soon after they arrive. I'm told they never waste much time,' their mother said quietly. She laid one hand on Ishani's arm. 'You don't need to do anything tonight. I'll take care of Umed.'

Ishani shook her head. 'Umed needs me.'

Priya peeled another piece of the cassava in her hand, running her fingers over the rind, searching for lumps and bumps and bits of skin that she'd missed. She tried to stop listening to the conversation between her mother and Ishani. But most of all, she tried not to think about the different lives Ishani and she would lead if her sister's dream came true.

Ishani, a scholar at glorious Kuwatta.

Priya, a prisoner in tiny little Disin.

She couldn't breathe.

'Umed has me and your sister,' said Priya's mother, her voice cutting through her thoughts. 'You should focus on the contest. Maybe it would help to visit Master Haripersad at sunrise for some final preparations.'

Ishani nodded slowly, looking at Umed, who seemed to be sleeping.

Priya put down the bowl and stood up. 'The cassavas are peeled.'

They both looked at her in surprise, as if they'd forgotten that Priya had been sitting there on the floor all this time.

'Is there anything else I can do?' she asked.

Their mother waved her away without looking at her. 'You can go.'

Priya's head felt heavy. In silence, she walked across the living room. Ishani kept her head turned away. Priya's bare feet made no sound. She headed to the room she shared with Umed and Ishani.

She piled up some hay in one corner and dropped down onto it. Bits of dried grass flew up into the air and came fluttering back down.

'I have a good feeling about this,' she heard her mother say. 'Maybe in a while, when you've saved up enough at Kuwatta and Umed is better, we'll be able to leave this country.'

'Leave?' echoed Ishani.

'Yes,' their mother said firmly. 'This isn't our country. Suryan is our home.'

'But, Mama, we can't just . . .'

Priya grabbed some hay and pressed it to her ears, so that all she could hear was her own breath and the thump of her heartbeat. For a moment, there was silence. For a moment, there was peace. Then the darkness behind her eyelids turned into loose teeth, into dark grey slime and into her brother's face, his dreamy eyes rolling back into the sockets.

+++

The next day, Priya got up before the sun rose and padded over to her little brother. Umed had not yet woken. But he was alive, he was breathing. He was still with them.

She gently stroked his cheek. His skin was still a sickly yellow colour, and he didn't respond to her touch.

Why? she thought again. *Why did all this have to happen now?* The blood moon, Umed and the scholar from Kuwatta.

Umed sighed softly. It was strange to see him like this, unconscious and silent. Normally, he couldn't sit still and paced restlessly along the dirt paths or around the house, wandering through his own imagination. And that sometimes got noisy, when yet again he failed to notice something, crashing into it and knocking things over. Umed's dreamworld had always been far more appealing to him than reality. Sometimes Priya wished she could disappear into his dreams too.

'I'm going to find a way to help you,' she swore, even though she knew there was little chance that she would actually find a solution.

Her mother and sister were still asleep when she began her daily chores. As she was sweeping the house, Ishani sleepily walked past her. The first rays of sunlight were creeping over the horizon. Ishani briefly kneeled beside Umed before leaving. The sound of the door closing woke Priya's mother.

'I've used more blue water on him,' said Priya, as her mother entered the room.

There was no reaction. Priya realised that something had changed. An unpleasant, tense feeling settled in her stomach. She said something else to her mother and didn't receive even a glance in response. No matter what Priya did, her mother was not going to speak to her. She barely even reacted to her presence. As if Priya were not worth her energy.

Priya made breakfast for herself and went outside, so she wouldn't have to endure the silence any longer. Out on the porch, she drank coconut water and ate her milk with rice, even though she wasn't hungry. She'd had to suffer her mother's silent anger before. After a few days, her mother usually got over it. But sadly that didn't make things any easier now.

In the early morning, the paths of Disin were bustling. The villagers wanted to get most of their work done before the sun was high in the sky and the heat became unbearable. They usually carried fishing nets and baskets back and forth, but today they were shifting logs and wielding axes.

The preparations for the contest had begun.

'I've seen her!' a small boy shouted, jumping up and down among the stream of people. 'I've seen the scholar!'

Priya stepped forward and listened closely, still scooping up her rice and milk.

'They're making the announcement sometime this afternoon,' a woman with a large basket of fish on her head said to a woman who went past with her arms full of wood.

Soldiers from Kuwatta were standing among the villagers. They were dressed in green uniforms with brown-and-black camouflage and had swords in the leather belts around their waists. Narrowing her eyes, Priya took a closer look. On each of their right arms, just below the shoulder, the emblem of a rising sun was woven into the fabric: the symbol of Kuwatta and, by extension, the entire rebel movement.

Many people wore that emblem. The soldiers from the warrior villages on the edge of the rainforest sewed the same symbol onto their clothes.

Priya tossed aside her scraped-out coconut. Her mother was right. If anyone would know how to help Umed, it was the healers from Kuwatta. But they never left the fort. So Priya would have to find a way to reach them instead.

Wiping her hands on her salwar, she went down the steps. As she reached the ground, she heard a chilling scream. Priya looked over to where the sound had come from. The people on the path were backing away. Logs fell to the ground and were kicked aside. Among the tangle of bodies, a group of men were dragging a woman along by her arms and her black hair. Her clothes were torn and covered in mud.

'No,' she sobbed. 'Not my baby. Please, spare my baby.'

A terrible realisation dawned on Priya.

One of the men had a bundle in his arms. A soft sound of crying drifted in Priya's direction.

The woman writhed on the ground, clawing in vain at the hands that pulled her along.

'Shut up,' snarled one of the men, yanking her hair. The woman groaned. 'You have given birth to a monster. That alone is a crime.'

'She's not . . .'

'And you kept it hidden,' said a woman, stepping out from behind the group of men. Her face was twisted in disgust. 'Not only did you bring a monster into our midst, but you hid it and endangered the entire village!'

The woman on the ground made a raw sound that seemed to come from deep inside her. 'No, no. She's just a little girl, a baby. She's not hurting anyone.' Her whole body shook as she spoke. 'I'll make sure she never harms anyone. I swear it on the Gods and the blood moon. Let me take her into the rainforest. We'll never come back.' Her words turned into a groan of pain as one of the men kicked her in the stomach.

Priya wanted to look away, but her body was frozen. A soldier from Kuwatta stood beside her, arms crossed and a grim expression on his face, watching the crowd jeering at the woman and her newborn daughter.

'Every blood child in Awaran is a potential danger,' said the man, who was holding the baby. He stepped over the child's mother. 'That's not a baby. That's a monster.'

Priya's ears were ringing.

'No,' screamed the mother, reaching out for her daughter. 'No!'

The man just walked away. The baby in his arms started wailing. She had only just been born. Had barely had time to taste life. And that brief taste was the only taste she would have anymore.

Priya took a shaky step back. This could have been her, over seventeen years ago. If her mother hadn't managed to outwit everyone.

One of the child's little arms slipped out of its wraps. The sight made Priya feel sick. Then furious. Her whole body was trembling.

She hated the villagers, Disin, all of Awaran. How did these people dare to call a baby a monster when they were the ones who were planning to murder a child? She wanted to yell in their faces. She wanted to snatch the baby and leave this cursed village.

Priya stepped forward and was about to block the way of the men who were dragging the woman. But a heavy hand landed on her shoulder. The soldier from Kuwatta pulled her back. From close up, she saw that he was Topuan, not Suryan, like the people of Disin. He had closely shaven hair, smooth brown skin and dark, watchful eyes.

'Stay out of it,' he said in Awuran, his gaze still fixed on the crowd.

Priya pulled her shoulder free.

'Get your hands off me,' she snapped at him in Suryan.

For a moment, his eyes flashed to her face. 'It won't make any difference,' he said coldly, in her language. 'With a crowd like this, there's nothing you can do.'

He stepped away from her to help an elderly man lift a log. The group had moved on, accompanied by loud cheers from those watching. Priya heard the woman howling for her daughter. She screamed as she was dragged away. She screamed as she disappeared into the trees. She screamed until the sound abruptly stopped.

And the silence that followed broke something inside Priya.

She started running. She had no idea where to. She just wanted to get away from everything. To disappear into the rainforest and never return to Disin. But she knew that wouldn't get her very far. Not only were there monsters, predators and poisonous beasts in the forest, but young girls who didn't take care often disappeared there, taken by people from other villages or attacked by robbers and lost forever.

She wouldn't survive the wilderness. She didn't know how. But she had to get away, no matter what it took.

Priya struggled through the crowd. The shouts of anger and irritation as she bumped into people passed her by in a blur.

The world around Priya faded away. She flew along the dirt paths.

Until she overlooked a fallen branch blocking the way and her foot caught on it.

Priya broke her fall with her hands and knees. Sand and stones grazed her skin as she came to a stop, groaning as a sharp pain flashed through her shoulder, which was already tender and sensitive from her previous fall.

She could hear the flowing water of the Cotari nearby.

Panting, Priya looked up. There were no concerned or angry people standing around her. No one snarling at her that she should watch where she was going. Somehow she actually wanted someone to pick a fight with her, so she'd have a reason to lash out at them. Furiously, she blinked her eyes.

Half of the village had gathered in the clearing by the river. Priya pushed herself to her feet.

At the very front stood some soldiers and a scholar from Kuwatta. The scholar stood in the middle of the clearing, surrounded by the soldiers and the villagers. She was taller than the soldiers on either side of her, but her stately demeanour also made her appear to rise above all the others.

Many people in Disin longed for the title she carried.

The soldiers who were trained at Kuwatta were taken only from the warrior villages on the edge of the rainforest or from large, influential settlements that trained soldiers all the time. At the fort, they were shaped into kaptens and bashas. Those were high ranks, not positions to which the people of settlements such as Disin, where no one learned to fight, could aspire. The village was too small and unimportant for that, its inhabitants too inexperienced in the martial arts.

The same did not apply when it came to scholars, however, who worked at the fortress as advisors and researchers. Remarkably, Kuwatta didn't discriminate when it came to the title of 'scholar'.

It didn't surprise Priya that people were staring at the scholar, partly because of her position, but probably also because of her appearance. Her smooth, dark skin, high cheekbones and wide nose indicated that she was of Luanan descent. Occasionally, the villagers saw Luanans, Topuans and Dalinese people from the warrior villages. But the groups of people in Awaran tended to keep themselves to themselves, and mixed settlements did not really occur. Although the different peoples worked together against their common enemy on the coast, the colonists from Freeland, they considered none of the others to be their equals, and they had as little to do with each other as possible. They did not belong together – and nor did they want to.

Except, that was, in Kuwatta, the centre of the rebel movement of the free peoples of Awaran, where emissaries from the different groups came together to form the guerilla army.

The scholar stepped forward and the crowd moved with her.

She was about to announce the contest – any moment now.

Priya's heart started beating faster. She couldn't help it.

A thought came to her: what if she took part in the contest after all? What if she thought only about herself and just gave it a try? Even though she wasn't really allowed. Almost her whole life, she'd dreamed of escaping from Disin, from this life, of going to Kuwatta. Why should only Ishani be given that chance and not her? Winning the contest was Priya's only safe way out as well.

Remaining in Disin was not an option. Even if no one found out she was a blood child, she would simply waste away until there was nothing left of her if she stayed.

In Kuwatta she would be able to live her own life, while also fighting against the colonists who had killed her father. Something for which she would never forgive them.

There was movement behind the scholar, who was standing directly in front of the korjalen that had brought her and the soldiers to Disin. When Priya stood on tiptoe, she saw that there were still some people sitting inside the boats.

The three village elders of Disin stepped forward. Leaning on their walking sticks, they stood beside the scholar, with their hunched backs and their wrinkled faces.

Priya pushed through the crowd, and a few people grumbled and pushed back. The villagers around her were shouting and whistling and cheering. A nearby group of men and women eagerly discussed which of them were going to participate.

Eventually, Priya made it closer to the front – and that was where she spotted Ishani. Her sister was gazing in adoration at the scholar.

Priya didn't know whether she wanted to vanish back into the crowd, so that her sister wouldn't see her, or whether it didn't really matter. If she took part in the contest, sooner or later she'd have to face her mother's anger – again. Before she could decide, Ishani suddenly glanced to one side and noticed her.

Her dark eyes widened but she didn't say anything. She just stood up straight and turned to look back at the scholar.

Priya stayed where she was.

In the circle, the village elders tried to address the crowd, but they couldn't make themselves heard above the hubbub.

It didn't often happen that a scholar from Kuwatta came to oversee the contest in little Disin. It was true that anyone was allowed to enter the contest, but that didn't mean the scholars always went to the trouble of visiting every last little corner of Awaran. Some of the travelling traders and the soldiers from the warrior villages even whispered that Disin had simply been missed out last time.

Most people wouldn't want to miss out on an opportunity to get into Kuwatta. The refugees, whose expertise was mainly in agriculture and fishing, were primarily focused on survival. The Suryans had not yet had the chance to flourish in the rainforest like the Topuans and the Luanans, who had lived there for a long time. They had plenty of people in Kuwatta who could influence the general. The Suryans, on the other hand, were, like the Dalinese people, regularly excluded from important decisions that were taken at Kuwatta. Or at least that was what Priya had heard lots of the villagers grumbling about. Winning the contest was a dream for many of them, a chance to make their voices heard and to join the fight against the colonists.

It was a dream that would also bring fame and fortune if it came true, as the winner's family were paid in gold for their efforts in Kuwatta.

Eventually, the village elders succeeded in silencing everyone.

'We thank you for your visit, Scholar Afounsowa,' said village elder Mathura in halting Awuran. He bowed his head briefly, a Suryan sign of respect. Scholar Afounsowa gave him a nod in return.

The crowd held their breath as they watched the scholar take another step forward. She, in turn, looked at the villagers with an expression that gave nothing away. 'The contest will begin at sunrise in exactly seven days' time. It will consist of two parts.'

She spoke fluent Suryan.

A ripple seemed to pass through the crowd, followed by a low murmur. Priya was also surprised by the scholar's words. She saw that Ishani had frozen. The test had existed long before their mother fled into the rainforest, all those years ago, where she was taken in by the people of Disin. But the contest had never had two parts before. It had always been a single written test. Their preparation – Ishani's preparation – with Master Haripersad had been based entirely on that.

'A written examination,' the scholar stated, 'and a physical test. Only those who complete both parts with outstanding results will be granted the honour and privilege of being trained in Kuwatta.'

Murmurs and whispering.

Priya blinked in surprise.

One of the village elders loudly cleared his throat. 'A physical test?' he asked warily.

'Kuwatta is a military fortress,' said Scholar Afounsowa. 'That should not be forgotten. Not even by scholars.'

'I understand.' The village elder looked somewhat defeated. 'Kuwatta is not a place for everyone.'

Kuwatta, murmured the crowd. Kuwatta, the residence of General Suapala. Kuwatta, where scholars were educated and heroic kaptens were trained. Kuwatta, where everything was possible.

People revered the place for its possibilities. But at the same time Kuwatta seemed almost too good to be true.

Priya felt as if her longing must be written all over her face. The idea of a physical test gave her hope for the first time. All her chores and hard work on the land had made her body strong. The villagers who had spent years preparing for the contest had buried their noses in books. Physically, Priya had an advantage over them.

'The nature of both the written and the physical tests will be announced just before the start.'

That came as no surprise. To ensure that no one could cheat, the scholars kept the details of the written examination secret. As a result, the topics to focus on remained something of a guessing game. People with friends in the large settlements near Kuwatta, where the scholars often held the contest, sometimes tried to extract information about what might be on the paper. Their efforts were in vain; it was never the same twice.

'May the moon shine long and white on every participant,' Scholar Afounsowa concluded. The village elders bowed to her once more. A brief nod was her only response.

As soon as Scholar Afounsowa and the soldiers disappeared, the crowd started moving again.

Ishani stayed where she was, her lips pressed into a thin line and her eyes darting around in panic.

The crowd began to disperse, giving a clearer view of the korjalen at the water's edge. The people sitting in them were not wearing military uniforms. They weren't scholars either. They clearly didn't all belong to the same population group and were presumably the people from other settlements who had emerged victorious from the contest. Each of them came from one of the four peoples that made up the rebel movement.

'Didi,' Ishani croaked. 'What am I going to do?'

Priya felt something inside her clench up. She already had enough problems on her mind as it was. *Ignore it*, she thought, *ignore all of it*.

'This isn't what I trained for,' Ishani added, her eyes wide.

People were still pushing past them. Priya felt shoulders bumping into hers, hands on her back, caught snatches of conversations about the meeting that had just taken place.

'Go to Master Haripersad. Talk to him about what you can do,' said Priya. She tried to walk away, but that only resulted in Ishani coming and standing right in front of her.

'Haripersad? That old man? How is he going to help me with the physical test?' Ishani said, shaking her head. Her voice was becoming more and more shrill. 'I've been preparing for this ever since I was a child. How can they suddenly add a physical test, when they've never done that before in the entire history of Awaran?'

Priya had never seen her calm and serene sister, their mother's favourite, in a state of panic before.

'I have to do this,' Ishani went on. 'I have to go to Kuwatta. If I don't succeed, then . . . What am I going to do with my life? What's going to happen to Umed?'

'Umed?' repeated Priya. She felt uncomfortable because she'd completely forgotten about her little brother for a moment.

'We need a healer from Kuwatta. When I get there, I can make sure we find one. Didi, you've always been so fit and healthy. Can't you help me with the physical test?' Ishani said, looking at her pleadingly.

Priya took some satisfaction in seeing her sister beg. Finally, Ishani felt a fraction of the pain and the despair that Priya carried with her every day. Her sister had the life Priya had always wanted, and that meant Priya's love for her had always been tinged with jealousy. But at the same time, she couldn't bear to see her sister in such a state. Instinctively, she wanted to protect Ishani and Umed. That was what she always wanted. She squeezed her eyes closed for a moment, trying to shut out the guilt.

She had decided to choose for herself.

But she couldn't do it.

Not completely.

'In a week's time? Shan, you're smarter than me.' Priya tried to smile. 'How much could you do to improve in a week?'

'I have to at least try. Are you going to help me or not? If not, I'll find another way. No problem.' The bitterness had returned to Ishani's voice.

Priya knew that she herself would fail the written test. A test Ishani had spent years studying for. But suddenly she had an idea. Maybe she could help Ishani with the physical test – and at the same time she could try to gain more knowledge about Kuwatta from her sister.

'Fine, I'll help you.'

A big smile appeared on Ishani's face. 'Thanks, Pri.'

She stepped towards her and for a second Priya thought her sister was about to give her a hug, but she didn't. Of course not. Umed was the only one who sometimes put his arms around Priya. Her mother and sister touched her as little as possible. Had there ever been a moment when she'd felt the warmth of her mother's body? She couldn't think of one.

'You're amazing!' Ishani was still grinning all over her face. That was unusual for her, and for once it made her look as young as she actually was.

Priya wondered if Ishani realised how much Priya herself wanted to go to Kuwatta, regardless of how much she loved her sister.

'It's no big deal.' Her smile felt like a grimace.

5

'THIS IS TOO EASY,' Ishani said a day later.

Her black curls were stuck to her forehead, and she was so out of breath that she needed to gasp for air after every word. She had heavy logs hanging on her back, tied together with a fraying rope.

Priya was trying to improve their stamina. Ishani was tall and slim; she didn't have the same sturdy build as Priya and Umed. Her studies also meant that she hadn't spent nearly as many hours working in the fields as Priya. She was fast, but she never kept going for long on their runs, even though she stubbornly insisted that she could handle them with ease. Priya would have been lying to herself if she didn't admit that it felt good finally to be better at something than her sister.

Priya rubbed her burning eyes and stifled a yawn. 'Shan, we've taken about a hundred steps since we last stopped.'

'That's the problem. You're making me stop too soon,' Ishani countered, after which she choked and started coughing. 'This isn't enough!'

Her usual calmness had given way to a fiery focus that Priya had rarely seen in her sister. Or maybe she just didn't know this side of her sister well enough, because they never really did anything together.

'There's no point pushing yourself too hard,' said Priya. 'You'll just damage your body.'

Ishani furiously shook her head.

Priya leaned against a tree as she tried to shift the ropes over her shoulders into a better position. But her hand landed right in the path of a colony of red ants. Hissing in pain, she frantically shook her hand to get them off.

They had long since left the main tracks of Disin behind. This deep in the jungle, the thin path they were following was partially overgrown, forcing Priya to lead the way, chopping at bushes and foliage with a machete. She made sure they stayed close to the river. As long as they could hear the Cotari, they'd be able to find their way back to Disin.

'Give your body time to get stronger,' she said to her sister, who was still frowning.

The contrast between Priya and Ishani could not have been greater. Her sister was dreading the physical test, while it gave Priya a glimmer of hope. Priya was even feeling more optimistic about the theoretical test. Ultimately, it was more about insight and creativity than about pure knowledge. Priya had often heard Master Haripersad drumming that into his students when she hid among the piles of books and the crooked bookcases while he taught them. Even so, he still made sure that his pupils knew the books about Awaran history, healing sciences and botany from cover to cover.

No one knew exactly what the general was looking for, so the villagers went on studying.

'Um . . . how many military fortresses are there in Awaran?' asked Priya.

'What?' muttered Ishani.

'How many forts are there in Awaran?' Priya repeated her question. 'I heard that the fort of Kuwatta was rebuilt.'

Ishani hoisted the logs higher on her back and marched on through the trees with a look of determination on her face. 'That's right. For a time, there were only seven forts. Since the reconstruction of Kuwatta, there are eight again.'

'And they're all under General Suapala's command?'

'Yes and no.' Ishani took a deep breath. 'He has authority over them, but they've been empty for years. Only Kuwatta is still in use.'

Priya slapped a mosquito on her arm.

Ishani stopped running. 'Are you trying to test me?'

'I was just curious.'

Priya already knew more or less how Awaran's rebel army worked. The general governed from Kuwatta, where they trained kaptens and bashas. They led the warrior villages at the edge of the rainforest. Those villages kept the Freelanders at bay and carried out flash raids to liberate pieces of land.

That was about the extent of her knowledge.

When they were younger, Priya had looked through Ishani's books during her brief visits to Master Haripersad. Partly out of curiosity, and partly because she couldn't stand Ishani always being such a know-it-all. But Priya wasn't very good at learning from books. Ishani only had to hear or read something once to remember it. Priya, however, had to put in a lot more effort. The information she read passed through her like water through a sieve. There was something that Priya never forgot, though: the long hours in the blazing sun on the plantations, the empty look in her parents' eyes, their hatred of the colonists. The image of the blood-soaked corpses – including her father's – on the plantations, just before they fled to the jungle over twelve years ago.

Umed had been only a few months old and Ishani was three, both too young to remember the events, but Priya had been five. Old enough to be aware of what was going on. The discontent among the Suryans on the plantations. The protests led by her father and a few others. The uprising that erupted against the colonists who controlled their lives. The terrible days that followed, when so many workers were slaughtered in front of their families as if they were animals. Her father's broken body in the scorching sun.

An execution, that was what they said. A lesson. A warning.

That was all.

Ishani set off on a weak sprint. 'I . . .' Her voice faltered. 'I heard a blood child has been born.'

And killed, Priya silently completed the sentence, studiously keeping her expression neutral. 'Ah.'

Ishani nodded. 'I know it's difficult with your . . .' She didn't finish her sentence, just gestured weakly in Priya's direction.

Priya raked one hand through her black hair, trying to shake off the memory of the newborn blood child. 'With my curse?'

'No. Yes. I mean . . .' Ishani tried again. Her breathing was shallow. 'It's hard for all of us, but now with Umed . . . I can't blame Mama for reacting like that. I just want you to know that ultimately there's nothing you can do about it. It's just the way you were born.'

'Sadly,' Priya responded coolly. It was the first time Ishani had spoken to her about her curse. Priya realised that she actually preferred it when her sister ignored it.

Ishani seemed to sense that and stopped talking.

They slogged through the rainforest in silence, until Ishani grunted and slowed down after hurdling a tree stump. 'This isn't working. I'm way too slow.' She hit a tree with the side of her fist, sending some birds fluttering into the air. 'This is unbelievable. I didn't just spend years working towards this only to fail because of a physical test that never existed before!'

'The others weren't expecting it either.'

Ishani snorted. 'What the others are doing and thinking is irrelevant. I'm not planning to lose.'

'But what if you don't win? What are you going to do?' asked Priya.

Ishani didn't answer right away. She leaned forward, resting both hands on her thighs. 'I don't know,' she said to the ground. 'There's no future for me except Kuwatta.'

But that's not true, thought Priya. Ishani had other options.

'If I don't win, I'll have to get married. After all, I'm almost sixteen, so I'm nearly old enough,' Ishani said, still leaning forward. She didn't mention the fact that Priya was seventeen and unmarried. Not that their mother would ever voluntarily let Priya leave.

'They'll introduce me to some nice Suryan man, and I'll have to look after him until I die.'

'You . . .'

'I can't do it.' Ishani stood up. Raw emotion showed on her face, naked and open. 'I just can't. I don't plan to tie myself to anyone. I don't feel the need, and I never will. In fact, I'd rather die.'

Priya didn't know how to react. She wasn't used to Ishani opening up like that. Usually, she hid her emotions behind a calm, neutral facade. It was clear to Priya that Ishani didn't want to go to Kuwatta just because she was intelligent. It was deeper than that.

But it wasn't as if Priya could give up for that reason. There was no other way to get into Kuwatta.

'Great,' Priya said finally. 'Hold on to that attitude when we go out again tomorrow.'

'We're heading back already?' asked Ishani. She pointed at the thin path they'd been following. 'We're not going to finish the route?'

'I don't know what you're going to do.' Priya turned her back on her sister. With one hand, she pushed the foliage aside and stepped over a stump. 'But I have plenty of other things to do today.'

'Like what? Mama doesn't mind you being with me today,' Ishani called after her. 'She knows you're helping me!'

Priya sniffed, even though Ishani couldn't hear her. Yet again Ishani was showing that she didn't realise Priya couldn't break the rules that easily. Ishani might get away with not doing her chores – she didn't have many anyway – but it was a different story for Priya. If she stopped doing her work altogether, her mother's silent treatment would soon come to an end.

A few seconds later, she heard her sister coming after her.

You're doing it wrong,' said Priya, pushing Ishani out of the way. Two days had gone by since they'd started their training, and Ishani had lost some of her fire.

'Watch closely.' With both hands, Priya dug into the soil and loosened the hard pieces of earth. Then she pulled up a few cassavas. 'Like this. If you pull them out one by one, it takes less effort.'

Ishani ran a hand over her sweaty forehead. 'My arms are burning. And my shoulders. And my back. Everything.'

'That's the idea,' said Priya, raising her eyebrows.

Ishani hung her head. But a moment later, she dug her hands deep into the earth and, with a determined look on her face, pulled four cassava plants out of the ground. 'Oh. Oh no.' Two roots suddenly shot loose – and Ishani fell over backwards.

Priya looked over her shoulder, too startled to do anything. Ishani scrambled into a sitting position and wiped a dirty hand over her cheeks and mouth, leaving them covered with mud. She looked up. 'Stop laughing.'

'I wasn't . . .' Priya's voice died away. She realised that the corners of her mouth had indeed turned up. For the past two days, Ishani had hardly left her side. At first, Priya had found it awkward, but she'd become used to it fairly quickly. Ishani could be nice when she wanted to, and Priya was secretly enjoying her sister's sudden affection.

She didn't want to get used to it, though. That would only make it harder to bear the pain that would probably be coming in a few days' time.

At that thought, the corners of her mouth turned down again.

'Don't you think it's strange?' Ishani suddenly asked.

'What?'

'That we never really talk to each other,' Ishani replied, digging her fingers into the soil. 'Sometimes I feel like I don't actually know you at all, didi.'

Priya nodded slowly. This was a conversation she didn't want to have. She knew the bond she and Ishani were creating now would soon be broken. Still, she struggled not to stare at Ishani in disbelief. There was of course a good reason why they never normally spoke to each other. Ishani spent every day with Master Haripersad while Priya worked on the land, fished, washed or cooked. Besides, Priya didn't always understand Ishani when she was gushing on about mathematical formulas, the history of Awaran or the types of soil in the rainforest. Sometimes she had the feeling that Ishani was showing off on purpose, but maybe that was just her own insecurity. There wasn't much to talk about when someone felt so distant from you.

'Three baskets,' said a gravelly voice, making Priya, Ishani and the other villagers look up from their digging. Two Topuan soldiers from a nearby warrior village were standing beside the villager who was loading the full baskets.

'You took two baskets last week,' the woman protested weakly in a mixture of Suryan and Awuran.

'That was before the colonists blew up some of our food supplies,' the soldier said impatiently. 'Or do the people of Disin want to fight against the Freelanders themselves?'

'We have permission from the general,' his companion said in a milder tone, taking a sheet of parchment from her breast pocket.

The villager reluctantly took the parchment. Priya didn't know if the woman could read, but the general's signature, which every child in Awaran could recognise, was probably enough.

'They're taking more and more,' muttered Ishani.

'The Freelanders keep sending more soldiers to the interior of the country.'

Priya was repeating what she'd heard the other villagers say. Working away quietly in the background meant that at a certain point people stopped paying attention to her and spoke freely in her presence.

Ishani didn't seem convinced. 'The Freelanders have always sent soldiers to the interior. The warrior villages should be able to deal with it without demanding more and more from us.' She pursed her lips and began tugging cassavas from the ground more aggressively.

Priya saw how, after a few helpless looks at the others, the villager gave in and handed the baskets to the soldiers.

+++

The next few days flew by. The villagers soon became used to the presence of the soldiers from Kuwatta.

Volunteers and soldiers had marked out a circle by the water where the contest would take place.

Occasionally, one of the winners from another settlement appeared in the village, but before they could strike up a conversation with any of the villagers, they were sent packing by one of the soldiers from Kuwatta.

During Ishani's physical training sessions, Priya tried to get more information out of her. Thankfully, Ishani saw it as a way to test her own theoretical knowledge. At night, Priya slipped away with Ishani's textbooks and read them by the light of the moon.

She rarely slept, but often dozed off for a moment, waking up in a blind panic. Her heart pounding, she snatched up her notes and started reading through them with burning eyes.

She didn't have enough time and, with every book she read, she became more and more aware that she knew nothing about the world.

Even so, in the short amount of time she had, she tried to memorise as much information as possible. During her trips to and from the Cotari, where she filled buckets with water, she recited formulas over and over. When she washed clothes, she secretly made calculations in the mud with a stick. When she worked in the fields, she ran through facts that she'd memorised during the night.

'The Freelanders speak Freeland, the Topuans speak Topuan, the Dalinese people speak Dalinese, the Suryans speak Suryan and the Luanans speak . . .' Priya mumbled to herself as she grubbed up the cassavas. Ishani was looking after Umed, so she was free to speak out loud.

'Luana is a continent, not a country,' said a voice beside her.

Priya smiled stiffly at the older woman crouching beside her who was digging for cassava. It was Maya, the wife of one of the village elders. She often brought coconuts and bananas for Priya's mother and other single parents in the village.

'There are so many different languages spoken there that the Luanans didn't understand one another when the Freelanders transported them to Awaran,' Maya added. 'The language they developed in the rainforest is a completely new one. We just call it Luan for the sake of convenience.' She gave Priya a wink. 'You studying for the test too?'

Priya looked over at where her mother was working. She'd lost a lot of weight since Umed had been in a coma, but she refused to sit still. Now, too, she was busily digging the cassavas out of the hard earth. She hadn't heard their conversation.

'Something like that,' Priya mumbled to Maya before turning back to her work.

+++

Healers came and went, but Umed didn't wake up.

'A healer from Kuwatta,' Priya had said to the soldiers she'd approached. 'I'm not asking for much. Just a way to get in touch with one.'

'I'm sorry,' the first soldier had replied in Suryan, scratching his chin.

'Hardly any of them ever leave the fort,' another said, with some sympathy.

'The healers only answer to General Suapala,' a third growled. Walking on, he added, 'If you want to talk to a healer, you'll have to get to the general first. Can't help you with that.'

It was an impossible task. And with every question Priya asked – with every plea – her belief that Umed would recover crumbled further.

On the fifth day after the announcement, she stood in front of their house, at her wits' end. Quiet voices floated out through the open window. Priya slowly raised her hand to open the door. On the wood, the symbol that protected them from the monsters of the blood moon was fading away. She'd always thought it strange that it didn't stop her, a blood child.

Then she pushed the door open and stepped inside.

Her mother was kneeling beside Umed. With one hand, she supported his head and with the other she was carefully giving him water to drink from a small bowl. Umed lay limp in her arms, but his throat was moving. He was drinking. Priya watched closely, waiting for him to start screaming again.

But that didn't happen. He remained quiet.

Beside them stood a man in a simple, brown tunic. His hands were behind his back and he was observing Umed as he calmly spoke to their mother. On his forehead, right between his eyebrows, there was a yellow line. Yet another religious healer that their mother had brought into their home. No one in Disin could help Umed, so Priya's mother often travelled with the traders to other villages to see if she could find a healer.

Every time she was disappointed, and every time she went back out again, looking for help for Umed.

Priya frostily greeted the latest healer.

He glanced at Priya, leaning forward and whispering something in her mother's ear. Her mother nodded. Then the healer started rummaging in the pouch at his waist.

Priya's mother put down the bowl and wiped Umed's forehead and neck with a cloth. Even in his strange, unconscious state, he suffered from frequent bouts of fever. He moved restlessly, letting out raw cries that went to her very core. With every scream, Priya winced, knowing that he wouldn't be in this state if they had returned home just a little faster.

The healer handed a few small bags to Priya's mother. 'Give him two lots of silverbloom and one of coriander mixed with cumin. Don't forget to rub his feet with finely ground charcoal.'

'We won't. Thank you so much for your help,' their mother said, touching the healer's feet as a mark of respect.

Then she headed to a wooden box in the corner of the room and took out a ring that she had brought with her from Suryan. Priya knew that their precious belongings were now almost gone. Before long they would have to pay the healers with cassavas, fish and what little sugar they had.

The healer tucked the ring away, laid his hand on Umed's forehead for a moment and then walked past Priya, who gave him a quick bow. The door closed behind him with a gentle thud.

Priya put down the pile of kitchen utensils that she'd washed with water and ashes. A pan of rice pudding was bubbling away on the nearby fire.

Priya felt her mother's gaze on her back, but when she turned round, her mother acted as if she couldn't see her. Priya pursed her lips and headed back outside. On the porch, she curled up in a corner and squeezed her hand into the opening of one of the rain barrels to pull out a textbook, some paper and a few nuggets of charcoal. It was time to go through Ishani's botany notes.

Two more days, Priya told herself.

Two more days.

She stayed reading on the porch until it began to get dark and she saw Ishani climbing the stairs.

When she stood up, she saw a bowl of cold rice pudding on the windowsill.

6

IN THE EARLY MORNING light, Priya closed her book and got out of bed.

The last two nerve-racking days had passed, which meant the day of the contest had arrived.

The wind carried the birdsong through the window as she got ready. In one corner of the room, Ishani lay sleeping on her stomach.

Priya crept out of their room. The living room was silent. Umed was curled up in the corner. As she went past, Priya glanced at his face. He seemed to be sleeping calmly, although he had a slight frown on his face.

She crouched beside him.

'See you this evening, Um,' she whispered, her voice as quiet as a breeze. She leaned forward and kissed him on the forehead. As she moved away, she saw his frown was gone.

Priya stood up and walked to the nearest window. The front door would make too much noise. She gently pushed open the shutters. Then she lifted one leg over the frame, grabbed the wood with both hands and swung her other leg over too. Outside, she didn't look back, but hurried down the steps. She listened. Nothing.

Before the silence could turn into the sound of her name, she started sprinting.

She ran until she reached the newly marked-out circular field. There were already some people standing around. Scholar Afounsowa wasn't there, but one of her soldiers was leaning against a pole that the villagers had knocked into the ground at the edge of the field.

Half of the circle was filled with forty or so wooden chairs and desks that had been made in the preceding days.

Above her, the dark blue night sky gave way to a paler blue. A dim light shone between the branches and leaves.

As Priya walked on, the soldier noticed her. He was clearly Dalinese. She gave him a respectful nod. He looked at her for a few seconds before his gaze drifted away. Her greeting went unanswered.

The other villagers who were there openly stared at her. Priya felt the sting of their gazes and the weight of their silent opinions pressing down on her. Disin was not a large village. Everyone knew everyone else. Priya saw the daughters of market women who her mother chatted with every week, the sons of farmers she often passed on the dirt paths. They nodded and smiled at her, and Priya briefly returned their greetings.

There were, of course, expectations about who was going to take part in the contest and who stood the best chance of winning the honour. She'd heard their names mentioned over the years. Priya was not considered to be in the running. She could hardly blame the villagers. Although everyone in Disin knew each other, Priya's mother had always kept her in the shadows. She was the ghost of the Chkadhari family.

More and more people came streaming along.

The buzzing of the crowd swelled.

Accompanied by soldiers, Scholar Afounsowa stepped forward.

'Good morning, people of Disin,' said the scholar, and the murmuring died away, 'and welcome to the opening of the contest. As you all know, this contest has two components. The first part is a written test, and it will take one day to complete. We are about to hand out the test papers. Anyone who secures a seat at one of the desks is guaranteed a place in the contest. We may have a few spare papers, so those who do not succeed in claiming a seat at a desk may be able to complete the test elsewhere. However, we cannot promise that we will have enough written tests for everyone.'

This caused muttering in the crowd.

Priya's gaze scanned the villagers. She could see around a hundred people, and she was sure most of them would want to take the test. Forty chairs and desks for a hundred people. So, more than half of them would be forced to drop out after the battle for a desk.

'Participants are not yet invited to take their seats,' barked Scholar Afounsowa, as a few young people were already stepping forward. They froze where they stood. 'I have not yet given the starting signal.'

Reluctantly, they went back to their places, and the circle was intact again.

Scholar Afounsowa waited for the silence to return. 'You may hand in your answers to me or to the soldiers at any point in the day. There are no rules about how long, short, detailed, in depth or superficial the answers should be. But as soon as the sun rises tomorrow, your chance is over. If you haven't handed in your test by then, you will be disqualified.'

Priya's gaze was fixed on the chairs and desks. Her body was as taut as a bowstring, anticipating the moment when the starting signal would be given.

The scholar continued. 'The second part is a physical challenge. Its exact form will be announced after the end of the first test. Bear in mind,' she added, 'that the winner of the physical test is not automatically the winner of the whole test. The written examination will, of course, also count.'

The villagers looked at one another, but no one felt brave enough to object in front of the scholar. Priya caught a glimpse of Ishani and leaned forward to get a better look at her. Her sister was standing with crossed arms on the other side of the circle. Her shoulders were hunched up. She was obviously nervous.

'So, that was the announcement. I hereby officially open the contest. The theoretical paper will be handed out as soon as all the seats are occupied.'

The crowd rushed forward as one, Priya running with them. Show-ing no mercy, people pushed and pulled her on all sides. She took an elbow to the cheekbone, a punch in the stomach. Nails scratched her arms. She didn't care. She just wanted a place. To take part. To win.

Out of the corner of her eye, she spotted a free desk and she dived towards it. Just before she got there, a skinny boy slid onto the seat. But her momentum as she flew at the desk sent her crashing into him. He fell from the chair and onto the ground as Priya landed on the seat with a thud. The boy scrambled to his feet. They held each other's gaze. Priya tightly gripped the chair beneath her and braced herself.

'Pri!' A hand on her shoulder. Startled, she looked round.

It was Ishani.

'What are you doing here?' Ishani asked, her eyes wide.

All the Gods.

'I . . .' She couldn't get the words out of her mouth.

'There are no chairs left!' cried Ishani, looking around in panic. Her voice cracked. 'I don't know what to do.'

'. . . my place!' the boy who had fallen yelled at her. His voice seemed to come from far away, drowned out by the noise of the crowd.

Priya clenched her jaw. She tried to see through the crowd of wrestling, pushing, pulling bodies. People were fighting for the last seats. Some of the villagers had already given up any hope of a desk and were besieging the soldiers for a test paper.

'Didi, help me. Please.' Ishani's voice sounded shrill. She grabbed hold of the desk and looked at Priya with big, tearful eyes. 'I have to win. I have to!'

Priya closed her eyes for a moment. She wanted to go to Kuwatta. Her mind was made up. But at the same time, she couldn't bear the panic and fear on Ishani's face. The big sister inside her was scream-ing at her to protect her sister. Ishani would never recover if she lost, especially at this stage. She wasn't like Priya.

'Please,' Ishani begged.

If Priya decided to do nothing, Ishani would never forgive her.

Priya breathed in deeply. She grabbed Ishani's wrist and gave it a tug. Ishani let out a cry. At the very last moment, Priya stood up and planted Ishani on the chair.

'Didi?'

'Make sure you don't lose your spot,' said Priya, disappearing among the throng of bodies.

Away. She had to get away from here. Before it really dawned on her what she'd just done.

The crowd had become a suffocating wall. With every step she took, Priya was pushed two steps back by the undulating motion of the mass of people. Bodies rubbed against her, fingers brushed her waist and thighs, breath feathered her neck. There was no escape.

'Get back!' a voice shouted. 'Everyone step back! None of you will get a test paper until the people who are sitting at the desks have received theirs.'

The group of people dispersed, and sweet, fresh air filled Priya's lungs.

She looked around.

There was not a single seat left. Two soldiers started handing out the test papers to everyone who was at a desk. They ignored the rest.

Ishani had managed to hold on to her chair. But Priya was left with nothing.

Priya's throat slowly squeezed shut because of the agitation and tension in her body. She refused to believe this was the end. Not while there might still be a test paper left over.

She searched for Scholar Afounsowa among the soldiers and the remaining villagers. There. The statuesque woman was standing outside the circle of people, safely near the riverbank. In front of her was a stack of splintered wood. Behind her, the river glistened.

Priya, though, only had eyes for the paper in her hands. The soldiers would be stormed as soon as they had finished handing out exams to the people at desks. Priya had little chance of reaching them first. And she didn't want to get stuck in the crowd again.

But hardly anyone would dare to speak to Scholar Afounsowa. Priya started moving. Faster and faster, so that her doubts couldn't get in the way of her reckless plan. Sprinting, she darted around the makeshift barrier that separated the scholar from the others. Her feet sank in the mud, and soon the river was up to her ankles.

Scholar Afounsowa spotted her. She glanced at the soldiers and then turned to Priya.

With one final, splashing step in the river, Priya came to a halt in front of the scholar. 'My name is Priya Chkadhari,' she said before taking a deep breath. 'Can I have a test paper?'

Priya held out her hand.

It was a moment before Scholar Afounsowa responded. 'Sorry?'

'The test paper you're holding,' Priya clarified. 'Everyone who's sitting at a desk has been given a test paper now. So, I'm entitled to one of the papers that's left over.'

For the first time since Scholar Afounsowa had arrived in the village, Priya noticed a touch of emotion on her face. A hint of a smile that softened the sharp lines of her face.

'You're in luck. I have the last test paper in my hands.' Scholar Afounsowa flicked through the documents she was holding, before taking a number of sheets from the pile and placing them on Priya's outstretched hand.

Priya's fingers curled around the test, but Scholar Afounsowa didn't let go at first.

'Look around you,' she said, and Priya did as she was told.

The soldiers had run out of test papers to hand out. The villagers who hadn't got their hands on a test crowded around, looking lost. They stared at Priya. They stepped forward. Their faces were twisted with jealousy. Hatred. Despair.

'If you want to win,' said Scholar Afounsowa, 'you should start running.'

And she let go of the test paper.

7

MORE THAN HALF OF the remaining crowd came after Priya.

Hesitantly at first, and then fast and furious.

With every step Priya took, the water splashed. Her feet sank into the mud, flowing water rushing past her ankles.

She wanted to run back around the villagers and up onto the bank, but they were too fast. She wouldn't be able to move quickly enough. So she rolled up the exam and clenched it between her teeth. Then she ran deeper into the river. Brownish-green water swallowed her up. The further she went, the stronger the current became. But Priya knew the river and its quirks. It helped that the current wasn't at its strongest at this time of day.

With every step, she pushed her feet into the sand and stood her ground. When she was about halfway across, she heard splashing behind her.

Priya kept going. One step, another step. The water dropped from chest height to her waist. The current was becoming less strong, so she moved forward faster. Reaching the opposite bank, she scrambled through the reeds and over the roots of the mangrove trees. Branches and sharp leaves hit her in the face.

Only then did she dare to look over her shoulder. Most of the villagers had given up their pursuit, but five of them had ventured across and were striding with determination against the current of the river. She had to stay ahead of them.

Priya slipped through the trees. Her clothes were sticking to her skin and large drops of water slid down her body. But at least the test had stayed dry. She took it out of her mouth and jumped over a low-hanging branch. She didn't pause, just went on running and running. By now, she was panting so hard that she felt light-headed. Her lungs protested, and her body groaned. But she didn't dare to stop.

It was only when she tripped over a rock and went sprawling into a bush that she finally came to a halt. Gasping, Priya lay there among the leaves and branches. She closed her eyes and listened. At first, all she could hear was her heart beating. Then the singing of the birds and the chirping of the crickets. No footsteps. No voices.

It looked like she'd shaken off the villagers.

At least for now.

Priya struggled to her feet and searched for a sturdy tree. When she'd found a suitable one, she clenched the test between her teeth again and started climbing. As soon as she was a good distance above the ground, she perched on a thick branch that was well sheltered. Three macaws on a branch above cocked their heads, peering down at her.

Priya unrolled the test. It was torn on one side, and she tried to smooth it out. At the top was a thin charcoal stick for writing. She detached it from the sheet. As she read through the first few questions, she sucked her bottom lip. Geology. She flipped through. Biology, history, botany. All of it written in Awuran.

Ishani was fluent in Awuran, both spoken and written. Priya could read the language pretty well, but her writing was poor.

She went back to the first page. Her skin prickled. She could hardly answer any of the questions. They didn't just require knowledge, but also insight and application. With some of the questions, she didn't even know exactly what was being asked.

She looked down at her hands, now dusty and blackened by the charcoal stick as she'd rolled it, distracted, between her palms. It felt as if the whole world was laughing at her for attempting the test.

Chewing her bottom lip, she leafed to the third page. Halfway down, she answered a question that she roughly knew the answer to. Occasionally, her practical experience helped her. When she came to a question about how to treat joint pain, she replied that the fat of a constrictor snake might help. With other questions, she could only guess at the answers, so she let her imagination run wild.

The longer she wrote, the more ridiculous her answers became. She wrote down all the stories, myths and legends she'd heard while working in the fields and in and around the house. Primeval creatures, vengeful spirits and blood children. All of them put in an appearance somewhere in her answers.

Frowning, she went on scratching down her answers in her sloppy handwriting until night fell and she could no longer read the questions.

+++

Priya searched among the branches for the sky. The test was pressing against her chest under her kameez. The twisting branches of the trees stretched far up above her, shielding the moon and most of the stars. The jungle showed a different face after night fell. It was full of whispering and rustling and secrets shrouded in leaves.

Finally, she caught a glimpse of the moon high up in the sky. From its position, she guessed it was just after midnight. Slowly, she climbed down from the tree.

Priya broke off a dry branch and used the end to push bushes and leaves out of the way. She poked it into a few dark places too, to check that there was no tigri kati or snake hiding there. She made sure to avoid the main paths.

Once she reached the river, she took out the rolled-up test and put it back into her mouth. Then she slowly lowered herself into the river, which was as black as the night sky. Here and there, waves glinted in the moonlight.

The current was stronger this time and Priya was almost swept away a few times. Panting with exertion, she reached the bank a little further downstream and then climbed ashore on a deserted, overgrown stretch of the river.

'There she is!' yelled a voice.

Priya froze. Did they still want to take her test even now? She swore under her breath.

'Yes! I see her! Quick.'

Priya clawed for the mangrove roots. With two large jumps, she was on solid ground. She heard rustling and footsteps rapidly approaching.

Gods. She had to get to the soldiers and the scholar. Listening carefully, she dived straight through the undergrowth, muttering a quick prayer to the gods to help her as she stuffed the test back into her kameez.

'Where did she go?' a voice shouted.

'What are you idiots doing?' another yelled. 'Spread out! Get her test! Bring it to me!'

Priya tried to run around her pursuers. She couldn't see a thing and kept stumbling over roots and rocks. But she knew she was getting closer to the round clearing. Through the dense vegetation, she could see the circle.

'Not so fast,' said a deep voice, as a man grabbed her. He pulled her backwards, twisting her arm.

Priya cried out. 'Let go of me,' she gasped.

'Not until you give me that test.' In the darkness, she couldn't see the man's face clearly. He was muscular, but short.

She stamped on his foot. He cursed. His grip weakened slightly and Priya pulled away. Judging by the sounds of panting and running feet, her other pursuers were also close now. Priya broke into a sprint, but two shadows darted in front of her. She skidded to a stop.

'This doesn't have to be difficult,' said one of the two. A woman. 'Just give us the test and we'll let you through.'

'And what then?' asked Priya. 'I only have one test. That's not enough for all of you.'

'Just give it to me,' panted the other person, a boy.

'Shut your mouth, Raj,' snarled the woman.

Raj. That was the name of the fisherman's son who lived three houses away. Priya made use of the moment to climb a tree. She was close to the clearing. She just had to buy some time and then . . . 'Scholar Afounsowa!' she shouted. 'I want to hand in my test!'

Her two assailants were yelling at each other. The woman pushed Raj aside and was the first to come climbing up after Priya. The muscular man came to join them.

'Scholar Afounsowa!' Priya screamed again.

One of her pursuers grabbed her ankle. She kicked the hand away and went on climbing. More hands. They pulled at her leg. At her clothes. Priya heard something tear. They got hold of her other foot. She clung to the trunk. It wasn't enough. More hands tugged at her.

She fell.

First onto a thick branch, which she hung on to for a moment. Now they were grabbing at her from above. Leaves came tumbling down past her. Priya glanced up at her assailants, who were still high in the tree, and pushed herself off the branch. With a thud, she landed on the ground.

Every second, she expected to feel hands tearing her clothes, looking for the test she was hiding. To her surprise, that didn't happen. The shouting gave way to sounds of protest. Priya's heart was pounding.

'Get up.'

Priya turned onto her side and peered upwards. Her breath was still hurried and she felt dizzy. Someone was looking down at her. Scholar Afounsowa, she realised a second later. Beside her stood two soldiers.

Priya pushed herself to her feet, reaching a hand into her wet kameez and taking out the test, which was damp, but – thank the Gods – still intact. Fingers trembling, she unrolled it. The inside was dry. Her answers were still written there.

'Is your name on it?' asked Scholar Afounsowa as Priya held out the completed test to her.

Priya nodded and the scholar took the test from her.

8

BY THE TIME THE stilts of her house came into view, she was almost dry. Priya looked back one last time to see if anyone was following her and then quickly climbed the stairs. There would be questions and blame. She hadn't shown her face all day and night.

But it was better to go inside anyway, so that she at least had a chance of shelter. She only had to keep this up for another few days. The end of the test was going to change her life no matter what, she thought to herself. Whether she won or not. She took a deep breath and headed inside.

The door creaked and all the heads in the room turned towards Priya. Ishani stopped in mid-conversation with their mother. Even Umed, in his strange sleep, turned his head towards Priya. The silence in the room felt thick and viscous. Oppressive.

No, thought Priya. This wasn't going to work. She couldn't do it.

She turned round.

'Priya,' her mother said.

Her stomach flipped.

'Where were you?'

How was she supposed to answer that question? Every answer would be the wrong one. 'Outside.'

'Look at me.'

For a moment, Priya closed her eyes. Then she turned slowly.

Her mother was scowling. 'Ishani told me you're taking part in the test.'

Ishani? It felt as if the ground was sinking away from under Priya's feet. Staggering, she took a step back. She'd known it was only a matter of time before her mother found out she was doing the test. But she hadn't expected the news to come from Ishani. It felt as if an unwritten rule of trust had been broken.

She swung to glare at her sister.

'You told her?' she blurted. She knew she sounded hurt, but she couldn't help it. She'd helped Ishani with the contest. She'd given up her own seat, so that her sister would be guaranteed a place. How *could* she?

Priya felt her curse stirring within her and she pressed one hand to her stomach. She had to keep it inside.

'Nearly everyone in Disin knows,' began Ishani, hastily rising from her cross-legged seat.

'That doesn't mean you had to be the one to tell her,' hissed Priya. 'Do you even realise how much this means to me?'

'To you?' cried Ishani. 'This is *my* future. It's what I've been working towards all these years. We can't both do this. There can only be one winner – and that title is mine.'

Priya wanted to hit something. It didn't even occur to Ishani that Priya, too, wanted more out of life than to stay in this godforsaken village. 'Says who?'

Stunned, Ishani took a step back. The calculating look that Priya had often seen in her eyes when she was solving tricky algebra appeared in her dark eyes. 'Everyone in this house, didi.'

'Leave Ishani out of this,' their mother said. 'At least she didn't lie.'

Priya took a sharp breath. Her hand clenched into a fist. So this was how it was going to be. Of course it was. 'Why is it a problem if I enter the contest? It's for everyone. What if I want to get revenge for Papa by fighting against the colonists?'

'Shut up about your father!' Her mother pressed her lips together, which was a habit of hers when she spoke to Priya. 'The test is meant only for the most intelligent citizens.'

Priya ignored the jibe. 'Ishani's been taught from an early age. It only makes sense that she has more knowledge and . . .'

'She's been taught because she has talent,' her mother said coldly. 'Besides, it's not Ishani's fault that Umed ended up like this. You're staying here and taking care of your brother.'

When she heard Umed's name, Priya's protest died away. Her mother was right in some ways, no matter how painful her words were. Ishani *was* more intelligent. Master Haripersad always glowed with pride when he spoke about her.

Ishani stared at a point just behind Priya's head. But when her eyes met Priya's, she seemed to shrink.

At first, Priya and Umed had received as much instruction as their sister about the history of their country, geology, the healing sciences and botany. But while Ishani picked up a lot during the lessons, Priya had to study the texts they were given to take home until late in the evening so that she could understand what Master Haripersad was talking about. Umed didn't turn out to have the same knack for study as Ishani either. Their education came to an end before the year was out.

Although Priya still went on reading in secret during her visits to Master Haripersad, she was well aware that Ishani knew and understood a lot more about the world.

'Go,' their mother said, with a nod to Ishani. 'And be careful.'

'I'll try to be home early,' Ishani said softly. Her arm brushed Priya's as she passed her. 'I'm sorry,' she mumbled almost inaudibly in Priya's ear. 'I couldn't . . .'

'Traitor,' Priya snapped back softly, and she felt her sister's muscles tense. A moment later, the front door closed behind Ishani.

Numb with anger and betrayal, Priya remained where she was standing. Her mother walked over to Umed and kneeled beside him.

Frowning, she held her hand to his forehead. With her slender body bent over her son, she looked frail and thin. Strands of her black hair had come untied and fell across her face. Priya and Umed had inherited their dark brown skin from her. Ishani's complexion was a shade lighter; her skin was a warmer shade of brown with a yellowish undertone, like their father's.

'We've had this kind of discussion before. You know very well why you can't participate.'

It took Priya a moment to realise her mother was talking to her.

'You're not going to Kuwatta,' her mother added. 'And you're not doing the test.'

'You can't forbid me,' said Priya. Her throat felt thick and sore. She had to hold it in. Her curse. Her emotions. Everything.

'As long as you're living under my roof, you'll do as I say,' her mother said. 'If you take part in that test, you'll find yourself in situations that will make you reach for your cursed powers. You've made that mistake before, and I don't want to risk it. It's too dangerous. You're staying with me.'

It's too dangerous. There hadn't been a day in her life when those words hadn't echoed through her mind. *She* was too dangerous. For her family. For Disin. For the rest of the world. The words had made her hate her own existence.

Priya couldn't take it anymore.

The four walls around her formed a prison. Her mother, Disin, all of Awaran; they were suffocating her. She wanted to get out, away from here.

'No,' Priya said, so quietly it could barely be heard. She took a step forward. 'No,' she said, more loudly this time, and her mother looked up. 'I've always done what you wanted me to do. I've done what you asked of me without complaining, day in, day out. I've done all the chores around the house for you. I didn't protest when my studies had to stop and Ishani was allowed to continue. I never complained about Umed having much more freedom to do what he wants.' Her voice was trembling, and she hated it. 'I even took care of him when needed.

This is the first time I've ever wanted anything for myself. I promise I'll do my best to control my curse. But you can't take this away from me.'

'You'd risk your family's lives for the sake of a contest?' her mother asked, raising her voice.

Priya didn't reply. If she opened her mouth now, everything was going to come pouring out. Desperately, she tried to keep her emotions under control.

With a few brisk steps, Priya's mother was beside her, roughly grabbing her arm. The left side of her face was twitching, a tic she had whenever she was under a lot of pressure. 'Stop this nonsense. You are going to do as I say – do you hear me?'

'No,' Priya replied forcefully, trying to pull her arm away. 'No, I won't.'

'Do you want all of us to die?' her mother said, shaking her. 'Isn't it enough that Umed's lying there like that? Do you want us all to end up like your father?'

That stung. Priya pushed at her mother's hand. When it didn't budge, she tried to pry her fingers away, one by one. 'Leave me alone,' she said, breathing heavily. 'Just leave me alone.'

But her mother refused to let go. She was frail and looked as if she might collapse at any moment, but her grip was like a heavy chain that Priya couldn't shake off.

The feeling of panic and powerlessness made Priya lose control, drowning in her own emotions. They came out like a tidal wave.

'I want to be free from . . . all of this,' Priya screamed at her. 'I've been a prisoner without a voice of my own for long enough!'

Her mother's face twisted with fury. And pain. And something that Priya couldn't place. 'A prisoner? You're the prisoner here? Is that what you think of my care and protection? Is this how you thank me?'

Priya was breathing heavily. 'You've never wanted me. Not as a daughter, and not as a person either. Just admit it.'

'You don't know what you're saying,' her mother bit back at her. 'You have no idea what I gave up for you.'

An ice-cold, painful feeling spread through Priya's body, pressing on her stomach, her lungs, her heart. It strangled her like a snake, until she was gasping for breath.

'I risked everything to have you . . .'

Enough. *Enough.*

'Then maybe you shouldn't have bothered,' screamed Priya. Her own voice hurt her ears. With a rough movement, she finally tore herself away.

Go away. Go away. Go AWAY! she cried out from inside herself.

The energy inside her exploded outwards, and Priya saw her mother being thrown across the room, as if she'd physically pushed her away. She slammed into a wooden cupboard and slumped onto the floor.

A sharp pain shot through Priya's head. No, she thought, staggering. NO. What had she done?

White dots danced in front of her eyes. She stepped forward to help her mother up.

'Don't touch me!' Her mother raised her hands, crawling backwards against the cupboard. 'Stay away from me.'

Priya froze, then looked down at her mother in horror.

She turned and ran out of the house.

+++

For a moment, Priya considered going to Master Haripersad. Then she realised that Ishani was probably with him. With no other options, she sought shelter in another villager's storage shed. Slumping down onto some sacks of rice, she leaned back against a stack of logs. She found a couple of loose cassavas and ate them raw to stop the rumbling in her stomach.

In spite of the heat, she was shivering all over. Slowly, shakily, she breathed out. She wrapped her arms around herself and rocked back and forth with her eyes closed.

After a while, she settled down and forced herself to try to sleep. Priya felt more lonely than ever. She missed her father, who in her memories spoke her name with such affection that she knew he must have loved her. She missed Umed, who at least could have given her some warmth with his stories.

She squeezed her eyes tightly shut and took a ragged breath. The physical test would begin tomorrow. This was not the time for dark thoughts. She had to be clear-headed.

Unfortunately, sleep wouldn't come. Her head was still throbbing painfully, and she couldn't forget the look of fear in her mother's eyes. Priya's mother had never looked at her with love, but she'd never been afraid of her either. Not like that.

'I am not a monster,' she mumbled to herself. 'I am not a monster.'

Her fear of failing the test and having to face her mother again was eating away at her.

If she lost, the rainforest was the only way out that she had left.

Eventually, she fell into a restless sleep.

9

'THE SUNRISE THAT MARKS the start of the physical test has arrived.' Scholar Afounsowa's tone was businesslike.

The people standing around the clearing made enthusiastic noises. But inside the circle itself, where the participants stood, there was a tense silence.

Priya hid a yawn behind her hand. She had come very close this morning to being discovered by the family whose shed she'd spent the night in.

'The physical trial will consist of bouts of combat. This is your weapon.' Scholar Afounsowa showed the participants a wooden stick. 'The rules are simple. To win, you must disarm your opponent or make them submit. Killing is clearly not permitted, but injuring your opponent is. You are allowed to stop only if one of us has given the signal,' she said, pointing at herself and at the two soldiers standing to her right.

In front of the soldiers' feet was a large pile of sticks. During Scholar Afounsowa's speech, they started handing them out to the participants, who nervously accepted them.

'The contest will take three days to complete.' Scholar Afounsowa pulled a rolled-up sheet of parchment from her clothing. She opened it up. 'The names of all those who submitted the theoretical test are written here. In the first round, you will fight against three opponents.'

Priya caught the stick that was thrown to her. She weighed it in her hands; it was heavier than she'd imagined. It felt strange to hold the long piece of wood, knowing she would have to use it as a weapon.

'If you win two of the three fights, you will advance to the next round. That is also the case in the second round. From the third round, you'll be out as soon as you lose a fight. Until we end up with one winner. And remember this,' Scholar Afounsowa said sternly. 'The winner of the physical trial is not necessarily the winner of the whole contest.'

'Now move apart. Make sure there are three steps of space between all of you,' the smaller of the two soldiers barked in Awuran.

The participants obediently spread out. Not so long ago, at least a hundred people had fought to get to Kuwatta. Now only forty-five remained.

The number of spectators, on the other hand, had dramatically increased. The villagers stood on the sidelines, yelling words of encouragement. Some pulled a participant they knew to the side and whispered in their ear.

Scholar Afounsowa brought her own stick down on a rock with a loud bang. Everyone looked up, startled. The competitors who had wandered off hurried back to the clearing.

'That's enough. Divide them into pairs,' she said to the soldiers. 'I want three pairs in the ring at a time. Make sure they have enough space.'

The soldiers stepped forward to follow the scholar's orders.

Priya was paired up with Monisha, a daughter of the farmer who lived next door to them. Her opponent was a few years older than her and taller. She reminded Priya of Ishani. Small-boned and slim, she was a competitor who had clearly prepared only for the theoretical component.

'Stand by!' one of the soldiers called to the three pairs.

Priya moved her feet apart for a better balance. Her opponent mirrored her movements.

The soldiers looked at the three pairs in the middle. One of them nodded at Scholar Afounsowa.

'And . . . fight!' the scholar commanded.

Priya had always been bad at waiting. She hated those moments when her skin prickled in anticipation. The doubts that came with waiting caused her to lose sight of her goal. Action, movement – that was what she loved. She spent enough time holding herself back. So she didn't wait to find out what Monisha was going to do.

She attacked.

The girl backed away, raising her stick in a reflex. Priya's stick smashed against hers. The shock went through Priya's hands, elbows, arms. Her opponent let out a cry. Priya darted forward, grabbed the girl's stick with her free hand and pulled it from her before she could regain her balance.

It was over.

Stunned, Priya's opponent stared at her empty hands, tears welling up in her eyes. 'No,' she said in a choked voice. 'No!'

One of the soldiers blew a whistle to signal the end of the fight.

'Come with me,' he said, nodding at Priya.

Her victory didn't really sink in until she reached the edge of the ring. Euphoria coursed through her veins. She might not have been a favourite when it came to the written test, but perhaps her physical power would make up for the knowledge she lacked.

In the next round, Priya was up against a fisherman in his fifties. He had a limp. Again, she immediately went on the attack. Priya turned, lunged and dodged. She barely felt the blows she parried or the ones that grazed her. Her body was glowing, her blood sang. She didn't care that she occasionally stumbled or that her stick missed its target more often than not. She was younger and more agile than her opponent.

And she hit harder.

Before she knew it, the fight was over.

Again, a soldier led her to the side. Priya saw that Ishani was fighting a girl who looked about twelve years old. Ishani was a full head taller than her opponent. But it was a tough fight. They were both out of breath.

Their sticks banged together. Their poor coordination sent the two girls crashing into each other and they fell to the ground, their sticks rolling away. They wrestled to be the first to reclaim their weapon. Ishani shoved the younger girl aside and reached out for her stick.

Priya felt a hand on her shoulder. A soldier had appeared beside her, and Priya saw that a middle-aged woman was to be her next opponent.

They walked past Ishani, who was still fighting for her victory. Before the other girl could scramble to her feet, Priya's sister pounced on her stick. Using her feet and her free hand, Ishani held the stick to the ground. Then she quickly snatched up her own weapon.

She had won.

Turning her stick in her hands, Priya faced her own opponent. This was her third and last fight of the day, and her body was sore and tender. It helped that the woman opposite her only managed to hit her once. Her blow also had much less force than those of Priya's previous partners.

It was only a matter of time before Priya, for the third time that day, knocked the stick out of her opponent's hands and won.

+++

Stumbling, Priya made her way along the dirt track. Her arms, legs, torso – *everything* hurt. Everything was on fire. During the fights, the adrenaline had kept her from feeling the impact of the blows, and her scratches and bruises were an irrelevance. But now she could feel every blow threefold.

She had no idea how she was supposed to survive the fights tomorrow.

She also wondered how she was going to slip into a shed in this state without being noticed. She couldn't even walk along the path silently. Around her, a dozen or so other participants who'd also made it through to the second round were heading home. None of them had emerged from the fighting unscathed.

The sun was already setting, so it was hard to tell one person from another. But Priya still recognised Ishani's silhouette from a distance. Her sister had brought her stick with her and was leaning heavily on it to walk.

Priya drew level with her. She didn't intend to start a conversation with Ishani, but her sister clearly felt differently.

'Didi.'

Priya walked on in silence.

Ishani dragged herself forward more quickly. 'Didi, listen . . .'

'I don't want to hear it,' said Priya in a flat voice. 'Save yourself the trouble.'

The dark line of trees behind the houses looked more appealing with every step she took. If she stayed near the edge of the jungle, spending the night there shouldn't be a problem. Maybe she could find a dry spot somewhere among the trees. Not in a shed, but under the starry sky.

Ishani grabbed her elbow. Her grip was surprisingly powerful. 'Listen to me. Mama asked me a lot of questions. I only told her you were taking part because she was going to find out anyway. Why are you so angry with me? You knew she'd hear about it sooner or later!'

'You don't understand why I'm angry?' Priya turned round furiously. Ishani let go of her. 'I helped you! And that's how you thank me?'

Ishani's mouth twitched. 'I still don't understand,' she said sullenly. 'This is supposed to be *my* victory. Why are you even competing? You don't really want to . . .'

'Just go away, Ishani.' Priya went to turn her back on Ishani, but her sister stopped her.

Two big grey clouds moved across the orange-pink sky above them.

'I've worked towards this all my life. It's not as if you're really in with a chance.'

Priya snorted. 'Without me, your dream of going to Kuwatta would already have gone up in smoke. Or do you think you'd have managed to grab a desk for the written test without my help?'

That hit a nerve. The hard look appeared in Ishani's eyes again. 'Fine,' she said. 'Suit yourself. If you'd rather be alone, then do whatever you want. That's what you've been doing all your life anyway.'

She pushed Priya aside with her shoulder, and then, dragging her leg, she walked ahead of her to their house. Fists clenched, Priya stared at Ishani's back. Yes, she'd always been alone. But not because she wanted to be. Priya stomped doggedly past their house. Two houses on, she leaned against the side of a shed. Her legs couldn't go any further.

She tilted her head back.

The first fat raindrops were coming down.

+++

Most of the second day went by in a blur.

Priya won her first fight. In the second fight, she lost her stick because of a clumsy mistake. Feeling sick with disappointment, she stood at the side, waiting for a soldier to come and fetch her. Winning really mattered now. If she lost her next fight, she couldn't go through to the final round.

'Wait here until I call you,' a soldier told her.

Priya watched the other fights. Ishani was on her second fight of the day. Priya tore her eyes away from the duel. She refused to pay any attention to her sister. Refused to give in to the painful lump in her throat that appeared whenever she thought about her family.

But the crowd was strangely quiet, eerily quiet. The air was charged, and Priya was starting to feel uneasy. Everyone seemed transfixed by the fight between her sister and her opponent in the middle of the ring. Priya reluctantly glanced in her direction again.

Ishani was fighting against Vikash.

Unlike most of the competitors, Vikash was solidly built. As the son of a village elder, he'd never gone hungry. With every attack he made with his stick, the muscles in his arms bulged. All those hours he'd spent in the village elders' korjalen sailing to trade in neighbouring villages were now paying off.

And her sister, Priya soon noticed, was clearly losing. She stood bent over with her stick in both hands and looked up at Vikash, her breath coming out in gasps. Vikash didn't look tired at all, just had a thin sheen of sweat on his face and shoulders. Although it could have been the rain.

Ishani ran forward with a shout. Vikash merely raised his stick. She slammed into it, bouncing back. Vikash hadn't even moved his feet. The corners of his mouth twitched upwards. He was playing with her.

'Do something,' someone called from the crowd. 'Give your opponent a break!'

Vikash looked up, annoyed. The spectator immediately shut up. Without taking his eyes off the crowd, Vikash parried Ishani's next attack. Then he took a step back and looked Priya's sister up and down. He seemed to be considering something before making a decision. He rolled his shoulders back.

And then he attacked.

After his first blow, Ishani fell into the mud. After his second blow, she was eating dust. After his third blow, she couldn't get up. But the stick was still clasped firmly in her hand.

Priya watched her, jaw clenched. She had made her wounded hands into fists. She couldn't watch. Ishani's tall, slender figure lay in the dirt, a filthy heap. Her dark hair had fallen from her plait and strands were trailing over her back and face.

Vikash had won. All he had to do was pull the stick from her hands. Ishani was no longer capable of fighting. But she was still trying to stand up.

Vikash watched her, bored. His stick came down on Ishani again. This time she stayed on the ground.

Priya flinched.

Ishani's hand opened up. The stick rolled over her fingers and then just lay there. Her skin gleamed with rain. She avoided the next blow by rolling onto her side. Her body was twisted, her gaze was blank. Priya knew that she was still conscious only because of sheer will-power. Her back was speckled with dark dots that grew into a large stain. Blood.

Priya stepped forward.

A soldier grabbed her by the arm and pulled her back. His dark eyes looked at her sharply. 'Stay out of it.'

'That's my sister!' she snapped at the man, trying to shake him off. Ishani screamed.

The soldier gripped Priya more firmly. 'The only ones who can stop the fight are your sister – and us. If you interfere, both you and your sister will be disqualified.'

That was enough to make her abandon her protests. She squeezed her eyes closed as Vikash raised his stick again. Every blow that struck Ishani felt as if it were coming down on her own body. Why didn't Scholar Afounsowa intervene? It was making her feel sick.

'. . . up,' croaked a hoarse voice.

An uneasy murmur went through the crowd.

'Stop!' ordered Scholar Afounsowa.

Priya cautiously opened her eyes.

The scholar was striding into the ring. Vikash was frozen in his attack, slowly lowering his stick. Ishani had clasped her fingers around the long weapon.

'Repeat what you just said.' The scholar held her hand up to Vikash and looked at Ishani.

'I . . .' rasped Ishani. 'I give up.'

Then she fainted. Priya ran forward. She knocked Vikash out of the way and sank down onto her knees beside Ishani. Hands shaking, she cupped her sister's face. The blood on her back and shoulders mingled with the rain. 'Ishani? Shan!'

But Ishani lay limp in her arms and Priya was dizzy with fear. Not again. First Umed and now Ishani. She was just about to start shaking her sister when Ishani took a shuddery breath.

'Ishani,' Priya gasped again, this time with relief.

'Give her to me.' A villager had come over to them, and she carefully took Ishani in her arms. Priya recognised her; she'd seen her talking to her mother before. Her name was Shanti. 'You're not done. They're calling you for the next fight.'

'What? No,' said Priya, leaning protectively over Ishani.

'My husband's a healer. I'll take her to him.' The woman examined Ishani's body, quickly and decisively. 'Can you let your mother know?'

+++

Priya dug her fingers into the mud.

Ishani was lying in the healer's main room. Her mother and Master Haripersad were also there. Priya had gone to tell the teacher, who had no interest in the physical contest and had remained in his own house with his books. He'd listened to her stammering explanation and had immediately set off to break the news to their mother, so that Priya could go and check on Ishani. It happened so quickly that he hadn't even asked why she hadn't gone straight home.

It hadn't taken long for her mother to come running.

So, now she was sitting here, against one of the wooden stilts under the healer's house, hidden behind enough foliage not to be seen. If she concentrated, she could make out what was being said. She bit her bottom lip to keep her emotions under control. Even winning her last fight and getting through to the next round hadn't brought her any joy.

First her father. Then Umed. Now Ishani. It was true – she was indeed cursed and she dragged all those around her into it with her.

'Priya!'

That brought her back to herself.

Master Haripersad had come downstairs and was looking around, searching for her. 'Priya!' he called again. He sounded worried.

Priya tried to make herself invisible. She wasn't prepared for the questions he no doubt wanted to ask her. And she certainly wasn't ready to explain her own choices and her dreams to him. Master Haripersad understood a lot about the world, but that was something he wouldn't comprehend.

'I know you're here somewhere.' Master Haripersad was still looking for her, but he was walking in the wrong direction. 'Why won't you come out, Priya? What's going on?'

Priya bowed her head. It was better to ignore him. If she was going to leave this life behind, then she would have to leave him behind as well. But something inside her wanted to go running to him and to pour everything out.

'Keep it inside,' she murmured to herself. 'Keep it all inside.'

She squeezed her eyes tightly shut.

+++

On the third day of the physical test, Priya dragged herself to the ring. There had been a lot of rain recently, and all that water had made an impact. Her feet sank into the muddy ground. Narrow streams flowed past her and towards the river.

Priya rolled her shoulders back. Her body was stiff and sore, after another night in a random shed. Her stomach was rumbling too.

'Come here,' a soldier barked at her.

Luckily, Priya wasn't the only one who was suffering after the knocks she'd taken in her earlier fights. Her first opponent of the day staggered towards her and struggled to assume a fighting stance. He was about the same age and height as her. Priya could see that his right leg was shaking.

She took a deep breath and tried to clear her head.

As soon as the start signal was given, she lashed out at his trembling leg. He'd been anticipating that and parried her blow, but still he almost fell. She hit again. He blocked it, taking a step back, which forced him to put his weight on his injured leg. He crumpled.

Priya tried to take advantage, but he was prepared. She couldn't find an opening. He parried nearly all of her blows and even managed to go on the attack himself a few times. Their sticks clashed together.

She realised that she was enjoying the fight – and that made her forget the pain. But at a certain point, she began to tire. The fight went on and on.

Her arms became heavier, her blows clumsier. At first, she'd been able to target her opponent's body quite successfully, but now she kept missing her aim. She was getting desperate. She couldn't keep this up for long. But the same was true of her opponent. His stick hit hers with less and less force. Even if they did hit each other, they were not going to inflict any serious injuries.

And then Priya made a big mistake. Tripping over her own feet, she flew past him. Triumphantly, he swivelled and brought down his stick on her arm. Pain flashed through her wrist – and she dropped her weapon.

But before it could hit the ground, she dived on it. With her knees in the mud, she grabbed her stick with her right hand – just in time. Instead of standing up, she swung the stick low across the ground with all her might, hitting the boy's injured leg. With a yelp of pain, he landed beside her in the mud – but he didn't let go of his stick.

Breathing heavily, they stared at each other.

He was the first to move. With his stick firmly in his hand, he crawled through the mud towards her. She tried to dodge as he lunged at her, but the pain in her body made her slow. He threw himself on top of her, his body weighing down heavily on hers. One arm pressed on her shoulders and throat. With his other hand, he struggled to pry the stick from her fingers.

Priya tried to get the stick under her body, out of his reach. Her fingers were slick with blood, sand and water. Meanwhile she tugged at his arm with her free hand. He was pushing so hard against her throat that she could hardly breathe. She spluttered violently. When his arm shifted a little, Priya seized the opportunity, sinking her teeth into his arm.

'Gods, you bitch!' he screamed, but he didn't let go.

She bit down. Tasted blood. He pulled back his hand and she leaped to her feet. Even though she was racked with pain, she still managed to shove him off when he tried to restrain her. With a crash, he landed on his back. Then, she was on top of him. For a moment, she struggled with his arms, trying to get the better of him, but as soon as she pressed her knee onto his wounded leg, he went limp. His raw cry echoed across the ring. Wet strands of muddy hair fell over her face, hitting his chin and neck. She pinned her stick across his shoulders, so that he couldn't get up.

He wasn't looking at her. Just staring at nothing, his face filled with pain. She pressed harder on his leg, until she felt a bone break and he started screaming.

Leaning over him, she pulled the stick from his hand. Then she let herself fall to the side.

'We have a winner!' the shout rang out across the ring.

Priya rolled onto her back. The world was spinning. Fine drops of rain fell onto her, cooling her face.

As she let go of both sticks, she heard footsteps. She looked to the side and saw a soldier coming towards them.

The soldier helped Priya's defeated opponent to his feet. They slowly made their way to the side, the boy leaning heavily on him, unable to stand on his right leg.

'Return to the edge of the ring,' the soldier called back over his shoulder. 'Your next opponent is almost ready.'

Priya tried to move, but it took a few attempts. She couldn't push herself up, because her grazed hands were so painful. She had no idea how she was going to win the next fight in this state. When she was standing upright, she took a few deep breaths in and out and then stumbled to the edge of the ring.

'Wait.' Another soldier blocked her way. 'He's ready. You can go to the middle.'

Priya looked around. Her stick slipped from her hands. It was Vikash.

As Ishani's bleeding and broken body flashed into her mind, a wave of fury washed through her.

The Topuan soldier bent to pick up Priya's stick. He held it out to her. She took it automatically. Her ears were buzzing.

She stood in front of Vikash, who was spinning his stick in his right hand. Apart from a few scratches on his arms and a swelling on his calf, he looked unscathed. Much better than Priya, with her battered and bruised body.

Priya braced herself and leaned slightly forward.

'Stand by!' shouted a soldier.

Vikash lazily assumed a fighting stance.

The rain was coming down harder.

'And . . . fight!'

Vikash darted forward. Priya just had enough time to raise her stick in defence. Then she made an attempt to attack. Their sticks clashed, blow after blow. She felt every impact shoot up from her sore hands and through her body. With each thump, her feet sank deeper into the mud. Her teeth smacked painfully together. He was stronger than her. She hit him more often, but it didn't make any difference. Every crash of his stick sent her more and more off balance, while he didn't even falter.

Her hands, arms and shoulders were screaming. She couldn't take it anymore. But she refused to give up.

She lashed out at his hip. He absorbed the blow and took advantage of the moment to whip his stick in her direction. Quickly, she ducked. The stick grazed her back. Biting her lip to hold in a scream, she stood her ground. She dived forward and wrapped her arm around his legs. Then she pulled him towards her with all her weight. He fell back and went crashing to the ground.

He kicked out at her arm, forcing her to let go. With a growl, he leaped back to his feet. His dark eyes were blazing. Priya needed more time to recover. Vikash hit out at her so quickly that she was unable to dodge his blow. The wood of his stick slammed into her shoulder and the side of her face. She fell to one side. An explosive pain. Blood and mud in her mouth. Red. White. Light.

Her stick rolled from her hands.

'Stop,' said someone.

No, she wanted to answer. *No, this can't be the end. I'm not finished yet.*

Blinking, she looked up. Dark spots were dancing across her vision, but she could still make out Vikash's expression.

He was looking down at her. There was no remorse on his face.

Priya was consumed by bitter disappointment. Within her, her emotions and her curse churned against the imaginary glass walls she had built around them.

Her whole body trembling, Priya crawled over to her stick. As long as she could move, it wasn't over. And she was not planning to give up. Vikash raised his stick for a final blow.

'Stop,' Priya hissed at him. Was that a command? No, wait, no. She mustn't use her curse. No matter how angry she was, that was not an option. Her head was about to explode.

'Enough, I said.' Scholar Afounsowa stood in front of Priya. Vikash disappeared from view.

Priya collapsed.

The fight was over. It even hurt to breathe. The side of her face was burning.

'Vikash is the winner of the physical . . .'

The voice faded away and the dark spots took over.

10

SHE COULDN'T HAVE BEEN unconscious for longer than a few seconds because she was still lying on the wet sand when she opened her eyes again. A soldier was leaning over her. She felt fingers gently touching the side of her head.

She winced. The fingers disappeared.

'Take her away.' She couldn't see who the soldier was talking to, but then she felt hands and arms sliding under her back and knees and trying to help her up. 'Can you stand?'

'No,' she murmured. She wanted to say more, but she stopped because the right side of her face was hurting too much to talk.

'You're going to be fine,' a boy's voice said.

Priya could see only blurred shadows. She closed her eyes again and tried to swallow. All she could taste was the metallic tang of blood in her mouth. Sand crunched between her teeth.

With the boy's help, she sat up. It took some effort not to fall straight back down again. The fights were over. A group of people stood around her, but she could only see their feet and legs, as she couldn't look up. One pair of feet stood out – their skin was a lot darker than the others.

Again she tried to speak. 'Ishani . . .'

'Your sister's going to be alright.' The same boy's voice. 'She'll probably be back on her feet in a couple of days. And so will you.'

'The winner will be announced in seven sunrises' time,' said someone further away. A soldier? Or Scholar Afounsowa. Noises sounded strange in her right ear.

'Then most of the competitors will have recovered sufficiently to . . .'

She didn't hear the rest. Hands slid under her back and knees, lifting her up. Unable to hold herself up, Priya leaned to one side. Luckily, it was the left side of her face that fell onto someone's shoulder. She could smell a faint scent of coconut.

She vaguely registered that it was the boy who had spoken to her before. His face was swimming above her head. She tried to say something, but her mouth wouldn't cooperate. Eventually she gave up and closed her eyes.

+++

Leaves rustled above her head.

Gradually Priya became aware of the world around her again. She was lying on a thin mat of woven leaves.

'Ah, you're awake,' said a voice on her left.

Priya turned her head towards the source of the sound. Just that simple movement was enough to send a series of stabbing pains through her head and torso. The right side of her face felt strangely tight. The sounds coming in through her right ear were muffled. She carefully reached up to explore the sore spot. Her fingers encountered a thick layer of ointment. Then she felt her right shoulder, which was wrapped in pieces of cloth.

A woman was stooping over a wooden bowl of steaming water, wringing out a brown cloth. Over her shoulder she called out, 'Another one's woken up!'

It was the woman who had taken Ishani under her wing – Shanti, one of the midwives in Disin, whose husband was a healer. She often stepped in to help her husband when there were too many sick or wounded people for him to tend to on his own.

The room was filled with a thick, damp haze that smelled of herbs, sweat and blood.

'Where am I?' croaked Priya, licking her dry lips.

'In the house of my husband, healer Sharman. As you can see, you're not alone.' Shanti gestured at the other people in the room. Most of them were asleep or whimpering softly. Priya recognised the boy whose leg she had felt breaking during the fight. His broken limb was now enveloped in bandages.

'The boy who brought you here said he wanted to take you to your own house, but that you panicked when you realised where he was going.' She was dabbing the sweat from the forehead of a middle-aged man whose entire upper body was bandaged up. 'So we just kept you here.'

Flashes of the fights were coming back to her. Vikash. The all-encompassing pain.

'Has . . .' Priya hesitated, fearing the answer. 'Has the winner of the competition been announced yet?'

Shanti laughed softly.

'That's the first question everyone has asked when they woke up here,' she said. 'Don't worry, girl. The announcement hasn't been made yet. It won't happen for another five sunrises.'

Priya nodded her thanks and winced. She tried slowly, very slowly, to get to her feet. Moving made her back burn painfully. Her second attempt almost made her scream. In the end, she rolled onto her left side.

Beside her were three gourds with cold food in them.

'Your mother came to see you,' said Shanti, kneeling down beside her next patient. 'And Master Haripersad. Shall I send for him? He was very upset.'

Priya let her head fall onto the mat. 'No.'

'What about your family?' asked Shanti. 'Don't you want to go back to them?'

'No,' said Priya. 'No, I don't want to see my family.'

Just then, a man came into the room. He kneeled beside Priya and swiftly began cleaning her wounds.

+++

For the very last time, they all stood at the circular clearing by the water's edge: the villagers of Disin. Tense and bursting with curiosity, they had gathered around Scholar Afounsowa, who stood with her back to the flowing Cotari. Behind her, the koraljen bobbed on the rippling water.

Ishani and Priya stood, with two other villagers between them, in the middle of the crowd. Her sister was leaning on a walking stick and Priya craned her neck – she couldn't see much because of all the people in front of her. With one hand, she rubbed the side of her face. Her cheek and ear were still painful. She could catch only glimpses of the scholar and her soldiers. Nervously, she looked around for her mother, but she didn't see her anywhere.

She did spot Master Haripersad, though. Luckily, he didn't see her.

'We thank you, people of Disin, for your hospitality and for the fighting spirit of your participants,' said Scholar Afounsowa.

A ripple went around the crowd.

'General Suapala,' said the scholar, 'sets great store by knowledge, by initiative, by intelligence, but also by courage, strength and justice.'

Shoulders hunched, Ishani kept her gaze fixed on the ground.

Priya had finally found a gap between all the heads, through which she could see Scholar Afounsowa. Her uniform was an immaculate green. Around her wrists were orange-red bracelets that made Priya think of the sky at sunset.

'Only competitors who demonstrate all of those attributes may call themselves winners. To our great pleasure, a villager who fits this description has been found in Disin.'

The scholar's eyes swept over the crowd. For a moment, Priya thought their gazes met. She breathed in sharply and tried to control the expression on her face. Then the woman in front of Priya shifted her weight and the scholar's face disappeared behind a large head of curls. Priya took a step to one side and stood on her tiptoes. The scholar had not shifted her gaze. But now it was clear that she wasn't looking at Priya. Her eyes were on someone close to Priya.

On Ishani.

And suddenly Priya knew. She felt it in her bones, in the rushing of her blood, in the ringing in her ears. In the end, the brightest of the villagers would be chosen to become a scholar in training.

And that, it seemed, was her sister.

Scholar Afounsowa kept her eyes fixed on Ishani.

Priya was supposed to feel happy for her sister. Was supposed to stay calm, because this was what everyone had been expecting. What *she* had been expecting. But instead, she felt only bitter disappointment. Felt yet another rejection travelling through her bones and leaving nothing but coldness behind. And she knew, she knew with absolute certainty, that she would not survive if she stayed in Disin. For years, she had kept her curse – kept herself – in check.

She couldn't do it any longer.

'. . . the one who will come with us to Kuwatta, to be trained there as a scholar, under the supervision of General Suapala,' said Scholar Afounsowa, 'is . . .'

The tension was almost too much for Priya.

'Isha . . .'

No, thought Priya, squeezing her eyes shut. Her curse was writhing uncontrollably, seeking a way out. *No. Stop. Stop. STOP.*

The scholar's voice caught in her throat. Her eyes glazed over. One of the soldiers tapped the scholar on the shoulder and whispered something in her ear.

Priya gasped. It felt as if something inside her were exploding. Her hands, which she was pressing to her temples, slid down her face. She became aware of a thumping sensation in her head. Horrified, she stumbled backwards. She was almost certain she hadn't commanded

Scholar Afounsowa to do anything, because her eyes and thoughts had not been focused on the scholar. But it had been a close thing.

It had almost gone wrong.

Almost, almost, almost.

'. . . Priya Chkadhari,' said Scholar Afounsowa.

11

THERE WAS UTTER SILENCE after Scholar Afounsowa spoke Priya's name.

Priya fell to her knees. The world was spinning. Spots of green, blue, white. Hazy shadows of people. Too many people. How was it possible that her name had been called? It wasn't right. She was almost certain that the scholar had been about to say Ishani's name.

Her fingers dug into the sand.

Ishani.

Priya looked for her sister among the shadows and found her almost immediately. Ishani, the only person Priya could focus on, was staring at her. Her eyes widened in surprise at first, then confusion, before narrowing to suspicious half-moons.

Priya bent forward, pressing her hands to her eye sockets. It felt as if someone had stuffed her skull with straw.

Ishani walked over to her and knelt beside her. 'What have you done, Pri?' she hissed. 'In the name of the Gods, what have you done?'

She hadn't done anything. Nothing at all. But Priya couldn't blame Ishani for her distrust. Knowledge, initiative and intelligence? They weren't exactly terms that described Priya. Now she was starting to doubt what had happened herself. Had she unintentionally used her curse?

'Priya Chkadhari,' Scholar Afounsowa repeated more forcefully. 'Step forward.'

Priya pushed herself to her feet. Ishani stepped back. Priya avoided her gaze. Warily, she inched forward as the group parted. Priya shook her head, but she soon stopped doing that when she realised everyone was staring at her.

'How did that happen?' she heard someone mumbling.

'It must be a mistake,' said another person. 'The scholar started to say someone else's name first.'

'Isn't that Ishani's sister?'

So, she wasn't the only one who'd noticed that Scholar Afounsowa had been about to say Ishani's name. Priya narrowed her eyes, attempting to decipher the expression on the scholar's face.

She forced herself to keep walking. Taking one step. Then another. Scholar Afounsowa waited until Priya was standing right in front of her. Her dark eyes were unreadable, her face was an emotionless mask. Priya could not fathom her. Throughout the entire competition, she had remained a mystery. The scholar almost seemed to be carved from stone. She had the same kind of cool tranquillity about her as Ishani.

Scholar Afounsowa placed her hands on Priya's shoulders and turned her around. The firm pressure of her hands was all that kept Priya from falling over.

'Behold, people of Disin.' Her voice was loud and clear. Powerful. 'Your winner. The representative of your village, the pride of Disin, the hope of Awaran!'

The soldiers banged the bottoms of their sticks on the ground three times. Here and there, villagers cautiously clapped. Priya's dizziness left her. She saw her former opponents staring at her. Somewhere in the sea of faces were Ishani and Master Haripersad.

'We're leaving at sunrise,' said Scholar Afounsowa more quietly. 'You may withdraw this evening to say farewell to your family and to gather your belongings for the journey. Try to limit the number of things you bring. You will be provided with everything you might need in Kuwatta and the korjalen are already carrying enough cargo.'

'There's no need,' said Priya, her tone flat. 'There's no one here for me to say goodbye to.' She was not going to set foot in her house again if she could help it – and she probably wasn't welcome there anyway.

The group of villagers began to break up. A few people tried to approach Priya, but the soldiers stopped them. The test was over. Their dreams of Kuwatta would have to be put on hold again until the next competition. There was work to do. Priya noticed Vikash standing at the front. To her surprise, she saw that his arm had been bound into position with wooden splints and rope. He gave her a brief nod and turned round. Priya relaxed slightly.

'If I'm not mistaken, you have a younger sister who also took part in the test. Ishani Chkadhari.'

Priya was immediately on her guard. 'Yes, that's right.'

Scholar Afounsowa nodded slowly. 'Go home,' she said. 'Say goodbye to your family. Pack your things. I'll meet you there tonight.'

It was not a request. Priya didn't dare to ask why the scholar wanted to visit her home. She just bowed her head and walked away.

Two weeks had passed since the contest had begun. It was more than a week since Priya had last spoken to her mother. She had watched her from a safe distance, with a pain in her chest and stomach that took her breath away. But spoken to her? Definitely not. The silk thread holding them together had broken when Priya had used her curse against her mother.

The thought of leaving her little brother behind was really painful, though.

Priya went home the long way, to make sure she wouldn't run into Ishani. She could still see the shock in her sister's dark eyes when Priya's name had been called.

Priya was afraid. Afraid because she couldn't say for certain whether or not she had used her curse. Afraid of Ishani's reaction, as her sister was clearly convinced that Priya *had* used it. Afraid of the reaction that Ishani's words might unleash at home.

After a long detour, she finally saw the house looming up ahead. Slowly, Priya climbed the stairs. Step by step. Foot by foot.

Before she reached the porch, the door opened.

'Come in,' her mother barked. Then she turned and walked ahead of Priya.

Priya entered the living room. Ishani was sitting beside Umed, legs outstretched and head bowed. Beside her was her walking stick.

'I've gathered up your belongings.' Her mother stepped forward with a small gourd. Priya took it from her. There was soup in it.

'Drink,' her mother ordered.

Out of habit, Priya did as she was told. She put the gourd to her lips and took a sip. A sharp, salty taste filled her mouth. It was the soup her mother usually made when one of them needed to recover after an illness.

Her gaze slid back to Ishani, who still hadn't said a word and had now taken Umed's hand in hers.

'Be careful on your journey,' her mother said. Her chin was trembling a little. 'Trust only yourself.'

Priya nodded and drank some more soup. She hadn't seen this coming. Her mother was acting as if there had been no argument. As if she hadn't spent her whole life fighting to keep Priya in line and forbidden her to do the test.

'And keep your secrets to yourself,' her mother continued. There it was. The warning. 'Don't tell anyone anything you might regret later.'

Priya lowered the gourd. Her mother was clearly struggling to keep her expression neutral, but her voice gave away her fear.

'She hasn't found out about it, has she? The scholar? She doesn't know you used your curse?' her mother asked quietly.

Again, Priya looked at her sister, who was avoiding her gaze. 'No,' she said to the side of Ishani's head.

'Then it's alright,' her mother said, pushing against the gourd in Priya's hands. 'Drink it quickly. It's too late to do anything now. I can't protest against a scholar's decision, no matter how much I might want to.' And Priya knew she wanted to do that very much. 'Whatever you do, make sure absolutely no one discovers your secret.'

Her mother watched closely as Priya gulped down the soup. Her tongue and throat were burning when she handed the bowl back to her mother. She wiped her mouth on the back of her hand and saw that her mother was looking at her expectantly.

'It's time to pack your things,' she said. She raised one hand and it seemed as if she was about to lay it on Priya's shoulder but then she changed her mind and lowered her hand.

Suddenly, Priya realised something. 'I can't leave the house,' she said, so painfully aware that no one wanted her there. 'The scholar's expecting to meet me here this evening.'

Her mother almost dropped the gourd. 'Why?'

'I don't know,' Priya admitted.

Ishani raised her head for the first time since Priya had entered. 'She knows, doesn't she? You deceived everyone,' she hissed venomously.

'Of course I didn't.' Priya's mouth became dry. 'What are you talking about?'

Ishani stood up. 'You know very well what I mean. You used your curse. She was saying *my* name, but then . . .'

'Ishani,' Priya's mother said sharply. 'Be quiet.'

'This was *my* future,' Ishani shouted, ignoring her mother. 'And she's gone and stolen it!'

Priya wanted to apologise, wanted to yell back at her, wanted to disappear and never return. She took a step back. In Ishani's dark eyes, she saw the shards of their sisterly relationship, now shattered, as she'd predicted.

'And what about you?' she spat back. 'Why don't *I* deserve this? Why is it only ever about how *you* feel and what *you* want?'

'That's enough now!' their mother intervened. 'We've already discussed this, Ishani. Hold your tongue and sit down. I don't want to hear another word.' Priya hoped that would be the end of it, but her mother turned to look at her and said in a cold voice, 'I will give you one chance, Priya. Did you use your curse?'

'No,' said Priya, without knowing for sure if she was telling the truth. Just a little longer and she would be away from here. Just a little longer and she wouldn't have to see how she'd ruined not only Umed's life, but also Ishani's. It was as if the world cruelly wanted to show her that she was a monster in more ways than one.

+++

The scholar arrived at nightfall. As Priya's mother was lighting the bundles of herbs to keep the insects at bay, there was a quiet knock at the door.

Ishani was the first to move. She got up from her place beside Umed and, with the help of her stick, she walked to the front door.

'Good evening.' Scholar Afounsowa had to duck to enter. A soldier followed her and closed the door behind them.

Priya saw that Scholar Afounsowa had exchanged her green uniform for a beige one. Her height and imposing aura made their living room feel small and insignificant.

Priya's mother wiped her hands on her orange sari and bowed deeply to the scholar.

'I am honoured that you have chosen my daughter as Disin's winner,' she said, still in the middle of a deep bow. She stood up and pressed her hands together, with the fingers pointing straight up – a Suryan greeting.

'She performed well in the test,' said Scholar Afounsowa, waving away the wisps of smoke that came wafting towards her. 'With such results, it is her right to travel with us to Kuwatta.'

Priya's mother nudged Priya, who hurried over to the herbs and moved them to a different corner of the room. The smoke changed direction.

'Forgive my impertinence, but why did you want to come to our house this evening?' asked Priya's mother.

'My visit was certainly not intended to subject Priya to any further questioning if that's what you fear, Mrs Chkadhari.' Scholar Afounsowa's gaze shifted briefly to Priya.

'But . . .' Priya's mother frowned. 'Then why are you here?'

'For Ishani.'

Priya looked up with a start and saw Ishani's head jerk up too. Her sister had been curled up next to Umed all evening, acting as if she'd become part of the house. The scholar's words brought her back to life.

'It has come to our attention that you have not one but two daughters who are extremely talented,' Scholar Afounsowa continued. 'So, I would like to ask you to give them both to Kuwatta, so that the two of them can work towards a free Awaran.'

'There can be only one winner.' Priya's mother stepped forward, standing in front of Priya. Her tone became suspicious, without losing its undertone of humility. 'Only one can be the best, not two, Scholar Afounsowa.'

'The general is looking for talented citizens. I am doing only what he asks of me. Besides, we have in fact never ruled out the possibility of multiple winners.'

That was true, but it had never happened before. Or at least Priya had never heard either Ishani or Master Haripersad mention it.

'Can't you just take my middle child?' their mother pleaded. 'She's worked so hard for years so that she might study in Kuwatta. My elder daughter will be more useful in Disin.'

Priya froze.

Being treated her entire life as if she were worth less than Ishani was one thing. It was something else entirely to hear her mother admit it out loud to the scholar.

'There are many possibilities at the fort,' said the scholar.

Those words did not go down well with Priya's mother. 'She will not be capable of taking advantage of any of those opportunities,' she insisted more urgently. There was a slight tremble in her voice. 'You must understand, I can't do without both of my daughters. My son was recently exposed to the blood moon . . .' Scholar Afounsowa's gaze shifted to the unconscious Umed. '. . . and I know my elder daughter. She's better off with me.'

'That's enough,' said Priya from behind her back. Her voice was quiet, her tone raw.

Her mother turned and cupped Priya's face in both hands. It was something Priya had often seen her do to Umed and sometimes Ishani, but she had never – *never* – done it to Priya. Her mother's hands felt narrow, small, bony. But they were warm. And they held her tight. The places where they touched Priya were almost burning, it felt so unreal.

'Mama,' she said in a small voice. 'I . . .'

'Listen to me, Priya,' said her mother, interrupting her gently but forcefully. 'They only have room for scholars and soldiers at Kuwatta. Do you understand what I'm saying? You will disappear there. Once you're at the fort, there's no way out.'

And there was the cold, there was the pain, there was the bitter disappointment.

Priya roughly pushed her mother's hands away. 'You've never believed in me, not for one single day, have you? No way out?' She snorted and took a step back. 'That's been true all my life. I was born in a prison and if I don't free myself now, I'm going to rot away until there's nothing left of me.'

'You have no idea what goes on inside that fort,' her mother whispered, with more intensity in her dark eyes than Priya had ever seen before. She was speaking so quietly that even Priya could barely make out her words. 'You have no idea what you're getting yourself into. If they find out . . .' Her voice faltered, and she closed her eyes. 'It's better if you stay in Disin.'

Unbelievable. It was unbelievable that she'd almost fallen for it. Her mother didn't love her. Priya was suddenly absolutely convinced of that. She had never loved Priya. All she cared about was other people not finding out that Priya was a blood child. It was all about *her*. It was about Ishani. It was about their family. But it was not about Priya. Ever since her mother had made the mistake of hiding her blood child at birth.

The only person in the family who actually cared about Priya at this point, blood child or not, was unconscious.

'I understand your concern.'

The scholar's voice seemed to come from a long way off. Priya tried to calm down.

'Kuwatta demands the utmost of its scholars and soldiers. But although my previous words might have given that impression, I did not come here to negotiate with you.' An icy tone had crept into the scholar's voice. 'If you refuse, you will be going against the wishes of General Suapala. You would be depriving him of valuable knowledge, development and progress, even though you know just as well as everyone else that the colonists on the coast are breathing down our necks. Are you prepared to pay the price for your disobedience?'

Priya's mother opened her mouth. Closed it again.

'That's not necessary,' said Priya. She strode past her mother, who was glued to the floor, and stood before Scholar Afounsowa. 'I'm ready to leave.'

'And so am I. If General Suapala requests my presence, I will not refuse,' said Ishani, coming to stand beside Priya.

A thin smile appeared on the scholar's face. 'Very good. Take their belongings,' she said to the soldier who had been watching in silence.

The soldier snapped into action. He walked to the bag containing Priya's few belongings, which her mother had already prepared. In one movement, he swung it over his shoulder.

Ishani went up to the soldier, spoke to him in a low voice and disappeared.

'I'll leave with you now if you don't mind,' said Priya, who was still standing in front of the scholar.

Scholar Afounsowa raised her eyebrows, but replied, 'As you wish.' Then she stood up straight. 'Let's leave it at that. Early tomorrow, at daybreak, we shall depart from the water's edge. For now, I wish the rest of you a good night.' She paused and then said, 'May the moon shine long and white upon all of you.'

With those words, she disappeared through the door that the soldier had already opened. Ishani was just coming back into the living room.

'I'll be there,' she said, handing the soldier the bag that she'd quickly packed.

Priya kneeled beside Umed. She pressed one last kiss on his forehead. 'I won't forget you, Um,' she whispered, as she swore to herself that she would find a remedy for him when she got to Kuwatta. Ishani was not the only one who could be counted on.

The scholar and the soldier had already gone through the doorway. Priya jumped up and strode to join them. Her emotions were in chaos, but she refused to look back. She refused to say goodbye to her mother, even though it hurt. Maybe that was why she didn't do it. Maybe she wanted it to hurt, so that she would know there had been some kind of love between them.

But before she was out the door, her mother grabbed her and pulled her back. 'Listen to me. I know you're angry with me,' she said, tightening her grip. 'But listen carefully: if you see anyone with a bleeding mouth, run away as fast as you can. Do you hear me? Even if they're staggering, wounded, even if they beg you for help. You run *away*.'

Priya pulled her arm free and stumbled outside.

'Do not listen, do not look, do not speak. By all the Gods, run away. RUN AWAY.'

12

FIVE KORJALEN SWAYED ON the river, close to the bank. The Cotari meandered into the distance until it disappeared into the green of the trees and the undergrowth, its brown-black water glinting, full of promise, beneath the rising sun.

Priya sat, knees drawn up, in one of the long, slim boats. She was surrounded by the winners from other villages and settlements. Luanans, Topuans, Dalinese and Suryans all sat together in the different boats, as if the invisible lines drawn between the free peoples of Awaran didn't matter here.

Priya rubbed the back of her neck. Scholar Afounsowa had taken her to the house of one of the village elders the night before, where the scholar had been staying since the beginning of the test. The elder had shown Priya to a place on the floor in a small room, which Priya suspected was a hastily emptied storage room. That wasn't a problem – she'd slept in much less pleasant places recently. Even so, it had taken her a long time to fall asleep, and she'd woken with a start, her body stiff.

Dreams of a screaming Umed, a sneering Ishani and people with blood-covered mouths had plagued her in the night.

She shivered at the memory and tried to shake off the images.

A movement in the corner of her eye made her look up. The winners in the korjaal next to hers were standing up and moving aside so that Ishani could step between them and take a seat in the middle of the boat.

Ishani glanced at Priya, but said nothing.

The riverbank was packed with curious villagers who had come out in the early morning to wave them goodbye. They were staring with interest not only at Priya, the official winner of Disin, but also at Ishani and the other winners.

Master Haripersad stood in the crowd. Priya's mother had not come, but he was there. Priya fiddled with the hem of her kameez. The mischievous twinkle in the teacher's eyes was absent today, but he smiled softly as he looked at her. And that smile made Priya shrink a little inside. He didn't look angry, even though she'd cut him out of her life without saying a word. No, he just looked sad.

I'm sorry, she thought. Even though it was too late for that.

The mumbled conversations died away, and people shouted their farewells. The last soldiers stepped into the korjalen.

One soldier walked to the front with a koela in his hand. He was the koelaman, who would use his stick to probe the shallow and dangerous parts of the Cotari, so that they could avoid them.

The ropes securing the korjalen were untied. The boats drifted out onto the slowly flowing water.

The knot in Priya's stomach began to loosen. Slowly, she breathed out.

'Hey!' shouted a boy, pushing his way through the crowd. Shocked, the villagers moved aside in all directions. 'Wait for me!'

Roughly shoving a couple of people out of the way in his haste, he ran along the riverbank, level with the korjaal. His skin was smooth and dark brown, almost black, and he had a red kamisa hanging around his waist. Priya guessed he was around her age.

Scholar Afounsowa glanced at him and rolled her eyes.

The boy took a run-up and jumped.

With a crash, he landed right in front of Priya's feet, making the korjaal rock perilously. The soldier at the front cursed in a language that she thought she recognised as Luan. The newcomer almost fell into the Cotari, but then he grabbed the edge of the korjaal with one hand and clutched Priya's arm with the other. She fell forward, slamming her nose into his shoulder. Her cry was stifled by his arm.

When he'd regained his balance, he gently pushed her back. She held her hands to her throbbing nose and glared at him, eyes blazing.

'Sorry,' he apologised in Awuran with a smile that brought out a dimple in his left cheek. His voice was soft and husky, with a lilting undertone.

Judging by his deep-brown skin, his wide, strong nose and full lips, he was of Luanan descent. She muttered curses at him in Suryan, knowing he wouldn't understand. He tilted his head and slightly narrowed his dark eyes.

'Kwasi,' said Scholar Afounsowa, and he turned round.

Priya warily felt her nose, found that it was still intact and lowered her hands.

By now the korjaal was sailing between deserted banks. There was no sign of any villagers. They had left Disin behind – and with it, her family and her old life.

She had expected to be relieved. But instead she was struck by a sudden sadness. It wasn't as if she regretted her decision to leave everything behind and never to return. But Disin was still the place where she had grown up. And the place where Umed remained behind. She wasn't going to see him again, and that was hard. Harder than she'd expected.

'You're late.'

'You're right, Scholar Afounsowa. But how could you leave me behind?' Kwasi said, clutching his chest with a pained expression.

A strange sensation came over Priya, and she ran her fingers over her shoulders and arms. And then she saw it. There was a black shadow moving over Kwasi's shoulder. Priya squeezed her eyes shut. It was a tarantula. Its hairy legs were climbing up Kwasi's shoulder and onto his neck. She closely followed the path the spider was taking.

Surely Kwasi must be able to feel it?

'I told everyone we would leave just before sunrise. I expect you, as a winner, to act responsibly,' Scholar Afounsowa said frostily.

'I was late. I'll admit it.' Kwasi reached back, holding out his fingers behind his neck, and the tarantula swiftly climbed onto his hand. 'But did you really mean to leave me behind? After all we've been through together?'

Scholar Afounsowa raised her eyebrows. 'First you leave the korjalen even though I discouraged all the winners from doing so, and then you got too involved during the test, even though all interference is forbidden.'

'I only . . .'

'Enough,' Scholar Afounsowa interrupted him. 'You're here now. Take your seat.'

The other winners in Priya's korjaal hadn't tried to talk to her yet, which was fine by her. They were far enough apart that they didn't have to touch one another. Two Topuans, one Dalinese, and one Luanan. And Kwasi and Priya.

It was strange to see them all together in this small space.

Kwasi let out a defeated sigh and, to Priya's dismay, dropped down next to her on the narrow bench. He hung his hand. The tarantula fell off his hand and scuttled away, and the tingling sensation that she'd felt faded.

Kwasi's leg touched hers and she immediately moved up a bit. Her abrupt movement made him turn to look at her.

'I noticed you didn't say goodbye to anyone back there. Not a family person?' he asked her. She shrank a little at that question, but he'd already turned away again.

Without waiting for her reply, he started stretching. 'I'm already so stiff, and we've only just sat down. It took three whole days to travel from where I lived to here. How long do you think it'll take to get to Kuwatta?'

He really did talk far too much.

However, it wasn't just her reluctance to talk that was preventing her from answering. Priya's Awuran was good enough to hold a conversation, but that didn't mean she liked speaking it. Ishani always laughed when she heard Priya speaking that language. Not out loud. That wasn't her sister's style. She just gave a little smirk.

'Forget what I said. It's not like any of us have ever been to Kuwatta before.' He puffed upwards, making the little black curls on his forehead dance. Then he smiled again and the dimple in his cheek reappeared. 'Did I introduce myself, by the way? The name's Kwasi. I'm one of the winners from Pijaro.'

Priya narrowed her eyes. So, he wasn't the only winner from his village either. Interesting. 'Priya Chkadhari. Winner of Disin.'

'Chkadhari,' repeated Kwasi. He looked at the other korjalen. 'There was another winner with the same last name. Your sister, right?'

She looked away. That wasn't something she wanted to get into.

'I didn't know it was a secret.' He leaned in closer, lowering his voice. 'I can keep it to myself. No problem.'

She backed away a little. 'It's not a secret.'

He leaned back and raised his hands in an apology. Then he crossed them over his chest defensively.

She rolled her eyes, and he responded with a grin.

'How did you know we have the same last name?' she couldn't resist asking. The Awuran words felt strange and clumsy on her tongue. The foreign language felt like a badly composed song whose notes shifted in all directions when Priya said them.

Kwasi didn't appear to notice that she was struggling for words. He rested his elbows on his knees. 'I was in the crowd. You might have noticed me.'

'No,' she replied.

Kwasi seemed to find her chilly reaction amusing. 'I was there during the physical test too. I even carried you to the healer. Like a hero. You were looking pretty rough.' He sadly shook his head.

'Wait.' Priya looked at him with renewed interest. 'That was you?'

'Yeah. It's just who I am. You're welcome, by the way.' He gave her a big grin. 'I was also there when the other Chkadhari was declared the winner. Oh no, *your* name was announced at the last second, of course. A lot of the villagers had opinions about that.'

Priya couldn't stop her thoughts going to her mother. 'What did they say?' she asked.

'They were speculating that your mother had deliberately kept you hidden away and was waiting to play her secret trump card. Others said you were jealous of your sister and that you'd bewitched the scholar with black magic.'

Priya sniffed to hide her hollow laugh.

'You don't believe me?' The supposedly offended tone he'd used when he spoke to Scholar Afounsowa came back into his voice.

'My mother didn't keep me hidden as some kind of trump card. She didn't have any high expectations of me at all.' She wanted to take back the words as soon as they'd left her mouth.

'Then she got you wrong,' said Kwasi to her surprise. He held her gaze, with nothing but curiosity and kindness in his dark eyes. 'I've seen you fight.'

His honest smile made Priya uncomfortable. She gave him a quick nod.

Kwasi seemed to settle for that. He stood up and walked forward. The korjaal rocked with every step he took. Priya followed him with her eyes as he strolled past the other winners to perch beside the koeleman, who gave Kwasi a look of irritation as he enthusiastically launched into another story.

Priya relaxed a little, relieved that at least he was leaving her in peace.

The korjaal that Ishani was sitting in sailed through the rapids right beside them. Priya's sister held her folded hands on her lap and gazed straight ahead.

Priya looked away. Her eyes should be focused forward, on Kuwatta, which, somewhere ahead in the distance, was waiting for her.

13

THE JOURNEY TO KUWATTA seemed to take forever.

At night, they moored somewhere on the riverbank and set up camp close by. The scholar slept in a tent that the soldiers put up for her. The rest of the group spent the night on the ground under the starry sky, dozing off to the sound of running water, the chirping of crickets and the crackling of fire. It was a blessing for Priya that the korjaal Ishani was in wasn't moored close to theirs. That meant she could avoid her sister.

During the daytime, Kwasi chattered away more than everyone else in the cramped korjaal put together. Within no time, he was friends with most of the passengers, although the soldiers took a little longer to warm to him. It was thanks to Kwasi that Priya found out that Disin was the last village where the scholar would be holding the test this time.

Although Priya struggled to get used to Kwasi's chattiness, she appreciated his presence. As long as he was talking, her unpleasant memories and thoughts lay dormant somewhere in the back of her mind.

'So, what's it like there?' Kwasi asked a Topuan soldier one day. 'Kuwatta.'

'It's a military fortress,' the soldier answered in a bored voice, rowing on. 'What do you think it's like?'

'Are the buildings really all made of jet-black stone?' Kwasi went on in the same loud whisper, as if he were telling a secret. But the whole korjaal could hear him, as he well knew. 'With towers so high that they touch the sky?'

Priya moved to one side, leaning forward so as not to miss the soldier's reply.

The soldier sighed. 'Yes, more or less. The black fort stands on a black stone bridge that's built on the edge of a waterfall. On most mornings, thick clouds of mist come drifting up and the towers look like they're wrapped in clouds.'

'And is it true that the general has four lovers?' asked the Dalinese boy who was sitting in front of Priya.

The soldier raised his eyebrows. 'Where did you hear that?'

The Dalinese boy blushed. 'Just something I heard in my village.'

Priya leaned further forward. 'Four lovers? Don't you mean political connections . . . um, alliances?'

All eyes turned on her and she became painfully aware of her clumsy Awuran. She swallowed.

'That's what I was told,' she said more slowly, moving back to her spot. She saw Kwasi's amused smile.

The soldier nodded. 'That's right. Political alliances, with firm agreements laid down. The general is of mixed descent and has entered into relationships with all four of the free peoples of Awuran to keep the peace and to give each group a voice. But he has only one wife.'

'Yes, right now. He has had several partners though,' said Kwasi casually, wiggling his eyebrows. 'And apparently he's also had a lot of children with them.'

'Kwasi!' said Scholar Afounsowa from her seat at the front of the korjaal.

'My apologies, Scholar Afounsowa.'

+++

Kuwatta's welcome came rolling towards them in the form of large clouds of mist. The fine drops made Priya's face damp. The overhanging trees and the reeds on the riverbanks slowly disappeared behind a light-grey curtain. Most of the soldiers stopped rowing. Priya sat up straighter and narrowed her eyes, trying to make out what was hiding behind the clouds, as her stomach clenched nervously.

In the distance, the sun came up, painting the mist in front of them a pale pink. The sky above was still a dark blue with endless twinkling points of light. Priya tilted back her head to take a better look at the stars, before the mist also concealed a large part of the sky from her.

A tingle ran along her spine. She rubbed the back of her head, but the gentle pressure didn't go away.

Then the glittering dots in the dark sky slowly descended. *Was this really happening?* It was impossible to grasp. She squeezed her eyes shut for a moment. Opened them again. The dots were still moving. She slowly reached out a hand in amazement as the pieces of pure light came close enough to touch.

Priya looked around. Kwasi had also tipped back his head. There was a deep frown line between his eyebrows, but he didn't move.

Like Priya, the other winners were standing up, tripping over one another in their attempts to touch the falling stars.

Priya reached for one as it came closer. The sparkles playfully scattered and drifted away before she could touch them. Without thinking about it, Priya chased after the stars. Stumbling, she followed the dots of light.

In the tip of the korjaal, she fell to her knees. The koelaman looked down at her with an irritated sigh. He'd had to move aside so that she didn't land on top of him.

'What is this?' she asked no one in particular. The tingling sensation down her spine had grown more intense.

Without waiting for an answer, she leaned over the edge of the korjaal. The water of the river, normally a brownish black, had taken on a translucent blue-green glow. The creatures swimming in it were giving off light.

This was incredible.

Priya cautiously moved her fingers towards the water. As her fingertips touched the surface, glowing fish jumped into the air. With a cry, she fell backwards. The fish spread their glittering wings. Droplets went splashing in all directions, in fiery sparks. To the right of the korjaal, a freshwater stingray slowly rose and swam through the air.

She slid back in alarm. 'Am I dreaming?'

'No,' said a voice. Scholar Afounsowa had come closer and was holding out one finger to a dragonfly. The moment her finger touched the glowing dragonfly, the insect burst apart in a rain of sparks. 'This is the magic of Kuwatta. This is the power that General Suapala possesses.'

Magic? The general used magic? The only sort of magic that Priya knew was black magic. And the villagers of Disin kept well away from that, because using it could summon vengeful spirits. Priya jerked her head to look at the scholar. 'What do you mean?'

'Everything will soon become clear,' was all that Scholar Afounsowa said.

Her face gave nothing away. Priya looked around to see if the others had heard the scholar. But they were all gazing ahead with wide eyes.

As the mist lifted, the fort finally became visible. It was built on a wide bridge of glittering black arches over the river. The overwhelming roar and the splashing water suggested that the river turned into a waterfall on the other side of the bridge.

'Wow,' Kwasi whispered. The other winners in the korjaal were also transfixed by the sight before them.

The river was so wide that Priya couldn't make out its banks in the receding mist.

In front of the fort, which towered majestically above them, were two large statues of black water panthers. They seemed to be looking right at them.

The fort itself, as far as she could see, took up the entire width of the river. At its centre stood a huge edifice, made from the same black stone as the bridge, which glittered under flaming torches. The various towers of the building descended like steps on either side of the tallest structure at its centre. Large grey doors, richly decorated with gold, formed its entrance.

On either side of the central building were two thick walls that shielded the building from the riverbanks. As they came closer, though, Priya saw that they weren't walls, but more buildings, made up of high towers of solid black stone. She reached up to her mouth to remove a strand of hair, blown into her face by the strong wind. The three huge structures in front of them, which made her feel so small and insignificant, were now taking up almost her entire field of vision. But the black bridge that the buildings were standing on continued even further. Priya caught glimpses of smaller buildings and huts made of palm leaves and reeds.

Kuwatta was magnificent.

But the closer the korjalen came to Kuwatta, the faster they seemed to go. They passed between the statues of the panthers.

'Aren't we going too fast?' asked Kwasi, who had appeared beside Priya. He looked rather nervous.

'Yes,' said Priya, shrinking back. 'Shouldn't we be stopping?'

'Hold on tight!' she heard someone shout from behind them.

A moment later, the korjaal shook. Priya fell forward but was just able to grab hold of the edge of the boat so that she didn't fall out. Kwasi crashed to the floor beside her.

Their korjaal glided up wooden ramps and onto the stone deck beneath the fort. A number of soldiers stepped forward, throwing thick ropes over their heads and across the boats. The ropes were then hooked onto the korjalen, which the soldiers pulled up across log rollers and onto the deck. Eventually they came to a stop, more or less level with each other

They had arrived in Kuwatta.

＊ II ＊

THE TREACHEROUS
SOUL ROAMS
THE NIGHT

14

AS SOON AS THEY came to a stop, a soldier stepped forward and held out his hand to Scholar Afounsowa. Silently, she took it and climbed smoothly from the korjaal. The soldiers who had accompanied them followed her.

'A fine display,' one of them said to a green-uniformed soldier on the deck, who grinned and bowed mockingly.

The winners, including Priya, hurried after the scholar and the soldiers from the boat. They huddled together, with their backs to the korjalen, so that the drops of splashing water didn't hit their faces. The deck was packed with soldiers in brown and green uniforms shouting orders as they pushed past each other with full fishing nets and baskets bulging with cassavas, coconuts and grain.

'These are the new recruits. I've got twenty-five probies and twelve soul-singers with me, including this group,' Scholar Afounsowa said, pointing at Priya, Kwasi and the six winners who had been in the korjaal with them. 'Gather the rest. There are a few cadets from warrior villages in the boat at the back too.'

Probies? Soul-singers? What did she mean? They must be ranks, but the names meant nothing to Priya.

The man gave her a nod. His gaze moved to the winners, who were standing together on the deck. Then he signalled to the other soldiers, who divided the new recruits into three groups. Priya and Kwasi's group and one of the other groups were made up entirely of young people, but Ishani's had winners of various ages.

On what basis were they being divided up? Priya couldn't see any logic. The cadets would be trained at Kuwatta to become kaptens and bashas. It made sense that their group consisted mainly of people who were strong and young. That wasn't the case with Priya's group. They were going to be trained as scholars. All the winners who were standing with her were around the same age as her, though. If it was about age, then Ishani should be assigned to the same group. Was she missing something? Was it expertise? Intelligence?

A dark thought, lurking in a corner of her mind for days, surfaced. Did they know about her in Kuwatta? Was Scholar Afounsowa aware that Priya was a blood child? Her eyes swept nervously over the dozens of soldiers who were walking around the deck. Most of them were wearing brown uniforms. Only the soldiers who had brought them to Kuwatta were wearing green. But they were all carrying weapons and had the symbol of a rising sun on their shoulders. If they actually intended to execute her . . . Priya's mouth went dry. Escape wasn't an option. She couldn't possibly win a fight against so many soldiers.

But she mustn't get ahead of herself. None of the soldiers had been surprised to see magic being used. In fact, Scholar Afounsowa had admitted that Kuwatta had magic.

Frightened cries rang out, distracting her from her thoughts. The nearest soldiers pushed Priya's group out of the way, just in time.

With a thud, a water panther landed on the deck. The feline towered above the tallest of the soldiers. Water poured from her dark grey scales, which glistened in the rising sun. Her tail slammed into an empty korjaal, which went flying back into the river. With yellow eyes, which seemed to be made of glass, she took in everyone on the deck. When she growled softly, the people standing closest to the creature quickly jumped back.

'All the saints,' she heard Kwasi say beside her.

A man was sitting on an ornately decorated saddle on the water panther's back, wearing a black uniform and with a perfectly straight back. One of his hands was covered with a black glove with gold details.

His proud, powerful bearing gave Priya the impression that he was a fully grown man, but when he turned his face in her direction, she saw that he couldn't be much older than her. His black hair, damp from the mist, curled onto his nape. And his eyes, the colour of which she couldn't make out from this distance, glided swiftly over the new group of winners.

'Step away,' barked a soldier who was standing near Priya and Kwasi.

Priya saw that the soldier and Kwasi had already moved back. A path cleared between the soldiers and the winners for the panther and her rider. Quickly, Priya followed the others' example.

'How many?' the young man in black asked the nearest soldier in a stern voice.

'Twelve soul-singers,' he replied.

'Who *is* that?' she quietly asked Kwasi, with a cautious nod towards the young man in the black uniform.

Kwasi leaned his head slightly towards her. 'You've never heard of General Suapala's youngest son? Reza is the only person with a water panther. They grew up together after Reza saved her from a boa when she was an abandoned cub.'

Priya had indeed never heard of Reza before. She didn't even know how many children General Suapala had, although Kwasi had said there were a lot.

People in Disin talked about Kuwatta, of course, but only the masters and the students like Ishani paid any attention to what really went on there. Most of the villagers were too busy fishing, planting, digging. Surviving. Priya wouldn't have considered details like that worthy of interest before.

The panther prowled past them, leaving a trail of water. From close up, the feline was even bigger than Priya had expected. Her back was more than two heads higher than Priya. Priya couldn't take her eyes off those powerful legs and gleaming scales. She may not have heard of the general's youngest son, but everyone in Disin knew about water panthers. She'd never come across a water panther that would obey a human before, though. They were regal creatures: proud, independent rulers of the jungle and the rivers that flowed throughout Awaran.

The panther pushed off the deck and scaled a massive black wall, zigzagging upwards with smooth bounds until she disappeared among the towers above. As soon as she was out of sight, the soldiers on the deck came back to life.

'You two.' The soldier who'd been given the task of dividing them up into groups looked impatiently at Kwasi and Priya, who were lagging behind. 'Follow the others.'

Priya looked at the rest of the group. There were twelve of them and, as in the korjalen, their group consisted of a mixture of Suryans, Dalinese, Luanans and Topuans. The majority were from the last two groups, the groups that kept most of the rebel movement running. Scholar Afounsowa and the soldier had said that there were twelve soul-singers. So, they must have been talking about their group.

Scholar Afounsowa came towards them and nodded approvingly. 'Follow me.'

Five soldiers on their left, and five soldiers on their right. That was how they were led onwards – winners captive between soldiers. Priya glanced furtively at her sister, who was in another group, accompanied by only two soldiers.

Ishani, though, was acting as if Priya didn't exist.

'Make way!' A group of cadets pushed past them. They were heading for the building at the centre of Kuwatta, which, judging by its position and lavish decoration, was the most important one, most likely the general's residence.

Priya's group turned off, leaving the noisy deck behind. They were taken to one of the tall buildings beside the central one. Its entrance was less impressive than the one to the building in the middle, but it was still lavishly decorated with gold and carvings, in a script that vaguely reminded her of Topuan. Even when she tilted her head right back, she couldn't see the top. All she saw was gleaming black stone reaching to the heavens.

Building almost the entire fort out of black stone in the tropical heat was a strange choice, she thought. Even in the early morning, Priya felt the heat radiating from the ground and walls.

'This is the Academy,' Scholar Afounsowa told them, as they stepped into a large entrance hall. Inside, the walls and tiles were the colour of a cloudy sky, with touches of gold here and there. 'It's where you'll spend every day for the weeks to come.'

Her announcement made some of the tension in Priya's body drain away and, with a lighter tread, she followed Scholar Afounsowa up a flight of stairs. The Academy was an airy building, with high windows and steps that seemed to go on forever. Not the kind of place where anyone would condemn blood children to death.

Priya ran her fingers over the carved banisters, enjoying the sunlight that streamed in through the large windows. 'Are the cadets taught here too?' she asked, a little out of breath.

She addressed her question to the nearest soldier, who gave her a look of irritation. He didn't seem bothered by all the stairs, unlike the winners, who were trudging away with sweaty faces, huffing and puffing. 'Yes,' the soldier finally said, with obvious reluctance.

'A number of your lessons will coincide with those of the probies and cadets,' said Scholar Afounsowa, who'd heard them. With a glance over her shoulder, she silenced Priya.

Kwasi, contrary as usual, took two stairs at once to get closer to the scholar and asked, 'So, what are we?'

Soul-singers, thought Priya.

'An important addition to the probies and cadets.'

'So, is that what soul-singers are? The name sounds kind of . . . dramatic, if you ask me.'

'Shut your mouth and keep walking, Kwasi.'

After yet another flight of stairs, Priya peered down through a window and saw that they were now high above the ground. The Keep – the scholar had told them that was the name of the large building in the middle – was on the other side, so her view wasn't obstructed and she was looking out on to a large part of the bridge. As the mist cleared, she could even make out where the bridge met the riverbank. The river flowing beneath the fort ended in the largest waterfall she'd ever seen.

Scholar Afounsowa led them to the highest point of the building, a round room in the narrow tower that rose high above the rest of it. The wind carried cool clouds through the high windows, filling the room with a light mist. Even from this dizzying height, Priya heard the waterfall roaring below.

'Sit down,' said Scholar Afounsowa. Although she spoke calmly without raising her voice, everyone immediately looked for a place to sit on one of the wide wooden benches.

It reminded Priya of the room where Master Haripersad taught, but his classroom was small and dark. This one was a lot airier and well organised.

Priya sat on the nearest bench. Kwasi slumped down beside her a moment later.

'This classroom is Master Yapoma's room,' Scholar Afounsowa said, looking over at the doorway, where a Topuan man was standing. He was wearing a simple light green uniform and had snow-white hair that reached his waist. His light brown skin was smooth, though, which made it hard to guess his age.

The soldiers by the door stepped aside to let him through.

'Welcome to Kuwatta.' Master Yapoma's voice was soft and pleasant to listen to. As he smiled, fine wrinkles appeared by his eyes. 'I look forward to getting to know you all better.'

'Why are we the only ones here?' asked a Luanan girl who had half risen to her feet. She was finely built with full lips and long black hair that fell to her waist in thin plaits. 'Where are the other winners?'

'Master Yapoma teaches the soul-singers, Nanu.' Scholar Afounsowa's gaze swept slowly around the room. 'People like you.'

'Soul-singers? What does that mean?' asked Kwasi, drumming impatiently on the tabletop with his fingers.

'We won the test,' said Priya, who was starting to feel that something wasn't right. 'That means we earned our places as scholars in training.'

'You have all done more than win the test, Priya,' said Scholar Afounsowa, glancing to one side. 'Go ahead, Somohardjo.'

One of the soldiers stepped forward. Her eyes ran briefly over Priya and the other winners, and then she closed them. Soldier Somohardjo's green uniform was steaming in the damp room. Priya only realised that something was going on when wisps of mist appeared, multiplying and becoming thicker as they curled upwards.

Priya slid forward to get a better view. Again she felt a slight tingling along her spine. It moved up until she felt an unpleasant pressure on the back of her head and under her ears.

The soldier raised her hand and let the mist revolve around it. Colourful flowers bloomed in circles, gleaming in the light of the torches.

'What *is* that?' asked Priya, full of disbelief and admiration. 'How is she doing it?'

'It's because she's a blood child,' said the Topuan girl next to Priya, who was resting her chin on one hand. She was watching the flowers with a slight frown on her face, but she didn't seem surprised. 'Like us.'

Priya blinked, too stunned to say anything.

Kwasi, beside her, cursed in a mixture of Luan and Freeland.

'We have chosen all of you for the same reason we chose Soldier Somohardjo, years ago,' said Scholar Afounsowa. 'Welcome to Kuwatta, children of the blood moon.'

15

A SHOCK RAN AROUND the room.

Some of the winners, including Kwasi, shot to their feet. Others froze on the spot, the fear and alarm clearly visible on their faces. However, there were also a couple who didn't seem shocked, such as the Topuan girl beside Priya, who remained quietly in her place.

Priya had no idea what to think. For days, she'd been trying to tell herself that she hadn't used her curse. That it had just been her imagination playing tricks on her. But Scholar Afounsowa had known the truth all along. Her worst fear had come true.

The terrible suspicion had plagued her all the way here. Her mother's words had hit home, but she didn't want to believe their cruelty. After all, where could she go if her future at Kuwatta turned out to be a lie?

Nowhere, it rang in her ears. *Nowhere.*

And now it was too late to escape.

In Awaran, blood children were seen as monsters. Now that their secret had been discovered, they were facing a death sentence.

But then a slight hesitation set in. An almost imperceptible tingle ran up her spine and spread throughout her body. Maybe she was jumping to conclusions? Why would they make them walk up all those steps to this room in the Academy if they were just going to kill them? It made no sense. Besides, none of the soldiers had drawn a weapon.

Scholar Afounsowa's voice cut through the misty room. 'The general has selected you to play a special role within Kuwatta.'

Even before the scholar had finished speaking, Priya felt that tingling sensation run along her back again. Only this time it was more insistent.

The last drops of fear left her, giving way to a strange kind of calm. Her heartrate slowed, her hands stopped shaking. She was calm. Content. The scholar didn't want to hurt her at all, she could see that now.

'I thought we were being trained to be scholars,' said the girl who was called Nanu. She was holding the wooden table tightly with both hands. Every time her posture relaxed, probably as a result of the strange tingling sensations that Priya was also feeling, she immediately tensed her muscles. Her dark brown eyes were combative. 'Isn't that why we took the test?'

'The test is designed to select intelligent citizens to be educated as scholars. However, on this occasion, it was modified for the first time to allow us to detect blood children more quickly,' said Scholar Afounsowa simply.

Priya fought against the strange, calm feeling that seemed to be taking over her own emotions. It was hard, because only a small part of her consciousness was aware that the feeling didn't match with what she was actually experiencing. *What are you doing to us?* she was about to ask. But before she could say the words, her fighting spirit abandoned her again.

'Many of you will have grown up with the notion that you were cursed, so you kept your gift a secret in order to survive. Out there, people are consumed by fear of everything associated with the blood moon. Primeval creatures, vengeful spirits and even their own children,' said Scholar Afounsowa, who had left her place at the front of the room and was gently guiding a boy who had stood up back to his seat. 'You have had to keep your gifts secret, so that their fear would not turn against you. But here, in Kuwatta, you are under the protection of General Suapala, and he sees your gift not as a curse, but as a blessing.'

'That's enough,' said Master Yapoma with a sideways glance at the soldier closest to him. 'What you're doing is more than a nudge in the right direction. Remember what I said: soft and light as a feather.'

The soldier mumbled something that sounded like an apology.

Priya shook her head. She was slowly regaining control of her emotions.

The meaning of what Scholar Afounsowa had just said was starting to sink in. All her life, she'd been told that she was a danger, that she had to bury her curse deep so that no one could find out it existed. And now someone was telling her that her curse was not a bad thing? That they were under the general's protection because he saw it as a *blessing*?

She didn't believe a word of it.

'Why would you say that?' she asked. She still didn't feel quite like herself. 'Everyone in the entire country thinks we're no better than monsters.'

'General Suapala values intelligence, knowledge and strength,' said Master Yapoma kindly. 'Therefore he also values blood children. Like the probies – the future scholars – and the cadets, you will be trained at Kuwatta and swear allegiance to the general.' He paused. 'However, the others are being trained to become scholars and regular soldiers, while you will become part of a special division of elite soldiers. The soul-singers division.'

Scholar Afounsowa gestured at the soldiers. 'Look at them. Each of them has been through the training and they're all blood children. Although we prefer the term soul-singers.'

The three soldiers were standing with their hands behind their backs and fixed expressions, waiting to receive orders. Their green uniforms were spotless and uncreased. They also had weapons – each had a dagger, a sword and a spear. Priya's gaze swept over their bodies, but she saw no signs of injury or malnutrition. They were blood children and yet they were treated well.

Priya felt another slight tingling sensation run along her spine and suddenly saw dozens of tiny spiders crisscrossing Kwasi's fingers. As in the korjaal, he didn't react to them, but now she understood why. He was creating an illusion, just as Soldier Somohardjo had done. Priya's power to make other people obey commands was clearly not the only form that the blood children's curse took.

It was dawning on her that she was not in danger. They really were being offered a place at Kuwatta. The panic she'd felt when she realised that the general knew she was a blood child – a soul-singer – had completely paralysed her. So she hadn't seen what was happening right in front of her. Soldier Somohardjo had used her curse, as had the soldier who had influenced her emotions. Kuwatta was training soul-singers to become soldiers.

They meant it.

Being trained as an elite soldier meant a permanent place at Kuwatta and a chance to fight against the colonists. It meant she could avenge her father and her fellow Suryans. Her blood ran faster at that thought. But that wasn't the only thing, although she found it hard to admit it. The feeling that the stick fighting had given her had remained with her. It was indescribable, almost addictive: the adrenaline during the fight, the euphoria when she won. Fighting for Kuwatta would give her a purpose. She would be able to make herself useful.

And she would be wanted.

Finally.

Yet something was gnawing away at her.

'How did you know we're cursed?' she said.

Master Yapoma rested one hand on the shoulder of the soldier beside him. 'Soul-singers who do not have their gift under control use it instinctively when they find themselves in difficult situations. Some of you deliberately resorted to your gift during the physical test, but for most of you it probably happened unconsciously.'

Priya thought back to the moment when the winner had been announced. Her despair, confusion and fear, all merging into each other, and then the uncertainty about whether she had used her curse or not.

'Did I use my curse when you announced me as the winner?' she asked Scholar Afounsowa. For the first time, she wasn't afraid to hear the answer.

'Yes,' came the answer to the question that had occupied her mind for days. 'We had our suspicions during the physical test, but we didn't know for sure until the announcement. That was the reason why I selected you at that moment. Otherwise I would have taken only your sister.'

For Priya, it felt as if the world had turned upside down. Her curse had been her salvation this time, instead of a punishment. Ishani had actually been right. Priya's gift had ensured that Priya – and not Ishani – had been announced as the winner. Just not in the way that Ishani had thought.

'This is not a casual invitation to stay at Kuwatta,' said Scholar Afounsowa, crossing her arms. 'As soon as we leave this room together, giving up or leaving Kuwatta will be considered desertion. Which is punishable by death,' she added.

The words were met with a charged, nervous silence.

Scholar Afounsowa looked at each of them, one by one. 'I will ask this once – and never again,' she said. 'If you do not want to take part in the training, then stand up now.'

Priya considered her options. Although it was likely that none of them had been the true winners of the test, their villages still thought they were. If they went home, people would ask questions. As far as Priya knew, no one had ever returned from Kuwatta after having been declared the winner. The villagers in Disin would never leave her in peace if she went back. Maybe Kuwatta wouldn't either. They might keep a close eye on her for the rest of her life to ensure she didn't reveal anything about their special training for blood children.

And why would anyone want to go back? Priya herself had no intention of returning to her old life while a future existed in which she could be stronger and more powerful. A future in which her curse – in which *she* – was appreciated instead of feared. Her mother had clearly been wrong. Kuwatta would not make her disappear; the fort was giving her a chance to rise above the rest.

Everyone was silent for some time. Beside Priya, Kwasi quietly drummed his fingers on the tabletop.

Then, with a scraping sound, a bench slid back. A Suryan boy stood up and shuffled forward, head hanging. He was followed by a Topuan girl who looked like she was about fourteen years old. She wrapped her arms around herself, making herself as small as possible.

The rest remained in their seats.

Scholar Afounsowa nodded at a soldier by the exit, who started moving. He led the two soul-singers into the corridor and did not return.

+++

'Go inside,' the soldier said.

Priya had paused in the doorway, full of awe. After the two blood children had left, the group had descended the many stairs again, led by Scholar Afounsowa. She had then escorted them across the square and into the Keep. If the Academy had been impressive, the fortress's Keep was incredible. Large halls with high ceilings and black walls alternated with corridors with ornate engravings and more gold than Priya had seen in her entire life.

However, Scholar Afounsowa hadn't given them a moment to stop and take a look. They'd climbed the spiral staircases at a murderous pace.

Eventually they came to a round room with a particularly high ceiling. Torches hung beside tall arched windows. A carpet of jaguar skins led to a platform with five black seats. There was a thin man in a black uniform sitting in the middle one, which was larger and more impressive than the others. He had several medals pinned to the left of his chest and the symbol of a rising sun embroidered on his sleeve.

It had to be General Suapala.

'I said "go inside", cadet.' The soldier gave Priya a shove and she stumbled through the doorway. The room was already half filled with winners, standing uneasily in their designated places.

As she looked around, Priya's heart swelled with awe and hope, and yet also with disbelief. She would never have believed it possible that she would be standing here today, in the heart of Kuwatta, at the core of the rebel movement. She'd often dreamed about it, but she still couldn't quite comprehend that it was actually happening.

The stone seat to the general's left was empty, but a woman was sitting on his right. She was a stately, classic beauty, with distinctly Luanan features. Thin black plaits were twisted up onto her head and she wore a black uniform with touches of gold. Perhaps she was his daughter. With an amused smile, she looked down upon the new students as they shuffled nervously back and forth.

Behind the seats stood four individuals in clothes with colourful designs. From this distance, Priya couldn't decipher their expressions, but she could tell that they were from different ethnic groups. Priya guessed they were the advisors who represented the different sections of Awaran's population.

The soldiers who had accompanied Priya's group told them to move forward and lined them up in neat rows behind the group of new cadets and scholars in training. Priya automatically craned her neck, looking for her sister. But when she realised what she was doing, she stopped.

Scholar Afounsowa walked forward and stood at the head of the group of winners. Turning, she issued a command – 'Salute!' – as she pressed her fists together and bowed her head.

In a wave of movement, the winners imitated her salute until even the soldiers at the very back were standing in the same position.

'General,' said the scholar, head still bowed. 'These are the new probies, cadets and soul-singers.'

'My thanks, scholar. At ease,' the general croaked in Awuran. Priya let her hands fall to her sides and looked up.

The general had the broad, powerful nose and jawline of a Luanan and the warm bronze complexion and sharp eyes of a Topuan. Priya saw a trace of Dalinese in him as well, or was it Suryan? She couldn't say for sure. He was the first person she'd met who had the blood of more than one ethnic group in him.

A movement above caught her attention. She looked up and saw how astoundingly high the stone ceiling was. It had been carved into an intricate work of art.

Far above them, several beams formed a network of paths. Priya saw a lonely figure standing on one of them. The light of the torches didn't reach all the way up there, so she couldn't make out his face. He crouched down. For a moment, his dark uniform lit up and she saw something gleaming at his side.

Whoever it was, he was observing them. Silent. Waiting. Watching.

Priya forced herself to look away and to listen to the general.

'You have all made a choice. For Kuwatta. For Awaran,' said the general. His voice gained in strength and was now clearly audible. 'As scholars, but also as soldiers.'

Everyone else remained perfectly silent. The general was not large or imposing, but rather thin and frail. Even so, he had an air about him that commanded respect.

'From this moment on,' said the general, 'you are no longer the children of your parents. You have no brothers, sisters, no cousins or aunts and uncles. From this moment on, you are not Suryans, Topuans, Luanans or Dalinese. From this moment on, you are *more*.'

'We are *more*,' repeated the soldiers and Scholar Afounsowa. Priya mumbled the words along with them. She wanted to believe the general; she *longed* to believe him.

'You are both the weapons *and* the shields. You protect us from the Freelanders, the oppressors and enemies who have torn apart, destroyed and murdered our flesh and blood. Cadets, probies *and* soul-singers together. No longer will you watch helplessly as this happens.'

'We will not!' said Priya with the soldiers around her. This time she didn't doubt her words. She was ready to destroy the Freelanders, just as they had destroyed her father – and her mother's spirit. Everything would have been different if it hadn't been for the colonists. Perhaps she would not even have been a blood child, since she would never have been born in Awaran, but in Suryan.

'From now on,' the general said calmly, 'you will fight back.'

'We will fight back!' shouted Priya along with the others in the room, and for a moment the tower they were standing in disappeared and she saw herself on the front line, fighting against the colonists.

'Salute!' shouted Scholar Afounsowa again, her voice loud and strong above the others.

Everyone in the room pressed their fists together and bowed their heads. Before Priya lowered her eyes, she saw that the general was smiling, which made the long shadows under his eyes disappear for a moment.

16

'KUWATTA MIGHT SEEM LIKE a maze at first,' said Novan as he led them out of the Keep. He was a second-year soul-singer and had been given the task of showing the new group around. 'But you get used to it. It helps that it's mostly the Keep that's complex. You won't spend much time there in the beginning.'

Novan had light brown skin and a wide mouth that was constantly in a warm smile. As soon as they'd sworn their allegiance to the general, Scholar Afounsowa apparently no longer found it necessary to accompany them.

Using his back and shoulder to avoid putting pressure on his bandaged arm, Novan pushed a door open.

'Why not?' asked someone from the group.

'Only high-ranking soldiers and scholars are allowed to enter the Keep without the general's express permission,' replied Novan. 'That's the major, kaptens, head scholars. And bashas, when they're doing so on behalf of their kaptens.'

'What if we want to see the general?' asked Kwasi, who had clasped his hands behind his neck and was sauntering along at the back of the group.

'Simple,' said Novan with a straight face. 'Break the rules. With a bit of luck, the general will want to see you.'

A few people chuckled, and Kwasi looked as if he was actually considering that option.

'Did you get that in a fight?' asked Makaku, a slenderly built boy from the Luanan village of Afogron, pointing at Novan's bandaged arm.

'Was it the colonists?' Nanu pushed Makaku aside to get a better look at Novan's arm.

'The Freelanders fight with muskets and bayonets. Are we going to train with those weapons too?' Makaku pretended to hold a rifle in his hands and shoot. He and Kofi, a quiet Luanan boy who was taller than everyone else, were the only ones in their group who came from warrior villages, and Makaku talked about the colonists almost non-stop.

'Let's hope not,' mumbled Kwasi next to Priya. He was peering at a narrow side entrance where there were no torches or kokolampoes. A dripping sound indicated that water was leaking somewhere. Priya slowed down when she saw dark shadows moving in the corridor.

'Why would we use our enemies' weapons?' a Topuan boy said, wrinkling his top lip. He was as thin as a rake and had straight black shoulder-length hair and dark, deep-set eyes that were now looking at Makaku in disgust. 'I'm not touching anything they made.'

That didn't go down well with Makaku. 'You Topuans are safely hidden away in the rainforest,' he said, 'but I've seen with my own eyes what they can do with their muskets and cannons.'

'Are you saying we're cowards?' hissed the Topuan boy, following it up with a flurry of words in Topuan. 'My ancestors were fighting the colonists before *your* people even . . .'

'That's enough, Paneke. You too, Makaku,' Novan intervened. His warm smile had disappeared and he pushed Makaku and Paneke apart. 'You heard what the general just said. Here you're fighting as soldiers, side by side. Hey!' He walked back and used his good hand to pull Kwasi out of the narrow corridor. 'We're not to stray from the main routes.'

With a sheepish grin, Kwasi gave him a thumbs up. Shaking his head, Novan pushed him forward and continued on his way. 'You'll have the chance to prove yourselves sooner than you think, so focus on your lessons,' he said to the group. 'That's the most important thing.'

Soon after that, they left the Keep and headed into a tunnel that ran through the bridge beneath the Academy. When they emerged from the tunnel, black fields came into view with, behind them, the low structures that Priya had seen before. She glanced back at the buildings behind her. Slowly, she looked ahead again, using her hand to shield her eyes from the sun. The black stone burned the soles of her feet.

The soul-singers had broken up into smaller groups. The Luanans and Topuans were walking together, their heads close as they talked in their own languages.

Priya, somewhere at the back of the group, gathered up all her courage and took a few big steps forward so that she was closer to Novan. 'How can we send letters to our families?'

Novan looked over his shoulder. 'Why would you want to send letters to your family?' he asked sharply.

His question caught her off guard. She looked at Kwasi, Makaku and Nanu; none of them seemed bothered. Priya had known they would be separated from their families in Kuwatta, but she hadn't anticipated that they wouldn't be allowed to write to them. And she certainly hadn't imagined that everyone here would accept it with such ease.

'Because ... Because I ...' she began, searching for words. She didn't know how to pronounce the Awuran word for 'medicine'.

Someone behind her sniggered, and she felt her cheeks glowing.

'Forget it,' said Novan before she could get her words out. 'Without the general's permission, nothing is sent. And he never gives permission to students. From now on, Kuwatta is your only family.'

+++

'This place ...' Novan said, tapping his knuckles against the wall of one of the barracks in front of them '. . . is your home. The boys will sleep here, and the girls will be in the barracks on the other side. You'll find the washrooms between the front and the middle barracks.'

'Is that where the other soul-singers are?' asked Kofi, speaking for the first time. He nodded at the barracks further to the back. Priya counted around ten of them. Those buildings looked a lot sturdier than the others. Between, there were smaller buildings, probably the washrooms Novan had mentioned.

Novan shook his head. 'No, that's where the cadets without gifts live. Like you, they'll be trained as soldiers, so you'll study most subjects with them. The only one they won't be doing is soul studies, of course. Behind the regular cadets are the probies.'

'The probies?' echoed Kwasi with raised eyebrows.

'Haven't you been paying attention? That's what the masters call the scholars in training. They're also known as windbags,' Novan added casually.

Priya paused by a line on the ground in front of the barracks and rubbed her foot over it. The white colour, the only piece of Kuwatta that was not grey or black, didn't fade.

'There are a few rules that all first-years – especially new arrivals – have to follow.'

Priya looked over her shoulder and saw that Novan was holding up three fingers. 'Firstly, always be on time. Secondly, except in the soul studies lessons, using your gift is not permitted. And certainly not on the ungifted. Thirdly, and never forget this: there is a white line on the ground in front of the barracks.' He looked at Priya as he spoke. 'And after sunset, it is forbidden to cross that line.'

'Why?' Kwasi immediately asked. 'I understand the first two rules, but why aren't we allowed to cross the white line after sunset?'

Novan sighed wearily. 'Did you come to Kuwatta to question everything, cadet? Those are simply the rules.'

Kwasi didn't reply, but he made a face behind Novan's back.

'The food is served over there.' Novan pointed with his good hand at a place beyond the line.

Priya looked again at the line beneath her feet. A little further on, right on top of the white line, there was a small wooden hut with a soldier in a brown uniform sitting inside. He was leaning back in his wicker chair with a large leaf over his eyes to shield them from the sunlight.

'Those are the study areas,' Novan explained, pointing at a number of open huts. 'Beyond that, you'll find the training fields.'

+++

Priya joined the girls, who were heading to their own barracks. There was a timetable nailed to the door, but before Priya could see what it said, Nanu pushed the door open and disappeared inside. Priya was one of the last to follow.

The building was smaller inside than the outside suggested – but that could also have been because of the semi-darkness. Two narrow windows near the ceiling allowed in a little light. It smelled of damp wood, just as everything in Kuwatta seemed to smell damp. As a gust of wind shook the barracks from side to side, Priya's stomach did a little flip.

The Topuan girl in front of her let out a muffled cry. Priya recognised her as the girl who had sat calmly beside her in the Academy. She was small, just coming up to Priya's chin, and her thin legs stuck out from under an ochre-coloured dress. With her oval face and big round eyes, she appeared to be the youngest of the group.

'What?' Priya, immediately on the alert, asked in Suryan before quickly switching to Awuran. 'What's wrong?'

'Oh.' The girl fiddled with the beads around her neck. 'It's nothing. Just that there's a lost soul in the corner. There weren't any in the Keep, so I thought . . . I hadn't expected to see one here. Unfortunately, she doesn't want to talk,' she added in an unhappy voice.

Priya looked at the spot that the girl was staring at. She saw nothing but darkness. 'You can see ghosts?'

'Yes.' A brief hesitation. 'Can't you? I'm Jupta, by the way. I won the test in Kwamapan.'

'Ghosts? No, I can't. My gift is that I can make people do what I want them to do,' said Priya. 'I'm Priya. From Disin.'

Nanu gave a sniff as she headed past them to one of the mats. Priya became painfully aware of her poor Awuran pronunciation again. She pressed her lips together. Jupta had turned away from her and was choosing a spot for herself.

There were five mats in the barracks, woven out of rope with a layer of dry grass beneath. At the foot of each mat was a pile of neatly folded clothes: their uniforms, with pairs of shoes next to them. As two of the soul-singers had already left, one of whom was a girl, one mat in their barracks would remain empty.

Priya heard laughter again and saw that Nanu was looking her way. She couldn't take it any longer. 'What's so funny?'

'I haven't seen many Suryans before,' said Nanu, looking Priya up and down. The rest of the girls in the barracks were silent. 'But the few I've seen weren't fit to be soldiers. And neither are you.'

'You don't know anything about me,' Priya snapped at her.

Nanu sniffed. 'I know everything I need to know.'

'Nanu,' Jupta said warily.

'I'll tell you one thing, Suryan,' Nanu continued. She came closer, the half-light creating a flickering shadow on her dark brown skin. 'You and your people don't fight. All of Awaran knows that. Give up your place on the front lines, kantrakti, then at least you can make yourself useful here.'

Priya felt white-hot fury rippling through her. Nanu hadn't used a truly pejorative term, not like the Freelanders did, but still, the word kantrakti – contract labourer – sounded like a dirty word coming out of her mouth.

'My father,' Priya said with clenched fists, 'didn't die in an uprising so that you could accuse us of being cowards.'

Nanu studied her briefly. 'So he wasn't as meek as all the rest. Congratulations,' she said coldly. 'That doesn't change what I just said. The rebel army has no use for the Dalinese and Suryans.'

Priya's natural instinct to hold everything in only just kept her from attacking Nanu. Priya hated the other villagers in Disin for what they did to blood children, but she couldn't stand this condescending attitude towards all Suryans. 'That's what all of Awaran says about blood children too, isn't it? That they're better off without us,' she said, staring right at Nanu, 'but look, we're still here now.'

That shut Nanu up.

However, Priya knew that Nanu, for all her sneering, had a point. The Luanans and Topuans actually fought wars against the Freelanders. That wasn't the case for the Suryans and Dalinese – who had been brought to Awaran as indentured labourers. There were uprisings and there were runaways, like Priya's mother, but there had never been any real organised resistance. They were part of the rebel army, but in practice that meant that for every ten Luanans or Topuans, maybe two Dalinese and two Suryans fought alongside them.

Priya looked at Mawar, the Dalinese girl in their group, but she was lying on her mat with her eyes closed, pretending not to hear them.

'That's not entirely true.' Jupta had kneeled down beside her mat. 'What you just said,' she clarified, looking up when no one responded. 'Blood children aren't seen as monsters everywhere.'

Nanu shook her head. 'Maybe not in Kuwatta,' she said before Priya could react. Her sneering tone was less caustic than when she'd spoken to Priya.

'No,' said Jupta firmly. 'We – the Topuans – don't see blood children as unnatural or evil. I've never had to hide my gift. The Freelanders might think blood children shouldn't be allowed to live, but that didn't come from us.'

The words hung heavy in the air. It was hard for Priya to process what Jupta had said. 'But that's impossible,' she said finally. 'How can your people see blood children differently when . . .'

But it *was* possible, said a little voice deep inside. The Topuans had been living in Awaran long before the Freelanders had set foot there – unlike the Luanans, Suryans and Dalinese, who had been brought to the country by the colonists. The Freelanders had been terrified of everything that took place during the blood moon – and they still were, according to Master Haripersad – which was why they thought children who were born at that time were cursed. The pieces of the puzzle were falling into place.

'Are you trying to say that the Luanans, Dalinese and Suryans just blindly accepted what the Freelanders told them?' asked Priya.

Even Mawar opened her eyes at those words and rolled onto her side.

'Well, yes,' said Jupta with an awkward shrug. 'That's what often happens when people encounter something they don't know or understand.'

Nanu made a sound that was a cross between a sigh and a sniff, but it was lacking her previous fire. 'Utter nonsense,' she muttered. But she sounded less sure of herself. Angrily, she strode over to an empty mat.

Priya stood frozen in place. She should feel glad to know that the original inhabitants of Awaran had never seen her as a monster. Instead she just felt bewildered. Deeply disappointed. And somehow hurt. All of which soon turned into a seething rage. She was furious with the Suryans, the villagers and her parents. Furious at what they'd done to her because of their false assumptions.

And yet it was hard to hate them completely, as Priya knew they were suffering too. They had just accepted what the Freelanders said, but Gods, somehow Priya couldn't hold it against them. They didn't know any better when they arrived in Awaran and they had been afraid. That awareness made Priya even more angry at the world.

A short knocking broke the silence. 'The first bell rings just before sunrise. Make sure you get up as soon as you hear it, because after the second bell you won't have enough time for breakfast. When the third bell rings, you're too late,' Novan called from behind the closed door, before his footsteps died away.

None of the other soul-singers looked in Priya's direction. She forced herself to walk to the last mat, the one closest to the exit. Stiffly, she picked up her uniform, which felt soft and clean, so she could take a closer look at it in the dim light filtering through the cracks in the walls.

She didn't care what Nanu or the rest thought. She wasn't going to give up her place. Not for anyone or anything. In Kuwatta she could at least make a difference. Avenge her father, find a remedy for Umed and – who knows? – maybe change the world.

The uniform consisted of a simple pair of brown trousers with a sleeveless shirt in the same colour. Her eyes slid down to the sturdy black shoes in front of the mat.

Priya picked one of them up. She'd never worn shoes in Disin. It hadn't been necessary. She ran her fingers over the shoe and squeezed it gently. The material, which she didn't recognise, gave a little. She put the shoe back down, moved her uniform aside and lay down on her mat. A gust of wind made the barracks shake, and her stomach twitched again. She grabbed her mat tightly.

Whispers and murmuring filled the barracks.

Priya felt intensely lonely.

But she was used to that by now.

17

PRIYA SAT UP WITH a start.

Something had woken her. For a moment, she didn't know where she was and she stared, disoriented, at the roof. As a drop of water fell onto her forehead, she gasped. Right above her head, there was a damp patch in the wood. She saw another drop falling and turned her head away, so it landed on her cheek.

It was only then that she realised how quiet it was in the barracks. Too quiet.

She looked around. The room was empty. The shoes beside the others' mats had disappeared. Outside she could just make out a vague chattering above the sound of the river. Voices, quickly dying away.

Priya rolled off her mat.

She was late.

Quickly, she swapped her salwar kameez for her uniform and clumsily crammed her feet into the shoes. She tossed her old clothes into the corner of the room.

Still tugging at the heels of her shoes, she ran outside. After a few steps, she changed her mind and walked back to look at the timetable that was nailed to the front of the barracks. Soul studies. Historical studies. Healing sciences. Combat training. Memorising the subjects, she started running.

She flew past the barracks. Despite her bad night, because of the shaking of the building and the constant roar of the waterfall, she was wide awake. Her snatches of dreams were filled with Umed's face, twisted in pain. Over and over, she jolted awake, out of breath.

She was quickly approaching the supervising soldier's stone hut and swerved to avoid it. And then she bumped into Kwasi, who was still pulling his shirt over his head. Quietly cursing to himself, Kwasi stuck his arm into a sleeve and turned to look at her.

His face lit up. 'Priya.'

'We're late.' She ran past him, almost stumbling in her unfamiliar shoes, but she managed to steady herself.

In the distance, she saw a group of people in brown tunics walking away from her. Priya started sprinting. Kwasi, shouting his mouth off as usual, was right behind her.

The students headed behind a building. Priya went even faster. Soldiers in brown and green uniforms watched as she ran past. Kwasi went on talking. Priya held up her hand to shield her eyes from the sunlight and scanned the surroundings for the other soul-singers.

There! There they were.

She recognised the tall, broad-shouldered Luanan boy at the back of the group: Kofi. He was the last to head into the Academy.

Priya and Kwasi crossed the huge field in front of the Academy. At the entrance, they were stopped by a soldier in a brown uniform. 'Name and rank?'

'Priya,' panted Priya. 'Cadet Priya. Soldier,' she added after a short silence.

'Let me . . . just . . .' Kwasi leaned dramatically against the wall. 'Cadet Kwasi,' he finally managed to gasp.

The soldier looked at their uniforms. 'You're new.'

Priya nodded. 'Yes.'

'And you're late.'

Priya swallowed the words of protest that were on the tip of her tongue. 'Yes, ma'am. Sorry, ma'am.'

Kwasi mumbled the words along with her.

The soldier nodded at the black field behind them. 'Ten laps. Then you can go in.'

'Ten?' Kwasi exclaimed. 'But . . .'

'Twenty.'

Priya glared at Kwasi. He slammed his mouth shut and locked his lips with an imaginary key.

'Dismissed,' ordered the soldier, and they both started moving at the same time.

+++

Bathed in sweat, they climbed the stairs of the tower where soul studies was taught. In just a short time, Priya had come to loathe the number of towers and stairs in Kuwatta. Her legs felt as heavy as lead. It was only sheer willpower that got her up the last few steps.

'All the saints,' said Kwasi, wheezing for breath. He stopped just in front of the entrance to their classroom. 'Do you think they chose this room on purpose, just to make us suffer even more?'

Priya felt a slight tingle run through her spine and shivered. She peered past Kwasi into the classroom. Master Yapoma, their soul studies teacher, was standing, arms raised, in front of the small group of soul-singers. His snow-white hair, braided with dark green beads today, was hanging down his back. He was wearing the same light green uniform as the previous day, which looked simpler and more practical than the military uniforms that the soldiers wore. Priya followed the line of his raised arms. Her eyes widened.

The ceiling of the classroom had disappeared.

Instantly forgetting how tired she was, she stepped forward. She saw dark, heavy rainclouds, typical of the monsoon season in Awaran, moving across a grimy grey-white sky. But there was no indication that the ceiling had somehow opened up. The black walls blended so perfectly with the sky that it was as though an artist had painted it with delicate brushstrokes.

'You two, over there in the doorway,' said Master Yapoma without looking at them. 'Tell me what you can see.'

The eyes of all the soul-singers moved from the sky to Priya and Kwasi. Priya's mouth went dry. Nanu was resting her chin on her hand, staring at the two of them. Jupta also had her round, dark eyes on them. The corners of Makaku's mouth curled up a little. Their gazes burned Priya's skin. All she wanted to do was hide behind Kwasi.

'An illusion,' said Kwasi, still staring upwards in amazement, oblivious to all the eyes that were on them. 'I have the same gift, but I've never managed to do anything like that.'

The master nodded and lowered his arms. 'But this isn't the only gift that soul-singers can possess. What other gifts are there?'

He had not yet given Priya and Kwasi permission to step any further into the room, so they were forced to stand there in the doorway, looking for answers to his questions as everyone stared at them. Priya felt uncomfortable, but at the same time very curious. Her curse – or gift, as she corrected herself – had always been a mystery that she wasn't allowed to think about, let alone explore.

Priya cleared her throat. 'I can use my gift to force people to obey commands.'

'I know another one.' Kwasi's hand shot up. 'Some soul-singers can influence emotions. As we experienced yesterday,' he added with less enthusiasm.

The teacher was still not satisfied. He looked around, raising his eyebrows, which were as white as his hair. 'What else?'

Priya's gaze fell on Jupta, who was clearly startled by their eye contact and fiddled nervously with the beads around her neck. Yesterday in the barracks, she'd said that she could speak to . . .

'Spirit-speakers,' someone behind her said in a monotone. 'Soul-singers who can speak to the souls of the dead.'

Priya looked round and saw that a black-haired boy had come to stand behind her and Kwasi. He tilted his head, so that the rays of sun coming through the window didn't shine into his honey-coloured eyes. The movement made his long gold earrings glint.

Priya couldn't say for sure what his background was, but she could see Luanan and Dalinese features in his face; a sharp jawline, warm ochre-coloured skin and medium-length black hair that curled at the back of his neck. She knew she was staring, and yet she couldn't take her eyes off him.

With his hands tucked deep into his brown tunic, which had clearly been made specially for him, and a face that showed no emotion whatsoever, he was a picture of boredom. Yet there was a strength about him that had nothing to do with his broad shoulders and agile build. Even without a trained eye, Priya could tell he must be a formidable soldier. She was about to look away when her gaze fell on his right arm. He shifted slightly, exposing his right hand. His hand and the lower half of his forearm were not flesh and blood, but a prosthesis made of some kind of black material.

Her eyes flew back up.

This was Reza, the general's son. Which explained his mixed blood.

His presence had not gone unnoticed by the other blood children – a buzz was going around the classroom.

'Deed-speakers, sight-speakers, sense-speakers and spirit-speakers,' the master recited, silencing the whispers. 'Those are the names we have given to the different kinds of soul-singers, based on the gifts that they possess. Now sit down. You too, Reza,' he said with more respect in his voice. 'And make sure you don't arrive late again.'

Priya stepped into the round classroom and headed to a desk right at the back. Sitting down, she pulled the heavy book on the desk towards her.

She ran her fingers over the letters on the cover. She couldn't decipher all the words but thought that one of them meant 'beginning'.

'During our soul studies classes, we are going to discuss your gifts. Gifts that originate in magic. And magic,' he said with more emphasis, 'is the core of soul studies.'

Priya grasped the book more tightly. She'd learned from a young age that magic was just as cursed as the blood moon and its children. Only those with evil intentions took an interest in such things.

Out of the corner of her eye, she saw that Reza had deliberately chosen a seat at the front where the other blood children would find it difficult to talk to him. Priya was a little surprised to see him in the classroom. If Reza was here, in their soul studies lesson, it could mean only one thing: he was a blood child. Was that the reason why the general had created a training course especially for blood children? But even if that was the case, it was strange that Reza should join their group. They were novices, while he had grown up in Kuwatta and must already know a lot more than they did.

'No, that's a deed-speaker. I'm a sight-speaker,' she heard someone say in a hushed voice. Kwasi had sat down beside Makaku and they were whispering to each other.

'Magic is seen by the ignorant as a fickle, demonic energy.' Master Yapoma looked up. The rainclouds were shifting. The sky slowly turned pale blue. 'In reality, just like any other science, it is subject to natural laws.'

'How did you do that?' asked Mawar, pointing at the sky. 'How is it possible to make everyone in the room see that? It's not real, is it?'

'Yes – and no. It's an illusion that sight-speakers can maintain by manipulating the soul of another person – or persons, in this case. In reality, it doesn't exist, but one might wonder whether reality itself is not a concept that humans maintain in order to make the world understandable.'

A faraway look appeared on Master Yapoma's face, and the air above them began to shimmer. He shook his head. The sky became a bright blue and then dissolved, to be replaced by a black ceiling.

'The first step is feeling,' said Master Yapoma, still a little dreamily. 'Feeling the soul in yourself. The souls of others around you. Close your eyes and focus.'

Priya sat motionless for a moment. She shut her eyes and concentrated. It took her a while to find it. A pulsating energy writhed deep inside her, hidden behind a shield that she'd erected to keep that energy – her curse – inside. But she didn't have to do that anymore. Umed, Ishani, her mother. They weren't anywhere near her now. She couldn't do anything that might hurt them. Carefully, she lowered the shield. The effect immediately swept through her body. An invisible burden fell from her. She grew warmer, as energy shot through her. Her fingers tingled.

She felt her curse. Her gift. Her soul.

Priya opened her eyes.

'Every human being has the same inside here.' Master Yapoma tapped his chest as he walked along the rows of desks and chairs. 'A soul. You are no different in that respect from the ungifted. The only difference between you and them is that the blood moon has given you *more*. You have the power to manipulate souls. There are a lot of opinions on that subject. Only Mother Earth knows if it's actually a good thing or bad. But here at Kuwatta at any rate the opinions of the rest of Awaran do not matter. In Kuwatta, we see the soul-singers as the core of our strength.'

Priya closed her eyes again. Slowly she shifted her attention to the others in the room. It was true – she could feel their energies burning. Points of light whose presence she'd sensed on the edge of her consciousness without ever daring to think about them before. She cautiously swept past them, shivering. Their souls were more intense now that she was open to them.

'I-I can feel something,' someone stammered.

'Very good,' said their teacher. 'Try to go further. Beyond these walls. What do you feel? Humans are not the only ones with souls. Cats, parrots, snakes and even insects. Every living creature possesses one.'

Priya wasn't interested in animals. She couldn't feel anything outside, but inside the room? That was a different matter. Kwasi. Jupta.

Makaku. Their souls felt warm and circled slowly at chest height. When she concentrated, she could feel more. Snatches of frustration. Slivers of impatience. Were those her emotions or theirs? The abundance of sensations was almost overwhelming. She gently tried to nudge their souls. It felt strange to touch them with only her consciousness. They yielded a little but didn't react. Maybe if she gave them an order, it would work on them.

But not with Kwasi. There were others she'd rather try out her gift on. They deliberately hadn't woken her up this morning. And she had not forgotten.

'In the days to come,' said Master Yapoma, 'we are going to hone the soul magic within you to create a deadly weapon.'

Priya stopped when she reached Nanu.

'Fall over,' she commanded.

18

AN ALL-CONSUMING PAIN SHOT through her head.

Priya groaned and slumped in her seat. She was losing control of her gift. The pain was getting worse. Her breath came in gasps. She didn't know how to make it stop. It was so incredibly painful that she couldn't think straight.

'Help me,' she murmured. She *begged*. 'Help me, please.'

She couldn't handle it. It felt as if her consciousness were being torn apart.

Suddenly she felt a cold hand on the back of her neck, which disappeared just as quickly. Then a hand slammed into her windpipe, leaving her unable to breathe. Coughing, she collapsed forward onto the table. The shock made it feel as if something had come loose.

She was free. Her soul was free. The pressure was gone.

'What . . .' she groaned.

'That's not what I understand by helping, Reza.' It was Master Yapoma.

'She's conscious again, isn't she?'

'Is she still alive?' she heard Kwasi saying in the background – which made her want to sit back up so that she could give him a withering stare.

'Of course she's still alive,' said someone else, and that was followed by a series of words in Topuan.

'Give her some space,' barked Master Yapoma.

Priya struggled to push herself up. Dozens of blurred faces were hovering around her. She blinked a few times. The faces converged until only three remained. She saw Kwasi, smiling with relief. Master Yapoma, who was standing right in front of her, was looking at her with a mixture of concern and disbelief. 'That,' he said tensely, 'was certainly not what I was expecting in my first lesson.'

Priya wondered in a daze if that was good or bad. Her guess was: bad.

'You see? It worked just fine.' Reza was standing on the other side of the teacher, his arms loosely crossed and his eyes fixed on her. In spite of his stance, which gave off the same boredom as before, his gaze was penetrating, even questioning, as if he were searching for an answer in her face. His slight frown said he couldn't find one.

Priya rubbed her forehead, which was throbbing painfully. Her hand moved down, stopping just above her throat. Had he really hit her? She still couldn't manage to speak.

Reza pushed himself back from the desk and leaned in towards her. 'You've got some nerve,' he said, 'using a command against your fellow students.' *Students*. In the plural. His gaze slid from her face to her throat and then down, to her hands, arms, chest, stomach.

Priya folded her arms over her chest, and he looked back up. What did he think he was doing? His light brown eyes were so cold and unfathomable. From this close up, Priya noticed that he was different from the others. Not just because of his status and his clothing, but also because of his soul – she couldn't feel it. That was curious, given that she no longer seemed to be able to keep her curse locked away. The world around her was suddenly filled with life. She could feel the faint energies of the ospreys circling the tower, of the insects crawling along the walls and of all the other soul-singers in the room. But she couldn't feel Reza's.

'Where's the gold?' Reza asked in a cold voice.

'What gold?' Priya exclaimed. Her vision was finally sharp enough to see beyond the faces in front of her. Behind Master Yapoma, Reza and Kwasi, a number of students were lying on the floor. Not just Nanu. She counted three of them, four, five. Most of them were frowning at her as they hoisted themselves to their feet.

But that couldn't be right. Priya had only aimed at Nanu.

'Where are you hiding it?' asked Reza now, which made her look up at him again.

Irritation welled up inside her, clearing the numbness that had clouded her mind. Was he accusing her of being a thief?

'Nowhere,' she said simply. 'There isn't any gold, unless you count all of this stuff surrounding us.' She gestured vaguely at the gold engravings on the ceiling and walls, the symbol of the rising sun carved in gleaming gold.

'She doesn't have any, Reza. You must be able to feel that too.' Master Yapoma pushed him aside. 'Try to breathe through your nose. In. Out. Keep going,' he said to Priya before turning to the others. 'This is what happens when you use your gift without training. Without self-awareness. Without control.'

'I've often used my gift,' Nanu objected, standing up and staring icily at Priya. 'That's never happened to me.'

'The more powerful the gift, the easier it is to lose yourself in it,' said Master Yapoma, and Nanu pressed her full lips into a thin line.

Priya breathed carefully through her nose, so that the air slid as softly as possible down her aching throat.

Master Yapoma's hand came down on her desk. He leaned forward to look her in the eyes. 'Soul magic is a weapon. Remember that. If you use more than you can handle, that same magic will tear you apart until there's nothing left of you.'

Priya gulped and tentatively reached her hand to her throat. Her eyes flashed briefly to Reza, who was still glaring at her with a dark expression. 'Understood, master.'

+++

The classroom where they were taught historical studies was a lot bigger than the soul studies tower. The class was about to begin, and the room was packed with students looking for a seat. Most of them were dressed in brown tunics that were a shade lighter than the soul-singers' uniforms; they were the cadets without a gift. There were also a few students in beige-coloured tunics – the probies.

Priya noticed that students with tunics of the same colour sat together, so that the room was soon divided in three. In soul studies, the Luanans and the Topuans sat together, but it was different in historical studies. It wasn't about where you came from. The soul-singers were excluded by both the regular cadets and the probies, so they were forced to sit together at the back of the room.

The only one missing from their group was Reza. He had disappeared after their soul studies lesson before anyone could speak to him and had not returned. Maybe that was just as well. Priya didn't know what she might do if he started to accuse her in that cold voice again.

'Sit down,' Scholar Afounsowa thundered across the room.

Priya chose a desk at the edge of the group of soul-singers. They probably wouldn't want to sit next to her after she'd thrown them to the floor with her curse. She saw Makaku pulling Kwasi onto a chair. The rest of the soul-singers avoided her gaze.

Jupta was one of the few who hadn't yet found a seat. She was about to sit down next to a student in a beige uniform, but he slid a stack of books onto the empty chair at the last moment. Jupta bounced back as if someone had slapped her in the face. Desperately, she looked around.

'Most of you know me as a scholar,' said Scholar Afounsowa. She closed a book on her desk and stood up. 'During your lessons, I am your teacher, your master. And you will address me as such.'

Jupta looked around, her shoulders hunched. She was lost in a sea of beige-coloured students. Priya couldn't bear to watch any longer. She gave the empty chair beside her a little kick. Jupta noticed and pounced on it.

'Thank you,' she mumbled.

Priya, who didn't know what to do with Jupta's gratitude, gave her a quick nod.

'In the past, Awaran belonged entirely and solely to the Topuans and other indigenous peoples of this land,' recited Scholar Afounsowa, walking past the wall, which was covered with various maps of Awaran. 'However, their lives changed dramatically when the Freelanders came.'

Scholar Afounsowa launched into a monologue about the colonists and the Topuans. Priya recognised much of it from the tirades that Ishani regularly delivered whenever she became obsessed with a subject.

Her sister always became so fired up when she was talking about the history of Awaran. Umed and Priya had no choice but to listen in silence. Until Umed finally had enough and told Ishani that 'no one's interested in that stuff', and they started bickering. Priya bowed her head, so that her black hair fell in front of her face; the memory wasn't a bad one, and yet it weighed heavily on her. The thought of Umed made her stomach ache.

She'd been in Kuwatta only one day, but she wondered if she was already too late. Their journey there had taken four precious days. Had Umed's situation improved? Was he awake yet? Or was he in desperate need of the medicine she had sworn to get for him?

'There were two wars. During the first war, the Topuans stood firm, but they lost large areas of land. Why was that?' Scholar Afounsowa looked around the classroom.

Priya tried to shake off her fears. Fear wasn't going to get her anywhere.

A probie's hand shot into the air.

Scholar Afounsowa gave the student a nod.

'Because of the diseases and the weapons that the Freelanders brought with them,' replied the student. 'The Freelanders used cannons and muskets, and the Topuans weren't familiar with such things back then.'

Priya's mouth went dry. The person who had spoken, at the front left of the classroom, was Ishani. Priya could see only the back of her head, but that was enough. She would recognise her sister's stiff, proud posture and nasal voice anywhere.

Of course, she'd known that she would run into Ishani again. But she'd tried to dismiss that thought.

'. . . the fort was destroyed before. The reconstruction of Kuwatta was a collaboration between the Luanans and the Topuans. Since then, they have joined forces in the war against the Freelanders,' said Ishani.

'Correct. But it's not the case that the colonists won the war entirely. Although the first war is considered a defeat, it's important to remember that the colonists have still not achieved what they set out to do. And what is that?'

Ishani's hand shot up again. 'Gain complete control of Awaran. The colonists act like they own the entire country, but in fact they're only in charge of the coast. That hasn't changed since the abolition of slavery and the arrival of the Suryan and Dalinese contract labourers.'

Priya was irritated by her self-confident tone. In Ishani's head, she was always the best in the group. The slumbering fury deep within Priya was starting to stir again. Before she knew it, she was raising her hand.

Scholar Afounsowa gave her a nod. 'Speak, cadet.'

'Well, if the Freelanders have better weapons and spread all kinds of diseases, why haven't they won yet?' Gods, she'd wanted to seem intelligent, but now she just sounded incompetent. 'I, um, assume it has something to do with the jungle,' she guessed, thinking frantically.

'Who can give me an answer?' Scholar Afounsowa's gaze moved to the side. 'You?'

Jupta ran her hands over her beads. 'Yes, master,' she said. 'My people know the jungle inside out. We know where every river flows, where every savanna is located and where every swamp can be found. We've used that knowledge to our advantage during attacks. The Freelanders, on the other hand, are no more than foreign invaders.'

Priya wondered if the Topuans actually thought the same about the Luanans, Suryans and Dalinese people with whom they were now fighting side by side.

'Their fine weapons are no match for Mother Nature,' Jupta concluded.

'Exactly,' said Scholar Afounsowa, and Jupta heaved a sigh of relief. 'In the guerrilla war that we are waging, our invisibility plays an important role. The jungle protects us; without it, we'd already be lost.'

19

HEALING SCIENCES WERE TAUGHT by Master Wiratma. With her stocky build, her face full of deep wrinkles and her long grey hair in a plait, she reminded Priya of the village elders in Disin. However, Master Wiratma possessed a vital energy that Priya had never seen in the village elders. Sadly, she put most of that energy into showing her preference for the probies.

'Any soldier who thinks combat training is more important for armed conflict than the healing sciences is sorely mistaken. In the best-case scenario, you'll be saved by a soldier who has been paying attention. In the worst cases . . .' Her voice faded away. 'You understand what I mean. I expect absolutely *everyone* here . . .' Her piercing gaze slowly swept over all the cadets and soul-singers. '. . . to pay close attention.'

Kwasi quickly hid a yawn behind his hand.

A probie raised her hand and asked a question, and Master Wiratma launched into a monologue about the venom of various snakes and frogs that could act as healing agents.

Priya listened for a while, but eventually she couldn't control herself anymore. She put up her hand and, without being asked to speak, she blurted out, 'How do you cure someone who's been exposed to the blood moon?'

Master Wiratma pursed her lips in displeasure. For a moment, Priya was afraid she wasn't going to answer the question, but then she said, 'To know how we can treat someone, we first have to find out what exactly it is that they need to be healed from. And what is that?'

It felt like a reprimand and Priya felt her face heating up. No matter how hard she tried, she always made herself look ignorant.

Several of the Topuan students raised their hands. Fortunately, they were the only ones; like Priya, the rest of the students didn't seem to know what the teacher was talking about. The cadets and probies looked at one another uncertainly.

The corners of Master Wiratma's mouth curled upwards in satisfaction, as if she had been expecting this reaction. 'Yes?'

'The blood moon brings out the ancient magic of the rainforest. The aura is an element of that: it's pure magic,' the Topuan probie said confidently. 'It's also why blood children are born only during the blood moon.'

'And why primeval monsters and vengeful spirits are more likely to attack at such moments,' Master Wiratma added, nodding at her. 'While the aura makes them more powerful, it makes ordinary humans weaker.'

So that was why Priya had never been bothered by the blood moon, but the rest of the villagers were terrified of it.

'At Kuwatta, we make sure that all of our students develop immunity to the aura. Who can tell me how we do that?'

'During every blood moon, a part of a person without a gift may be briefly exposed to the moon,' said Jupta in a low voice. 'It will make them sick, but not seriously, because the aura touches only part of their body for just a short time. After a few exposures, a natural resistance develops.'

Master Wiratma nodded and finally a hint of approval seemed to appear on her face as she looked at a soul-singer. 'Very good.'

'But what if the aura *does* make someone seriously ill?' Priya stubbornly persisted.

'I'm curious too, master,' said Ishani, coming to Priya's aid after being quiet all this time. 'I've read that gold dust is used. Is that true?'

Of course Ishani was already trying to get to the bottom of it, even after this short time.

'Gold powder, sieved from the river,' said Master Wiratma warily. 'Mixed with black claw plant and a few drops of the Cotari. But the ingredients aren't the problem. It's the preparation of the tincture, which is a very delicate process. Each of the ingredients must be heated to a different temperature, and they need to be combined at the right moment. But as I said, we use different methods at Kuwatta,' she added sternly. 'The remedy is intended as a last resort and can be prepared only by experienced healers.'

+++

'We've been here one day,' sighed Kwasi at lunch, 'and look how much work they've already saddled us with.' He shook his head. 'It's too much. My head's about to explode.'

'All those stairs don't help,' groaned Nanu.

'And then they go and serve the food here,' Kwasi said, sweeping his hand around. They were by the barracks, which meant they'd soon have to walk all the way back to the Academy for their next lesson. 'I'm telling you, they did this to make us suffer.'

'Just be glad you're not a probie. Then you'd have to cram even more information into your head,' Kofi said, putting him in his place. He bit off a piece of the jarabaka in his hand. Then, frowning, he dug out a fishbone from between his teeth.

Priya, at the end of the table, shovelled down her bravoe soup as quickly as she could. Before her was more food than she'd ever been given in Disin and she wasn't planning to waste anything. As she ate, she swatted away the red wasps and the big black flies that surrounded her plate.

Kwasi smiled, and the dimple in his cheek appeared. 'Even if I wanted them to, the probies would never accept me.'

Mawar pushed aside her gourd, which was still half full. 'You'd think people were still telling them that blood children are monsters, even though Kuwatta is trying to teach exactly the opposite.'

The instructors at Kuwatta were indeed doing their best to teach the probies and regular cadets that they now formed a team with the soul-singers. In their botany classes, their teacher even went so far as to analyse the powers of the soul-singers, to make them easier for the probies and regular cadets to understand. Not that it had helped much so far.

Priya looked at the other tables.

The soul-singers sat at a long table that was a little apart from the probies and regular cadets. None of them dared to go and sit with the other students, not even Kwasi. The lessons in historical and healing sciences had shown them that the soul-singers were on their own. On several occasions, Priya had seen probies and regular cadets swerve to avoid her in the corridors. The invisible lines were clear even at Kuwatta: even your own people didn't want you if you were a blood child.

Makaku shoved Kwasi aside to grab a mango. 'How did you actually win the test?' He added something in Luan and grinned.

'I didn't,' replied Kwasi, his mouth full of banana. 'Scholar Afounsowa chose someone else and then came to my house later. Suddenly said she wanted to take me too.' He shrugged. 'How could I refuse? All my brothers and sisters were over the moon. And my parents had been dreaming of Kuwatta for years. It was more their dream than mine.' Kwasi sighed. 'Not that I'm not grateful,' he quickly added.

Kofi nodded thoughtfully. 'The same thing happened to me. I won the physical test, so I didn't really stop to think about it.'

So, Scholar Afounsowa had been acting secretively elsewhere too, not only in Disin. That didn't surprise Priya, but she was surprised that the fort apparently hadn't done this before. It wasn't usual to take several 'winners'. If it had happened often before, then surely

Ishani would have heard about it and told them about it at home. So it must mean Kuwatta had recruited blood children in a different way before. And something had happened to make them change their methods.

Priya split open a coconut with a knife that was on the table and held it above her mouth to catch the milk. Nanu looked at her as if she was some kind of filthy insect, which only confirmed what Priya already knew. She was tolerated by the other soul-singers, but that didn't mean they would include her in their conversations. Particularly not after the stunt she'd pulled during soul studies.

'It's strange,' Jupta said to Paneke. The Topuan boy was poking listlessly at his food, even though his skinny body could have done with a good meal. 'I only saw a dead person's soul in our barracks on the first day. But in the Keep and the Academy . . . nothing.'

Paneke asked her a question in their own language.

'Did you hear it last night too?' Kwasi said, leaning forward to Nanu.

'What?' Nanu said impatiently.

'The screaming.'

Priya lowered her coconut. Mawar, who had just stood up, sank back onto the bench.

Nanu rolled her eyes. 'Very funny.'

'I heard it too,' said Paneke, joining their conversation. He turned to the Luanan soul-singers for the first time. 'It started as soon as the sun went down.'

The other soul-singers had fallen silent. Priya waited for Kwasi to burst out laughing. He often made stupid jokes – and he was always the one who laughed loudest at them. But this time he looked serious.

'All I heard was the river,' mumbled Makaku beside him.

Then the bell rang, and they all snapped to attention.

+++

'Pathetic,' sneered Master Ramsaroup as he walked along the lines of soul-singers and cadets. Reza was among them, this time dressed in a crumpled black uniform and with a tired face.

Priya stood up a little straighter as Master Ramsaroup passed her. The master of combat training had angular features and was small but tough-looking. The most striking thing about him, though, was the collection of scars on the right of his face – four pale-pink lines that ran down from his eye and stopped just above the corner of his mouth.

There was a sword at his side, the top of its hilt inlaid with gold.

Priya held her breath, afraid he was going to focus on her, but he walked past. Slowly, she breathed out.

Although he was very intimidating and she preferred to avoid his gaze, she was glad that a Suryan was their master of combat training. Nanu was wrong: Priya's people could fight back. And she was going to show her – and all the other soul-singers.

'I asked for soldiers and this is what they sent me.' He looked in disgust at the soul-singers as he spoke. The regular cadets, sons and daughters of soldiers from warrior villages, were probably just about acceptable as far as he was concerned.

Kwasi was humming beside Priya. He had a distant look on his face that reminded her of Umed whenever he drifted off into his dream world. She was about to give Kwasi a nudge, but their master was too quick for her.

He turned quickly, bringing his face close to Kwasi's, and asked in a dangerously quiet voice, 'Is there something you'd like to say, cadet?'

Kwasi's eyes widened. 'No, master.'

'Then I don't want to hear anything from you. Understood?' barked Master Ramsaroup. Startled, Kwasi took a step back and bumped into the person behind him.

'Got it, master. I won't do it again.'

Master Ramsaroup concluded his inspection. 'As many of you have clearly never held a spear or a sword in your lives, we'll have to start at the very beginning. First of all, the most important rule: when I give you a command, you obey.'

Priya resisted the urge to wipe the sweat from her forehead.

'It doesn't matter what the command is. If I tell you to climb the highest tower of the Academy, you will climb. If I tell you to jump into the river, you will jump. Is that clear?'

'Yes, master!' they chorused.

The grey clouds shielding the sun unfortunately weren't making it any cooler. The black training ground they stood on made the heat even more unbearable. Had the people who built the place deliberately chosen black stone for that reason? When Kwasi had complained about all the stairs and the long way to lunch, she hadn't taken him seriously, but now she wondered if there was some truth in his words. Maybe Kuwatta really did want to make them suffer.

Master Ramsaroup stood in front of the group. 'Thirty laps of the field.'

Reza shot off like a flash. A handful of others, including Kofi, followed him. But most of them, including Priya, stood dazed for a few seconds. The command wasn't unexpected, but it was so hot that Priya couldn't bring herself to take the first step. Out of the corner of her eye, she saw the edges of the field rippling in the heat. Reza grew smaller and smaller in the distance. He was the fastest of the group by far, with Kofi some way behind him.

'Do I have to repeat myself?' yelled Master Ramsaroup. 'Because I hate repeating myself.'

Gods, she had to do this. She hadn't come to Kuwatta to stay weak and invisible. Biting her bottom lip, she took the first step, then the next. The rest of the group soon followed. The first lap was torture, the second was agony, and after the third Priya stopped counting.

Master Ramsaroup didn't say much. The only words that came from his mouth were: 'Again.'

And again.

And again.

Until Priya couldn't hear the Cotari for her own panting, and black spots appeared before her eyes. Some of the cadets collapsed. Priya didn't know what happened to them. Some of them disappeared, and she saw others back up and running a little later. Their bodies became vague blurs. A few times she staggered and slumped forward, longing for the cool shade. Her clothes, drenched in sweat, stuck to her body.

She had no idea if she'd actually completed the thirty laps by the time Master Ramsaroup told them to stop. Then he moved them to the edge of the field, where they were somewhat sheltered by the banana leaves hanging over a fence. He drilled them mercilessly, quickly switching from one exercise to another. Now and then, he gave them a short break to let them drink water. Makaku stuck his head straight into a bucket of water and had to run another lap as punishment.

They ended with push-ups. First with their hands flat, but then on fists, until the skin chafed from Priya's knuckles and they began to bleed.

'Did I say you could take a break?' Master Ramsaroup's voice boomed across the field. He kicked Kwasi, who was lying on his back, exhausted. Kwasi rolled over miserably and pushed himself back to his feet.

Jupta, who had collapsed yet again, quickly pushed herself back up too. Through strands of hair, Priya could see that her arms were trembling.

Priya clenched her jaw and went on with her push-ups. *Ten, eleven, twelve.* She counted under her breath. Beads of sweat slid down her forehead onto the black stone below. Her muscles cramped up, but that was nothing compared to the pain that was blazing through her knuckles.

When they finished, all she wanted to do was drag herself back to the barracks and curl up on her mat. But the sun was slowly sinking towards the horizon, which meant she didn't have much time left to find the healing rooms. She still didn't know how she was going to send Umed's remedy to him as soon as she had her hands on it. But that was a problem for later.

She waited until Master Ramsaroup dismissed them and then slipped away without the others noticing. She didn't dare to ask the master where she could find the healing rooms. He'd probably send her straight back to the barracks, as the sun had almost set. She was prepared to miss her dinner to get this done. She'd tried desperately to find a better moment, but without luck. Kuwatta didn't give its students any free time, so now she had no choice but to try this approach.

The black fields were colossal and there were no buildings to hide behind, so she had to be quick. Priya noticed soldiers walking around the outer edges of the training ground, and she quickly strode across the middle. She didn't look back. Not even when she heard someone shouting. The voices grew louder, and Priya picked up her pace. Just for a moment, she forgot how tired she was.

She soon reached the Academy. Torches illuminated the black stone. Priya pressed her lips together. There was no way through other than the tunnel that led beneath the building. Her legs couldn't go any faster, so she kept close to the wall and cautiously peered round the corner.

She took a chance and ran towards the gate. Three steps before she reached it, someone grabbed her arm.

'What,' said Reza quietly, 'do you think you're doing?'

He pulled her back and she fell against him. Priya's eyes were still on the gate. As the two guards spotted them, they gripped their spears. She'd been caught. Furiously, she turned to look at Reza, who only then let go of her arm. He glared down at her with an unexpected intensity. Orange-red rays of sun sharpened his jawline and turned his eyes the colour of molten gold.

Priya didn't know who she was more angry with: him for stopping her, or herself for not noticing his presence in time. It didn't help that she still couldn't feel his soul. It was as if he'd put up a wall around his spirit. A wall she couldn't get through.

'First you accuse me of theft,' she growled at him, jabbing his chest with her finger, 'and now this. Why can't you leave me alone, cadet? And before you ask me again: no, I don't have any gold on me.'

He stared at her finger. Then at her face. 'Cadet?' he echoed.

'Is there some other way you'd like to be addressed?' Even though they were taking the same classes, Priya was well aware that they weren't equals. Cadet or not, he was still the general's son. But that didn't mean she was going to grovel to him.

'I need to get to the healing rooms,' she said in an agitated voice before he could reply. Then she turned to walk on.

He grabbed her arm again. 'That's not going to happen.'

She pulled her arm away and glared at him. 'Why not? You're worried I'm going to steal medical supplies now too?' Actually, she hadn't entirely ruled out that option if the healers refused to help. But she obviously wasn't going to tell him that.

'Why do you need to go to the healing rooms?' Reza said, raising an eyebrow. 'Are you injured?'

Well, no, not really. Unless her grazed knuckles counted, but there was no way she could bring herself to say that. 'It's not for myself,' she said more calmly. Reza's face was still emotionless. How could he feel so empty, both inside and out?

'The sun's about to set.' Reza's gaze went to the sun, the edge of which was already touching the horizon. Soon Priya would be going to bed not only with empty hands but also an empty stomach. 'Whoever it is who needs the medicine, unless they're on their deathbed, it'll have to wait until tomorrow.'

'That's no good,' she said, frustrated. 'There's not enough time between our lessons.'

'Why can't you just . . .' he began, but then it began to dawn on him. He narrowed his eyes. 'This is for someone outside Kuwatta, isn't it? That's forbidden.'

'You don't even know what I . . .'

'I know enough,' he interrupted her, moving closer to her. This near to him, she could feel the heat of his body and see the dark circles under his eyes. 'Whoever it is, when you came to Kuwatta, you made a choice. Kuwatta is your life now, we are your family. Everyone outside no longer matters.'

'Family?' She snorted. 'You're my family?'

'Even if you get your hands on the medicine, you'll never be able to send it to them,' he said, ignoring her jibe. To her frustration, his words hit home. Even though she already knew that somewhere deep inside, she still didn't want to believe it and now he was forcing her to confront the facts.

'Is there a problem here?' one of the guards said, walking over to them.

'Cadet Priya is new,' said Reza, still staring at Priya. 'Will you escort her back to the barracks? The sun's about to set.'

20

ONE LAST SHOVE AGAINST Priya's back sent her stumbling into the barracks.

The door slammed behind her, and the room was sunk in darkness. It took her eyes a moment to adjust.

'Ah, the lost princess has returned,' Nanu said, rolling over on her mat.

Priya ignored the comment and staggered to her own mat, where she collapsed, exhausted. Her empty stomach was rumbling and yet again she cursed Reza under her breath.

She could not hear the deep, regular breathing of people who were sleeping. The room was perfectly silent. Glancing around, she saw that Mawar and Jupta weren't there.

Priya braced herself and pulled off one of her shoes. Pain flashed through her foot. There were blisters on her heel and toes. She tossed the shoe aside. The other shoe followed. This time she knew what to expect and was better prepared for the pain.

As soon as she was done, she sat with her back against the wall. The wood creaked under her weight. The wind slipped through the cracks, playing with her hair.

'Forbidden?' she muttered, thinking of Reza's words. For her perhaps. But clearly not for him. He was allowed to walk straight on while she was brought back. Didn't he understand how ridiculous he sounded when he said they were family? As the general's son, he had privileges she couldn't even dream of.

Frustrated, she kicked one of her shoes, barely feeling the pain. Even at the heart of the rebel movement, there was nothing she could do to help Umed. As her hands made fists, the wounds on her knuckles opened up again and a thin trickle of blood seeped between her fingers.

It took Priya a few attempts to get back on her feet. She walked out of the barracks. The wind howled, blowing sand in her eyes. For a moment, she thought she heard a scream above the wind. She froze and listened, but all she could hear was the whistling of the wind and the roar of the water. Nothing else.

Treading carefully, to protect her sore feet, she managed to reach the washroom. She pushed the door open with her shoulder. There were three girls already there. Two probies, whose conversation immediately fell silent, and Mawar, alone in the corner and washing herself. Priya stumbled silently past the probies, and then the two of them quietly resumed their conversation.

In the middle of the room, on the right and left, two holes had been made in the ground, close to the wall. These openings allowed river water to flow in through a long channel in the ground so that there would always be fresh water for washing.

Leaning on the wall, Priya slowly lowered herself and immersed her feet in the flowing water. It was painful, but it was nothing compared to what she'd been through in combat training. After a while, she also pushed her hands into the water, breathing out with a hiss as the water washed away the blood and dirt.

The wind tugged at the hut, making it shake back and forth. Through the narrow window high above, she saw the slim curve of the crescent moon against the blue of the night sky. Light-grey clouds scudded by peacefully.

Here at Kuwatta, she heard none of the sounds she used to hear in Disin. There was no twittering of birds or chirping of crickets. No shrieking of monkeys or croaking of frogs. No rustling of the leaves as the wind stirred the trees. At Kuwatta, there was nothing but flowing water, strong gusts of wind and black stone.

A piercing scream broke through the rumbling of the waterfall. There was no doubt about it this time. Priya froze.

One of the probies gasped. 'What was that?'

'Maybe the senior students are training?' suggested the other, with an anxious look on her face.

'Yes,' the other said with a nod. 'Maybe that's it.'

Priya caught Mawar's eye on the other side of the washroom. Unless the soldiers were fighting to the death, she couldn't imagine that the scream was part of any training session. It wasn't the cry of someone sparring with a fellow soldier; it was a scream that chilled her blood. The kind of sound someone might make when they were being tortured. It reminded her of the desperate cries of the woman who was killed in Disin along with her baby. Goosebumps rose on Priya's arms and shoulders. Were they executing people?

Mawar was the first to look away. She turned and left the room. The sliding door slammed behind her.

Priya scrubbed her hands more thoroughly. This was just a distraction. It didn't matter if Kuwatta was hiding secrets from her. The fort was the only place where she could become stronger, better. She had no plans to leave. Her biggest problem now was how to get Umed his cure.

+++

Someone was poking her shoulder. Once. Twice. Three times.

That's enough.

Priya lashed out. And made contact. For a moment, there was peace. But then she felt another push against her shoulder. Struggling, she opened her eyes. Jupta's face was hanging above her.

'What?' Priya grunted.

Jupta looked over her shoulder and back again. All Priya wanted was to sink back into a dreamless sleep, but it was already too late for that. She was becoming aware of her surroundings. Her feet – ice-cold, swollen and wrinkled – were half in the water, and her head was lean-ing against the wall at a cramped, painful angle. Was she going to be late again? Priya shot to her feet, ignoring her aching body.

Behind Jupta, two cadets whose names Priya didn't know were washing. One of them was concealing a smile behind her hand; the other wasn't even bothering to hide it.

'What time is it?' asked Priya. 'Has the first bell rung?'

Jupta didn't answer. A frown appeared on her face. 'What did you say?'

Gods. Priya had automatically spoken in Suryan. She shook her head to clear her mind and then repeated her questions in Awuran. As she spoke, the sound of the bell echoed around the room and the two girls behind them started washing more quickly.

Jupta raised her finger. 'That was the first one.' She kneeled beside Priya and looked at the blisters on her feet. 'I've got something that might help. My parents gave me a salve before I left. Seems they knew more than I thought,' she added, pulling a face.

'Do you miss them?' asked Priya, even though she could already guess the answer. Jupta spoke lovingly about her parents. There was no hint of resentment or anger.

Jupta shrugged self-consciously and nodded. 'And my sister. They didn't want me to go,' she said with a small smile. 'Not that I was going to let them stop me. I worked far too hard for this.'

'Did you win the test?'

'Yes, although I'm wondering now if I really did. Maybe I was chosen because of the theoretical test too, or maybe just because of my gift.' Jupta shrugged again. 'I always dreamed of becoming a scholar.'

'And now here we are,' said Priya quietly.

'And now here we are,' Jupta agreed just as softly. She looked at the side of Priya's foot. 'Maybe you should tear your old clothes into strips today to bandage up your hands and feet. The water's made your skin go all soft.'

Priya relaxed a little. 'Thank you,' she said slowly, the words feeling strange. 'Thanks for waking me up, too.'

Jupta gave her a shy smile. 'You helped me too.'

The two other girls, who had now finished washing, pushed past them to reach the exit, and Priya took a step back. The door slid shut behind the last of the two cadets.

'But still,' said Priya, rolling her shoulders to loosen the muscles. 'The others don't like me. I'm sure it'd be easier for you to ignore me.'

'They don't hate you. That's not it.'

'It certainly looks a lot like it.'

Jupta's expression changed, becoming distant, and Priya narrowed her eyes to scan the room. 'Is that ghost with us again?'

'What?' Jupta looked at her in surprise and then burst out laughing. 'No, sorry. No, the dead person disappeared yesterday. There aren't many souls lingering in Kuwatta.'

'Oh.' Priya coughed to hide her discomfort.

'It's more . . .' Jupta absentmindedly tugged on the coloured beads around her neck. 'I was just thinking. It's not that they don't like you. It's more that they can't deal with it. We've all learned to live separately, of course. That's all changed dramatically at Kuwatta, but it doesn't change the fact that it'll take time. To me, you all have such unusual customs. The way you look, your clothes, your language. Even your accent when you speak Awuran is new to me.'

'I try to pronounce the words correctly,' Priya said defensively. She reached out to slide the door open. If she didn't hurry, the second bell was going to ring and she could forget about her breakfast. Her stomach felt so empty after missing dinner the night before. She wasn't going to make the same mistake again.

'You do pronounce them correctly,' said Jupta with a small, apologetic smile, holding Priya back. 'It's just that it's different. Not bad, but different. We're used to ignoring one another – that was the unwritten rule. And now we suddenly have to learn to live together.'

'What about you?' Priya asked from the doorway. 'How do you see me? As an intruder?' She hadn't forgotten how Jupta had spoken about the Freelanders. The Freelanders and Suryans were, of course, very different from each other. One group were conquerors, while the other group had been taken to work in a strange land. And yet they did have one thing in common: they were not originally from Awaran. And neither were the Luanans or the Dalinese.

Jupta picked a bit of fluff off her tunic. 'Suryans don't know Awaran the way we know her. You don't hear the secrets that the jungle whispers to us, and you don't feel the pain and joy of the earth. But,' she said thoughtfully, 'Awaran wouldn't make you into blood children if she wanted to disown you. Just because you don't come from here doesn't mean we can't fight side by side.'

Priya weighed Jupta's words in silence as they left the barracks. Essentially, it wasn't much different from what her mother often said: that first and foremost they remained Suryan. Sometimes Priya didn't know what she thought about the question herself. Her home was Awaran. But was it really the land where she belonged? According to the Topuans, they were strangers from distant countries; according to her mother, they were guests who would one day return to their own homeland. And according to the Freelanders, they didn't belong anywhere, because the Freelanders were the lords and masters of the world and the Suryans were merely their subordinates.

But Awaran was all she knew. The only land on whose soil she had walked, whose air she had breathed and water she had drunk. Awaran was the land that had given her life, the land she was fighting for. She knew nothing else. So why did she sometimes feel like a traveller with no destination?

21

THE WEEKS THAT FOLLOWED went by in a whirlwind.

Combat training, much to the relief of many of the students, was moved to the mornings, when the heat was more bearable. Still, it was only a slight improvement, because Master Ramsaroup ramped up the pressure with every lesson. With his tough training, their muscles were soon stronger and their fitness had improved considerably.

While Priya's hands had bled at first during the push-ups, within just a few days calluses had started to appear. Her shoes stretched and the blisters healed with the help of Jupta's ointment. Even the endless running around the black field didn't get her out of breath as quickly.

But she had no time to think about how she was going to get her hands on the remedy for Umed. And she certainly didn't have the energy. By the time the lessons were over, she was so exhausted that the edges of the real world were starting to blur. All she really wanted to do was to curl up on her mat and not get up again. But instead, she practised her combat techniques, her languages and her gift into the late evening hours, by the light of a kokolampoe.

Priya often worked through the night to improve her language skills, studying not only texts in Awuran, but also in Topuan, Luan and Freeland. As she had no real talent for most subjects, except for soul studies and combat training, she had to work twice as hard as many of her fellow students – and three times as hard as people like

Jupta and Ishani. But that didn't stop Priya. She had no intention of being inferior to anyone.

'If he survived the first few days, the chances that he'll die are slim,' said Jupta. She was sitting cross-legged with a book about botany in her hand and watching as Priya tried to take control of a bat's soul without affecting the whole colony.

In the weeks that had flown by, Jupta and Priya had grown closer, partly because Jupta was still the only one who seemed to like her and who actually talked to her. To be fair, Kwasi also spoke to Priya, but his attention was all over the place. He would enthusiastically strike up a conversation with Priya but then the next moment he seemed to have forgotten she existed.

'But the chances of damage are high,' Priya objected, her eyes returning to the bat in the air. By now she'd done her research. 'I just want to be sure he makes a complete recovery.' That was the least she could do for Umed. 'And because of *him*, it's all become even more difficult.' By 'him', she meant Reza. Since their encounter in front of the Academy, the whole class had been accompanied to every lesson and back to the barracks by an older student or a low-ranking soldier. Slipping away had become virtually impossible.

Jupta made a sympathetic sound as she turned a page of her book.

It was a beautiful cloudless night, so the black training fields and the Academy in the distance were clearly visible, even in the dark. The moon shone brightly and the stars glittered in their thousands above their heads, as the students eagerly practised their techniques and lessons. The soldier sat in the hut in front of the barracks as usual, keeping an eye on them to make sure they didn't cross the white line.

The bat whose soul Priya was wrestling with skimmed over her head and flew away. 'Gods, why won't it work?' she wailed, burying both hands in her hair in frustration.

Since their first soul studies lesson, she'd failed time and time again to use her gift in a focused and deliberate way. She could feel her power, but she couldn't seem to aim it at one person at a time. She always dragged others into the command. It didn't matter that she wasn't great at 'feeling' either, as Master Yapoma called it – sensing the presence of souls in her surroundings. Her range appeared to be limited to the classroom and a few steps outside. Spirit-speakers, like Jupta, could easily tell how many students were walking round inside the Academy.

Jupta suddenly scrambled to her feet, the book in her hands falling to the ground. 'Did you feel that too?' she asked, with big dark eyes.

The bat had come closer, but Priya had abandoned her attempt to control it. 'What?' asked Priya and then she saw the look in Jupta's eyes, the same look as on the first day. 'Was it a dead person's soul?'

Jupta shook her head. 'No. Wait . . . it's gone. It came from the Keep. A strange energy. Something I've never felt before.'

Priya looked at the Academy, which was shielding the Keep. 'What do you mean?'

'I don't really know,' Jupta said with a helpless shrug. 'It was a short burst of energy, but it was really sharp. Like a bolt of lightning.'

That was strange, but not particularly surprising. Priya had expected Kuwatta to experiment with weapons and magical powers so that they could use them against the Freelanders. If they were already conscripting blood children into their army, then this wasn't much of a leap.

'Jupta!' Paneke was waving at Jupta. 'Are you coming?'

Priya ran her hand over her face, which was damp because of the heat. 'You go ahead,' she said to Jupta, who was looking at her questioningly and a little guiltily. It was easier for Priya to pretend she'd made the choice to train separately. 'I'm not going to stop until a bat is sitting on my hand.'

+++

Master Breeveld, their strategy lecturer, ran one bony finger along the twisting dotted line on a map of Awaran that indicated where the influence of the rebel army ended and the colonists' began. 'This is now also the line where the rainforest begins. The Freelanders had all of the jungle by the coast felled for their plantations and big houses.'

He tapped the five warrior villages, which were positioned exactly on the line. 'Our first line of defence. They're separate from each other, but make no mistake: they work closely together to carry out their attacks on the plantations.'

He moved his finger to a spot between two of the warrior villages. 'There are some swampy regions between the warrior villages. The Freelanders have fallen foul of them during their military operations on a number of occasions.'

Paneke raised his hand. 'Have they ever broken through the line?'

Master Breeveld nodded gravely. 'The fort has been rebuilt several times for a reason. On those occasions when the colonists reached our fort – which was not in the same location as the current Kuwatta – we were forced to surrender it. We learned the hard way how to adapt. But they've never defeated us. They have made incursions, but then always fell apart again. You there, tell us why.'

'Jungle madness, diseases and organised attacks from neighbouring villages that know the rainforest better than they do,' Ishani immediately rattled off. Priya suspected that Master Breeveld asked her to speak up so often because he was sure she would give the right answer and he would not have to correct her.

'And by vengeful spirits and primeval monsters,' Jupta added from her seat beside Priya. She knew an incredible amount about the rainforest and what had taken place there. Priya had come to realise that this was the difference between the other groups and the Topuans, who had lived and roamed throughout Awaran for centuries.

'Explain.' Master Breeveld removed the small round glasses from his nose and polished them on his robe.

'Primeval monsters are attracted to violence. Deep in the rainforest, the colonists found it hard to defend themselves. And the vengeful spirits . . .' Jupta absentmindedly ran her fingers over the beads around her neck. 'Vengeful spirits can be summoned by anyone, if black magic is used. When there's a group of them, they can do a lot of damage. The colonists employ many methods, but they make sure to steer clear of the vengeful spirits. They're more likely to be the victims of their violence than the instigators.'

+++

'You're distracted again,' Master Yapoma said to Priya. She gave an irritated sigh, exhaling the breath she'd been holding. 'The focus must come from within,' he continued. 'Look deep inside and form the invisible shield around your soul. Strengthen yourself against intruders. That's the only way to protect yourself against other soul-singers.'

For Priya, who had spent her whole life closely observing her surroundings so that she knew how she should act, that felt unnatural. It would have been easier to create a shield to protect other people from her than to create one to protect herself. She only knew how to hold everything inside.

Most of the other soul-singers seemed to be having less difficulty. Only Nanu and Makaku were shifting restlessly back and forth with pained expressions.

'Can't I just command them to keep their distance?' she suggested.

'No,' said Master Yapoma sharply. 'I've told you many times before that quality is better than quantity. If you can't do exactly what you want to do with your gift – *without* accidentally dragging several souls into your command – then you will fail, cadet. The same goes for this shield.'

Priya hung her head and sighed. She obviously understood why he was so insistent about her having proper control of her gift. She was a soldier, and soldiers worked as a team. If she couldn't influence who she was using her gift on, then there was a good chance that she'd be commanding not only her enemies but also her fellow soldiers. That was, to put it mildly, impractical.

'Try again,' he ordered.

They were sitting together in front of the Academy. The master had taken a look out of his tower and decided that they would continue their lesson in the open air today. So they were sheltering under the banana leaves, in lotus pose on the black stone, and forming invisible shields around their souls. Or at least trying to.

Priya opened one eye to see that Master Yapoma was standing with his back to her, and she leaned over slightly to Jupta. 'Is Kwasi not here again?'

'Late,' Jupta whispered back, without opening her eyes. 'As usual.'

'Unbelievable.' Priya tugged at the front of her tunic, which was sticking to her skin in the sweltering heat. Kwasi was so loud that his absence left a noticeable silence. But their group seemed to be even smaller today. 'Mawar,' she said, as it dawned on her. 'Mawar's missing too.'

And Reza, but that wasn't unusual. The general's son came and went when it suited him, and none of the masters ever said anything about it.

'Mouth and eyes closed, cadet,' said Master Yapoma. 'All I want to hear is your breathing.'

Caught out, Priya sat up straight. She closed her eyes and reached inside. Her soul shot off in all directions, and she couldn't hide her frustration. In an attempt to calm herself, she breathed in and out three times. She tried to weave an imaginary shield around her soul. Fluid and flexible at first, but then stronger and stronger. More and more solid. *Keep others out*, she thought emphatically. *Protect me.*

Her nose was itching. The shield in her mind dissolved. Gods, not again.

This was so much harder than she'd imagined.

'Why do we need to do this?' said an irritated voice. For a moment, Priya thought the words had tumbled from her own mouth, and she opened her eyes. But no – it was Nanu who had spoken. She had half risen to her feet. 'It's not as if we're going to fight against other soul-singers. The Freelanders hate blood children, just like the rest of Awaran.'

'Not everyone hates blood children,' Jupta muttered quietly.

Master Yapoma's expression hardened for a moment. But he wasn't like Master Ramsaroup, who would have immediately punished Nanu for this open resistance.

'Tell me, cadet,' said their master, 'which of the soul-singers' gifts is most valuable?'

Nanu frowned. 'No idea. The gift of the sight-speakers?' she guessed, as she was a sight-speaker herself and often manipulated others' senses for her own amusement.

'Try again.'

'Deed-speakers?' she said reluctantly.

Master Yapoma shook his head.

Nanu furrowed her brow and sat back down. 'I don't understand.'

'Sense-speakers,' said a voice behind them. Priya turned her head and saw Kwasi approaching in a pair of makeshift sandals crafted from bark, reeds and leaves. His dark brown skin was gleaming with sweat and his cheeks had turned a deep red. She guessed he'd had to do some kind of exercise as punishment again.

'Explain,' said Master Yapoma. He didn't seem surprised at Kwasi stumbling late into his lesson. None of the masters did anymore. Occasionally Kwasi got away with it, but more often he missed half of the lesson because he was having to do some kind of punishment.

'That can't be right,' said Makaku, laughing. 'People who can influence emotions in a war? What good are they to Kuwatta?'

'I see there is still work to be done on your knowledge of this subject, cadet. Sense-speakers do not so much influence emotions. They influence the energies that make up the soul. Which includes emotions but goes much further. Kwasi, why don't you tell us why this makes them Kuwatta's best soldiers?'

Kwasi put on a serious expression. 'Human beings often talk about a soul when what we actually mean is the energy flowing through our bodies. Animals, plants and even certain stones are also made up of energies. They may not be exactly the same as the energy in our bodies, but they can still be influenced. And sense-speakers can influence all of those energies and use them as weapons.'

Master Yapoma nodded approvingly. 'That's right, cadet. Sit down.'

'Thank you, master.' Kwasi pressed his fists together and sank down in the nearest spot, right between Jupta and Priya. Priya's surprise that Kwasi had sat with them and not with Makaku gave way to irritation as he pushed them aside with his arms and legs to get more space.

'Keep your sweaty limbs to yourself,' Priya hissed at him. He deliberately waved his hands in her face, so Priya kicked his leg. Jupta gave a loud sigh.

'Sense-speakers,' said Master Yapoma, 'are the most powerful soul-singers. Not only when it comes to building mental shields, but also for mentally breaking other people. Their affinity with energies allows them to easily throw their opponents off balance by manipulating their emotions. They can also fuse more quickly with the power contained in gold.'

'I don't understand, master,' said Jupta, who had moved forward. 'Do soul-singers here use gold?'

Master Yapoma gave her a slight smile. 'Look around you, cadet. The fort isn't made of black stone and gold just for decoration. Gold is the only kind of metal that contains magic. Which is why the scholars at Kuwatta are so fond of it. No matter what kind of devices they make, they always include gold in them. It also amplifies the powers of soul-singers. Especially sense-speakers.'

'So why don't we just use gold all the time?' asked Makaku, throwing his hands in the air. 'If it makes everything so much easier, I don't understand why we have to do all this training.'

'Sense-speakers are powerful not because they can physically do the most damage, but because of their flawless control. It's what makes them the best soldiers that Kuwatta has.' A sharp undertone had crept into his voice. 'Using gold without control will not make you a better soldier and it certainly won't protect you from enemies, who are hidden everywhere.' He was looking at Makaku, but Priya felt that he was speaking directly to her. 'These exercises are there for a reason.'

22

'ATTENTION!' ROARED MASTER RAMSAROUP above the sound of the rushing water. He'd taken them to the foredeck, where stone and boards seemed to sway along with the river and fine drops of water splashed their faces.

Priya stepped aside a little, so that her arm wouldn't touch Reza's. They were lined up neatly in front of Master Ramsaroup and pressing their fists together; the soul-singers at the front and the regular cadets at some distance behind them.

Reza's water panther, Kohóna, lay stretched out under the palms at the edge of the field, rolling lazily on her side but still keeping an eye on them. She followed the general's son almost everywhere.

'Cadet Mawar will no longer join your lessons. The general has decided to end her training.'

Priya waited for more explanation, but Master Ramsaroup left it at that. Out of the corner of her eye, she saw Jupta frowning. Mawar had been missing since the day before. Priya hadn't thought too much about it at first – until Mawar didn't show up for dinner and her mat remained empty all night.

'So, what's she doing instead?' Kwasi said, trudging towards them. He'd arrived late and had to run an extra twenty laps around the field.

Master Ramsaroup looked as if he was thinking about giving Kwasi more laps to run. 'Mawar is serving the army,' he said abruptly.

That wasn't the answer Priya had been expecting. When she'd accepted the general's offer to be trained as a special soldier, she'd thought her future was fixed. It hadn't occurred to her that she might be placed elsewhere – or, in other words, be thrown off the training course. After all, deciding to quit was not an option.

'Make no mistake,' Master Ramsaroup said as the murmuring started. 'We are both instructing you *and* assessing you. The general is aware of everyone's progress. He decides if you are worthy of your place here – or if another role in Kuwatta would suit you better.'

The chatter came to an immediate stop. Only the river beneath them continued to rage on.

Master Ramsaroup struck the stick against the palm of his hand. 'At ease,' he commanded. Everyone obeyed. He divided them up into groups of four, so that they could spar with one another and learn to work together at the same time.

Reza and Nanu were up against Priya and Kwasi. That was fine by Priya. They were the two people at Kuwatta who annoyed her most.

'Parry and disarm,' she heard Master Ramsaroup shout. 'Make use of the moves you've learned over the past few days.'

Nanu sneered at Priya, but Reza's attention was elsewhere. His face was unusually tense; usually he just stared into space, looking bored. Priya followed his gaze and saw three people at the edge of the field: two in green flanking a woman in black.

'That's the major,' Kwasi said, answering the question she hadn't asked. He stood beside her, a hand raised to keep the sun out of his eyes. 'I noticed her walking around.'

'Give me a different opponent.' Reza had taken his eyes off the major and was looking over his shoulder at Master Ramsaroup. He pointed half-heartedly in Priya's direction. 'Someone who's not her.'

Priya couldn't believe her ears.

He was the only one who could say that kind of thing in front of an instructor and get away with it. It was infuriating. Priya didn't even dare to think the words, let alone say them out loud. She'd heard that cadets could be dangled over the edge of the fort on a rope if they committed serious offences. That sounded exactly like the kind of thing that might happen if she were to defy her teacher like that.

Master Ramsaroup came towards them. 'I'm not here for your enjoyment.'

That was an exceptionally mild reaction.

Reza shook his head. With his black hand, the prosthesis, he pointed at Kofi. 'He's better.'

The other students cast furtive glances at them, and Priya clenched her jaw. Nanu, who was standing beside Reza, let out a snorting sound that sounded suspiciously like a laugh. Was Reza really trying to get rid of Priya because he thought she wasn't good enough to face him? In front of all the other students? She was white hot with rage.

'No,' Priya interrupted the two of them, causing their attention to shift to her. 'I don't want anyone else.' She raised her chin slightly. 'I refuse to switch.'

Master Ramsaroup looked at her impassively for a moment, which made her skin prickle. Then he placed a hand on Reza's shoulder and walked on. 'Teams will not be changed.'

'Why did you do that?' Kwasi said, prodding her arm. 'He's the general's son. Have you seen him in our training sessions? We're going to die.'

'Ah, the art of exaggeration,' Priya muttered with her eyes fixed on Reza, who was glaring at her. She couldn't read minds, but she suspected he'd love to throw her down the waterfall. And that only confirmed her decision.

She reasoned that she'd learn more quickly if she fought against Reza, since he knew what he was doing. At least Kwasi wasn't exaggerating about Reza's fighting skills – he was amazing. His power, technique and speed were way ahead of the rest of the class. But then he'd grown up at the fort and had more experience than everyone else put together. But if Priya was honest, that wasn't why she'd stood her ground.

All she wanted was a chance to punch him in the face. Even if it was just once.

His rejection made her furious. Nanu still believed that Priya didn't amount to much because she was Suryan, and the other soul-singers, except Jupta and Kwasi, mostly ignored her. It made no difference that she always kept up in their lessons and was maybe even one of the better students. Priya tightened her grip on the stick.

She'd had enough of being told over and over that she was worthless. And she still hadn't forgiven him for stopping her when she was looking for the healing rooms.

'I don't think this is a good idea,' said Kwasi, somewhere behind her. Was he trying to hide? 'Did I mention how much I hate fighting? My aim is to live my life as a pacifist.'

'Are you serious?' She glanced back over her shoulder, looking at him in disbelief. 'You're training to be a *soldier*.'

'Not by choice!' he objected. 'Well, maybe a little. But I thought I was going to be educated as a scholar. How was I supposed to know it would turn out like this?'

'As a scholar, you're still working for the army.'

'But at least I wouldn't have to use my own hands to kill people!'

His reasoning made no sense at all.

'Can we get started?' Nanu asked impatiently, slapping her stick against her palm. 'Or are you going to stand around chatting all day?'

Priya took a step forward and turned to the side in readiness. She crooked her finger to summon Reza closer. He just rolled his shoulders and stayed where he was. His expression hadn't changed, but the air between them felt charged. Then she caught a sudden glimpse of his soul, hidden behind a thick shield – a flash of frustration. Priya's heart leaped at her discovery. This was the first time she'd felt his soul.

'And . . . fight!' shouted Master Ramsaroup.

Nanu, unable to wait, sprinted forward, holding out her stick like a spear. Priya stepped aside, bringing Kwasi into full view. He let out a cry and ducked, so Nanu's stick missed him by a mile. Growling, she tried to regain her balance and turned round.

Priya counted on Kwasi, in spite of his yelping, to keep Nanu busy for a while. She swung her stick in Reza's direction.

He easily dodged her attack. 'Nice try.'

'You think? I wasn't even trying,' she said drily, taking another swipe at him.

With a sharp movement, he knocked her stick aside. She blocked his hit, but it took more effort than she cared to admit. She was surprised to see that he'd used his black hand. He was able to move it, and yet the hand clearly wasn't made of flesh and blood.

A tingling sensation ran down her neck. Alarmed, she looked up and reinforced her mental shield. Using your gift during combat training was forbidden. Even so, she felt him brushing against her consciousness once again. He wasn't here to spar, he wanted to defeat her as quickly as possible, and he wasn't wasting any time.

His stick flashed in her direction. It was only her reflex reaction that allowed her to block him. The impact made her feet slide back. That was a close one. Again she felt his gift brushing against her soul. At the same time, he started moving. She dodged his next attack and felt her mental shield starting to tear under his pressure. His gift was worming its way into her. She felt her energy fading. So he was a sense-speaker. Wonderful.

With all her strength, she pushed back, trying to seal the mental crack in her shield. But then his stick smashed into her shoulder, upper arm and hand. Her weapon slid from her hand and rolled away. A cry escaped her mouth. He slammed his ordinary hand into her windpipe, cutting off her voice.

The force of his blow made her fall backwards, his gift crashing through her defences. He infiltrated her emotions, playing them like musical instruments. Her mind told her she had to fight back, that she couldn't give up, but the touch of his gift kept her relaxed and docile.

He sat on top of Priya. 'Surrender.' Reza looked down at her, his prosthesis resting loosely on her throat. Up close, she could feel and see that it was made of shiny black stone woven through with very fine gold thread.

Priya stubbornly pressed her lips together. Even that small act cost her a huge amount of energy.

It wasn't as if he had to press her physically to the ground to declare his victory. This was nothing more than a show of force. Through her hazy, eerily contented emotions, she noticed that the corners of his mouth were slightly turned up. For anyone else, the change was too minimal to pass for a smile. But this was Reza. In the weeks she'd been at Kuwatta, she had never seen him smile.

She knew she shouldn't confront him. Just because he was breaking the rules didn't mean she could afford to as well. But something about his smug attitude meant that she didn't really care. He was getting under her skin, driving her crazy. And maybe that was what pushed her over the edge.

His gift was deep in her soul, but not so deep that he had every part of her in his grasp. She breathed through her nose, scraping together all the remnants of willpower and energy that she still had in her. In spite of everything, she had an advantage: he was using his gift on her, so she could feel his soul. He was no longer beyond her reach.

Reza tilted his head. 'Surrender.'

She slowly breathed out and then braced herself.

The corners of his mouth went down again. He seemed to realise that something wasn't right.

'Get. Out. Of. My. Body,' she said – and she *pushed*. Physically, mentally, she didn't know. All she knew was that she wanted him as far away from her as possible. He was an intruder, a parasite, and she was going to destroy him – until there was nothing left of him.

Orange-yellow light exploded behind her eyes, but this time she didn't lose her willpower or her grip on her gift. He was going to leave her body, no matter what. She pushed, and pushed, and *pushed*.

Until she felt him start to give way. The space he occupied within her body was becoming smaller and, drunk with victory, she kept pushing. 'Get out of my body,' she muttered under her breath.

Black spots were dancing before her eyes.

'Stop.' Master Ramsaroup in the distance.

The weight on her fell away. Reza had stood up. Breathing slowly through her nose, she tried to focus. A lock of his black hair fell over his eyes as he looked down at her with a tense expression that she couldn't fathom.

'Not as invincible as you thought?' she said in a choked voice.

'You lost,' he responded tonelessly.

'But I still pushed you away.'

'You can think what you like.' With those words, he turned his back on her.

Priya pushed herself up onto her elbows. Around her, all the fighting had stopped and the cadets were staring at her. The major and the other two soldiers were standing, arms crossed, behind Master Ramsaroup. Blood dripped down onto her clothes. Cautiously, Priya reached up to touch her nose and realised it was bleeding. Her head was still pounding from the force she'd used.

She fell back onto the ground with a smile.

23

'DEFIANCE, CAUSING INJURY AND using your gift.' Master Ramsaroup slammed his stick onto the stone. 'I don't even know where to begin. Have you forgotten that you are not permitted to use your gift in any lessons except for soul studies?'

Heads bowed, Priya and Reza stood in front of him. Above them was a soft rumbling, and large drops of rain fell from the dark grey clouds, spattering onto the black field, which, except for them, was now deserted. Priya held her arm up a little, so the rainwater could cool the pain. Reza had not been holding back.

'I'm sorry, master,' said Priya, bowing her head a little deeper.

Reza just sniffed and looked to one side.

'The purpose of my lessons is not for you to show others how wonderful you are!' snarled Master Ramsaroup. 'And look at me when I'm talking to you!'

Reza slowly turned his head to look at the teacher. 'My apologies,' he said.

That only made Master Ramsaroup even angrier. The pink scars on the right side of his face stood out white against his red face. 'Go and tell that to your father.'

'What?' Reza looked up in alarm. 'I didn't . . .'

'Spare me your words. You're not here for my sake, Reza, but for them. If you can't even manage that, then you can explain why to the general.'

Priya glanced at Reza out of the corner of her eye. She guessed that when Master Ramsaroup said 'them', he was referring to her and the other soul-singers, since Reza showed up only occasionally during combat training and soul studies. But if that was right, what did he mean about Reza being there for them? Reza didn't seem to care much about her or the other soul-singers.

'And as for you,' said Master Ramsaroup, turning to Priya for the first time. She stood up straighter. 'You attack without any strategy, your footwork is a mess and you use your gift like a fool. What exactly did you hope to achieve?'

She clenched her jaw. That hurt. Priya knew she was no match for Reza, but she'd done her best with her form and her footwork. If she did break the rules, she at least wanted to put on a good show, so she didn't end up like Mawar.

'For the next month, cadet, you will clean all the student washrooms.'

Unbelievable. He couldn't really impose this punishment on her while Reza got away with a little chat with his own father, could he?

'But . . .'

'Silence, cadet. You start in two sunrises' time.'

She closed her mouth.

Great Gods. There were a dozen washrooms, used by over a hundred students. She didn't even want to think about how long it was going to take her. Boiling with rage, she glared in Reza's direction, even though she knew deep down that she'd brought the punishment upon herself.

'And now you're dismissed. I don't want to see the two of you any longer.'

+++

A day later, Priya clutched her books to her chest as she walked to her strategy class. Other students pushed past her, chatting excitedly. After getting an elbow in her ribs and a hand in her face, she moved to the side of the stairwell. Another bunch of students was streaming upstairs, quickly heading up the narrow steps. Priya searched for a familiar face in the sea of beige and brown tunics.

'So, where is it?' she heard someone say.

'You'll see it soon enough,' another student promised. 'It's clearly visible from the very top of the tower.'

Curious, Priya decided to follow them before they disappeared from sight. Faster and faster, she climbed the steps. The voices flowed into an ocean of sound that swelled in volume the higher she went.

'Didi.'

Something in Priya's stomach tensed up, and she stopped. Ishani. It wasn't just her sister's voice that she recognised. Her sister's soul was now as familiar to her as Jupta's. She hadn't done it consciously. Priya would rather have ignored her sister's existence, but she couldn't shut out Ishani's presence when she was nearby.

Ishani came out of a classroom and walked into the hallway by the stairwell where Priya was standing. Like the other probies, she was wearing a beige uniform and her dark hair was twisted into a neat bun. In her hands, which were covered in black smudges, she held a lump of material that Priya didn't recognise.

'I don't think we have anything to say to each other,' said Priya, her eyes on the students who were pushing upstairs past her. Until now, they'd managed not to exchange a single word. Not even when they were standing right next to each other. Priya didn't feel ready to break that unwritten rule yet.

She didn't want to do this. She couldn't.

'I have some news.' Ishani's soul was moving restlessly, alternating between nervousness, resentment and reluctance. So at least someone was worse at shielding her soul than Priya was.

'Not interested.' Priya walked on.

Ishani stood in front of her. 'Wait. I . . .'

Priya slowly lifted her head, so she could look Ishani in the eyes. Whatever her sister had to tell her, she didn't want to hear it. It was true that she missed her at times. Sometimes she even remembered the bickering with her brother and sister with affection. But that was more out of habit.

She hadn't forgiven Ishani for what had happened during the test, and she certainly didn't intend to apologise for using her gift when the winner was announced.

'What? Are you in the mood for throwing accusations at me again?' asked Priya. 'I thought we'd decided to ignore each other.'

Ishani shrugged. It was a typical Ishani gesture, one that Priya only saw when her sister was uncertain. Which didn't happen very often. Priya looked away.

Dozens of students were running upstairs, pushing Priya aside. Frowning, she rubbed her arm. What, in the name of the Gods, was making them all so eager to go upstairs?

'They're going to look at the damage to the Keep,' Ishani said softly. 'If you go up the tower, you can see the hole in one of the walls.'

Priya forgot her anger for a moment. 'How did that happen?'

'Because of the blood children, of course,' said a Suryan boy who appeared beside Ishani. He was wearing a beige tunic like hers. Another probie. He was big-boned with a deep brown complexion and thin lips that were pulled into a sneer. 'Seems things got out of hand during a practice fight. As always happens with those cursed ones.'

'Rohan,' said Ishani in a warning tone.

'What?' The boy raised his eyebrows. 'It's true, isn't it?'

Priya snorted. She couldn't believe she'd come all the way to Kuwatta just to have to listen to the same narrow-minded opinions all over again. Although the masters kept stressing that the soul-singers were essential in the war against the colonists, Priya still found it hard not to see herself as a monster. It was what she'd heard all her life. So there must be some truth to it, mustn't there?

She could sometimes ignore the feeling, as she was so busy with her training and studies. But this boy had almost succeeded in undoing all her hard work. She hated the way his words tore open the old wounds so easily.

'Forget it.' Priya walked on, deliberately bumping her shoulder into Rohan. He swore in Suryan and tried to give her a shove back.

'I've got some news,' Ishani called again. 'From home.'

Priya stopped. She turned round. A conflicting mixture of fear and hope filled her heart. 'What did you say?' She turned and headed back down the stairs. 'Did they send a letter? How's Umed? Have they been able to heal him?'

'I've . . . Wait, no, what I mean is . . .' Ishani seemed to be struggling for words. Priya felt the frustration pouring off her. After a moment's hesitation, Ishani held out her hand. On her palm was a thin, ragged length of red-orange string – the bracelet that Umed had worn on his wrist for years. 'Sometimes I go through the post that's delivered to Kuwatta. It's one of my work assignments. This came in last week, along with a note. They were asking for medicine.'

She didn't go into any more detail, but Priya didn't really care. 'And did you send the medicine?'

Ishani's face clouded over. 'No.'

'Why . . .'

'That was all I wanted to pass on to you,' Ishani said, interrupting her abruptly.

'You can't be serious. Umed needs us!'

'I am doing what I can,' Ishani snapped. 'If you think you can do better, then you can send the medicine he needs yourself, can't you?'

Priya's fists clenched. She was about to go on the attack, but then Ishani's soul flickered. As usual, Ishani wasn't showing much emotion on her face. But she couldn't conceal her soul from Priya any longer. It was growing dimmer and smaller, as if she was trying to hide.

'As if she'd ever manage to do that,' snorted Rohan.

'Shut your mouth, probie.' Priya was finding it harder and harder to keep her annoyance under control.

Ishani glanced at him. 'Stay out of it.'

Rohan narrowed his dark eyes to half-moons and continued to stare at Priya, rolling back his shoulders to make himself look bigger. He clearly did not intend to stay out of it. 'Can't stand the truth, blood child? Is that it? Everyone in Kuwatta knows they only let you monsters in so you can fight on the front lines. Using monsters to defeat monsters. Know your place.'

Some of the students who were walking past turned their heads to listen.

The rage flaring up inside Priya made her cheeks glow. How *dare* he speak to her like that?

A quick glance at his posture and his self-satisfied soul told her enough. He thought he had more power than her, but he was wrong. Maybe in Disin he'd be right, but in Kuwatta their roles were different. She was worth just as much as him. Maybe even more. He might be good at studying, but in physical combat she was by far his superior. As a probie, fighting wasn't his focus. She took a threatening step towards him, intending to demonstrate that to him once and for all. His eyes widened and some of his bravado seemed to crumble. One blow would be all it took.

But that would mean breaking the rules again. And she couldn't afford to have more punishment. Certainly not after what had happened to Mawar. She had to be perfect so that she would rise through the ranks – which she desperately wanted to do. Gods, this was frustrating.

'Too chicken?' scoffed Rohan, noticing that something had changed. He stepped closer to Priya.

Ishani slapped him on the shoulder and he flinched. 'Don't you know how to listen, or something? I told you to stay out of it!'

Ishani's movement caused the object she'd been holding to fall from her hand. It bounced, landing on the step in front of her. Now Priya saw that it was a lump of shiny black material woven through with golden threads, so fine that they were barely visible. She'd seen it before – in Reza's prosthesis.

'There you are.' Jupta came rushing down, grabbed Priya's arm and pulled her up the stairs. 'You know you're going to be late? Have you seen the hole in the Keep? It's incredible. A lot of people think it was the Freelanders, but that's rubbish. I'd have felt them coming. Hey, hang on, was that your sister?'

'Just keep walking,' said Priya.

They weren't the only ones hurrying to get to their lessons in time. Lots of students, who must have been up to the highest point of the Academy to see the hole in the Keep, were noisily running downstairs past them.

Slightly out of breath, Jupta and Priya finally reached the second-highest floor. They rushed into the corridor, coming to a sudden stop when they saw their strategy master standing in the doorway.

'The bell has already rung,' he said with a slight smile that did not bode well. 'Report to the soldier on duty at the entrance to the Academy. And then I'll see if I have room for the two of you in my lesson.'

Priya could have killed Rohan and Ishani. The fact that Ishani had confirmed Umed was still alive – which she'd already figured out for herself, with Jupta's help – didn't outweigh her punishment.

At that moment, Kwasi, panting heavily and with a look of delight on his face, appeared at the top of the stairs. 'You're not in the classroom yet! Does that mean I'm on time?'

24

THE FURY OF THE strokes as she'd started scrubbing all those hours ago was long gone.

Priya was kneeling on the wooden floor, miserably leaning forward with a cloth clutched in her hand. She'd almost finished this room, but the prospect of having to clean at least four more washrooms made all the energy drain from her body.

And because she'd been late, she was going to have to do this for another week.

Priya sat there for a moment longer and then tossed the cloth aside. No matter how fast she worked, this was still going to take her most of the night. It was time for a break.

Outside, it had started to rain. Priya didn't seek shelter but let the shower cool her. The scent of damp soil and wet stone, always present in Kuwatta, grew stronger with the rain. Some cadets and probies were still out training or studying by the light of a kokolampoe, but most had already left for their barracks.

Priya was not in the mood for seeing anyone, so she made her way between the barracks and walked on. With one hand above her eyes, she gazed at the river and the hazy dark grey horizon beyond. What would it take to send a single korjaal that way with medicine for her little brother?

A great deal, as it turned out.

She walked closer to the edge of the bridge, looking down at the wavelets breaking against the black stone of Kuwatta. A large dark green snake slithered on one of the boulders sticking out of the river, its scales glistening in the moonlight.

Her gaze moved to just below her feet, where the mighty black pillars carried the fort.

And that was when she saw the face.

Priya missed her footing.

There was nothing for her to hold on to. She slammed onto the black surface and slid over the edge. With her outstretched hand, she grabbed the ledge just in time, the side of her body hitting the pillar with a bang. The pain was almost enough to make her let go. Almost.

'Gods,' she panted. Her grazed arms were bleeding. Beneath her, the Cotari raged wildly onwards. She was hanging above the water with drops splashing her and no foothold for her dangling legs. Panicking, she used her gift to reach out to the people who were walking around above her.

She found Jupta's soul first. Then Kwasi's. Was he somewhere nearby? Without stopping to think, she sent both of them a short, powerful command to tell them what had happened and to lead them to her. Priya hoped she wasn't going to mess up and draw other people into her command.

That was when she heard someone shout and looked down. Kwasi was hanging on the inside of the same pillar as her, holding on to handles that had been hammered into the bridge. He was leaning back, so that he could see her better.

'What . . . What are *you* doing here?' she blurted. She couldn't believe her eyes. So it was his face she'd just seen in the darkness.

'Enjoying the view.'

'Kwasi, I swear, when I get to you, then . . .'

'Fine, fine, I obviously wasn't enjoying the view. But can you do me a favour and come over here before you fall in the river?'

'How am I supposed to do that?'

'Look. Here.' He pointed to a notch on the side of the pillar. She had to turn her body to get there, but then she was able to climb further to the side. From there, she'd be able to reach the handles that Kwasi was holding.

'What then?' she asked. 'How do we get back up top?'

'It's a lot easier than you think,' said Kwasi. 'Just trust me.'

Surprisingly, she *did* trust him. Priya didn't usually find it easy to trust people and she wasn't friends with Kwasi the way she was with Jupta, but there was something about him that made a lot of people like him – and that included Priya. He was also one of the few people at Kuwatta who didn't seem to have an issue with anyone else – probies, regular cadets, Suryans, Dalinese, Topuans. He appeared to see everyone as an equal.

Priya swung her legs to the side but found it hard to get a foothold. Her feet kept slipping, and one of her shoes almost fell into the river.

'Give it another go,' Kwasi encouraged her, and she tried another time.

This time she managed to get a grip with her feet. She grabbed hold of the notch with her hand. She'd done it.

'Priya?'

Priya looked up.

'Priya, are you there?'

'Jupta?'

'Yes!' There was a scraping sound and then Priya saw Jupta looking down. 'How did you end up there? No, don't answer that yet.' She held out her hand. 'Grab my—' Abruptly, she fell silent, her dark eyes staring blankly into space.

'What's she doing here?' Kwasi whispered in alarm.

'Did you feel that?' Jupta asked at the same moment. She shifted and small pebbles went tumbling down into the dark depths. 'There's something out there.'

'Tell her she needs to go away or to come down here, but that she can't stay there,' said Kwasi. 'There are soldiers on the way.'

Priya felt the two soldiers he was talking about slowly heading towards them. They weren't soul-singers – they would have noticed them long ago. 'What does it matter if they see us?'

'Oh, all the saints.' Kwasi grasped her arm and pulled her towards him. She grabbed one of the handles. 'What do you think they're going to say if they see us here, right next to a secret tunnel?'

Priya gaped at him. A secret tunnel? And that's where he was trying to steer her to? How did he even know there was a tunnel here? Still, it was probably the best option. Priya didn't want to think about what the punishment would be if they were spotted hanging beside a tunnel they apparently weren't supposed to know about. As she quickly considered her options – her arms and legs were starting to hurt – she felt more pebbles falling as Jupta shifted position. Then Jupta's legs were dangling over the edge and she nimbly climbed down to the spot Priya had just left.

Now there was no turning back.

'Right. I'm here,' said Jupta, as soon as she was hanging comfortably, and she blew at the strands of hair that had fallen into her face. 'Where do we get inside?'

Priya blinked, too bewildered to say anything.

Kwasi grinned. 'Leave that to me.'

He climbed further to the side, fished a dagger out of his trousers and dug the blade into a thin opening until the stone began to move and the outline of a hatch became visible. Priya, who was hanging in front of it, quickly moved aside. Kwasi grabbed the edge of the hatch with his fingers and pulled. Priya went to his aid, and the hatch creaked open.

Priya peered inside, seeing nothing but darkness. But it wasn't as if she could go any other way. So she and Jupta followed Kwasi into the dark hole. Once they were inside, she saw that the tunnel was so narrow they couldn't stand next to one another. Water dripped through cracks in the wall, making puddles by their feet. Luckily, it wasn't as dark as it had looked from outside. A faintly flickering torch lit up Kwasi and Jupta's faces, casting shadows across their cheeks and foreheads.

'That went a lot better than the first time I tried it,' said Kwasi, wrapping the blade of his dagger in a piece of cloth. Then he tucked the knife into his clothes. 'Almost killed me,' he said, shaking his head sadly.

'Where did you get that from?' asked Priya. Part of the hilt was still sticking out of his waistband.

Kwasi waved his fingers in front of her face. 'Magic.'

'Where does this tunnel lead to?' Jupta had gone on ahead of them. 'The Keep?'

'If you go that way, yes.' Kwasi sounded proud of his illicit escapades. 'It does mean crossing the white line underground though.'

'And if you go the other way? Can we reach the mainland?' Jupta asked thoughtfully.

Kwasi shrugged. 'Maybe?'

'If this tunnel goes towards the Keep,' pondered Priya, 'could we perhaps go to the healing rooms? Would you be able to take me there?'

Kwasi nodded thoughtfully. 'Hmm. Yes, that should work. There's a whole network of tunnels under the ground. I haven't gone too deep so far. Didn't want to risk getting lost. But we can try. Why do you want to go there?'

'Medicine for my little brother. He was exposed to the blood moon,' she said without stopping to think about. It wasn't as if she had to worry about Kwasi reporting it to the administration. The boy spent his free time in forbidden tunnels.

Kwasi whistled. 'Wow. That's tough.' Then he gave her a casual shrug. 'No problem. I'll take you there.'

This was the chance Priya had been waiting so long for. She probably wasn't going to get any closer to the Keep any time soon. She still didn't know how she was supposed to send the medicine, but she could worry about that later. First she actually needed to get her hands on the remedy.

'And you've never met anyone on your expeditions?' asked Jupta, looking over her shoulder.

Kwasi shook his head. 'No, but . . .' Digging his hands deep in his pockets, he stepped forward. Closer to the torch, he opened his hands. 'Just beyond the Academy, I've occasionally come across this grey slime – and in the slime there were . . .'

'Teeth,' said Priya, finishing his sentence. Kwasi held at least a dozen milky-white teeth in his hands. 'I saw exactly the same thing just after a blood moon.'

'Lucky for us there's no blood moon today then.' Kwasi put the teeth back into his pocket and walked past Jupta to take the lead. 'I don't want to find out what kind of monster leaves behind grey slime and human teeth.' But despite his words, his eyes were gleaming.

Priya realised that this must be what he was up to whenever he showed up late for lessons: discovering secret entrances and exploring hidden tunnels. While she was doing her best to live up to the expectations of Kuwatta and the general, Kwasi was off doing his own thing. He was an average student in class, certainly not the same level as Ishani or Jupta – or even Priya – but, in his own way, he was also longing for more.

Kwasi led them along the narrow tunnels, turning left and right, and occasionally appearing to search the wall for some kind of sign. They went along wide tunnels, narrow tunnels, low tunnels and tunnels with high ceilings. They walked for ages, and Priya began to lose all sense of time.

'Wait,' whispered Jupta as Kwasi took a right at a T-junction. She grabbed him by the back of his tunic and pulled him back. 'There it is again.'

'What exactly can you feel?' Jupta's tone had made Priya shiver. There was an urgency in her voice that she hadn't heard before. This wasn't the quiet Jupta she knew. The dark shadows and narrow corridors made Jupta's eyes look even bigger. The beads around her neck seemed to glow in the light of the torches.

Jupta walked in the opposite direction, and Priya and Kwasi exchanged a look of confusion, but decided to follow her anyway.

'This isn't the way to the healing rooms.' Kwasi pointed back over his shoulder with his thumb. 'We have to go that way. You're heading towards the middle of the Keep now, and we need to go to the back.'

'It's the soul of a dead person.' Jupta didn't stop. 'There are more of them! So many more! Why wasn't I able to feel them before?' The corridor ended, and Jupta came to a stop at a closed door. In front of it, a dense line of spears was planted in the ground, their tips angled towards the door. Jupta wriggled her hand between the spears and tried to open the door, but it wouldn't budge. 'They're through there.'

Priya grabbed her shoulder. 'I'm sure if they want to come through, they don't need our help.'

'But that's the strange thing,' Jupta said quietly. 'They don't come. They never come. We've been at Kuwatta for weeks. Why is it that all the souls of dead people don't want to communicate?'

That was admittedly unusual. But Priya didn't want to jump to conclusions without all the information. Maybe there were no souls because the more experienced spirit-speakers who were already at Kuwatta had some special purpose for them. What was stranger to Priya was the spears. If Kuwatta wanted to keep enemies *out*, why were the spears pointing at the door that led deeper into the Keep?

'Listen. Someone's coming,' said Kwasi, moving closer to them. Priya felt a tingling sensation along her spine and tried to throw up a shield. She was just too late. A spider scuttled along Kwasi's arm and disappeared into his shirt.

Jupta gasped.

Priya turned and saw that they'd missed a narrow, almost in-visible entrance about halfway down the tunnel they'd just walked down. The wind outside was picking up, blowing in water mixed with sand. Then she felt a chaotic, agitated energy coming towards them, and all three of them backed away, on their guard.

A quiet, squelching sound could be heard, just above the wind.

A man came stumbling towards them. His silhouette was shrouded in shadows, his body contorted unnaturally.

Priya pushed Kwasi and Jupta behind her.

The first thing she noticed about the stumbling man was his tattered clothing. Ripped black scraps of fabric hung around the hunched body. He drew closer, becoming more visible in the weak light of a torch. There was no sign of the healthy, warm complexion that most of the inhabitants of inland Awaran had. This individual's skin had a drab, greyish undertone. His hands dangled aimlessly. There were strange scratches and marks on his legs and arms.

He raised his head.

Something dripped between his cracked lips, down his chin. He grinned and his teeth glinted with dark red liquid. Blood.

In spite of her horror, she couldn't take her eyes off him.

If you see anyone with a bleeding mouth, run away as fast as you can, Priya heard her mother say inside her head.

She took a shaky step back.

Do not listen, do not look, do not speak. By all the Gods, run away. RUN AWAY.

The monster attacked.

THE STARS
IN THE SKY
GO OUT
BEFORE OUR EYES

25

KWASI SCREAMED.

A starting signal for the world exploding into chaos. More screaming. More footsteps. More horrific panting.

Priya slammed into Jupta and tried to drag her away. But there was no way out. In front of them, the monster with the bleeding mouth was stumbling towards them, and behind them was the door with the spears. The blood drained from her face. They were trapped.

'Give me your dagger,' Priya said to Kwasi.

'What?'

'Give it to me!' she growled and he handed it over without asking any more questions. She clutched the weapon tightly.

Right at that moment, another figure came running into the tunnel. Priya's heart shot into her throat. But it wasn't a monster. A soldier in a brown uniform threw his axe at the monster's neck, clearly aiming to cut it in two. But the monster rushed towards them, so he missed, his weapon clattering against the wall. All Priya could do was stare, paralysed with fear, as the monster made straight for them. Its movements were unnatural, the sounds it produced were not human.

The soldier followed the monster's line of movement and caught sight of them. 'What are you doing here?' he yelled. Then he sprinted towards the creature, grabbing it around the neck with one arm before it could reach Priya. There was a struggle as the soldier held on to the monster while trying to keep it away from his body.

'Go!' shouted the soldier. 'Run!'

Jupta was the first to move. She pushed Priya and Kwasi forward until they started running too. Holding her breath, Priya squeezed with Kwasi and Jupta past the monster and the soldier. She tucked Kwasi's dagger into her tunic.

Before they left the corridor, they heard the soldier screaming. And screaming. And screaming. The sound was so sharp that it cut straight through Priya's body. She made the mistake of looking back, almost stumbling over her feet. Why hadn't she helped him? Why was she such a coward? For weeks now, she'd been training to fight, training to kill, but right now it was as if her body was refusing.

'Priya!' screamed Kwasi. That was when she realised she'd stopped running. 'We have to get out of here. Now!'

With trembling fingers, Priya reached for Kwasi's dagger. Her only weapon. She turned and ran back.

The scream was cut short. Priya ran into the tunnel. The soldier had fallen to one side and slumped against the monster, which scooped him up and tore his throat open. Blood sprayed from his neck and, gurgling and jerking, he fell forward. The monster tugged at his body, pulling off a strip of flesh. The soldier moved like a ragdoll in the monster's arms, no longer a person, but a corpse.

Priya gagged.

Her fingers found the hilt of the dagger, wrapped themselves around it. Trembling, she stepped forward, vaguely aware that Jupta and Kwasi had appeared behind her.

The monster's hands tore at the wound, tearing open the stomach and chest, so that the entrails came sliding out. Clumsily, the monster tried to catch the organs in its hand.

As she stared at the corpse in the monster's arms, Priya thought: *This is it. This is what Kuwatta has been hiding from us.* The screaming and shouting, the rule about not crossing the white line at night, the hole in the Keep. Everything fell into place. Kuwatta was fighting monsters in their midst.

She held the dagger in front of her. *This* was what they were being trained for. And if she wanted to get out of here alive with Jupta and Kwasi, she had to put all her lessons into practice. She swallowed the bile that rose into her mouth.

Jupta gasped. 'What is that *thing*?'

The monster stopped chewing and looked back, alerted by Jupta's voice. Its eyes were milky white in the light of the torches. Beneath its skin, its soul pulsed, a chaotic mass of flashes and threads, too weak for a living person, too strong for a corpse. Neither alive nor dead.

Dropping the corpse, the monster headed towards them. Wary at first, it sniffed loudly, nose in the air. As soon as it caught their scent, it came straight for them.

'Stay still,' said Kwasi. 'I'm trying to create an illusion.'

He stared frantically at the monster. At first it seemed to be having an effect. The monster slowed down, shaking its head. But after a brief moment of confusion, it appeared to refocus and came for them again.

'It's not working,' groaned Kwasi, sweat trickling down his temples. 'Why isn't it working?'

The creature was too close. Any second now . . .

Priya assumed a fighting stance. Inside, she was screaming with fear, but she couldn't just stand there and wait for it to reach them. She'd already spent too much of her life hiding.

Whatever happened, she didn't intend to go down quietly.

Just before the monster reached them, she shoved Kwasi and Jupta backwards. Then she ducked and felt its arms go over her head. She tried not to look into its strange, glassy eyes. Without slowing, she rolled on, landing in a crouch next to it, and kicked it in the kneecap. The bone broke under her foot, and the monster fell with a long, drawn-out scream. Adrenaline shot through Priya's body.

So, apparently her body did know what to do. Her mind might not want to fight, but her body had stored the exhausting lessons and knew which lines and angles to follow to break another body.

The monster tried to get to its feet, but she pulled it back by its tattered clothing, so that it fell in front of her. She slammed her elbow into its windpipe, and it collapsed onto the ground. It gasped, gurgled, more blood dripping from its mouth, which it opened wide.

Priya drew back the dagger and plunged it into the monster's chest in one fluid movement. Right where its heart was.

It went limp. Its soul dimmed even more. Panting, she stood over it.

'Wait!' cried Jupta. 'Go . . .'

The monster shot forward in a flash, its milky eyes bulging. Startled, Priya tried to back away, but its hands were already gripping the front of her tunic. It pulled her closer, screaming in her face, splattering her with mucus and blood.

How was that possible? She was sure she'd stabbed it in the heart. It shouldn't be able to get back up.

Its hands went to her neck. She trembled and tried to lash out, but it held on. So she tried to gain a hold on it with her gift.

'Let go,' she commanded.

It clutched her throat even more tightly.

'Let go!' she screamed.

It roared.

Again, heart pounding, she tried to grasp its soul, but it shot off in all directions. It was too volatile, fragmented and flickering to control. It wasn't working. It wasn't working. It wasn't *working*!

'Priya!' screamed Jupta.

Her windpipe was slowly closing. Her fingers clawed at its hands. She. Could. Not. Breathe.

All she could see was its strange pair of milky eyes and its grinning, bleeding mouth. Black slime dripped down its chin. Something white wriggled out from between its teeth.

Her vision blurred. She tried to grab the dagger, which was sticking out of its chest. Her hands slid off the hilt.

Slowly, the world turned black.

Then the pressure on her throat suddenly loosened.

The monster fell. Sweet air rushed into her aching throat. She staggered backwards, sank to her knees.

Jupta was standing beside her, both hands holding her weapon – a lump of stone that was wet on one side, as she'd just smashed it into the skull of the monster, which was now lying on the ground, screaming and roaring.

Jupta's face was smeared with blood. 'You good?'

'Yes. Th-Thanks,' Priya croaked in response.

'Out of the way!' Kwasi yelled behind them. Jupta dropped the block of stone, grabbed Priya by the armpits and dragged her aside. Kwasi flew past them, aiming the axe at the monster's neck. The axe got stuck halfway, and the monster started convulsing. Kwasi abandoned the weapon, and Priya quickly scrambled to her feet.

'The soldier,' panted Kwasi as they ran back down the narrow corridor. 'He's coming this way.'

'He's what?!' replied Priya. 'We just saw him die.'

Jupta looked back. 'Something's wrong. He feels like a . . .'

She didn't need to finish her sentence – all three of them could now feel the soldier's chaotic, agitated energy coming towards them. An ice-cold fear took hold of Priya, and they began to run even faster. The soldier had turned into a monster like the one that had just attacked them. Which meant that the three of them might end up the same.

'Wait!' Kwasi skidded but stayed upright and didn't slow down. 'You're going the wrong way!'

'Which way should I be going?' she yelled back.

'I . . . I don't know where we are anymore.' He threw his hands in the air. 'Try left!'

She turned left. At least the corridor they ended up in was bigger than the previous one. But there was no end in sight. It was a hopeless situation. They couldn't go on running forever – sooner or later, the monster was going to catch them. They had to kill it. It was the only way they'd be free to search for an exit.

'Keep running,' Priya yelled to the others, as she turned round.

She focused all her attention on the monster. A dagger in its heart didn't work. But a stone against its skull or an axe in its neck – that *did*. Its head must be its weak spot.

The soldier was coming closer, dripping blood from its open wound and trailing guts.

Disgust and anger formed a ball in her stomach. She concentrated all her energy in a fierce command: *Smash your skull*. The monster moaned and groaned until she felt its jagged soul beginning to break under her gift. Gritting her teeth, she kept her gift fixed on the monster. She mustn't deviate. Only the monster must break. She must not pull Kwasi and Jupta into the command.

It took all her energy, and she could have cried when the monster finally gave in. With both hands, it grasped its own head and smashed it into the ground with tremendous force. Over and over, Priya made it slam its head against the stone. Until its skull was crushed, and she could no longer tell where its ear ended or its mouth began. Until its convulsions ceased, and its soul was extinguished like a flame.

Jupta took her by the arm and pulled her away. 'That's enough. It's dead.'

Breathing heavily, Priya let go. Black spots danced before her eyes. She gagged again, and this time the contents of her stomach came up. She couldn't believe she'd just killed a soldier, someone who had trained here, just like her, and fought on the same side.

Jupta gently rubbed her back. Meanwhile Kwasi ran his fingers over the walls, searching for signs that might lead them to an exit above ground.

Priya's gaze returned to the soldier's corpse. White maggots were wriggling out of its torn stomach and slowly crawling towards them. That couldn't be good. She stepped away.

Jupta's hand stiffened on her back. 'More of them are coming.'

'How many?' asked Priya.

'About five . . . maybe more.' The fear in her voice was unmistakable.

Kwasi lowered his hand. 'I still can't see exactly where we are, but I know from experience that there are a number of hatches that can take us back above ground. Pay attention to the ceiling. If there's a hatch, you should be able to see its outline.'

'But how are we going to shake off so many monsters?' Jupta asked in a worried voice.

No one answered. They just started running again. Priya kept glancing back over her shoulder, waiting for the first glimpse of grey skin or a bleeding mouth.

Through the thick black walls, Priya heard lots of noise and muffled shouts, but the sounds were drowned out by the shrieks of the monsters that were pursuing them.

Priya looked round and saw Jupta nervously touching her beads. 'They're close.'

'Here,' Kwasi said, panting as he pointed at a new opening. They skidded to a stop. Another big tunnel – they all looked the same to Priya by now.

But she soon noticed that this one was different. In the ceiling and on the walls, she could make out gold under a thick layer of dust. The roaring of the river was clearer from here, too. However, the most important difference was the open stone door. As Kwasi ran through it, with Jupta and Priya close on his heels, the monsters came round the corner behind them. Priya glanced over her shoulder again.

Jupta's prediction was accurate – five monsters with bleeding mouths were coming after them.

The three of them shoved at the door with all their might, trying to close it. It was made of such thick stone that it moved excruciatingly slowly. Priya watched as the monsters quickly came closer. 'We're not going to make it.'

'Keep pushing!' yelled Kwasi.

'If I . . .'

'Oh, all the saints, Pri! Push!'

She pushed. Harder than she'd ever pushed in her life, and with every second that passed her heart sank further. The door clearly wasn't made to be opened and closed quickly.

The door was still a quarter open when the first monster crashed into it. But the three of them didn't give up. They kept pushing, even when the monster squeezed its body halfway into the crack and got stuck there.

Jupta cursed. 'Behind us,' she croaked. Her hands were still on the door, but she seemed to have frozen.

Those two words nullified their entire plan. Priya looked over her shoulder. Two monsters were standing behind them in the corridor. One of them was bent over a corpse, trying to tear a leg off with both hands. The other was staring straight at them. Then it put its nose in the air and screeched, drawing the other monster's attention.

Priya felt the other group of monsters pressing against the door. Nails scratched at the stone. She stood with her back to it.

The two monsters in their corridor shrieked and came running towards them. Bumping into each other, they fell over, stood up again and continued in a tangle of hands and feet. One had had lumps torn from its torso and arms; the other was missing some of the flesh from its jaw, exposing its skull.

'This is it, then. We're lost. We're going to be torn to pieces. We're going to die,' rattled Kwasi. 'It's like I said to my father, "Your son's a pacifist. Are you sure Kuwatta is the right place?" But he wouldn't listen! And now I'm stuck here in this monstrosity of a . . .'

'Kwasi,' said Priya.

'Yes?'

'Shut up. I can't concentrate.'

Jupta was stubbornly pushing against the door. 'On what?'

'On stopping them,' said Priya with more confidence than she felt. 'Keep pushing.'

Ignoring her pounding headache, she gathered up all the energy within her. She wouldn't be able to carry out an attack like the one before. Not only was her control too poor for that, according to Master Yapoma, but she didn't know if she had sufficient energy. These monsters had complicated souls and her headache told her that she was already testing her limits. Sheer terror was all that was keeping her going. Priya gulped.

It was sink or swim.

The monsters had almost reached them. They were clawing towards them. Jupta pressed herself flat against the door.

Stand still, Priya commanded all the monsters in front of and behind them. *Stand still*, she screamed again in her mind. Her head grew hotter and hotter as she repeated her command over and over again.

The monsters faltered. Priya could feel their souls jerking and struggling under her command. But she knew it wasn't enough. She couldn't get a grip on them. There were too many of them and their souls were too chaotic and too painful to control. All she'd done was slow them down.

'Stand still!' she screamed out loud as a monster's hand grazed her shoulder. Its touch triggered a new wave of adrenaline. And for the first time in her life, she completely let go. The last remnant of control, which she'd clung on to all her life – she let it go. There was an explosion inside her body, and her gift came tumbling out like an avalanche. The air seemed to crackle.

Her gift hit like a bomb.

The world around her froze. The monsters, the air – and Jupta and Kwasi too. No one moved. A second later, Priya dropped to her knees in their midst, felled by a headache that seemed to be tearing her apart. As she clutched her head with both hands, she felt the monsters pulling themselves away from her.

Priya fought desperately to keep control. A new wave of pain loosened her grip even more, and she groaned. The closest monster shot free from her control and began screaming. She squeezed her eyes shut, so she wouldn't have to see its hideous face as it tore her apart.

But suddenly the screaming stopped.

A thud onto the ground. Another.

Warily, Priya opened her eyes. For a moment, she could see the world in duplicate, and she couldn't decipher exactly what was happening in front of her. Sounds echoed in her ears. The pain in her head made her feel sick.

After what seemed like an eternity but was probably just a few seconds, the world came back together again.

The tip of a sword was sticking out of the mouth of the last of the monsters, which stood right in front of her. The others lay on the ground, their necks cut through. Priya blinked. With a slurping sound, the sword was pulled back. The monster collapsed, revealing the person behind it – its killer.

The man was dressed entirely in black, except for some glittering gold. He had a high rank, judging by the amount of gold. His nose and mouth were concealed behind a black mask, and a black hood was pulled down over his head.

His only identifying feature was the right hand, inlaid with gold, which was holding a long sword.

'Reza,' croaked Priya. How was it possible that he'd taken out all those monsters so quickly?

'What are you doing here?' said Reza, his voice muffled by the mask.

Behind him, a monster appeared out of nowhere, and Priya grabbed Reza in shock. His muscles tensed under her hands. Just as she pulled him towards her, a black shadow emerged from behind the monster. Yellow-green eyes, claws, and a pattern in the glowing lines of her black fur. Reza's water panther. The monster fell beneath the panther's paws as she struck hard and fast. Huge jaws closed around the creature's neck. The water panther ripped off the monster's head and tossed it aside.

'You can let go of me now,' said Reza, looking down at Priya.

Priya quickly let go.

26

REZA ESCORTED THEM THROUGH the tunnels.

His water panther padded silently as a shadow behind them. As they headed outside, Reza slew more of the monsters with such ease that it was clear he did this often. Priya, Kwasi and Jupta walked with him, in a daze.

Reza didn't need to study any walls for hidden signs that would lead them to the surface. Judging by his confident stride, he knew exactly how the network of secret tunnels fitted together and where he needed to be. It wasn't long before she saw the cloudy night sky ahead of them in the distance.

'How did you do that?'

It took Priya a moment to realise Reza was talking to her. It was even longer before she was able to answer. Her mouth was dry, her head was pounding, and the world seemed to be a surreal nightmare that she couldn't wake up from. The large hall of the Keep, which had once seemed so immaculate and elegant, was now a battlefield. Priya's stomach turned at the pungent metallic smell of blood, and she tried not to look at the broken bodies they walked past. Several soldiers ran past them into the Keep.

'What?'

Reza wasn't looking at her; his light brown eyes were scanning the surroundings as he loosely held a short sword with a golden hilt in his right hand. With one finger of his prosthesis, he pulled down his mask from over his mouth. 'You just immobilised at least twenty rabidos. Are you wearing gold?'

Was he accusing her of being a thief again? 'No.'

'What are rabidos?' asked Kwasi, grey-faced. He went on staring at the corpses around them, even though it just made his face turn even more grey.

'The monsters we saw, right?' Jupta didn't look much better. Fingers trembling, she touched her beads. 'Where did they come from? And why don't we see them during the day?'

Outside, the sound of the river was drowned out by orders and shouting.

'Rabidos, the monsters with the bleeding mouths, are the children of the Dedekedre, the monster that's had Kuwatta in its clutches for over a century,' said Reza. Priya struggled to catch what he was saying. 'They don't tolerate heat very well. They only occasionally attack in the daytime during the monsoon season.'

A monster that had held Kuwatta in its grip for a century. No wonder the rumours said that those who made it to Kuwatta never returned.

The Keep, with all its black towers, gold ornamentation and complex layout, suddenly seemed a lot less majestic. It was not a palace. It wasn't even a fort, thought Priya. Under the blue of the night sky, she saw the building, for the first time, for what it really was: a prison.

Suddenly she realised why Kuwatta was constructed entirely of thick black stone to trap the heat, and buildings that were more like walls. The fort wasn't designed to make them suffer, as Kwasi had once complained. It was made to contain the rabidos – and the Dedekedre.

'Kapten Reza, I'm here to take cadet Priya to the major.'

It took Priya a couple of moments to recognise Novan in his green uniform with a spear in his hand and a mask dangling around his neck. The second-year student who'd given them a tour of the fort on their first day looked a lot less cheerful now. Gravely, he pressed his two fists together as he looked at Reza.

'The general will decide what happens to them, soldier,' Reza responded sharply. He looked at Novan as if he were an insect he wanted to crush. 'Not my sister.'

The general? Priya felt warm and cold at the same time. So apparently not only the major was already aware of their disobedience, but also the general?

'I can explain,' began Priya, even though she had no idea how she was going to get out of this.

'There's not much to explain.' Reza turned, slightly frowning, with his hand on his prosthesis. She tried to catch his eye, but he seemed determined to avoid her gaze. 'Every soul-singer in and around the Keep felt you.'

What had they all felt? Her gift?

'I have orders from the major,' Novan insisted. 'If the general has different orders, I'm to report that to her.'

'Why just me?' Priya asked Novan. She'd broken the rules along with Jupta and Kwasi, and she'd expected to be punished. What she hadn't expected was that she would be separated from them and treated differently.

'She didn't say.'

Reza's jaw was tense; he was clearly not pleased. 'Of course she didn't,' he muttered. His eyes flashed to Priya, who saw a conflict in his eyes that was hard to interpret. Novan had addressed him as 'kapten', so his rank was lower than his sister's, who was a major. Without a direct order from the general, he couldn't defy his sister. 'Take her, soldier,' he said finally. Then he looked at Jupta and Kwasi with a quick nod. 'You two, come with me.'

Novan nodded and pressed his fists together again. Reza didn't respond to the gesture. He took Jupta and Kwasi with him, both of them looking anxiously over their shoulders at Priya. Priya tried to give them a confident nod.

Making their way between the bodies of other soldiers, the three of them soon disappeared. Priya walked with Novan in the opposite direction. It was becoming clear to her that Kuwatta was a machine; during the daytime, students were trained to fight against the colonists, while at night a war was waged against the rabidos. Groups of ten to twenty soldiers, most of them in green uniforms, were disappearing into the Keep, led by two soldiers in black. Like Reza, they wore black masks over their noses and mouths. A range of swords, spears and axes hung on their backs.

'The major isn't unreasonable,' said Novan. 'There's no need to be concerned.'

That just made her worry even more.

'The sun,' a soldier near Priya suddenly whispered. Novan slowed and looked at the horizon. Priya followed their gaze and saw that the sky had taken on a red hue. The monsters' screams and roars subsided, as did the shouts of the soldiers and the clashing of weapons.

'The sun,' repeated Novan.

It sounded like salvation.

27

'TAKE A SEAT, CADET.'

Novan had taken her through a side entrance back into the Keep and upstairs, floor after floor, until Priya lost count. They'd come to a stop in front of a stone door with words in Old Topuan engraved on it. Novan had knocked and, as the door opened, Priya was blinded by the sun reflecting off the many gold decorations in the room.

The major was sitting at a large desk, writing intently on a sheet of parchment. In front of her desk was a wide stool with a jaguar skin over the seat. With lead in her shoes, Priya walked forward and pressed her fists together. 'You wanted to speak to me, Major?' She bowed her head and felt her aching neck protest.

The major put down the quill she'd been writing with and leaned back in her chair. 'Sit,' she invited her again. Priya did as she was told, then waited a few seconds before glancing up.

Major-General Aïda had gathered her thin black plaits into a bun, and she was wearing a black uniform. Her shoulders and chest were free of gold, but the gold on her ears and in her hair more than made up for it. Gold thread was woven into the two plaits on either side of her face.

Behind her stood two soldiers with spears in their hands.

Major Aïda's eyes appraised Priya's dishevelled appearance. 'You have shirked the punishment that was imposed on you, entered

Kuwatta's secret tunnels without permission and crossed the white line.'

Priya waited for the words that were hanging heavy in the air.

'That is forbidden, cadet. And for good reason.'

'I am sorry, Major,' Priya said, looking down at the floor. Was she really sorry? Absolutely not. At least now she knew the terrible secret that Kuwatta was hiding. But she knew those were the words she had to say.

'You spent half the night in dark, narrow corridors, trying to get closer to the Keep,' the major continued in an icy tone. 'Tell me. Why did you go to so much trouble?'

'It was an accident,' Priya began. 'I fell over the edge of the bridge and discovered one of the tunnels by chance.'

The major raised an eyebrow. 'Where exactly did you fall over the edge? In the vicinity of the Keep? That's where the three of you were found.'

'I, um, no . . . I have a little brother in Disin,' Priya said to the surface of the desk. 'He was exposed to the blood moon a few weeks ago. No matter what I do, no one will let me anywhere near the healing rooms, so when I was in the tunnels, I thought . . .'

'And what about your friends?'

'I called them to me when I was hanging from the edge of the bridge.'

'And rather than pulling you up, they followed you into the tunnels?'

Priya opened her mouth, closed it again. She couldn't come up with an answer. So, she just mumbled 'I'm sorry' again. She knew she'd broken enough rules to be hung over the waterfall by her feet.

The major didn't react at first. Priya cautiously looked up. The major clasped her hands together and even though her dark eyes were on Priya, her expression made it clear that her thoughts were elsewhere. Priya tried to read the major's emotions in her soul, but she felt nothing. She used her gift to probe further but encountered a shield. She immediately retreated.

'I might not be a soul-singer,' the major said slowly, 'but I do know how to protect myself. Stay away from my soul.'

Priya bowed her head again, mentally kicking herself. 'My apologies, Major. I absolutely wasn't trying to use my gift to manipulate you, just to read how you were feeling.'

'Really?' To her surprise, Major Aïda laughed. The sound was clear and cutting.

Priya shifted restlessly. 'Why am I here?' she blurted out.

The sly smile on the major's face still hadn't entirely disappeared, and it was making Priya uneasy. 'For a number of reasons. Count yourself lucky that I waylaid you before you had to explain yourself to my father. He's a lot less forgiving.'

'Am I going to be punished?'

'Do you deny the accusations?'

Priya noticed that the major didn't specify which accusations, so she didn't answer her question.

The major seemed amused by Priya's silent rebellion. She pushed aside the inkwells on her desk and gathered the documents she'd been working on into a neat pile. 'I'm not going to punish you, cadet. That's not why I sent for you.'

Her words didn't make Priya feel any better.

'It won't surprise you that there's a strict hierarchy in place at Kuwatta. My father has his own policies, with which I must also comply, so all I can tell you is this: in my opinion, Kuwatta does not value soldiers like you highly enough.'

'Soldiers like me? What kind of soldier am I?' If she meant soul-singers, then it was strange that only Priya was sitting in front of her.

The major leaned forward. Her eyes were so dark that they seemed almost black. 'Hm,' she said. 'You soul-singers always have the same look. Pain, anger, fear. Raw emotions that swim in your eyes and make you go further than the average soldier would.' She leaned back again. 'But it's been a long time since we brought a soul-singer with as much power as you into Kuwatta.'

'How do you know my gift is powerful, Major?' Priya asked in confusion.

'I command the general army in my father's name. That includes the soul-singers who report to me. Do you not notice yourself how powerful your gift is?'

'I only . . . I don't know exactly what I did,' she stammered. All she knew was that the world around her had frozen for a moment, leaving her with a severe headache.

'Chaotic. Inexperienced. Uncontrolled,' Major Aïda summed up. 'But with so much raw power that it doesn't matter. My spirit-speakers felt your attack all the way up here.' She tapped her desk.

Priya didn't know whether to be happy with the compliment or not. Master Yapoma would probably shake his head if he heard what the major had said. According to him, control was an important factor for success. Without control, you could hit friend or enemy. The major, on the other hand, was all but purring with contentment.

'Why do you think Reza found you so quickly?' asked Major Aïda. 'He felt it too. Were you using gold?'

Priya shook her head, unable to say anything.

'Amazing. Truly amazing,' said the major, full of admiration. 'I've told my father many times: people like you are the future if we want to win the war.'

'Which war?' asked Priya, stunned by the major's praise. She felt like she couldn't breathe. The major was looking at her as if she were a plaything that she simply must own. 'The one against the colonists or the one against the monsters in Kuwatta?'

'Both.'

Priya gulped. She had agreed to be trained as a soldier. It shouldn't matter what war she was fighting. There was a reason why Master Ramsaroup had given them such ridiculous exercises in their lessons. When it came down to it, she was being trained to follow orders. So why did it feel as if the world she knew had gone up in smoke?

During every training session, she'd imagined that one day she would use everything she learned against the colonists. The people who had caused the greatest misery in her life. That was what she was prepared for.

'Is that why you changed the test?' asked Priya. 'So that you can find blood children faster and use them in these wars?'

'Yes,' said the major with a sigh. 'It's an exhausting task tracking down blood children in a country where most people reject them as soon as they're born.'

That's one way to describe the murder of blood children, Priya thought bitterly.

'Fortunately, my father also understood the need. A small change to the test was all it took to make it easier for us. Given the number of participants, it meant that the blood children came to us instead of the other way round. Of course, I made sure that there was a spirit-speaker on Scholar Afounsowa's team. Spirit-speakers can discover blood children most successfully.' The major's casual tone made it sound as if she were describing something as prosaic as supply and storage at Kuwatta.

'Why go to the trouble of keeping the rabidos hidden from us if that's what we're here for?'

'Practical reasons. Take a look at yourself, cadet.' Major Aïda gestured dismissively at Priya. 'You look like you could pass out at any moment. We don't have time to comfort crying children. Whatever they might say in the warrior villages, soldiers aren't born, they're made. And that process takes time.'

'Ah,' was Priya's weak reaction.

'The idea was to let you focus on your training and lessons for the first few months. Of course there are always a few cadets who break the rules and find out sooner,' she added, eyebrows raised.

Priya bowed her head and muttered her apologies again.

'You don't have to express your regrets to me. You and your friends are the only ones who will suffer,' the major said, picking at a fingernail.

'Tomorrow you will be informed that from now on you will be fully involved at Kuwatta.'

'What does that mean?'

'That you can be summoned in the night. Consider it a promotion,' the major said, all smiles.

Priya clasped her knees with both hands to stop them shaking. She didn't know how she would manage to face those hideous monsters again. The image of the corpses in the corridors and main hall wouldn't let go of her. So many soldiers had fallen, and probably more of them had been turned into rabidos. Priya wasn't so much paralysed by the fear of death; it was the thought of becoming a rabido that made her stomach churn. The only positive in all of this was that it might make it easier for her to reach the healing rooms and to get her hands on a remedy for Umed.

The major tapped her fingers on her desk, and Priya looked up again. 'I'm not done yet,' she said. 'I need soldiers. Powerful soldiers I can trust. Soldiers who can be my eyes and ears and directly follow my orders.'

Aha, so *that* was why she was here.

Priya looked at the soldiers behind the major, both following their conversation with expressionless faces. 'You want my loyalty.'

'*Complete* loyalty,' the major corrected her. 'Starting with the fact that not a single word spoken here ever leaves this room.'

'And what do I get in return?' Priya asked slowly.

The sharp smile was back. 'I can make sure your brother receives his medication. In addition, you will not be punished without my permission. You will be under my protection.'

Medicine for Umed? Priya was expecting a lot, but not that. She tried to keep her emotions under control, even though she knew it was a lost cause. Everything inside her was screaming at her to accept the offer. The major was the only one with a rank high enough to defy an order from the general. Still, it couldn't be that simple.

'The general has forbidden it, Major.'

'Luckily, that's not a problem for me.'

That was an ambiguous answer. It might mean that the major could change the general's mind – or that she would go against his orders. As the major was putting together a team of her own, Priya guessed it was the latter. Which meant the major was committing treason for some reason and that Priya had now inadvertently ended up in some conflict between the major and the general. Although she had to admit that, in a way, she only had herself to blame.

'How do I know you'll keep your word?' she asked warily.

'I'll make sure you receive a message from your brother to let you know that the medication has been received,' said the major. 'One message. And that's all.'

Priya nodded. That was more than she could expect from the general. 'Fine,' she said, before she could change her mind. She was already in too deep and had broken too many rules to be left empty-handed now.

'Good,' said the major with the sweetest of smiles, 'because accidents can, of course, always happen.'

Priya's mouth twitched. Those words confirmed what Priya had felt in the air: that she didn't really have a choice. Not if she wanted to stay alive.

28

NOT HAVING SLEPT FOR almost a day, more asleep than awake, Priya trudged after the soldier who led her back to her room. She dozed off before her cheek hit the mat. Her dreams, which she later remembered only vaguely, were peaceful and pitch black at first but then shifted to monsters with bleeding mouths, narrow, dark tunnels where she became trapped, and broken bodies. Until they, too, faded away and Priya dreamed about her father for the first time in ages.

She smelled the delicious scent of coconut and sugarcane that always lingered on him and heard his warm, deep voice. Only she could no longer remember his face. She hadn't been able to for years now. In her dreams, he always remained a faceless figure. Yet in her younger years she had cherished those moments, as dreams can influence reality. For a moment, just a moment, she had felt like he was with her again. She often used to beg him to come back. Even though she didn't remember him very well, he was still nicer to her than her mother. At least in her dreams.

The days of begging in her dreams were long gone for Priya. Her father wasn't there, and he wasn't coming back. He had died a hero, but he wasn't *her* hero. He couldn't be. He hadn't been able to rescue her from a terrible life in Disin. She'd had to do that herself.

'Priya,' her father said in her dream.

'Pa?'

He smiled. She didn't know why she felt it so clearly, as he had no face. And yet the smile was there, and she felt the urge to fall into his arms. No, she thought. No, she was a soldier now. She mustn't appear weak.

'Priya!' her father suddenly cried.

Priya shot upright. Still half asleep, she groped around, finding nothing but air and fell to one side, landing with a thud. Groaning, she touched her neck and shoulder. It wouldn't surprise her if they were already covered in bruises. And a couple more would be joining them now.

Daylight shone in through a small window. The sky was blue, although the edges were turning pale yellow here and there. Soon it would be evening again, and the monsters would be back.

'Sorry!' called Jupta. 'You were shouting, so I tried to wake you up.'

Priya blinked. She was lying on the floor of a simple room and had rolled off her mat. 'Where are we?' she asked dozily. This wasn't the barracks where they normally slept.

Jupta helped her to her feet. 'Still in the Lodge. I wonder if they're ever going to let us return to the barracks.'

Ah, the Lodge. She vaguely remembered being taken there after the conversation with the major. It was the other building beside the Keep, the twin of the Academy, which she'd mistaken for a big black wall when she'd seen it from the korjaal. Looking back, it wasn't that far from the truth. The Academy and the Lodge didn't only shield the Keep, they were also an extra barricade against the rabidos if they ever escaped. The designers of the fort had clearly given a lot of thought to it. As they had to the strategic position of the fort itself, right above the edge of a waterfall.

'Kwasi was just here. He should be back any . . .'

'Jup, have you seen Mawar yet?' Kwasi came bursting into the room, immediately closing the door behind him. 'Seems she found out about the monsters too, and that's why . . . Oh, Pri, you're awake. How are you doing? What did the major say to you?'

Kwasi's face still had a grey tint, but his usual enthusiasm had returned. He sat down by them, cross-legged, and scooted a little closer. 'I've sent a letter.'

'Well, I suppose it was . . . Sorry, you did what?' Priya looked at him blankly.

'Sent a letter. Addressed to the general,' said Kwasi in serious tones. 'Told him I can't fight on the front lines and that I'd appreciate it if they could find another role for me. Maybe as a scout for . . .'

'I've heard they use spirit-speakers for that,' Jupta interrupted him. 'Our senses extend much further than those of other soul-singers.'

'But can you read tracks? Map out a route by using the stars?' Kwasi asked angrily. 'Or discover secret passages in a heavily armed fortress, all on your own?'

Jupta just rolled her eyes.

Priya bit her bottom lip to stop herself from smiling. She hadn't expected to feel any kind of happiness so soon after such a traumatic night. Yet she felt a wave of affection pass through her, sitting between two people who – as she could now admit to herself – she genuinely cared about.

'Maybe not,' said Jupta with a sigh. She patted his arm indulgently. 'But even if we could, it wouldn't make any difference in here.'

Kwasi lost some of his fire. 'Mawar told me we're supposed to go and fight those monsters too.' He continued in a hushed voice. 'What do you think? How about we go back into those tunnels and see if any of them head towards land?' They both stared at him. 'I guess the answer is no,' he muttered.

'I'm wondering how those monsters – the rabidos – came into existence.' Jupta pulled her knees up to her chest and rested her chin on them.

'According to Reza, they're the children of the Dedekedre,' Kwasi said with a shrug.

'That just makes me even more confused,' said Jupta. 'The Dedekedre? I have no idea what that's supposed to be.'

'So the Topuans don't know about the Dedekedre and rabidos either?' asked Priya. She'd been hoping Jupta would give them an explanation. If Priya could understand the monsters' place in the world, what their purpose was, then maybe they'd be less terrifying.

Jupta shook her head. 'No, I've never heard of them. Not in the stories that are told; and I've never read about them anywhere either. I've certainly never felt anything like the rabidos' souls before. They're almost human and yet they're completely different. I don't understand how something like that could come into existence. Even as a spirit-speaker, I couldn't fathom their emotions.'

Kwasi nodded at Priya. 'Pri, you were able to manipulate them with your gift. Not even I could resist you.'

'Me neither,' added Jupta.

Priya shifted uncomfortably as they looked at her. 'I didn't mean to,' she said. 'It just happened. I was so . . . *terrified*. It was all too much for me. Something inside me came loose.' She could hear herself how muddled she sounded.

Kwasi fell backwards, stretching his arms above his head. 'Well, whatever it was, it saved our lives.' He put his thumb up. 'I'm happy.'

There was a quiet knock on the door of their room. The doorhandle lowered and the door opened a crack. Mawar peeked in. Her black shoulder-length hair had been clipped just above her ears and she was wearing a dark green uniform. 'The general wants to see the three of you after dinner.'

+++

The general stared at them from his lofty position in the Great Hall.

Far beneath their feet, the battle against the rabidos had already begun. However, there was no sign of it up above.

The general was sitting on his imposing black throne, which was crowned with black and gold spearheads. Next to him, on a slightly lower seat, was the major. The place on the other side was empty, as it had been the first time Priya was here. Behind him stood a Topuan woman and a Luanan man in traditional dress – two of the four advisors who represented their own peoples.

Scholar Afounsowa was also present, standing diagonally behind the general's seat. Priya had heard that she was not simply a master, but also a head scholar: she led a specific research project and a team of scholars and probies. As a head scholar, she was allowed to address and advise the general directly, like a kapten, who led a team of soldiers.

'What do we have here?' the general said wearily.

Priya, Jupta and Kwasi stood before him, heads bowed.

Scholar Afounsowa walked out from behind his throne. Priya looked up at her. A few days ago, Priya had been sitting at a desk in her lesson. Now the scholar stood there as a loyal advisor to the general, dressed in a beige-coloured uniform, with an angisa in the same colour wrapped around her black hair. 'Three cadets who entered the Keep through the underground tunnels last night.'

'Hm.' The general rubbed his chin. His gaze lingered on Priya. 'How long have they been at Kuwatta?'

'About one and a half lunar cycles.'

'Schedule them for part-time lessons and back-up. They can join the third-rank soldiers in their room.'

'They're soul-singers, General,' said Scholar Afounsowa.

The general let out a deep sigh, steepling his fingers. The first time Priya had seen him, she'd noticed the greyness of his skin and the dark circles under his eyes. This time he looked even more frail. 'Names?'

'Cadet Kwasi, cadet Jupta and cadet Priya, General. I reported about them yesterday.'

'Ah.' The general nodded. He turned his attention on them, and the look in his eyes was clear this time. 'That's right. I remember now.' He waved Scholar Afounsowa aside, and she stepped out of the way. His eyes swept through the room. 'Where is my son?'

'Kapten Reza is fighting tonight, General,' said a soldier near the platform. He was wearing a black uniform and a gold bracelet.

Probably a kapten. 'There was a complication with a door in one of the tunnels.'

Priya felt a shift in the major's soul when Reza's name was mentioned. It was minimal, almost imperceptible, but she was paying close attention. Her energy expanded and then contracted again, as if she were trying to keep herself in check.

'We can handle the matter without him, General,' the major said with a sharp smile. She placed her hands on her crossed legs. 'If I might make a suggestion: put them in a team where they can gain experience until we know how to beat the Dedekedre.'

The Dedekedre. Reza had said that the rabidos were her children and that she had had Kuwatta in her clutches. So they were planning to defeat the monster that led the rabidos? Priya hadn't known that. She'd assumed they were only holding the Dedekedre and rabidos captive.

'Fine,' the general agreed. 'Schedule the soul-singers on Reza's team.'

The smile on the major's face froze.

'He's had long enough to find members for his team,' the general continued. 'The part-time lessons still stand. Report cadet Priya's progress to me personally.'

Priya felt the weight of the general's gaze on her. He must have mentioned her specifically for a reason. She tried to find a clue in his soul, even if was just a shift in his energy. Something that might tell her more about his intentions. She encountered nothing. The general had firmly closed off his soul, and she didn't dare to push too hard. She didn't want him to realise what she was doing.

Priya could only guess what his motives might be. The general must know about her power. It couldn't be a coincidence that he'd placed her with Reza, who could keep an eye on her. But he was at the head of the army. He didn't have to stage this show of power.

Unless he felt threatened. Priya looked at the major. She was still sitting in exactly the same position.

Behind him, Scholar Afounsowa pressed her fists together. 'As you wish, General.'

+++

Reza's sleeping quarters were on one of the top floors of the Lodge. Priya had expected nothing less. Now she knew that under the ground, rabidos roamed the tunnels of the Keep at night, she understood why all the high-ranking soldiers and teaching staff lived on the higher floors.

Clutching his note, in which he had requested her presence, she knocked on his door, which was less finely decorated than the door to his sister's rooms.

As Reza opened the door, Priya took a step back. She'd been expecting a reaction, a brief 'Enter' or maybe a 'Yes?', but not this. He just stood there in the doorway, looking as if he'd just got out of the bath. His black curls were damp. His feet were bare, and he was dressed only in the bottom layer of his black uniform; his shirt hung open, revealing part of his chest.

It was unfair that he was so handsome.

'Come in.' As he pushed the door open further, she saw the three rings gleaming on his right hand. He turned and walked back into his room. Priya followed a second later, the note crumpled in her hand.

Reza dropped down onto a soft chair and motioned for her to take a seat opposite him. 'So, I hear you've been assigned to my team.'

'That's right.' She remained standing. His rooms were furnished simply and practically. Priya didn't see many decorations, animal skins or engravings. The only signs of gold were on his uniform, his hand and in his ears. Her gaze lingered on his arms.

'It was a rabido, if you want to know.' He raised his arm. She saw the white scars on the stump. 'Bit my little finger. I was ten years old, and the whole of Kuwatta must have heard my screams. Unfortunately, the pain only got worse. So . . .' He made a gesture as if he

· 232 ·

were chopping his hand off. 'It's the only way to make sure you don't change.'

'Why did you want to see me?' asked Priya, although the question she really wanted to ask was: 'How on earth did it happen?' Reza had grown up here. Both the general and Reza himself knew all about the dangers posed by the monsters. It seemed unlikely that the rabidos would have climbed this high up into the towers, which meant Reza, at the age of ten, had been down below at night.

Reza took an orange fruit, an awara, from the small table in front of him. He didn't eat it, just rolled it in his fingers. 'What has my sister promised you?'

Priya sniffed. 'Why don't you ask her yourself?'

'As of today, you're part of my team, cadet,' said Reza in an icy tone. 'That means that I'm your kapten.'

Unfortunately. 'And the major is your superior.'

He stood up, came closer, stopped right in front of her. He smelled of fresh grass and of the rainforest just after a downpour. 'Do you know how my father keeps the fort running? By ensuring that everyone, no matter where they come from, blood child or not, works together. He's the heart of this fortress. You've sworn loyalty to him, not to the major.'

Priya began to grasp the full extent of her deal with the major. The serious consequences if the general decided to punish her for disobeying him. Did this count as desertion? She didn't know. But she had a strong suspicion that the general had instructed Reza to watch her closely.

It was too late to back out. For herself, and also for Umed. Reza and the general had both made it clear to Priya that no post would be sent to any relatives she'd had to leave behind. The major was her only chance of having medicine sent to Umed.

'If you have a problem with the major, you'd be better off asking her questions than me,' said Priya, taking a step towards him. 'Kapten,' she added casually.

Reza leaned forward until there was only a hand's breadth between them. His eyes were the colour of dark honey. For a moment, his gaze wandered down, lingering on the bruise on her neck before he looked up again.

'You're playing a dangerous game, Chkadhari. You understand that, don't you?' he asked quietly.

She did indeed.

'What I'm doing is not your problem, Kapten,' she said, still looking at him. Priya felt warm under the intensity of his gaze.

'It's unbelievable that they expect so much from your energy, your strength, and yet . . .' He slowly shook his head, a smile breaking through the clouds on his face. She went on looking at it, even though it wasn't exactly a warm smile. She was surprised because she still had never seen him smile properly before. It annoyed her that he had such a hold on her. That she even noticed the droplets of water glistening on his black lashes.

He stared back with a strange kind of curiosity and, she noted a moment later, a hint of anger in his eyes. 'I have no idea what exactly it is that you're fighting for.'

She was fighting to survive. That was all she'd done her entire life. She stood there for three heartbeats before taking a step back and pressing her fists together. 'If that was all, I'll return to my room, Kapten.'

As she walked back, she wondered if he'd used his gift on her.

29

ONE DAY OF REST was all that Kuwatta gave them after they had almost been eaten by the rabidos.

Priya shoved a big piece of roti into her mouth as she headed down to the ground floor with Kwasi and Jupta. Their lunch break at the Lodge was hurried and more about gulping down enough fuel to get them through the day than to provide any enjoyment.

At night, the two lower floors of the Lodge were used to group the army into teams that would then disappear into the Keep, led by a kapten and his right hand, a basha. During the daytime, it was for training sessions and lessons.

'This way,' said Kwasi, pushing Priya into a different corridor. His sense of direction came in handy in the new building.

Their lessons were in a new timetable that was displayed in the large hall on the ground floor. Kuwatta was a machine, and that became even more apparent in the Lodge. Many of the soldiers were active at night, and it was quieter during the daytime. Even so, the soldiers who hadn't had a night shift were training. And there were always scholars studying. The focus in this building was on combat training and soul studies. Those were the only lessons taught in the Lodge. The Academy was reserved for the cadets and probies who knew nothing about the rabidos and the Dedekedre.

Outside, a crowd had gathered around a ring of white sand. Inside the ring, two soldiers in green uniforms faced each other.

'We've got combat training here soon,' Jupta said with a shrug.

Priya walked up to the ring. 'Then we might as well go and watch.'

Among the jostling, shouting crowd, she found Mawar, the soul-singer who had left even before Jupta, Kwasi and Priya. At least that was what Priya had thought at the time. Was that what the rest of their group thought about them now? Was it what Ishani thought? But even if they did think that, it was only a matter of time until they learned about the existence of the rabidos too.

The soldiers in the ring, a man and a woman, neither of them much older than Priya, had not moved from the spot and were looking each other straight in the eyes. Priya could feel their souls simmering. Thick shields kept the bystanders from exerting any influence on them, but their energy was so fierce, so explosive, that it was almost palpable. Although they were holding up their shields, Priya had no doubt they were using their gifts on each other.

The female soldier, who looked Luanan, inhaled sharply, blinked and jerked back her head, most likely reacting to illusions Priya couldn't see.

The male soldier, clearly Topuan, raised one corner of his mouth and mockingly bowed his head. With a growl, the female soldier ran forward. The male had already raised his sword. They whirled around each other.

Priya could barely follow their movements. Their swords flashed before her eyes. At first, she just heard the metallic sound of the swords clashing and the grinding noise as they slid past each other. Sometimes sparks even flew from the swords. But at a certain point in their fight, something changed.

It began with patches of darkness. Priya thought it was her eyes – until the darkness began to move and to turn into objects. A second sword barely missing the female soldier, a dagger whizzing out of nowhere towards the male and passing right through his body. They were sight-speakers. They were manipulating not only each other, but also the spectators. Their gifts were so powerful that they were forcing everyone around the ring to see whatever they wanted them to.

When she realised that, Priya tried to shield her soul from them. The illusions flickered before her eyes.

'Let it happen,' said an older soldier beside her, who had noticed the tension on her face. 'It makes it more interesting when you can see how they're manipulating each other.'

Priya followed his advice. The soldiers' movements slowed down, dissolving into a blur.

The male soldier ran up against the black wall and did a back-flip. His intention was to bring the other soldier down, but then his opponent disappeared. And so did he, the moment he landed.

Priya looked around in confusion – and there they were again. Their swords clashed in silent combat. All around them, multiple versions of the two soldiers fought one another. This was not a fight in which physical strength would prevail. The winner would be the one who could defeat the other's soul.

One version of the female soldier landed on the ground with a thud, slamming her fist into the centre of the ring. The illusions around her were blown away. Priya took a step back as the female soldier's energy crashed into her and passed straight through her body.

Kwasi stood gaping beside Priya. 'I didn't know sight-speakers could do such things. Do you think I could do that too?'

'Thought you were a pacifist.'

'Um, yes. That's true, but hypothetically speaking . . .'

Secretly, Priya was just as impressed by the fight as Kwasi was. She might not have been a sight-speaker, but the way these soul-singers fought with their gifts was breathtaking. It looked like art, a dance full of passion.

'So, which one do you think is better? Reza's protégée or the major's?' the older soldier beside them asked another man in a green uniform.

In the ring, the two soldiers danced around each other. Priya didn't see any more illusions but, given the number of swings and swipes on both sides, she had no doubt that the two opponents were still trying to outdo each other with their gifts.

Until something changed. The female soldier grazed her opponent's thigh with her sword. He jerked back.

'Letitia's the better of the two,' the cadet beside Priya said in the decisive tone of someone who was sure he was right. 'The major's protégés are the best soldiers around, but they're not the best warriors. Reza has experts on his team, not regular soldiers. When it comes to one-to-one fights, the members of his team are always going to win hands down.'

Right at that moment, Letitia held her sword to her opponent's throat. The man clenched his jaw tightly. His face slowly turned red, and he cried out.

Letitia stepped away from him and he sank to his knees, limp as a ragdoll, bowing his head. The female soldier stood in front of him and pressed her fists together. Sheathing her sword, she left the ring, tying up her black hair, which had come loose in the fight.

Along with the rest of the crowd, Priya stepped back to let Letitia through. As she walked past them, Priya spotted a tattoo of a water panther on her upper arm. Suddenly, Letitia stopped, took a step back and looked at the three of them, one by one. 'Kwasi, Jupta and Priya, I assume,' she said. She had a deep voice and clear brown eyes.

Kwasi cleared his throat. 'Um, yes. That's us.'

'I'm the basha of Reza's team. Follow me.' Letitia spoke in short, direct sentences, in a tone that made it clear she would not take no for an answer.

+++

Letitia led them to an open space between two wooden storehouses. Reza was already there, leaning against Kohóna as he spoke to a Topuan boy. Mawar was nearby with her hands buried deep in her pockets, kicking a stone.

'I have the newcomers, Kapten,' Letitia announced. 'Are we all here now?'

Reza looked at her and stood up straight. 'Askan is missing. He's on the schedule for tonight.'

'Again?' Letitia walked over to a sack that lay between Kohóna's paws. The water panther sniffed at her clothing as the basha shook out the contents of the bag. It turned out to be gold bracelets. She handed them out to the group.

Priya felt a rush of energy go through her body as she touched the gold. She blinked in surprise. The energy made the pain in her neck and shoulder fade into the background.

'Oh no. Not for me.' Jupta raised her hands defensively as Letitia held out a bracelet to her. 'I don't wear gold.'

'Topuan, huh?' Letitia lowered her hand a little. 'You sure you don't want to try?'

Jupta firmly shook her head. 'I know what gold can do. I also know about everything that gets killed in the search for gold.'

'What do you mean?' asked Priya.

'They find this stuff . . .' Jupta pointed at the bracelets with undisguised disgust. '. . . by throwing quicksilver into the rivers. Poisoning everything that lives in the water. So, I'm not interested in the enhanced powers.'

'In a distant future, when the wars we're fighting are a thing of the past, I'll agree with you, Topuan,' said Letitia. 'But sadly, right now, I can't afford to.'

'Let her.' Reza stepped forward, rolling his sleeves up to the elbows. 'If she wants to fight without gold, then she can fight without it.'

Priya rubbed the gold bracelet. She didn't dare to look at Jupta as she slid it onto her wrist. She wanted to be as strong as Jupta and the other Topuans and to refuse the gold, but she also had to admit that she understood Letitia. The memory of the monsters in the Keep would not let go of Priya. If gold gave her a better chance of surviving, then she couldn't refuse the bracelet.

Reza didn't train his team in the same way as Master Ramsaroup. He didn't correct footwork or demonstrate techniques. Instead, he assumed that they'd already got it figured out. He made Priya, Kwasi and Jupta fight opponents with more experience and told them to use both their gifts and their combat sticks.

Priya found herself facing Letitia and in the first few moments was overwhelmed by the tingling sensations running along her spine. She barely managed to keep her mental shield intact. Her poor defence resulted in three big new bruises. Dizzy with pain, she stood her ground, images of rabidos flashing before her eyes. She *had* to learn how to deal with it.

And she did. No matter how many blows she took, how many times it seemed like her mental shield was about to be torn in two, she remained standing. And her refusal to give up grew even stronger when, after a short rest, she had to face Reza. She narrowed her eyes suspiciously, still annoyed that he'd thrown her so off balance the night before.

Just you try manipulating my emotions again, she thought as she lashed out at him.

The last time they'd fought each other, Priya had been clumsy and inexperienced. A novice. This time she was able to block his stick while also resisting him mentally. But it wasn't easy. Reza was a head taller than her and a lot heavier. When he hit her, she saw stars. She wasn't going to win the fight by brute force.

After Reza's first two hits, Priya stopped trying to parry his blows, instead dodging them and looking for an opening. Reza didn't fight like Letitia, who had dramatic flair and relied on her gift. The precision of Reza's blows was unparalleled, as was his control over his gift. His movements were fluid, and his execution was lethal. She knew he didn't intend to stop until she was lying at his feet, defeated.

'So, where's this amazing gift of yours now?' he asked after Priya had dodged another blow. 'Vanished?'

'Shut your mouth,' she hissed back. *Down*, she commanded. She threw the command like a knife in his direction, but it smashed into his shield. Even with gold, she wasn't going to get through his barrier.

And the worst thing was that she was starting to get tired. She couldn't keep this up for ever and she was *not* planning to lose. She refused to.

She was getting desperate. Sloppy. Reza knocked the stick out of her hands. A moment later, her back slammed against the wooden side of one of the storehouses. Dizzy, she looked up. Reza was standing over her.

'Kapten?' she heard Letitia say.

'Is that all you've got?' asked Reza.

Priya clenched her jaw. It wasn't over yet. He was trying to take over her emotions. She felt his gift breaking through her shield. This time, there was nothing beautiful about the way he fought.

There was something frightening, something paralysing about the helplessness you felt when your emotions were being taken over. Priya saw a red haze in front of her eyes.

'Show me,' Reza demanded. 'Show me why you're worth so much.'

It sounded like a command, but at the same time it wasn't. He was furious. No, that wasn't it. He was bitter. And jealous. Of her?

In a sense, Priya was always trying to stay in control, and the only way she could do that was by keeping everything inside. Because that would protect her family; otherwise her gift would have been too wild, too *much*. But now she'd had enough. She loathed and detested the boy in front of her, who had distrusted and manipulated her right from the start and who could probably singlehandedly ensure that she was thrown down the waterfall. She wanted him out of her soul. Out of her thoughts.

In her mind, she let herself fall over the edge, releasing the last remnant of her self-control.

Kneel before me, she thought with such intensity that the world began to spin.

Her gift, amplified by the gold around her wrist, exploded behind her closed eyes. She focused on just one word. 'Kneel,' she croaked. Her gift poured out in waves. She cut through Reza's shield, felt his raw pain, dark jealousy and – she gasped – his loneliness. He didn't fully yield, but enveloped her with his own soul, and it seemed as if he felt her as much as she felt him. For a moment, it was as if they were one, merged into a single person. She pulled back with a jerk. *Kneel*, she snarled at him with her thoughts.

Then she crumpled. All the strength had drained from her body. Panting, she fell to the ground. The headache was so bad that it took her a few attempts to open her eyes.

In front of her, everything was still.

Reza's entire team was kneeling before Priya. Reza was the only one who had fallen to just one knee, not both. Gasping, he leaned with one arm on his knee. He was looking at her from under his eyelashes. She saw astonishment. Was he impressed?

'Well?' asked Priya, massaging her temples. 'Was that enough or do you want more?'

To her surprise, he laughed.

+++

A week later, they were summoned to fight the rabidos.

'The Keep consists of five rings.'

Priya stood with her hands behind her back, side by side with the six other soul-singers who were part of Reza's team. They were in a small room on the ground floor. Judging by the number of maps and documents on the walls, it was often used for meetings.

Priya looked at the people beside her. Besides Kwasi, Jupta and Priya, there were Mawar; the Topuan spirit-speaker named Ryan; and a Luanan sight-speaker, Askan. Half of Reza's team, including Priya, had been added only a few days ago. And Mawar was a fairly recent addition too, perhaps also on orders from above. Priya understood now what the general had meant when he said Reza's team needed to be expanded.

'It's usually pretty quiet in the third ring. There's the occasional rabido running around, but usually it's just soldiers repairing weak doors and walls,' said the basha, Letitia, using a stick to tap the crumpled map of the Keep that hung on the wall. 'Most of the fights take place in the second and the first rings. The inner ring is almost impassable because of the number of rabidos. That's where they hide when the sun comes up and the outer rings become too hot for them.' Her stick moved closer to the centre. 'Finally, there's the core, which is where the Dedekedre is located.'

Reza was sitting on the edge of a desk, twisting his prosthesis until something clicked into place and, satisfied, he let go. Since Priya had forced him onto one knee, he hadn't challenged her again during their training sessions. In fact, she had the feeling that he was avoiding her.

That was fine by her, as he kept popping into her mind even when he wasn't speaking to her. She didn't do it consciously. Sometimes she was just walking along, and she suddenly felt an echo of his feelings and thoughts running through her. Which was the last thing she wanted. She just didn't know how to stop it happening.

'We are defending the first ring,' said Reza, stretching the fingers of his prosthesis. It was still fascinating to see how a piece of stone mixed with gold could respond to his will.

Priya focused on the movements he made, trying not to think about the monsters, trying not to think about them coming at her and . . .

Kwasi raised his hand.

Reza looked up. 'Yes?'

'Why does Kuwatta keep the existence of the Dedekedre secret?'

Reza frowned. 'That . . . has nothing to do with what I was just saying.'

'It's been on my mind.'

'Because those are the general's orders,' Reza responded impatiently.

Kwasi bowed his head and made a face at the ground. Knowing him, Reza's answer was certainly *not* enough. It was a good question, insightful even. If the monster was that dangerous and soldiers were dying all the time – as she'd witnessed for herself a few days ago – then it would be useful to have more soldiers at their disposal. The different regions might be willing to send more soldiers if they knew how much was at stake.

If you see the man with the bleeding mouth, run away.

Her mother's voice echoed through her head. Her mother knew rabidos existed. It was the only explanation. Maybe she didn't know about the Dedekedre, but she did know about the rabidos. But Reza – and probably the general too – seemed to think that no one outside Kuwatta knew about the existence of the rabidos. Priya felt that she might be risking the safety of her mother and little brother if she asked too many questions, so she kept her mouth shut.

'We have the situation under control,' said Reza. 'The Dedekedre has been trapped for a century. That tells you all you need to know.'

The basha pushed forward a wicker basket. 'Your new uniforms. Made to measure. They're made from an extra-tough, waterproof fabric that will keep out parasites and protect you from rabido bites. As soon as you get to the third ring, it's mandatory to put a mask over your mouth, so that flying parasites can't enter your mouth or nose.'

Her speech was meant for Priya, Jupta and Kwasi. The other soul-singers were already wearing dark green uniforms – or, in the case of Reza and the basha, black ones. Their masks dangled under their chins, and they had straps to attach their weapons to. Hoods and knee-high black boots completed their uniforms.

'I think I've covered everything,' Letitia said, checking a tiny piece of paper that she fished out of one of her pockets. 'Yes, that was it. We'll go and pick up the weapons soon.'

'I have a question.' Reza's gaze shot in Priya's direction. His face remained neutral, and his soul was almost undetectable among the others. But still Priya felt a difference. She didn't know if it was a side-effect of their bizarre merging a week ago or if Reza was deliberately revealing his soul to her.

'What's the most effective way to kill a rabido?' she asked.

'Simple.' This time it felt as if she could sense him brushing against her soul. 'Cut its throat.'

30

THE TIP OF THE sword hanging on Priya's back jabbed into her side.

She ran her fingers over the straps, checking they were still securely buckled and holding the sword in place. As she had no sheath, the blade was wrapped in pieces of cloth. Once she'd drawn her sword, it wouldn't be easy to put it back. She pictured herself trudging back in the morning, dragging the sword behind her.

Reza led the way during their walk to the first ring, speaking to the Topuan spirit-speaker, whom he trusted. A number of daggers hung from the spirit-speaker's waist.

From the second ring of the Keep, there were no windows in the dark corridors. She couldn't see the sky, which would have helped her to judge whether the rabidos were about to attack, and that didn't help to ease the butterflies in her stomach. But at least she couldn't hear any screeches or drumming footsteps yet.

She ran her fingers over the gold bracelet around her wrist, as if that might give her extra energy.

'Close the door,' said Reza, looking back. The door in front of him was already closed, and the basha checked the spears in the ground in front of it, ramming them in more firmly. 'Halfway down this corridor there are some plates that you can press to make doors appear.'

The emergency exits. Priya remembered them from the drawings. The locking system allowed only a small opening to appear each time and you had to press other buttons to keep moving forward. The doors, which worked using magic drawn from gold, opened and closed at lightning speed. The complex locks meant the monsters were less likely to spread throughout the building.

Kwasi was right at the back. Uncertainly, he looked behind him and then forward again. Shoulders slumped, he went off to close the door. By the light of the torches, the greyness seemed to have left his skin. But he still didn't look quite like himself. Priya could feel the energy of his soul spinning off in all directions, performing dizzying somersaults. She was about to go and help him, but then saw that the Topuan soldier had beaten her to it.

The door soon slammed shut, and Jupta grabbed Priya's hand. At that moment, the Topuan spirit-speaker said, 'They're coming.'

Behind her mask, Priya's breathing sped up.

'Keep calm.' Mawar came to stand beside her. 'You're not doing this alone.'

'I'd rather not be doing it at all,' said Kwasi. 'But sadly you can't always get what you want.'

'Oh, Kwasi,' sighed Jupta, even though she looked like she couldn't agree more. She pulled the spear off her back. 'There are so many of them,' she said anxiously.

'Assume positions!' Reza called from the front.

His team swiftly moved into the required 2-3-2 position, which he'd explained to them earlier. Priya headed to the centre and pulled the sword from her back. She could already hear the rabidos coming closer and feel their prickly souls. Their slapping feet echoed along the corridors. Their shrieks, somewhat muffled by the stone, were shrill.

The impact as the first rabidos slammed into the door made the building shudder. Priya instinctively crouched and gripped her sword more tightly. It was sweltering inside her new uniform, and she was already sweating, even before the fight had begun.

The stone door, which had once seemed so solid and impervious, now looked like nothing – and it was all that separated them from the rabidos. As far as she could feel, hundreds were running towards them, as if they could smell the soldiers from miles away.

Piercing shrieks – the high-pitched sound hurt Priya's ears. They pounded over and over again on the stone door, which groaned under their weight. The door was becoming looser, moving back and forth on its hinges. Screaming, the rabidos threw themselves at it again.

The first parasites were already crawling through the narrow opening. The yellow-white maggots fell writhing to the floor and steadily crept forward. Leaving a blood-red trail, they came towards them.

Priya breathed deeply in and out, trying to stay calm. Beside her, Kwasi shuffled restlessly back and forth.

'Stand still,' said Reza. 'They can't get through your boots. Just stamp on them if they come too close.'

More high-pitched screaming. Another loud bang against the door. The top hinges came loose, and the stone door tipped towards them. The screeching grew louder.

'How many are in the corridor ahead of us?' asked Reza.

'Thirty,' his spirit-speaker replied calmly.

Jupta nodded. 'But there are more on the way,' she added quietly. Her eyes widened. 'Oh, Gods.'

The door tipped further. Priya saw the first faces, their mouths wide open, dripping with blood, their eyes full of madness.

'Stay in position,' ordered Reza, drawing his sword. 'Letitia and Kwasi, forward.'

Letitia obeyed at once. Kwasi took longer, coming to a stop just behind her.

Priya's ears were buzzing. The noise that the rabidos made was overwhelming.

The door gave way. The rabidos and the door fell to the ground, sending clouds of dust flying up. Behind the fallen door, another wave of monsters appeared. Their mouths gaping, they shot forward. Dead rabidos lay there, trampled by the others, and parasites crawled from the carcasses and broken skulls over the edge of the stone door.

Priya took a step back. Beside her she felt Mawar's soul stir.

'Sight-speakers!'

It worked to an extent. The screaming subsided. The rabidos became disoriented, some of them smashing their heads against the stone. Others clung to the first line of spears that were stuck into the ground. Even pierced through, they tried to crawl forward. The rabidos behind them clambered over them. Hands and feet were gored by the spears, but that didn't bother them. It was working, but it wasn't enough. Letitia closed the gaps, felling one after another with her short swords.

'Deed-speakers, forward,' barked Reza.

He was talking about Priya. Deep down she knew that. Somewhere. But the sight of the rabidos made every thought in her head dissolve like Suryan ink in water. She took a step. And another. Mawar, the other deed-speaker, had already joined the sight-speakers. The group of rabidos that had climbed over the spears was brought to an abrupt halt. Letitia kept going, as fast as an arrow, backed up by Kwasi. Priya could see from the tension in his body that he was doing his best not to run away. Reza plunged a dagger in the neck of a rabido as it almost sent Kwasi flying.

Priya was nearly there.

She saw the monsters with their bleeding mouths gaping, limbs at strange angles and parasite-riddled wounds. Their unhealthy grey skin was smeared with blood and slime. She saw them. She heard them. And that was all she could do.

A rabido was coming straight for Jupta, who had her back to the creature. Priya's breath caught in her throat. She had to do something. But her legs wouldn't move. She could feel the rabido's soul, full of sharp edges. Instinctively, she enveloped its soul and forced it to step aside.

The rabido swerved, narrowly missing Jupta. Priya felt a slight pressure in her forehead and temples. The rabido's chaotic soul struggled in her grasp.

Then Reza thrust his right hand, shaped into a point, into the monster's neck and pulled it back just as quickly. The rabido's soul was extinguished.

The pressure on Priya's head disappeared.

More rabidos pushed past Letitia and Kwasi. Reza and Jupta also disappeared among the monsters.

One of the rabidos leaped past Reza. He looked back and caught Priya's eye, but then two other rabidos distracted him, one of them pouncing on the spirit-speaker, who fell with a scream. Within seconds, he disappeared under a mountain of rabidos.

Priya took a shallow breath and raised her sword. The escaped rabido came closer. She lashed out with her sword. Too slow. She slashed at its stomach, and parasites rained down onto her shoulder. Grimacing, she tried to knock the maggots off her uniform. The rabido smacked onto the ground beside her. A female. Her belly was open, and she was screaming. She was screaming so loudly. But her hands still snatched at Priya. She grabbed Priya's ankles, pulling and pushing herself forward and leaving streaks of red behind.

Priya froze.

Someone dived in and shoved Priya aside with a shoulder. Her feet came free. A sword swung down and into the rabido's neck, where it remained.

'What do you think you're doing?' Mawar was standing beside her. She'd drawn two short swords and was staring at Priya as if she thought she'd lost her mind. 'Are you planning just to stand there the whole time?'

'No,' Priya shouted back. The hilt of her medium-sized sword was clammy in her hands. 'No, of course not.'

Mawar tugged on the sword that was still stuck in the rabido and cursed. 'The others don't seem to be having the same problem.'

The rabido writhed and struggled in its death throes. More and more maggots came crawling from her belly, where her intestines bulged out of her wound. Priya tried to breathe calmly through her nose.

Mawar pressed a foot against the rabido's shoulder, pulling her sword free. The rabido shrieked. Mawar let her sword fall again. This time, the head almost came off completely. Blood spurted up, drenching Mawar's uniform. A few drops landed on her face. The rabido jerked and shuddered. Finally, she lay still.

'All the saints! My arms.' With a look of disgust, Mawar wiped her sword on the rabido's limp body and took a step back. 'Don't aim at the chest and stomach. That's where most of the parasites are.'

'Thank you,' said Priya. Breathe in. Breathe out.

'Don't thank me,' said Mawar. 'There are plenty more where that came from.'

'I know.' Priya felt the sword in her hand. She stamped on a few parasites that were wriggling around their feet, hoping none of them had crawled inside her uniform.

Something inside Priya had broken when she saw the rabido die. A glass wall had been shattered, giving her room to move again. Cut the throat, Reza had said, and that was the only way. Together with Mawar, she moved forward. More and more rabidos were slipping into the corridor.

Based on numbers alone, they were greatly outmatched. It helped that the rabidos didn't have enough space to come running at them all at once. In terms of strength, though, they were . . . still in bad shape, thought Priya bitterly.

Priya raised her sword as the first rabido came storming towards her. She couldn't summon a command – she was too distracted by the turmoil around her. Now she understood why, during their combat training, Reza had made them take on four or five opponents at once. In fights like this, there was no logic. There was only chaos.

She blinked, and a monster appeared beside her. Grabbing a dagger with her free hand, she stabbed it in the shoulder. Then she kicked it aside.

Another rabido came running along the wall, its tongue hanging out of its mouth. Glassy white eyes that saw nothing and yet were fixed on Priya. Chunks bitten out of its thighs and arms. She could see the toothmarks. One of the other rabidos must have done it. Even with such serious wounds, it was still standing upright, but Priya could see that its body was shaking. It could barely hold itself up.

Somehow she felt sorry for it. So she waited until it was close enough, spun on her axis and put all of her strength into the attack as she slit its throat. She meant to decapitate it with one blow and to spare it the pain. It didn't work. As had happened to Mawar, her sword got stuck. The rabido stormed onwards, pulling Priya's sword from her hand.

'Shit.'

Mawar was ready. She tried to jump out of the way and to finish Priya's botched decapitation. But she missed and sliced off its arm. The rabido raced past, clutching her uniform with its remaining hand before it fell. Its fingers clawed into Mawar's uniform, throwing her off balance. With a growl of irritation, she shoved the monster backwards. Priya felt for its soul, trying to force it to lie still. When that didn't work – there wasn't enough time – she kicked it aside, pushed herself forward and grabbed Mawar.

'The emergency exit,' panted Mawar. She drew a long knife and angled her upper body to slice through the neck of a rabido that was approaching from behind. 'There are too many of them. I don't understand why the general decided to have us fight here.'

Priya could only see the ceiling. There were so many rabidos swarming around her – as she waved her dagger at random – that she could barely make out the walls. Where were Jupta and Kwasi? Among the chaotic souls of the rabidos, she could hardly feel their presence. And her arms were getting tired. How was she going to keep this up all night?

Then Mawar disappeared.

'Mawar?' Growling close to her ear. It was a sharp-edged soul. Priya knocked away the rabido's outstretched hands. Then she thrust a dagger into its neck and slashed. She shoved the dying rabido backwards, trying not to look at the blood that was spurting out of it.

'Mawar!' she screamed. Where was she? Why couldn't Priya feel her anymore? Panic, fear and frustration merged until she exploded inside.

'Out of my way,' she roared, and the world obeyed her command. Crackling energy – in her, around her. She held it in the palms of her hands. It felt so good. She was no longer weak and small but was made up of pure power. The release, the ease as everyone around her listened to what *she* wanted. All the rabidos in the room stumbled aside, clearing a path down the centre of the corridor. The screaming didn't stop, but it became less overwhelming, as if the monsters had come to a joint decision to reduce their screaming.

The soldiers in the corridor were affected too and had stepped aside, some not as far as others, depending on how well they were able to resist her command. Only Reza stood in the middle of the corridor with his sword raised in an attack that was no longer needed. He looked back, and there was the headache that Priya had been expecting. It blinded her. Gasping, she leaned forward, pressing her hands to her thighs and trying to remain upright. The world was spinning.

'. . . here!' she heard a muffled voice somewhere below. 'Open the emergency exit.'

Priya scanned the floor and saw Mawar's green uniform in a blur among the black spots before her eyes. She dragged her half to her feet and headed for the wall. With great difficulty, she pushed a number of rabidos out of the way. A bit longer. Just a little bit longer. And then she could let go.

She didn't know if Mawar had been bitten and she hoped that wasn't the case, but there was no time to check. If she let go now – mentally and physically – she didn't know if she'd be able to find Mawar again.

'Halfway . . . Wall,' Mawar gasped. She was leaning heavily on Priya, but still fending off rabidos with her long knife. 'I'll cover you.'

Priya ran her fingers over the wall, feeling the bumps and indentations. Her headache was so extreme that she was seeing the world in triplicate. She was nauseous with pain and felt like she was about to vomit. She knew she couldn't take much more.

'Now, Priya!'

Sweat ran down Priya's back as she searched the wall. Swaying, the soldiers tore themselves away from her command. The rabidos followed. There was no more time. They were coming. There! Lines. Forming a rectangle. Desperately, she pushed. She could have cried with relief when the wall gave way. With a swishing sound, the emergency exit opened.

Priya stooped to get a better grip on Mawar, but a rabido smashed into her and she fell against the sharp doorway. As one of its claws got stuck in her plait, tears welled up in her eyes. She grabbed hold of the monster and shoved it backwards. Another rabido leaped on top of her. With both hands, she pushed against its neck and collarbone to keep its biting mouth away from her head. Her dagger. She needed her dagger.

Then the rabido was gone. Air, finally, air. Where was Mawar? An arm slid around her waist and dragged her into the emergency exit. Priya didn't hesitate for a moment. She jerked back her elbow. Her free hand found the dagger she was looking for and, in one fluid movement, she pulled it from her boot and thrust it backwards – only to be stopped at the last moment.

'All the saints, Chkadhari, it's me,' Reza said sharply in her ear. 'Close the door.'

'Mawar's still . . .'

'She's been bitten. *Close* the door.'

'No!' Mawar clawed her way towards them. Her face and clothing were smeared with blood, and she was kicking fiercely behind her. Priya could see that her clothes were torn somewhere around her midriff – and her stomach was wounded. Priya rested her hand on the button to close the door, but she didn't press it. She couldn't.

'Use your gift!' screamed Mawar. 'I can't do this on my own. Help me! Please!' she begged.

Get back, Priya thought frantically, and the stabbing pains in her head intensified. Focus, she needed to focus. Why couldn't she do it again? Gods, the rabido was getting too close. She threw her dagger at the monster that was looming over Mawar – and she hit it in the chest. It barely even slowed it down. She'd known that it wouldn't, and she was furious with herself. She knew a knife in the heart made no difference. *Get back*, she thought again.

Reza placed his hand on hers.

He pressed.

A rabido bit Mawar's thigh. The door slid shut, with Mawar's body wedged in it. She screamed. The rabidos shot forward and Priya realised they'd only stayed at a distance because Mawar had commanded them to. Some pounced on Mawar, while others tried to reach Priya and Reza through the half-open door.

Mawar wailed. The light in her eyes went out as Priya watched. All the fire and vitality disappeared, giving way to madness. Tears of blood streamed down Mawar's brown cheeks. Her soul shot off in all directions, becoming agitated, chaotic.

Mawar opened her mouth and screamed.

'No.' Priya doubled up and pushed herself back, closer to Reza. 'No,' she wailed again. No, no, no, this couldn't have happened. It was a dream. It must be. Mawar couldn't be . . .

Reza pressed another button and a door opened behind them. He pulled Priya backwards and closed the door in front of them, and, just like that, Mawar – the rabido – was gone. Priya's throat felt painful and swollen. She wanted to howl. Instead, she turned round in Reza's arms and glared at him.

'Open the door. Where's the button?'

He took hold of her hands and squeezed them between their bodies. 'Stop it.'

She struggled to get free.

'What do you want to do?' He held her firmly in place. 'Do you want to die? Is that the plan?'

'My friends are out there!' She wanted to kill him. Where was her dagger? 'What kind of kapten are you? You're sitting here safely, while out there . . .'

'They already took an emergency exit. *Stop* moving.'

'Mawar . . .'

'Isn't alive anymore.'

She stopped, suddenly exhausted. Inside, she felt hollow and empty. His grip on her weakened. Tears ran silently down her cheeks. The space was small, intended for one person. Reza had half picked her up and pulled her inside, so she was practically sitting on his lap. She slumped against him, feeling his warmth and his soul within. He was stable and calm and yet she sensed something that she didn't understand, something that made her suspicious.

'Why?' she asked, her head on his shoulder. Outside, she could hear the rabidos raging on.

Reza moved a little, and she shifted in his arms. 'This is normal. All soldiers have to defend the fortress.'

'The first ring is close to the core. And we're inexperienced. *Why* was this plan chosen?'

Silence, and then: 'I warned you.'

Her head shot up. 'Are you trying to say the general did *this* on purpose?' She looked around to demonstrate what she meant by 'this', even though there wasn't much to see in the dark room. Had it been a test? Reza didn't react, and that turned her disbelief into rage. All she'd wanted to do was to help her brother. That was all. 'He has a problem with the major. And apparently now with me, too. Kwasi, Jupta, Mawar – they have nothing to do with that.'

'You're the new wonder of Kuwatta.'

First the major and now the general. A wonder? Priya felt anything but. Master Yapoma had never given her any indication during their lessons. Her gift was strong perhaps, but it was also unpredictable.

She hadn't even been able to help her friends. In fact, every time she used her gift, it felt like she'd done something bad and was being punished for it with a massive headache.

'Mawar's gone. All of us were nearly lost. What good are we to him if we're dead?' She gave him a furious shove. Much to her frustration, he didn't move. His muscles were as hard as the black stone around them.

'You're of less use to him if you're not the wonder the major makes you out to be.'

It wasn't just the major; *he* had just called her the same thing. 'What do you mean?'

Reza stared at her impassively. 'Your gift,' he said finally, and she felt annoyance in his soul, sensed bitterness in his words. 'He wanted to see how much it was worth.'

'Wasn't it enough that I almost brought you to your knees?' She was struggling to understand why the general had opted for this course of action.

'That was against humans. As you've noticed, rabidos are different.'

'And? Did I pass the test?' Priya spat.

'You'd better hope not,' Reza said quietly. 'If you have, he'll own you. Or destroy you.'

Had he actually saved her life or not? Ultimately, he was the one who would report back to his father. Priya stared at him. At the dark bloodstains on his jaw, the lines of his shoulders and throat, the black hair clinging to his temples and neck, and finally at his eyes, which glinted in the gloom and held a certain darkness within. For the first time, she wasn't curious about his soul, and she withdrew completely, afraid of what she might find. His warm body pressed against hers.

Even so, she shivered.

31

INSIDE THEIR QUARTERS, IT was silent. Priya lay on her mat, staring at the ceiling. She didn't want to look at her clothes or her hands. Even though she'd washed herself and changed her clothes, in her mind she could still see the blood.

It wasn't right. Mawar had been taken away weeks ago and had survived every fight since then. She'd been better than Priya. Stronger. Faster. Less afraid. This wasn't how it was supposed to end for her.

Jupta sat against the wall with her knees drawn up and her face pressed to them. Priya couldn't tell if she was crying; sometimes it seemed like it, but at other times it sounded like she was whispering words. She didn't know if she was so upset because of what had happened to Mawar or because of everything they'd seen last night – and she couldn't bring herself to ask.

Priya's eyes were burning, her throat felt painfully swollen, and her insides were upside down. But the tears didn't come.

Why hadn't she been faster? Why had she watched like a coward as Mawar had breathed her last breath? She didn't deserve to be alive when Mawar . . . When Mawar . . .

She pushed away the emotions before they could take her over completely, and she could no longer be sure of herself. Before she felt so much that she couldn't take it any longer. She bit hard on her bottom lip, tasting blood.

'Do you think we can save them?' Jupta suddenly asked.

Priya looked at her. 'The rabidos?' she asked, and Mawar's face appeared in her mind again. Her brown eyes, pleading, hopeful, afraid, until they clouded over, milky white, filling with blood and madness. Swallowing hard, Priya tried to ignore the image.

'Yes. I'm increasingly getting the feeling that . . .' Jupta leaned back, stroking her beads with one finger. 'Most of the rabidos are still wearing parts of their uniforms. Torn and covered with blood, but you can still see what it is. And their souls . . . They're the souls of neither the dead nor the living, and yet there's something in them that's still human. Can't you feel it? Every one of them was once like us, Priya. We're fighting against ourselves. Against the monsters we can become.'

Priya tried to imagine some way to rescue them, as Jupta had said, but she couldn't think of one. The rabidos were not open to reason. Priya had felt their souls. They were made up of pain and an insatiable hunger for human flesh. How could anyone communicate with that?

Priya stood up.

'Where are you going?'

'To see the major,' she said. 'I can't just sit here doing nothing.'

+++

'You just beat me to it,' said Major Aïda, clasping her slender fingers together on her desk. Her black plaits were loose down her back this time, and there were faint traces of white and red warpaint on her face. 'Speak, soldier.'

'Did you know what the general was planning?'

'Yes, and no. I knew you were going to be summoned. Every soldier in Kuwatta must obey the call.' It didn't escape Priya's notice that the major no longer spoke of her as a cadet. Since she'd encountered the rabidos, she'd risen in the military hierarchy. Whether she wanted to or not.

'I thought it unlikely that he'd put you on Reza's team and test your gift that way.' The major leaned back, the corners of her mouth falling slightly. 'I suspected something more like a demonstration in the Great Hall.'

The general had made the decision, Reza had carried it out, and the major had known about it. The major might have been irritated, but she seemed largely unconcerned. If Priya had hoped for any form of empathy, that hope was now gone. 'You promised to protect me, Major.'

'I knew he wouldn't let you die. Reza will have been instructed to guard you with his life. My little brother is the best soldier in all of Kuwatta.' The major spoke in a neutral tone, but Priya felt the tension in the air. 'As I assume you've seen for yourself by now.'

'And has the general seen what he hoped to see?' Priya asked, her jaws clenched.

The major studied her briefly and then leaned forward with a sharp smile. 'Oh, don't give me that look, soldier. You probably think me cold and unscrupulous, but I can't control everything. It's my father who is the general, not me. And if you knew what was down there, you'd understand our choices.'

'Rabidos,' said Priya. 'I've seen them.'

'They're only the shield of the true monster that dwells deep in the core of the Keep. I'm sure you've already heard about her. We call her Dedekedre – death cellar – because she rarely shows herself to us and seeks refuge deep under the ground, where it's colder and darker. She appeared over a century ago during a blood moon, along with many other monsters, and her power is devastating. She devoured village after village, settlement after settlement, until one of my ancestors constructed Kuwatta to contain her. The rabidos are her children, and she is their mother. And every night she sends out her offspring to gather human flesh for her.'

Priya stared at her. 'I don't believe it.'

'Deep inside, you know it's the truth.' The major's voice became softer, lower. 'Kuwatta is a prison, and we are its guards. If this fort breaks, if our soldiers are not enough, then the world is lost.'

Priya saw the rabidos in her mind's eye – their writhing bodies, their bleeding mouths and eyes full of madness. If they offered just a hint of what the true monster in Kuwatta could do . . . Priya had suffered many fears in her life. The tense undercurrent of fear that had dominated her life in Disin, panic when she arrived at Kuwatta, terror when she came face to face with the rabidos. But the fear flowing through her veins now felt different. It was a primitive, all-consuming terror – not only for her own life, but for the whole world. How was it possible that Kuwatta had so many soldiers under its command and still had not managed to defeat these monsters?

'Why does Kuwatta keep this hidden?' she struggled to say. She hoped the major would be less cryptic than Reza. 'Why aren't soldiers being recruited and trained on an even larger scale?'

'Those are the general's orders.' The major leaned back again, crossing her arms. Her lips were pressed into a thin line. 'And the orders of the previous general. Kuwatta keeps its gates closed. According to my father, it would not benefit the forces outside Kuwatta if they knew about the monster. They need to focus on the Freelanders on the coast.'

That seemed like a weak excuse to Priya. Judging by the major's expression, she thought the same.

'And do you agree?' asked Priya.

'Why do you think you're here, soldier?' said the major slowly. 'And not in front of the general?' She gave a frustrated sigh. 'I've tried several times to change my father's mind. He refuses to listen.'

'Is that why you're recruiting an army of your own?' It was a bold question, and Priya only asked it because her life was already at risk. The possibility of dying at any moment brought certain freedoms with it.

The major's eyes narrowed. For the first time, something dark appeared in her eyes, reminding Priya of Reza. 'I'm trying to convince my father that we will not defeat the Dedekedre this way. There comes a time when words alone are no longer enough.'

And there it was. The crux of the conflict between the major and the general. It wouldn't surprise Priya if the general knew what his daughter was doing – or at least had a strong suspicion. It made sense that Reza, who seemed to follow his father's every order, had tried to question Priya about the major. But the general hadn't openly confronted the major with her treason. Not yet, in any case. Did that mean he feared much of his army would rally behind the major?

'And there's no way to defeat the monster of Kuwatta?' asked Priya. Surely there must be something they could do?

'No,' said the major curtly. 'The probies and scholars are still searching for a solution. Until they come up with something, our soldiers have to go out every night to keep the prison intact.'

Goosebumps rose on Priya's arms.

One of the soldiers behind the major shifted. It was the slightest of movements, but the sound caused Priya's body to tense, immediately wary of danger.

The major seemed amused by her reaction. Then, with a wave of her hand, she changed the subject. 'As interesting as this conversation is, it's not why I wanted to see you. My little brother has been ordered by the general to patrol the area around the fortress for the next few days. You're going with him. Be on your guard.'

It was not a request. 'Outside the fortress? Not here?'

A slight frown line appeared between the major's dark eyebrows. She tapped her fingers on the desktop. 'I've been informed that our scouts have found slime and human teeth out there. It happens occasionally. Kuwatta keeps a lot at bay, but it's not watertight. And if there really are rabidos wandering about the rainforest, they need to be eliminated before they reach the surrounding villages. As I'm sure you understand.'

Priya, too, had found grey slime and a human tooth outside the fort – back in Disin. During the blood moon. Had she been mistaken? Was it just normal slime? And animal teeth? It must have been. A rabido outside the fort was possible, but all the way back home in Disin? That was unthinkable. If that were the case, surely both the general and the major would be aware of it.

The major took her silence the wrong way. 'The medicine is on its way to your brother, of course. I hope to receive a message soon.'

Her words were no more than another display of her power. Even if Priya didn't want to help the major, she would have to agree. Umed's health – maybe his life – depended on it.

'Ah,' said the major, as if something had just occurred to her. 'Probie Ishani is constantly asking about you. Your sister? I've agreed that she can see you.'

Priya couldn't believe her ears. 'She can't come here. She'd have to go through the Keep.'

'It's fine during the daytime. But don't worry.' She smiled her sly smile. 'The choice is yours. You can go to her, or she will be brought here.'

An obvious threat, which Priya could do nothing about. As if Umed's life wasn't enough. Beneath the desk, Priya pressed her clenched fists into her thighs. She didn't want to see Ishani. But she also didn't want her sister's life to be in danger. Ishani wasn't like her. She couldn't handle a sword, only knowledge. 'I'll go to her.'

'Excellent.'

32

ISHANI WAS POKING A lower-leg prosthesis with a rod. With complete concentration, she studied the black stone in front of her, oblivious to Priya, who was standing in the doorway of the small laboratory. In this part of the Academy, there were only probies and scholars, dressed in their beige tunics or uniforms.

About a week had passed since Priya had last seen her sister. But it felt like years. Next to Ishani stood a Suryan boy, who she frowned at as he gave her some unsolicited advice. Priya recalled that his name was Rohan, the irritating probie she'd wanted to hit.

Priya cleared her throat.

Ishani looked up. The metal rod fell from her hands, but Rohan caught it before it hit the floor.

'You wanted to see me,' said Priya, when Ishani didn't move.

'I thought . . .' Ishani's voice died away. She took an awkward step forward, her shoulders slightly hunched. The lines of her face and her chin reminded Priya of their mother. 'They said you . . . I didn't know . . . Where were you, didi?'

Ishani couldn't get her words out. She was stuttering, something Priya had never heard before. Previously, it would have given her satisfaction; she hated the way her sister always remained calm and found the right words for every situation. Maybe because Priya herself, in spite of her attempts to suppress everything, always went around feeling inside like she was about to explode at any moment.

Priya walked into the lab. On the long tables, there were more pieces of black stone, chunks of gold and tools. The black stone was propped upright in a wooden support so that it could be shaped with knives and chisels. 'Are these the magical prostheses?' she asked, without responding to Ishani's question.

Ishani pressed her lips together.

'Yes,' Rohan replied, still tinkering with the leg. 'Seems you paid attention in your lessons.' It was a weak taunt, maybe because he was paying more attention to the prosthesis than to Priya.

'We fuse the gold, specifically the magic within it, with stone,' Ishani explained. 'And then we cast it in the right shape. The magic in it reacts to the human soul. People outside Kuwatta act as if only blood children are magical, but the soul of every human being actually has a little magic. So it works for them too. The only downside is that the magic drains energy from the soul. The more you demand from your prosthesis, the more it takes . . .' Her voice faded, and she cleared her throat. 'But that's not why you're here.'

Priya didn't know what to do. Warn Ishani? Tell her about what was going on? Or keep everything hidden from her? All she really wanted to do was to run away. And she decided to do exactly that. 'I've managed to have the medicine sent to Umed,' she said, because she owed her at least that much. 'I'm glad you're well.'

She turned and left the lab.

'Wait!' Ishani came after her and grabbed her arm in the corridor. 'Why do you always do this?' she asked agitatedly. 'Why do you always run away from me? Don't you care that I was worried?'

'*You* were worried?'

'Why are you so angry again?' Ishani gripped Priya's hand tightly. 'You're acting like this is all my fault. And you always did exactly the same at home. I'm sorry I told Mama you were doing the test. I was just so furious, and I . . . I took it out on you. I wanted it so badly and I couldn't stand that you were doing the test too, because it felt like you were trying to take away the place I'd been working so hard for all my life. You're right. I was only thinking about myself.' She shrugged helplessly. 'But weren't we both doing the same thing?'

Priya trembled. She was trying with all her might to keep the bad memories and thoughts inside. This was exactly why she didn't want to come face to face with Ishani, why she ignored her sister and avoided her at Kuwatta. Because Ishani took her back to Disin, back to her mother's rejection and to the miserable situation that Priya had so desperately wanted to escape. Every time Priya saw her sister's face, that feeling of inferiority came flooding back and she turned into an ugly version of herself.

'Leave me alone, Ishani,' she said, pulling her hand away.

'You can't run away now. Come on, Pri. I'm trying to patch things up.'

Priya swung to look at her. 'Do you really want to know the truth? Fine. Our situations were not remotely similar. I was worth nothing, while the world lay at your feet. Perhaps Mother did save me, but that sacrifice drained any love for me from her heart. She gave me nothing. Nothing. And you . . . You didn't think for yourself. You just did everything she said.' Priya's voice was pure venom; the taste in her mouth was bitter. 'Maybe I did try to take Kuwatta from you, but at least you could have made a life for yourself afterwards. I was suffocating, Ishani, and nobody cared.'

'If you'd told me this before . . .'

'The fact that I have to tell you says it all. You weren't bothered if I was happy or not. Mother tossed me aside time and time again, and you couldn't have cared less.' Priya spat it out at Ishani, even though she felt more and more miserable with every word. This speech was not meant for Ishani. She clutched the front of her own uniform, digging her nails into her chest to drive away the pain inside.

'That's not true,' said Ishani. 'I *do* care. Why can't you see that? And if Mama didn't love you, she wouldn't have saved you.'

'I wish she hadn't. It would have saved me a lot of pain and suffering.'

Ishani gasped. 'Don't say that,' she said, her voice thick with emotion. 'Never say that again.'

'You have no idea, do you? You probably just didn't want to see it. There was not one day in my life when my own mother took me in her arms. She never kissed me goodnight or lovingly stroked my cheek. She didn't touch me. No one touched me, except for Umed. And that includes you. It wasn't until we got here, to Kuwatta . . .' Priya pointed at her hand. 'That you could even bring yourself to take hold of my hand. Did you really not see that, Ishani?'

Ishani's expression was horrified.

'She loved me?' Priya gave a snorting laugh, the sound hollow and lifeless. 'I may be alive because of my mother, but the daughter she really wanted died on the day I came into this world during the blood moon. And she never let me forget that.'

Her mother, who had fled from the colonists and survived with a stubbornness that Priya might have admired in another life. Her mother, who had unthinkingly accepted the opinions of her oppressors, and therefore seen her own daughter as a monster.

'I . . .' Ishani's voice died away.

She looked lost and confused, and that made Priya even angrier. She had no right to look like that. Not when she'd had the loving childhood Priya had always longed for. Ishani might be more intelligent than Priya, but she was clearly unaware of the privileges she'd grown up with. The love, affection and warmth that Priya had missed out on because of the moment of her birth.

The love Priya felt for her sister had always been bitter. Full of jealousy and envy.

'I . . . I'm just tired of being angry, didi,' said Ishani, her chin trembling. 'I don't want anything to happen to you. That's all I really wanted to say right now. I know I've made mistakes. Please believe me.' She took a deep breath. 'And I don't believe she didn't love you, even though she hurt you so badly. She rescued you for a reason.'

Priya turned away from her. What Ishani said was true, but she didn't want to hear it. In her own twisted way, their mother had indeed saved Priya. She'd even warned Priya about the rabidos and fought to keep her in Disin, where there were no monsters. Although that was debatable. And yet that didn't make it any better. In fact, it made it worse. Because how can you love someone and at the same time make their life a nightmare?

Priya's head hurt. This time Ishani didn't stop her when she walked away down the corridor.

33

PRIYA BREATHED IN THE outside air.

It was swelteringly hot in the rainforest – hotter than Kuwatta – and insects were buzzing all around. A black scorpion scuttled up the tree trunk beside her and a colony of red ants, each the size of a fingernail, marched past her feet.

Priya blew the air back out and took another deep breath. It tasted different, better, more familiar. The constant roar of the water was gone. The birdsong made her step lighter, and the wind rustling in the leaves lifted some of the weight she was carrying on her shoulders. The rainforest was helping her to forget the conversation she'd had with Ishani the day before.

Monkeys scattered, shrieking, as Kohóna, Reza's water panther, darted past Priya and jumped, zigzagging from tree to tree. Kwasi ran after her, more slowly. Laughing, he threw himself into a tree, nimbly climbing upwards.

Letitia looked up, startled, as leaves came tumbling down onto her head, and then seemed relieved when she saw it was just because of Kohóna. Sleeves of her black uniform pushed up to her elbows, the basha led the way, hacking out a path for the others. With every flash of the blade, Priya saw the claw-like scars on her forearm and the scar where the little finger of her right hand should have been.

'I've missed this so much,' cried Kwasi, swinging himself higher and sending more leaves swirling down onto the head of a grumpy Letitia.

Deeva, the new Suryan spirit-speaker on Reza's team, looked up with a smile. She was the only one with a pistol at her waist. It was a weapon rarely employed at Kuwatta, although the colonists used them all the time.

'Wow,' Priya said to Jupta. Kwasi had disappeared somewhere above them, but his cries of delight were still clearly audible. 'He wasn't lying when he said he was at home in the trees.'

'I'll admit it.' Jupta nodded. 'Outside of Kuwatta, he'd make a pretty good scout. Albeit an eccentric one.'

Reza – or the general – had decided to take his team on an expedition. His spirit-speaker and Mawar had been replaced by Deeva and Novan. Like Priya – and Mawar before her – the second-year student was a deed-speaker. He also fought with them at the Keep now, as could be seen by the haunted look in his eyes. His smile had weakened to a watery, thin version of his previously warm grin. To Priya, his presence felt like the major's latest cunning plan. He was, after all, another of her confidants. It seemed she didn't think it was enough just to send Priya; she needed someone else to report back to her. Was Novan there to keep an eye on Reza or on Priya?

'Stop!' Deeva held up one hand and stepped over a rock and some plants. Pushing aside the leaves of a young banana plant, she leaned forward.

Reza hurried over to her. 'Kwasi!' he called up before coming to a stop in front of Deeva.

'Yes, boss?' came a voice from among the trees.

'Down here!'

Deeva was holding something between her thumb and forefinger. Priya knew before she even saw it that it was a human tooth. In the spot where it had been found, there was a small puddle of grey slime.

'The sun hasn't set yet,' said Jupta, peering up to where patches of blue sky could be seen between branches and leaves. 'So it's still too hot for the rabido. It'll be hiding in a cool place somewhere.'

Kwasi crouched between them. 'It won't be long before the sun goes down,' he said. Twigs and leaves were sticking out of his black curls. 'Present, boss!' he added to Reza.

Priya didn't entirely trust Reza, and she didn't like him either. But unlike Priya, Kwasi and Jupta had reacted fairly mildly when she'd told them about the test and the punishment they'd been subjected to. Kwasi thought they could hardly blame Reza for following his father's orders. He understood that Kuwatta had to be defended, which meant sacrifices had to be made. He didn't agree with Priya's thinking – that Reza had also played a part in his father's cunning test, or at least he didn't think it really mattered. Jupta had just shrugged and wearily closed her eyes during their discussion.

Reza stopped and ran his hand through the loose mounds of earth around the slime. 'Dig this up,' he said. 'I want to know what's beneath.'

+++

Among the dense trees, it seemed almost as if night had fallen as the stiff, hunched figure of the rabido was pulled from the ground. Dark sand clung to the female's grey, sickly skin, and its eyes were closed. Only the mouth was a little open, revealing black gums and rotting teeth in the dim twilight.

'All the sainted saints,' muttered Kwasi.

'Put it down over there,' Reza said, pointing at a small clearing, and Letitia and Novan followed his instructions.

'It's still alive,' Jupta said, kneeling down beside the rabido. 'Only it seems to be . . .'

'. . . asleep,' Deeva said, completing her sentence. 'It's in some kind of dormant state.'

'I bet it'll wake up as soon as the sun goes down,' said Priya. 'Can you sense any more sleeping rabidos nearby?'

'Let me see.' Deeva closed her eyes. 'No, I can't feel anything, but that's not saying much. Even to me, the soul seems really weak.'

Priya couldn't feel anything at all. If Jupta and Deeva hadn't both said the rabido was alive, she would have assumed it was a corpse.

'I can feel a group of souls closer to the coast though.' Jupta got back to her feet. 'Living people is my guess. They're quite far off.'

Deeva nodded. 'Yes. I can feel the same.'

'How many souls?' Reza asked.

Jupta frowned. 'About twenty?'

'Eighteen,' Deeva said, correcting her with a smile. 'Not bad.'

Jupta proudly responded to her smile.

'Letitia, tie it up,' said Reza, nodding at the rabido. 'Make sure it can't get away when the sun goes down. We'll take it back to Kuwatta tomorrow.'

'You don't want to kill it?' the basha asked in surprise.

'It's the clothes,' Priya replied before Reza could speak. 'The rabido's not wearing a Kuwatta uniform. That's odd.'

Reza looked at Priya over Jupta's head. 'Exactly,' he said after a brief silence, and Priya felt the reluctance rolling off him. She gave him her sweetest smile. 'Novan,' Reza said more slowly, looking away from her. 'Make up a fire.'

Priya strode away before Reza could also give her an order that she'd reluctantly have to follow. They were setting up camp, so she could make herself useful looking for food and preparing a place to sleep. She didn't need to be given any orders for that.

As she was picking some cherries, balancing on tiptoe on a fallen tree, she noticed his presence. In the dim light – the rainforest was dark even on the sunniest of days – he was not visible. He didn't need to be. She felt the warmth of his energy, reacting to it almost instinctively. Automatically, she turned towards him. But then she slipped.

Cursing in Suryan, she tried to regain her balance.

Reza emerged from among the trees, holding out a hand to her.

She swatted him away. Her treacherous body wanted to accept his help, but she couldn't. She mustn't give in to his help, give in to *him*. Since she'd forced him onto one knee during the fight and their souls had merged for a moment, she was intensely aware of Reza. As if part of her had remained with him.

She jumped down from the tree, further away from him. 'Don't touch me.'

His eyes became a little darker, and he let out a brief, incredulous laugh. 'You don't have to make it any clearer, Chkadhari. The feeling is entirely mutual, by the way.'

'What exactly? Disgust? Loathing? Do you have any idea how much I hate you? Because of you, Mawar died before my eyes.' She was lying. That wasn't all she felt for him, but she forced herself to concentrate on the emotion she could control. On everything that should make him a terrible human being. On his brokenness, no matter how much it resembled her own. She wanted to hate him. She wanted to hate him so much that it hurt.

And yet.

He tried to conceal his irritation, but she felt slivers of it in his soul. And there was something else. Regret, maybe. Grief. Bursts that were as fleeting as the air, and yet so real. 'She'd been on my team for some time before you joined, Chkadhari. She should have been able to handle it.'

'But had she ever been to the first ring before? Had she ever fought so many rabidos at once?' Her heart was pounding so wildly that he must be able to hear it. It was the only sound that hung between them.

Reza said nothing.

'I thought as much,' she said scornfully. 'You didn't speak up against the general, did you? I know soldiers are needed to keep the rabidos captive, but to sacrifice those same soldiers for a demonstration . . .' She shook her head. 'Are people's lives really worth so little to you?'

He took a step towards her. His presence made her skin tingle. 'Do you think you and your friends are the only ones whose lives are constantly at stake? That you're the only one at Kuwatta who's being sharpened into a weapon to be used in the war – whichever war that might be?' His voice was dangerously quiet, even calm, although his soul was not. He was a master at controlling his emotions as far as the outside world could see, but he couldn't hide his soul from her anymore. Even his shield, normally so impenetrable, didn't keep her out now. His defences had been broken down, so she felt the sincerity of his words.

That made her bite back the poisonous words on the tip of her tongue. All she could do was stare at him.

Reza broke their eye contact by shaking his head. 'You might be the wonder of Kuwatta right now, Chkadhari, but that's what I've been all my life,' he said. 'You have no idea what kind of sacrifices I've had to make.'

The words lingered between them, becoming almost tangible. Priya looked at his eyes and saw more than his usual steely gaze. The pain she felt in his soul was visible there, and in the frown lines on his forehead, the downturned corners of his mouth. She thought back to the moment when their souls had connected. To the loneliness she'd felt in him, the anguish, the jealousy.

Reza tore his gaze away and made to walk off, but she stopped him, her hand on his shoulder. 'Is that how you lost your hand?'

Silence. She registered his hesitation. For a moment, she thought he was just going to leave, but he turned round, his fingers on the spot where his other hand had once been.

'You were ten years old,' Priya continued. She noticed that her voice was trembling. 'Did he send you to the tunnels at that age?'

He studied her face, as if he might find some answers there.

'Yes,' he replied eventually. 'I was under the command of my oldest brother. He was the captain of the team we entered the tunnels with.' His face was half in shadows and his voice was neutral, but she felt his emotion. 'He was going to protect me as we went deeper and deeper into the Keep, in search of the Dedekedre. We found her, but I didn't defeat her.'

He hadn't succeeded, but now they had her: Priya.

The parallels between herself and Reza were not lost on Priya. Both of them had been used by powerful people, although his exceptional strength had been discovered sooner, as he had grown up there. Since she'd arrived at Kuwatta, she'd heard many stories about his combat skills and his gift. He was Kuwatta's best soldier, the general's sharpened weapon. Just as Priya was the major's new plaything, the soul-singer the major could use to openly challenge the general, because Priya was the first to match Reza's strength. The first to bring balance.

'Where's your oldest brother now?' she asked quietly.

'I assume he's wandering around somewhere in the tunnels of the Keep,' he said, without a trace of emotion.

'I don't understand, Reza.' Priya stepped forward to get a better look at his face. 'Why do you follow all the general's orders, when . . .'

'What you're hinting at is treason, soldier,' he interrupted her. 'My father is pragmatic, not cruel. You don't know what you're talking about.'

Priya's anger surfaced again. Was he really trying to justify it? She'd had enough. 'I do know what I'm talking about, as you're well aware. And you know that I'm working for the major. That's why you've been told to keep an eye on me, isn't it?'

Reza sniffed. 'My sister has no idea what she's doing.' He roughly ran a hand through his hair. 'She thinks she's the saviour of Kuwatta, rallying all the soldiers to her cause. The general doesn't make rash decisions. The answer isn't as simple as she thinks, or he'd have chosen that route himself.'

Priya grabbed his hand and pulled him towards her. 'What else do you know?' she asked, searching every part of his face for the truth.

'I know that she sows division. Which could mean the downfall of Kuwatta.' Reza looked down at her, his eyes impossibly dark. 'I know that you . . . Gods, get out of my head!'

He sounded tormented. Priya was about to let go of his hand, but at that moment his fingers curled around hers. They were warm and rough, covered in calluses. She couldn't back away; she was trapped in his soul. There was no tingling or warning of a strange presence. But she could feel him as if there were no barriers between them. As if he were completely opening up to her, even though that couldn't possibly be true. He hated this just as much as she did. She couldn't escape from him, and he couldn't escape from her. They were each other's prisoners.

'Get out of my head.' His voice was powerful, but his soul said something else. Priya could feel his conflict – a slight contempt, but also something that seemed like anticipation . . . and desire. Something that felt so special that her whole body began to tingle.

The air between them was charged. His body was at a distance that could be bridged in a split second.

'This is your fault,' she hissed with all the resistance she could muster. She didn't like him, and yet she wanted him with every fibre in her body. It wasn't fair. It made no sense. It couldn't be real. 'You're manipulating my emotions, so that I . . .'

'So that you what?' His gaze descended, lingering on her lips. His eyes seemed a little darker than usual. 'I'm not doing anything.'

'Liar.'

He tore his gaze away from her and stumbled backwards. The crackling charge disappeared. The forest seemed darker than ever.

Priya tried to get her heart under control. She took a few slow steps back, her fingers to her chest. 'Stay away from me,' she whispered to him.

She was talking to the shadows and trees. He was gone.

34

PRIYA WAS STARTLED AWAKE by the snapping of a twig. Kuwatta had taught her to sleep light.

She sprang to her feet, her hand moving to the sword beside her. Kwasi was not far away, and he rolled over. His dark eyes glistened in the night; he was wide awake too. He took one look at Priya, pushed himself up and grabbed his spear.

'What did you hear?'

Priya pressed her forefinger to her lips and crept forward in a crouch, towards the sound. Deeva, who was on guard, had left her post. Reza wasn't there either. A nervous twitch ran through her belly. The shadows of trees and plants danced in the moonlight that shone through the branches. None of the shadows belonged to humans. The only sound she heard came from the buzzing and chirping insects, interspersed with the soft snores of the sleeping soldiers.

Kwasi had set off in a different direction. She could just about make out his silhouette among the plants. She saw him crouching near the rabido, which was tied to a tree. Letitia had made a gag and tied it in and around the monster's mouth, so that the screams were muffled. Nothing could stop its writhing, though, not even tying up its hands, feet and torso.

When Kwasi remained in the same spot for a while, Priya walked over to him, keeping a close eye on the surroundings.

She leaned in towards him. 'Found something?'

'Yes.' He raised his hand. In the centre of his palm, surrounded by slime and earth, there were three teeth. 'What do you think? Reckon they belong to our friend?'

An ice-cold feeling made its way through Priya's body. This wasn't from the tied-up rabido, and Kwasi knew that too. The slime hadn't been there earlier. 'We have to tell Reza,' she said.

A white shadow appeared among the trees. Priya grasped Kwasi's shoulder, her grip a little too tight. He looked at her questioningly, and then followed her gaze. His eyes grew wider. Something wasn't right. Rabidos were many things, but not silent. Whatever they did, they did it with lots of screaming and grunting. Priya scanned the surroundings, extending her gift further than she was used to, and felt the souls of several unfamiliar people around them. With the exception of two, they were some distance away, but it wouldn't take them long to reach them. They were clearly heading their way.

'We have to get back to the others,' she said, pulling Kwasi to his feet. 'Now.'

'Yes, I, yes . . . Exactly.' Kwasi ran with her, holding his spear in his free hand. Priya tightened her grip on the hilt of her sword while keeping a sharp eye on the surroundings. She placed her feet carefully, so as to make as little noise as possible.

Enemy soldiers and rabidos being found close together? That was bad news. Even if the rabidos devoured their enemies – as a small part of her hoped they would – that just left them with a larger group of rabidos that would have to be killed before they attacked the nearest villages.

As soon as they got back to their camp, Priya and Kwasi shook the sleeping soldiers. 'Wake up!'

Novan jumped to his feet, looking wildly around. 'What's up? What have we found?'

'The right question is: what's found *us*?' Priya said over her shoulder.

Jupta sleepily sat up. Her dark eyes, gleaming in the moonlight, immediately widened, and Priya helped her to her feet. 'It's the group

I mentioned earlier,' she said, giving Priya's hand a quick squeeze. 'And judging by their souls, they're not coming to talk.'

With her back to the rest of the team, who were now fully awake and standing up, Priya scanned the surroundings.

Something wet touched her neck. When she looked back, she saw that the water panther had come up behind her and was nuzzling her. Kohóna looked at her drowsily, and Priya felt the urge to reach out and stroke her. Instead, she gazed ahead again.

To their left was the edge of a swamp, and the ground where they were standing was soggy in places. The wind rose, rippling the water between the dark grass. The reflection of the white moon, partially visible between the leaves, became blurred. Shadows moved among the trees. Priya's knuckles turned white around her sword. She cautiously stepped forward a little. Not too much, but enough. The shadows grew bigger, detaching themselves from the trees and coming closer. Priya felt the hostility radiating from their souls, but also, surprisingly, a certain curiosity.

'Retreat.' Reza stepped out of the darkness, running towards them. 'Back to back. Kohóna, out of sight.'

Kohóna growled quietly, leaping into the darkness.

The first shadow stepped out of the trees, becoming visible in the moonlight. The figure wore white trousers and a dark jacket, the precise colour of which was hard to make out in the night. In his hand was a long outline: a musket with a bayonet. Back in Disin, Priya had heard of rebels who had broken away from the general and Kuwatta and used the weapons of the colonists. Groups of people who didn't agree with how the general was approaching the fight.

Then the soldier's face emerged from the darkness, and Priya was gripped by a cold fear. They were barely a day's journey from Kuwatta, deep in the rainforest and far from the coast of Awaran. To get here, the soldiers would have had to go past a number of warrior villages. It shouldn't be possible, and yet her eyes were not deceiving her.

It was a white man.

A Freelander.

'Well, well,' said the man. He had a long face and a full beard, which looked dark brown now, but was probably paler in the sunlight. His thin lips curled into a smile, making the white of his teeth stand out against his suntanned – or burned, it was hard to say – face. 'What do we have here? Ah, a bunch of coloured folk, all together.'

Even without the lessons of Scholar Afounsowa, who insisted that they learned to read and speak various languages, so that they could decipher historical documents, Priya would most likely still have understood most of what he said. Awuran had a lot of loanwords from Freeland, almost as many as it had from Middle Luan.

Behind the man were two other soldiers from Freeland, half shrouded in shadows and with one hand on their swords. On their backs, Priya could make out the silhouettes of other, larger weapons – muskets, she guessed. The rest of their team stood further back, invisible among the trees.

'A pleasure to meet you. The name is Colonel Johan van Huyzen.' The man spread his hands, as if to show that he had no bad intentions. The gesture was in stark contrast to his soul, which was made up entirely of cold and sharp edges. 'And which one is your leader?'

Priya felt Reza's soul swell, almost crackling with energy. He was extremely tense. 'That would be me,' he said in unaccented Freeland.

'And what should I call you?'

'Kapten,' Reza replied.

'Excellent!' Johan stepped further into the clearing. The rest of his group remained silent, as did Reza's soldiers, and the chirping of crickets and the croaking of frogs filled the air. But then Priya heard the rabido. She couldn't see it from here, but its muffled screams and wild writhing were clearly audible.

'I'll be brief, gentlemen. And ladies,' added the colonel after a glance around their group.

Only four other Freeland soldiers had stepped forward. The other members of the party, whose souls she could feel, were still hiding among the shadows of the plants and trees.

'I'm looking for Kuwatta, Kapten,' said Colonel Johan with a cheerful smile. 'Could you tell me the fastest route? According to the charming residents of the village a day's journey from here, I should be on the right track.'

This time, all the souls in Priya's team flared brightly. Priya felt Jupta's agitation, Kwasi's panic, Letitia's alertness. A day's journey from here there were only a few small farming and fishing villages. Priya couldn't recall their names, but they certainly weren't the large warrior villages – there were hardly any of those deep in the rainforest. A team of – she reached out with her gift again – *ten* colonists had broken through their lines of defence and had already passed through ordinary civilian villages – that was serious.

A ripple ran through Reza's soul: was it annoyance, anger? It happened too quickly for Priya. 'I'm sorry,' he said in the same neutral tone as before. 'I can't help you with that.'

Johan's smile disappeared. 'Then can you tell me why you're dressed in a uniform, coloured man?'

A scream from the rabido rang out. The gag must have come loose. Colonel Johan looked around. 'What was that?' he barked. 'It sounded like a . . .' His voice died away, and his head slowly turned forward again. He studied Reza for a moment. 'How is that possible? That was a zom, wasn't it?' The colonel sounded astonished.

He'd called it a 'zom', but he clearly meant the rabido. So, the Freelanders were aware of their existence. Priya's head was spinning. She sought for possibilities, for explanations for this impossible situation. Only the Dedekedre made rabidos. That was right, wasn't it? They were not creatures of nature, like water panthers, primeval monsters or even, in a way, vengeful spirits. Their team's mission proved that the general didn't take it lightly when a rabido was wandering around outside the fortress. This was a life-threatening situation. If this colonel knew about rabidos, did he also know about the Dedekedre?

Reza smiled, his lips closed. 'Why are you looking for Kuwatta, Colonel?'

'The governor of the Republic of Awaran has some business to discuss with Kuwatta. That's why,' said Colonel Johan, something dark creeping into his voice. 'I speak on his behalf.'

Priya noticed that the colonel was speaking for 'the Republic of Awaran'. The Freelanders considered themselves the rightful owners of the entire country.

'Couldn't he send a letter?' asked Priya. Reza's gift briefly stroked Priya's soul, and she shivered involuntarily. She had to stop herself from reaching out to him. Was that a warning? What was he trying to say?

Colonel Johan's attention moved to Priya. 'Excuse me?'

'The governor could have sent someone to deliver a message to one of the warrior villages. They would have made sure that the message reached the general in Kuwatta.' Priya waited for Reza to interrupt her, but he didn't. Like the others, he looked at her in silence, his face unreadable. 'Isn't that what you're here for?'

'The general?' The colonel laughed. It sounded hollow and full of hate. 'Is that what he calls himself? No, girl, we don't send nice letters to the rabble out here in the jungle.'

Priya was amazed that, after all those years, she could still sense, in this colonel, the plantation owner that her parents had once worked for. Even the general in Kuwatta, clearly a born leader, didn't possess the self-confidence that all white men seemed to swan around with. It wasn't so much arrogance, more a deep conviction of their own superiority.

'So, you're here to kill everyone at Kuwatta?' The words came rolling out of her mouth before she could stop them. Although she wasn't sure she even wanted to. 'With twelve men?'

Actually, no. If they were planning to take Kuwatta with twelve men, then it was indeed arrogance.

'How do you know how many . . .' Colonel Johan fell silent. He beckoned to his soldiers in the shadows and strode towards Priya. She tightened her grip on the hilt of her sword, and she felt Reza coming to stand beside her.

Colonel Johan came to a stop in front of her. The last hint of friendliness had gone from his face. He looked her up and down. 'Well, well,' he said, and Priya felt goosebumps rise on her arms. 'Is this a *blood* child? Have you sunk so low that you'd allow such filthy monsters into your midst?'

Priya blinked, overwhelmed for a moment by the primitive hatred – and flashes of fear – in his voice. As a result, she realised a moment too late that he was moving. His bayonet gleamed in a thin strip of moonlight. Before he could strike, Reza held a dagger to his neck.

'You will not touch her,' he said to the colonel in a dangerously calm voice. Reza's energy washed towards Priya, warming her like a blanket. 'Not with your bullets, not with your knife and most certainly not with your hands. You understand?'

Priya, now over the initial shock, considered forcing the colonist to stop breathing. A brief command, so she could watch him struggle. She couldn't believe she'd given him an opening. Just because he'd uttered a few condescending words. She should be used to hearing that sort of thing by now. And Reza, of all people, had come to her aid. As if it couldn't get any worse.

The colonel flashed him an unpleasant, vicious grin, which matched the hostility in his soul, and raised his hand.

'Down!' screamed Letitia.

They all dived to the ground.

The first gunshot sent the animals in the vicinity fleeing. Priya felt their souls darting off in all directions. The bang hurt her eardrums. The next shot came soon after. This one was closer. She heard a whistling sound. A bullet flashed past Priya, narrowly missing her as she dived out of the way. It left a white-hot trail by her ear.

Priya landed on her side, pressing back her sword so the blade didn't touch Reza. He fell in front of her and immediately pushed himself up onto one arm. Low enough that he wouldn't show above the undergrowth they'd ended up in, high enough to look at her.

'Wait for my signal,' he said. A breath later, he'd disappeared among the trees.

Priya moved forward a little and looked out across the clearing, where several people were standing. Most were wearing white trousers and holding muskets. Colonists. She couldn't see Reza anywhere. One of the soldiers was looking at her. With quick movements, she slipped backwards into the undergrowth. She had to get away. Right now. She crawled over sand and plants as more gunshots made her heart pound and her ears ring. Panting, she crept across the ground until she found shelter behind a hollow tree.

Disoriented, she looked around. She saw something moving among the nearby bushes, but she didn't know if it was a friend or an enemy. First she needed to calm down, so that she could feel its soul. She slid her sword into the straps on her back.

There was Kwasi. And Jupta. Reza . . . Where was Reza?

Another gunshot. Followed by an 'Oof'. Someone fell to the ground nearby.

Priya saw Deeva lying there. The soldier's hands went to her stomach, where a patch of blood was blooming like a flower. Priya saw that she was pressing her lips tightly together, trying with all her might not to cry out and give away her position.

Priya peered between the plants. Then she drew her dagger, put it between her teeth and crept low across the ground until she reached Deeva. She dragged her fellow soldier deeper into the bushes so that they were sheltered and cut a strip from her trouser leg to stem the flow of the blood.

'No,' whispered Deeva. 'I've got this. I'm fine.' But she wasn't. When Priya looked at the wound, her spirits sank. The bullet had ripped through Deeva's body just under her ribcage. Judging by the dark colour of the blood that was streaming from the wound, she'd been hit in the liver. Priya knew from her healing sciences lessons that she couldn't solve this. Deeva required immediate treatment from healers.

'Let me do this,' Priya said. With trembling fingers, she continued to bandage the wound. 'When this fight's over, then . . .'

Deeva smiled. The colour was draining from her face as Priya watched. They both knew she wasn't going to make it. 'I can feel twelve of them.' Deeva groaned and pressed her fingers, which had turned blue, to her head. 'You have to . . . break their souls.'

She was dying, and all Priya knew about her was her name and what her gift was. 'Where do you come from?' she asked, as more shots were fired above their heads. The clashing of swords grew louder, and she leaned in closer to Deeva. 'Where in Suryan?'

Reza pushed against her with his gift. Was that his signal?

Deeva smiled weakly and closed her eyes. A thin layer of sweat gleamed on her deathly pale face. 'Don't speak, sister . . .'

Sister. 'Yes,' said Priya, gripping her hand. 'We are sisters.'

'I wanted to get out of here,' the Suryan soldier struggled to say. 'As soon as I could. I wanted to go back to . . . Suryan . . . where we belong.'

Her words echoed the words Priya had often heard from her mother's mouth: longing for the distant land that they came from, where they were seen as equals. Where they weren't in constant conflict with people who looked down on them or thought they didn't deserve a place in their country.

What would that feel like?

Priya had never heard a bad word about her country of origin. From what her mother said, Suryan was a paradise they'd been torn away from by a bad decision and a whole lot of lies.

'And you will return,' said Priya, squeezing Deeva's hand. In the background, she heard shouting and footsteps. Reaching out for any souls she didn't recognise, she grabbed the nearest two. 'You will return,' she whispered to the soldier, while at the same time, with a fierce burst of energy, making the two enemy soldiers slit each other's throats. It was a lot easier now that all her fury was focused on them. She barely even noticed the headache.

Deeva's gaze emptied. Priya gulped, closed her eyes and let go of her hand. She crawled low across the ground to another tree and drew her sword. Kwasi, Jupta and Letitia were fighting side by side against five colonists. Partly with their gifts, partly with their weapons. Somewhere nearby, Priya could feel four more enemy souls. Somewhere among them was Reza.

Swiftly, she ran through the undergrowth, adrenaline racing through her body. The souls of the six colonists were surprisingly docile – they clearly had no experience with soul-singers – and she had no difficulty gaining control of them.

She raised her sword.

'Wait!' shouted Reza as she emerged from the bushes. He was standing, arms raised, among the soldiers. One of them was bleeding from three different wounds and looked as if he was going to collapse at any moment. Another had lost a hand but wasn't doing anything to stop the gushing blood. The rest stared ahead with glassy eyes and dreamy smiles.

Priya tried to slow down, but she had too much momentum. She could have thrown her sword aside, but she didn't want to. A moment later, she'd run through one of the colonists with her sword. His flesh yielded more easily than she'd imagined. More easily than a rabido's.

She didn't know if she liked that thought or not.

35

HE SLOWLY SLUMPED TO one side. Priya didn't let go of her sword and back away until he hit the ground. Her revulsion for the man merged with her own self-disgust.

'Step back, Chkadhari.' Reza was clearly still using his gift on the Freelander at Priya's feet. The man groaned quietly but didn't move.

Priya stared at her hands and then at the bloodstain on the left side of his chest, which was growing larger and larger. A thin layer of sweat had formed on his white skin. His eyes rolled back in his head. She had done that. Her sword had hit him somewhere between the ribs and sunk halfway into his chest. It was only Reza's influence that made him look peaceful as he drowned in his own blood.

'Priya!' Reza was talking to her with more urgency now. 'Get back!'

She leaned forward and pulled her sword free. It came out with an unpleasant sucking sound – most likely his lung filling with blood. The man started jerking and Priya was transfixed, unable to look away. She stepped back, trying to keep breathing calmly. This was fine. She'd killed rabidos. This wasn't so different.

Almost stepping on a body right behind her, she quickly stepped aside. It was Novan. His dark eyes were staring into nothingness. Her gaze moved downwards – his neck had been destroyed by a gunshot and his stomach ripped open by a stab wound. Priya felt sick again. And furious. She kneeled beside Novan to close his eyes. Then she shook her head and tried to pull herself together.

No matter where the colonists went in Awaran, they always had to use force. They had taken the coast of Awaran by force, taken the free peoples of other lands by force and made them work for them by force. As far as Priya knew, they had never reached out to any people of colour or seen them as legitimate, equal human beings. The colonists always had to be the ones who had the power.

Stepping backwards, she came to Reza, who was keeping the last surviving colonists under control, including Colonel Johan. There were three large scratches on Reza's right cheek but otherwise, to her relief, he looked unscathed. Letitia, along with Jupta and Kwasi, stepped out from among the trees, and Jupta tied the colonel's hands together.

Priya counted the nearby souls. Other than the four soldiers that Reza was restraining, she couldn't feel any living colonists left. Most of the surviving colonists were also dying, thanks in part to her. The fight was over, she concluded. They were surrounded by corpses. But still she couldn't relax. Her senses were on edge.

'Stay close,' said Reza tensely. 'Something else is coming.'

Letitia, Kwasi and Jupta stepped forward. Priya took a small step back, so that she was closer to them. They stood in a circle, with their backs to each other.

With her free hand, Priya pulled out the long knife that was strapped to her thigh. The rainforest filled with an orchestra of animal sounds again: monkeys, birds and insects.

'Deeva didn't make it,' she said with a dry mouth to Reza, although he must have already felt the loss of Deeva's soul.

Reza nodded. She felt him moving. 'Here.' He held out a gold ring to her. 'Put this on.'

'I . . .' she began.

'Show us what kind of wonder you are, Chkadhari.'

She took the ring and pushed it over her middle finger, which it was still a little too big for. As soon as the gold came into contact with her skin, a bolt of energy shot through her and the tension in her shoulders eased, along with her nagging headache. Reza's soul beside her seemed to become even brighter and more vivid.

A jagged, chaotic energy was coming closer. Shrieks echoed among the trees. The rabidos. It was a miracle they hadn't attacked their group sooner. Priya saw Colonel Johan's eyes bulge. His face was drooping, he was still under Reza's control, but his eyes darted back and forth. Priya had no doubt that Reza had deliberately freed part of his soul, so that the man couldn't react but was still aware of what was going on around him.

'I took out three of them,' said Reza, twisting the wrist of his prosthesis and giving it a quick shake. 'The rest fled as soon as the colonists got here. Kohóna's hunting them down.'

'How many of them are left?' She quickly reached out with her gift. 'Five?'

He glanced at her. 'Six.'

Priya rolled her eyes.

Letitia cursed in Luan. 'The filthy beasts. They really are everywhere.'

'I thought there were just one or two,' said Kwasi miserably. 'How can they have spread so quickly?'

Priya hoped that the one escaped rabido had simply come across a small group of traders in a deserted part of the rainforest. Six rabidos on the loose were a problem. An infected village was a disaster that could turn into a nationwide plague – and that was the last thing Kuwatta needed.

'Spirit-speaker,' said Reza, as if he was thinking the same. 'Are they the only rabidos you can sense?'

It took a moment for Jupta to realise he was talking to her and not to Deeva. 'Yes, Kapten,' she hurried to say. 'I don't feel any others.' Then her breathing faltered. 'But I do feel a primeval monster. Medium-sized. Slowly heading towards us.'

Letitia clicked her tongue. 'It was a question of time. We have to get out of here before it reaches us. We wouldn't survive that encounter.'

'Can't we just leave the rabidos to the monster?' Kwasi suggested hopefully.

'No,' replied Reza.

Kwasi sighed, shoulders slumping.

And then the first of the rabidos came from the trees, a white shadow running in the darkness. Priya braced herself. Their bleeding mouths and shrieks were no longer new to her. She wasn't alone, and she had a gift that could bring everyone nearby to their knees. In addition, Reza's training had prepared her better.

She could do this.

'Jump,' said Priya. She didn't use too much of her gift. By now, she knew from experience that this more subtle approach worked better on rabidos. Particularly when it was just one of them. It was hard to get a grip on their souls, because of the state they were in. They offered no controlled resistance, so a nudge in the right direction was more effective than a forceful command. And easier. Then she didn't need to worry about using too much and losing control.

However, the gold on her finger, which strengthened her gift, caused her to miscalculate. Her command reached further than she intended, brushing her teammates' souls. To her relief, they were able to ignore it.

The rabido jumped.

Priya met it halfway down, slitting its throat with her knife. As it fell, three other rabidos emerged behind its back. Reza moved past Priya. With his slender sword, he slashed through a rabido's throat. Then pierced another's neck with his prosthesis. Without a struggle, they fell to the ground.

'Show-off,' muttered Priya. Next to Reza, his soul close to hers, it seemed at times as if their souls were merging again, which was still an unreal feeling. Their training sessions and combat lessons, when she'd always been so focused on Reza, had taught her how he moved when he was fighting. She knew his footwork and style of attack inside out.

That made them a better team than either of them would have liked to admit.

She pulled a dagger from her boot and threw it straight at the last rabido's head. The knife slid into its eye socket.

+++

When the sun came up and they knew they had escaped the primeval monster, they returned to the clearing and, in silence, buried Novan and Deeva. None of them could manage to say much, but Kwasi mumbled something that sounded like a prayer. They threw the bodies of the colonists in a heap. Letitia sniffed and said she'd gladly watch them rot, but ultimately she was one of the first to start digging a large grave. It helped that they were near a swamp, which made the ground easier to dig. After half a day, they went on their way with a stiff rabido in a sack and a furious Colonel Johan van Huyzen. Both of them would be further inspected and, in the colonel's case, interrogated by the general.

Without pausing, they marched back to Kuwatta over the course of the morning and afternoon, reaching the fort as evening fell – which made Priya both relieved and anxious. The colonists were practically breathing down their necks. Kuwatta didn't have enough time or resources to fight two battles at once.

It was enough of a problem that rabidos were moving through the rainforest. The rest of Awaran was clearly not as safe from the monsters as the general had thought or claimed.

'Halt.' Reza held up one hand and their little group came to a stop. They were at the edge of the river, just hidden behind a row of trees and bushes.

Letitia grabbed the colonel, who had a sack over his head, by the back of his jacket and gave it a tug, so that he fell over backwards with a yelp. 'Behold Kuwatta, Colonel.' She pulled the sack off his head, giving him a clear view of the fort.

'I'll check the surroundings,' she said to Reza. Walking past Kohóna, who was washing her front paws, she disappeared into the forest.

Colonel Johan let out another cry when he saw Kohóna. 'What . . . What *is* that?'

'My water panther,' Reza drawled in Freeland. 'Would you like an introduction?'

'No!' Then he spat a few more words in their direction. Priya guessed they weren't anything pleasant.

Puffing and panting, Kwasi heaved on the rope tied to the sack with the rabido inside, adjusting it on his shoulder. 'I don't know how much flesh this one's eaten, but I suggest we put her on rations.'

Kohóna stretched slowly and came to stand beside Kwasi, sniffing at the sack on his back. Kwasi jumped. 'Oh, Kohóna. Hello.'

Jupta crouched down, rummaging through the colonist's belongings. They'd taken his musket, bayonet and other weapons from him, along with his bags. Priya saw a half-full knapsack, a pile of clothing and some food.

'What's this?' Jupta said, prodding something white.

'Bread,' said Priya. 'Mouldy bread, to be precise.'

Jupta tossed it over her shoulder, pulling a face, and went on searching his bags. She dug out a few useful tools and small daggers, which she attached to her own uniform. She threw the rest aside. 'What a load of junk,' Priya heard her say. The colonel had stopped screaming by now and was studying them with his glassy blue eyes. Again, she remembered the cruel white boss who'd ruled the plantation where she'd lived as a little girl. The man who had murdered her father. But in her memories, the features of both her father and the colonist had always been vague and changeable. Now that a white man was lying in front of her, she couldn't take her eyes off him. He was tanned by the sun, but still clearly white. In some places, there were patches of red, where his skin was burned.

One thing was certain: he was going to stand out at the fort.

'Boss!' Kohóna had pressed her face to the back of Kwasi's neck, and he was standing perfectly still. His wide eyes were screaming for help. Priya heard the water panther make a rumbling sound. Kohóna was purring.

Reza looked up, disturbed, but the sharpness left his eyes as soon as he saw Kohóna. 'She likes you,' he said, amused.

Just then, Kohóna nuzzled Kwasi's shoulder. But her head was about half the size of his body, so he stumbled and almost went tumbling into the river.

'Didn't see anyone. We can use the korjaal to get to the Keep,' said Letitia, coming towards them. 'Or head along the bank and onto the bridge. But that means the cadets and probies will see us.'

Reza nodded. 'We'll take the korjaal.'

36

AS SOON AS THEIR korjaal slid up onto the deck, Reza grabbed Colonel Johan by his collar and pulled him out of the boat. The Freelander barely struggled. His body had gone limp, as Priya had anticipated. He'd barely had anything to drink and refused to take any food from them.

'Where's the general?' Reza asked a soldier in a brown uniform. 'I need to speak to him at once.'

'Kapten! Um, I don't know . . .' The soldier looked back uneasily at another soldier in a green uniform who was approaching, clearly having heard them.

'The general's in a meeting with his advisors in the Great Hall, Kapten,' he said. 'He doesn't want to be disturbed, unless it's an emergency.'

'This *is* an emergency. Out of my way.' Reza dragged the limp colonel to the entrance of the Keep. No one tried to stop him. In fact, most of the soldiers stepped aside, and the guards at the entrance hurried to open the doors for him. One of them stared at the colonel's bound hands, his eyes widening.

'Letitia, come with me,' said Reza halfway down the large hall. 'The rest of you go to the Lodge. Stay there until you're called.'

Priya thought for a second that she'd heard him wrong. She took a few large strides until she was standing beside him. 'You're sending us away now?'

He kept walking. 'The general has ordered me to shield potential prisoners from the rest of Kuwatta until he has questioned them.'

His jaw was tense again, as often happened when his father was involved. He clearly didn't plan to say anything more. She knew he didn't have the authority to do so. Certainly not when others were around.

And yet she couldn't accept it. Because she knew what was going to happen. She and the rest of Reza's team might have caught an enemy, but they would never find out why the colonists were sniffing around. Just as no one understood why the general kept his gates shut to extra troops. Reza kept insisting that his father knew what he was doing and that protest, in whatever form, only created division. But for how long could people swallow orders without getting answers to their questions? Priya was beginning to see why the major no longer obeyed her father.

'We were witnesses,' said Priya. 'You can't send us away. We have a right to more information.'

'A right to information?' That made Reza stop in his tracks. He turned his head to look at her, narrowing his honey-coloured eyes. 'Do you hear yourself, Chkadhari? You are soldiers. Your obligation here is secrecy until the general makes his decision.'

Reza must know that she would tell the major. Not just because she wanted to, so that someone else would know about it besides the general and their team, but also because she had no choice. The major had threatened both Umed and Ishani for a reason. She was counting on Priya bringing her confidential information.

Priya really wanted to use her gift to force Reza to take her, but she knew that would only cause problems. He was looking at her as if he knew what she wanted. And maybe he did; she couldn't really hide her feelings from him anymore.

She couldn't change his mind. She knew that by now. But just the thought of having to wait for answers, when she didn't know if any would be forthcoming, was driving her crazy. She wanted to know how the colonists had almost made it as far as Kuwatta, but above all she wanted to know *why*. What did Colonel Johan want to say to the general of Kuwatta?

Kwasi gave an exaggerated cough. 'Nothing to see here,' he said as two soldiers walked by.

Priya ignored him and stepped closer to Reza. 'Did the general know that there were Freelanders near Kuwatta?' she asked.

Reza's energy became darker. She could feel his irritation. 'I think he suspected.'

She was surprised that he answered honestly. 'Did *you* know?' she continued.

A second passed. 'No. And that's enough questions,' he said, cutting her off. 'You've heard what the general wants.'

Gods, he could be so incredibly irritating with his blind obedience to the general. Did he ever think for himself?

'Step aside, soldier.' Letitia pushed her back with a look of warning. Then she walked away with Reza, while Priya remained behind with the others.

✦✦✦

The major was not in her room.

She wasn't in the Great Hall either. That was where Priya had run first, even though Kwasi and Jupta had yelled after her that it was the worst possible idea. Priya obviously wouldn't be admitted to the room, but she didn't need to be. She only wanted to know if Major Aïda was also present at the meeting. The soldier who was on guard told her that she was not. He could have been lying, but Priya didn't think that was likely. She cursed herself for making the wrong choice. She should have gone straight to the major's room. Reza or the general had probably made sure by now that the major was somewhere Priya wasn't allowed to go.

'If you see the major, then let her know that Priya is looking for her,' Priya said to the soldier who was standing guard in front of the major's quarters. Then she took a second look at him. 'Wait . . . Paneke?' she exclaimed.

'Priya.' Paneke gave her a little smile. 'So you're still here. We thought . . . Well, that's all history now.'

He was dressed in a green uniform. And he was standing in front of Major Aïda's quarters. 'Yes,' said Priya. And then she asked, 'How on earth did you end up in the Keep?'

Paneke rubbed the back of his head. 'After the three of you – Kwasi, Jupta and you – disappeared, everyone started to get uneasy. Mawar going . . .' Her name gave Priya a stab of pain. 'Most of us could just about accept that without asking too many questions. But when you three vanished too, we could tell that something was up. We tried to cross the white line one night.'

'We?'

'Kofi, Nanu and I.'

That meant only two soul-singers were being taught at the Academy now. It also meant that Paneke knew about the existence of the rabidos. Especially since he was still in the Keep when the sun could go down at any moment. 'Have you been summoned yet?'

Paneke shook his head. 'Nanu and Kofi have. But the major would rather keep me here.'

Priya had to give the major her due; she was good at intercepting and recruiting soul-singers. 'Do you know where the major has gone?'

'No idea. A soldier came with a message. And she left in a hurry.'

'Ah, here she is.' Kwasi had appeared at the top of the stairs and was looking back over his shoulder. 'Jup, you still there?'

'Why did you run off like that?' Jupta blurted as soon as she emerged from the stairs, out of breath.

'What are you two doing here?' Priya asked. 'Reza said we had to go to the Lodge.'

'Yeah. With the emphasis on "we".' Then Jupta noticed the soldier beside Priya. 'Paneke?' she exclaimed. 'What are *you* doing here?'

Priya took advantage of the moment to escape. Unfortunately that meant that she had to go past Jupta and Kwasi to get downstairs, but if she was quick, maybe she could slip away before they realised what was going on. She was pretty sure they'd come after her, but she could worry about that later. First she had to try to shake them off.

Priya didn't quite know what she was going to do, but she had a suspicion that she was about to break some more rules. And she didn't want Jupta and Kwasi to be involved.

She made it down three steps before she saw Kwasi standing in front of her. Caught off guard, she jumped aside, so she wouldn't go crashing into him. A moment later, she realised what he was doing and she threw him out of her soul. 'Are you serious?' she asked, looking back angrily.

'Look, it's not my fault if you don't protect yourself.' Kwasi shrugged and tried to look innocent. 'And stop running away from us all the time. It's starting to get annoying.'

'Right,' said Jupta. 'I agree with Kwasi.'

'Thanks, Jup.'

'You know I hate it when you call me that.' Jupta walked up to Priya and grabbed her arm. 'Now please tell us why you're running around the Keep like a crazy person. We know you often speak to the major and don't share everything with us. Don't look at me like that. We share a room. I notice things. Why do you want to be there when the general questions the colonel? What isn't he telling us? What aren't *you* telling us?' The stream of questions came out in one breath.

'I . . .' began Priya. 'You're not going to go to the Lodge if I ask nicely, are you?'

Kwasi spread his hands and smiled. 'That depends how . . .'

'No,' Jupta interrupted him. 'The truth. Now.'

37

'WHEN THEY'VE FINISHED QUESTIONING him, they'll need to put the colonel somewhere,' said Kwasi a little later. Priya had just finished telling her story. 'I bet they'll throw him in the dungeons.'

'The dungeons?' Priya couldn't remember the general or the major ever having put anyone in a cell during her time at the fortress. Neither could she remember them ever having publicly condemned anyone to death. But with a monster like the Dedekedre in your basement, you probably didn't have to. People disappeared so often in Kuwatta.

'I've studied the floorplans in the Lodge,' Kwasi said, rubbing his chin, as Jupta steered him into a narrow side corridor where they could talk without being disturbed. 'There are some small cells near the scholars' labs.'

'Why there?' Priya frowned. 'What are the scholars doing to prisoners?'

'That doesn't matter,' said Jupta impatiently. 'We have to decide now who we want to speak to – the colonist or the major.'

'The colonist,' Priya answered immediately. She could talk to the major later. But she guessed that wasn't true for Colonel Johan. 'Wait, who says you're coming along? I can't risk anyone finding out that you're missing.'

Jupta sighed. 'Stop making decisions for us.'

'And what's the worst they can do?' said Kwasi casually. He was smiling, but there was no sign of the warmth and the sparkle in his eyes that usually accompanied his smiles. 'Keep us here? They're already doing that. Make us fight the rabidos until we die? They're doing that too. Anyway, you need us. How else are you going to get past all those soldiers without being seen?'

'And find out exactly where Colonel Johan is being held?' Jupta added. 'If anyone can find him, it's me.'

Priya opened her mouth. Closed it again. They were right. Priya had no say here. This was their decision, and it was their own lives that they were risking.

And they were right – she needed them.

✦✦✦

Soon after that, they were standing in a corridor closer to the Great Hall, but far enough away not to be within range of Reza's gift. Or at least that was what Priya hoped.

With Jupta's help, they hadn't had much difficulty locating the colonel, Reza and the general. As Kwasi had predicted, they were at the cells near the scholars' laboratories, close to the Great Hall. The only problem was that if Jupta could feel *them*, that meant the general and Reza would be able to do the same if they had a spirit-speaker with them. Which they most likely did. It helped that Reza hadn't sent any soldiers looking for them yet.

'The major isn't in the Keep,' said Jupta. 'She must be somewhere outside the building, but I can't reach beyond the edges of the Academy and the Lodge.'

'Not a problem,' said Priya. 'That already tells us everything we need to know.'

Jupta nodded, still concentrating hard. 'Scholar Afounsowa is with the colonel, too.'

Priya slid down the wall, burying her hands in her hair. 'I have no idea how we're going to reach the cells without being seen.'

Kwasi patted her on the back. 'Who says you have to do that?'

She looked up incredulously. 'How else are we going to get to the colonel? It's not as if they're going to let us through. It wouldn't surprise me if Reza has stationed twenty soldiers to guard the Freelander,' she added.

'There are ten of them,' Jupta said helpfully.

'But those soldiers aren't you,' said Kwasi, pulling Priya to her feet. 'You can force all of them to step aside with your gift.'

'Not Reza.' Unless she threw all of her power at him, but even then she didn't know for sure that she'd win the fight.

'Then we'll make sure Reza and the general are out of the way.' Jupta blinked and looked ahead again. 'Who can get both of them to leave their post?'

'The major,' said Priya slowly. A plan was starting to form inside her head. 'If the major enters the Keep, I wouldn't be surprised if the general and Reza stop her personally. She already has too many soldiers in the army who obey her directly, so they can't be trusted. But we don't know where the major is.'

'Leave that to me.' Jupta smiled. 'She must be somewhere in the fort. I'll find her.'

+++

To make the plan work, they first had to head further downstairs, with the shrieks of the rabidos becoming louder. That would hopefully make the spirit-speaker who was with the general and Reza think that they were giving up.

'As soon as you feel Reza and the general heading down, run back upstairs,' said Jupta. She gave them quick hugs and continued on her way alone, towards the screaming rabidos. Priya waited anxiously, desperately hoping that Jupta knew what she was doing and didn't end up in the tunnels with the monsters.

'This probably wasn't what my parents had in mind when they sent me to Kuwatta,' said Kwasi, nervously drumming his fingers on the wall. He was no good at sitting – or standing – still. 'Oh well, they can't say I didn't warn them that this wasn't for me.'

Priya felt a tingle move down her spine but didn't bother putting up a shield, because she already knew it was Kwasi, even before she saw the spiders walking around his feet. 'Did you use your gift like that in the village where you grew up?'

Kwasi shrugged. 'There are spiders everywhere. No one suspects a blood child when they see one. Not even my parents.'

She followed the route of a long-legged spider. 'Why spiders?'

'You heard of Anansi?'

'The spider who always outwits everyone else.' Master Haripersad had told Priya the *Anansi Tori*. That almost seemed like a different life now.

'Yes, that one.' Kwasi smiled, and the dimple in his cheek appeared. 'When I was little, I used to pretend I was Anansi. I turned my situation around and pretended it was my idea to keep it a secret that I was a blood child, so that I could fool the entire village. And when I made the spiders appear, they were my accomplices in the plot.'

Priya understood that Kwasi had dealt with his loneliness in his own way. 'We all keep hurting each other,' she whispered. 'This land is broken.'

'Awaran is a mosaic,' replied Kwasi, just as quietly. 'Beautiful and colourful, but the cracks are painfully visible.'

They waited in silence until Priya felt Reza descending to the lower levels. She shot to her feet. Kwasi didn't realise at first, and she had to pull him up by his arm. 'He's going downstairs,' she said in an excited voice. 'Jupta's done it.'

Reza came racing down, followed at some distance by the general and a few soldiers. Priya waited until they were far enough beneath her and then sprinted along the corridor and back up towards the cells. She didn't look over her shoulder to see if there were any soldiers coming after her.

'There,' Kwasi panted behind her, as they skidded into the right corridor.

At the end of the hallway, there was a line of three cells, but only one was occupied. Colonel Johan van Huyzen was sitting with his ankles and hands clamped in a wooden chair. The pungent smell of sweat and human waste mixed with the metallic scent of blood was intense. Feeling queasy, Priya tried not to breathe through her nose.

The soldiers who'd stayed behind immediately came towards them.

'Brace yourself,' Priya said to Kwasi, who gave her a dramatic salute. Priya rolled her eyes and looked ahead again. *Get out of my way*, she thought, casting the command in their direction like a dagger. It shattered their shields, and they meekly moved aside. Kwasi hissed and also took two steps before regaining control of his body.

Priya walked forward. On the belt of one of the guards, a soldier in a green uniform, there was a bunch of keys. Priya hadn't let go of her command yet, but she could feel the soldier resisting. Kwasi took the keys.

'Wait.' Priya stopped Kwasi, who was about to walk on, and leaned in towards him. 'Can you make me white?' she whispered in his ear. 'For the colonel?'

He looked doubtful. 'I can try,' he whispered back.

'Make sure I'm wearing the same uniform as him. No, make it look better than his. Be creative.'

'Remember that it was you who asked for this,' he mumbled, looking amused as he slid the key into the lock. As the wooden door of the cell swung open, he waved her inside.

Priya put on a neutral expression and walked into the cell, with Kwasi following close behind.

'Barricade the door,' she said quietly.

The colonel showed no indication of having heard them. His head hung back, and his eyes were closed. His shirt had been taken off, and his torso was a blood-smeared mess. When Priya looked closer, she saw that they'd cut off his right hand. The stump was clumsily wrapped in scraps of material.

'Hello,' Priya said, coming to a stop in front of him.

He did not respond.

The colonel was too tall for the chair. It was only the clamps on his arms and legs that stopped him from sliding off. His straight blond hair clung to his forehead, slick and soiled by a mixture of sweat and blood.

Priya heard the sound of several soldiers running upstairs.

They had no time. She gave the prisoner's chair a kick, and he screamed. He sat upright, his eyes widening when he saw her.

'Hello,' Priya said again. 'Colonel.'

'Th-That's impossible . . .' stammered the colonel. 'That's impossible . . . How are you still free?' He shook his head. 'No. This isn't real. This is *not* real,' he said, opening his eyes even wider as if that might help him to see her more clearly.

Priya cursed under her breath. 'I'd like you to remain calm, Colonel,' she said soothingly. 'We don't have much time.'

'How did they find us?' he raved.

'You mean: how did *you* find Kuwatta,' Priya corrected him impatiently. 'And yes, how exactly did you do that?'

'I just . . . They helped us . . . It's not . . .'

'*Who* helped you?'

But he seemed to realise that something wasn't right. His blue eyes studied her. There was a feverish gleam to them. Had they already broken him? She hoped not.

'The monster's alive!' he suddenly screamed. 'They're . . .'

Kwasi tapped Priya's shoulder. 'We have a small problem.'

'Get out of there!' The female guard was rattling the cell door. Kwasi had used a long stick to barricade the door. The wood was cracking as the guard shoved at the door. 'Fetch Reza,' she called over her shoulder to the other guard, who ran off.

'Blood child,' the colonel whispered. It was beginning to dawn on him. 'You're cursed. You're all cursed!'

Those words *again*. It was maddening. All her life, she'd heard those words. She'd had enough. She did not want to hear them anymore. Priya grabbed him by the throat and started to squeeze his windpipe. 'This can be easy, or it can be hard, Colonel,' she hissed. 'So, why don't you make it easy for yourself? Tell me why you were looking for Kuwatta.'

To her surprise, he began to laugh. His cracked lips started bleeding and his teeth turned red. But his blue eyes were suddenly bright and lucid. 'You're acting as if we are the villains here, but look at you, look at what you're doing. Torturing. Killing. Allowing blood children to mix with humans. You're animals. Kill me. I don't care anymore. It just reveals your true animal nature.'

'How does it feel?' she asked quietly. She wanted to hurt him. She wanted to *break* him, as the Freelanders had broken her father. 'How does it feel to be at our mercy? To be less than we are?'

'I will never be less than you.' He stated it as a fact.

'And yet here you are, colonist. Without an army. Without weapons. Apparently you're not as superior as you believe.'

'Are you really that ignorant?' He grinned. 'Your buildings, your uniforms, your swords – they're all just imitations of ours. There's not one thing that you've invented yourselves. Our vision isn't plucked out of thin air, kantrakti. It might take you people a while to see that. But no matter. We're not going anywhere. In time you'll come to understand.'

The insufferable arrogance in his words wasn't mere bragging. He truly believed it. That awareness was what scared Priya most. Because at times she had indeed wondered if the Freelanders were better than them. They ruled half the world. Their weapons were more advanced, and it was also true that the rebel movement had learned a lot from them. Even the magical prostheses that Kuwatta was so proud of were based on Freeland technology. How was that possible if they were all equal?

But then she remembered what Master Haripersad had told her many years ago. About how the Freelanders had adopted various sciences, inventions and wisdom from the Suryans. How great and rich the societies of Suryan, Central Luana and Dali had been before their communities were suppressed with violence.

'There is no better or worse, beti,' he'd grunted. 'There is only change, and change occurs in different places in different ways. Sometimes it's seen as an improvement, sometimes as the opposite, but it's rarely that black and white. And it is certainly not the achievement of one people. It's a process that's going on all over the world.'

'Pri.' It was Kwasi. 'The door's breaking.'

Priya had run out of patience. She hit the colonel in the face, and his head snapped sideways with the force of the blow. *Stop breathing,* she commanded him, and his soul sent the message to his body. She broke through his mental shield with ease – if he had even raised a shield at all. All he could do was glare accusingly at her, his eyes bulging, as he tried with all his might to resist the actions of his body.

He lost the fight, as many unwitting people have lost a battle by focusing their attention on the wrong place. Instead of trying to get a grip on his soul, he was attempting to control his body, oblivious to who was actually in charge.

She watched as he turned red.

'Now tell me,' said Priya softly. 'Why did you come here?'

'Monster,' he spat.

'This is getting boring, Colonel.'

She released her hold for a moment, so that he could take a wheezing gasp. 'We gave you people a chance,' he snarled, trying to catch his breath. 'A place to live and to work for a world where we can live peacefully side by side. And look how you respond. With violence and bloodshed. Monsters, that's all you are. Monsters who don't deserve to live.'

'You want to exterminate us?' she asked, forcing him to take shallow breaths. 'Just try it.'

Behind her, she heard the wooden stick splinter. The cell door burst open.

'We are already doing exactly that,' the colonel snapped at Priya. 'You wait. It won't be long before this fort collapses. She's already defeating you.' Then he fell silent.

Priya felt someone grabbing her from behind. 'Who's defeating us?' she screamed, trying to pull herself free. Colonel Johan just smiled, showing his blood-smeared teeth again. A terrible suspicion stirred deep within Priya. This could not be coincidence. The rabidos roaming around outside. The monster in their midst, which they fought but couldn't overcome.

Her arm was painfully twisted up her back. Priya turned and kicked out behind her. 'Let go of me,' she growled at her assailant. It turned out to be Letitia, and Priya fired off a command. For a moment, the grip on her arm loosened, and she pulled away.

Kwasi was on his knees, pushed to the ground by two soldiers in black uniforms. Reza appeared between them. 'Why,' he growled through his mask, 'do you never do as I ask? Why, Priya?'

'Why should I listen to you when you do this kind of thing?' Priya knew she didn't stand a chance of getting away. 'Down,' she commanded the basha, who was trying to grab hold of her. Reza came towards her, and she fired the same command at him. It was a bluff. In a flash, she drew her dagger and held it to the unprotected flesh between his mask and uniform.

'Did the general know the colonists sent the Dedekedre?' she asked, close to his cheek. 'Did you know?' He didn't reply. 'Tell me!' Priya screamed in Reza's face.

She tried to keep her focus. Reza was a statue in her hands. He could tear straight through her mental shield with his gift if he wanted. He could push her away and try to overpower her. She wouldn't make it easy for him. But he had more soldiers, and she was already exhausted by the command she'd used to control ten people.

Reza nodded, almost imperceptibly.

His confession cut through Priya. He was not her friend. He never had been. So it made no sense that she felt personally betrayed by him. Her feelings didn't matter. The issue was that he and the general had kept this secret from Kuwatta. And if they were keeping that secret, what else?

Priya eased the pressure on the dagger and leaned forward. Reza's pupils were large black pools of bottomless water.

'I hate you,' she spat from the depths of her heart. 'I hate you so much.'

She couldn't stand that even now her gift seemed to long for him. But then she stopped resisting it. *Let him feel how much I despise him*, she thought.

Reza stiffened.

Priya squeezed her eyes shut for a moment. 'Take us to the major.'

'I can't do that.'

'I'm under her protection. She knows that I'm here. Do you want to undermine her authority too, Reza?' Taking a chance, she whispered in his ear, 'Is your father powerful enough for that? Will he be able to keep the army under control?'

Reza tensed under her touch. Goosebumps rose on his neck.

'Take us to the major.'

38

THE HEAVY STONE DOORS swung open.

In front of Priya appeared the largest room she had seen in Kuwatta. It was even bigger than the Great Hall, with a lofty ceiling and high windows with wooden shutters. An obvious difference from the other rooms in the fortress was the wooden panelling. Combined with the small square windows and shutters, it made the room resemble the plantation overseer's mansion.

The decorations in the room, however, referred to the different ethnic groups: carvings of Topuan letters on the ceiling and Luanan-style paintings along the wooden walls, Suryan cushions on the seats and fine Dalinese statues on the floor. Kokolampoes burned on the walls.

'They made her.' Major Aïda strode into her father's quarters, with Priya following on her heels. Her head was pounding; the exhaustion was taking its toll. She'd been awake for more than twenty-four hours. After the major and the general had arrived at the cell block together, the major had sent Priya and Kwasi to her room. Some time later, she arrived there herself and questioned them until Priya could no longer think straight. She'd hoped – in vain – that she would be allowed to go to her own room after that.

The general, in his black uniform, was sitting at a wooden desk and writing on a sheet of parchment. Behind him stood Scholar Afounsowa and another advisor; they stepped back, shocked. The guards who had been standing outside the room ran after the major. She paid no attention to them. She was furious. 'She doesn't come from the forests of Awaran. They *made* her to exterminate us. And you *knew*. How could you keep that to yourself?'

The advisor next to the general made a sound of disapproval. He pressed his hand to his chest. 'This is most inappropriate behaviour for a major.' The guards stepped forward, their swords half-unsheathed. The major's soldiers also began to draw their weapons. Everyone in the room was looking at either the general or the major, waiting for their signal.

General Suapala was the first to wave aside the weapons. 'I shall be the judge of what is inappropriate. Step forward, daughter.'

The soldiers moved back. The major motioned to her soldiers to lower their weapons. They obeyed her at once.

With a venomous look at the major and Priya, the advisor returned to his place. 'Of course, General. My apologies.'

'You may all leave. I wish to talk to my daughter alone,' the general said wearily. He raised himself slightly from his slumped position, but soon slipped back. 'That includes you, Mr Darwati.'

'But,' spluttered the advisor, 'someone has to advise you.'

'If I want advice, I'll ask for it.'

'Of course,' the advisor immediately replied humbly. He pressed his fists together and walked away. Scholar Afounsowa followed him, with more composure.

Priya's eyes darted from the major to the general. She turned to go, but the major stopped her. 'Not you,' she said, her face unsmiling. 'You're staying here.'

The major waited until everyone else had left the room and the door closed behind them. 'She was made by the colonists,' she said, a lot more quietly this time.

The general intertwined his fingers on his lap. His cheeks were sunken and the blue-black circles under his eyes were even more noticeable than the last time Priya had seen him. The bones of his hands protruded so much that the skin around them was taut.

'You lied,' said Major Aïda. 'To the peoples of Awaran. To those who obey you and trust you. To your own children.'

But not to all his children. Priya softly ran a finger over the hilt of her dagger.

'Why?' the major said almost inaudibly.

The general was silent for some time. Rubbing his thumbs together, he stared at a point behind Priya and his daughter. Priya thought for a moment that he was not going to respond or that, if he did, it would be a denial. But neither happened.

'For a long time, it wasn't clear,' he said finally. 'I still wonder if it's even possible.'

'The evidence is in front of us every night, Father.' The major stepped further forward. 'The Topuans have greater knowledge of souls and magic. They—'

'Have never succeeded in doing such a thing,' the general said, finishing her sentence for her. 'Creating a monster of this size and power is an extraordinary feat. If they had succeeded, I would have been informed about it by the scholars and my advisors. After much . . . encouragement, the colonel told us that the Freelanders used multiple souls to create the Dedekedre. They used a didibri dragon as a host for the souls. For the Topuans, it is sacrilege to abuse souls in this way.'

A didibri dragon. Priya gulped. She held the corner of the general's desk to keep herself upright. She could hardly comprehend what she was hearing. Didibri dragons were shapeshifters, but in their normal form they had scales like reptiles, with razor-sharp teeth and twelve tails. Priya had heard that they could also be summoned like vengeful spirits during the blood moon.

The major looked unimpressed. 'They used black magic.'

The general did not reply.

'You had no right to keep this information from the people,' the major snapped at him. 'You had no right to keep this information from *me*. I have ordered hundreds of soldiers to fight a monster I thought we didn't understand.'

'We don't understand it.'

'Of course we do!' Aïda stepped forward, her dark eyes blazing. 'The colonel has explained it to us in detail, General. She was created by them and sent to exterminate us. We could have recruited soldiers on a large scale among the free peoples, so that we had greater force. Maybe then we could have destroyed her before this all got so out of hand. Instead, we're still fighting her every night, while the Freelanders out there on the coast . . .' She shook her head. 'It wouldn't surprise me if they're working on a new Dedekedre to finish us once and for all.'

'I would have told you, if you hadn't been plotting for a number of years to take my position, Major.' The general's voice was razor sharp. 'You are a decisive commander who inspires soldiers, but you jump to conclusions and you make rash plans.'

The major took a sharp breath. 'Father . . .'

'It's "General" to you, Major.'

The major pressed her lips together. 'My apologies, General.'

The general rubbed the bridge of his nose with a thumb and forefinger. A deep frown line had formed between his eyebrows. 'Have you noticed that the Freelanders have left us alone for a long time, in spite of their ability to create the Dedekedre, daughter? Why do you think that is?' The major did not react immediately, and the general looked at Priya, eyebrows raised. 'Do you have any idea, soldier?'

She was startled by his sudden attention. Throughout the conversation so far, she had been an observer. She hadn't imagined that he would speak to her.

'I . . .' began Priya. 'I've heard that the Freelanders don't know our jungle well enough.'

'I have no doubt that you have indeed heard that.' The general leaned back in his chair. 'The Dedekedre has plagued the resistance for almost six generations. Long before the two of you were born, our people were already fighting her. And over a century ago, during a blood moon, we were teetering on the brink of ultimate defeat. Our fort had fallen, our soldiers had been reduced to a handful of survivors and with every lunar cycle a village fell prey to the Dedekedre.

'My grandfather, the general at the time, knew that the end was near. But in his desperation to ensure the survival of the Luanans and the Topuans, he decided to launch one last attack. He gathered a small army of blood children, made up of both villagers and soldiers, and lured the monster into the ruins of Kuwatta. It was the first time a general had used the resistance of soul-singers to defend Awaran. Perhaps because he was a wise man, but most likely because he was a blood child himself. A secret he kept well hidden.'

A shiver ran through Priya's body. It was *her* people who had ensured that the resistance had not collapsed. *Her* people who had protected Awaran when the people who considered them monsters could not.

'My father was just a boy, and he had no gift. But he told me how my grandfather, together with the other soul-singers, brought the monster to her knees. They set her on fire and built the first layer around her with black stone to keep her captive. Her roars were deafening. It wouldn't surprise me if the Freelanders heard it on the coast. Sadly, that was not the end of the story. The monster, severely weakened, cast off her mortal body. The parasites survived the attack and hid in the cracks of the ruin, unseen by the naked eye.

'My grandfather, unaware of this, hunted down the remaining rabidos and informed the Freelanders that the rebels of Kuwatta would bow to no one. To lend force to his words, he sent the blood children after the colonists. The legions of Freelanders at the edge of the jungle hadn't been expecting that. Their army withdrew to guard the boundaries of their plantations. Around ten years later, slavery was abolished. But it didn't just stop there. The colonists didn't surrender Awaran. This land was a source of great profit for them. So they soon started shipping Dalinese and Suryans to Awaran to work for them as cheap labour.'

The major's energy had calmed, losing its sharp edges. Priya wondered how many times she'd heard a different version of this story.

A version in which some of the details had been conveniently omitted. Priya knew that the Great General, General Suapala's grandfather, had died during the last battle. And he had left a wife, three sons and two daughters. His oldest son, General Suapala's uncle, died ten years later in the middle of the night during a violent attack by his opponents within the rebel movement. He died without children, so General Suapala's father succeeded him.

'Our continued survival depends on the façade that we uphold. I closed off Kuwatta to the outside world so that no one knew the Dedekedre was still alive – including the Freelanders. The colonists could have sent more of her kind, but they have not. Whatever they did to create the Dedekedre, it took a great deal of effort. They hadn't been counting on a victory for our side,' the general concluded.

'And now something has changed,' the major said quietly.

A muscle in the general's cheek twitched.

'They suspect that the Dedekedre is still alive,' said Priya, as it began to dawn on her. 'That's why Colonel Johan came. To see if their suspicions were correct.'

'Someone has leaked our secret.' The general shook his head, as if he couldn't believe it. 'That's the danger when a lot of people know about a secret and start making their own plans, Major.'

The major pressed her lips together. 'That still doesn't explain how the colonel was almost able to reach Kuwatta. The warrior villages—'

'Have been under attack from the colonists for weeks,' said the general. 'Which suggests that the Freelanders found out some time ago that the Dedekedre is still alive.'

'But they didn't report colonists advancing into the rainforest, General,' the major said, pacing the room. 'I've read all their reports. The attacks are described, albeit somewhat superficially. But they don't say a word about enemy intruders in the forest.'

'They were unable to do so. The colonists were clever about it. They distracted four of the five warrior villages with brief incursions and stormed the fifth without the rest realising. Then they captured the soldiers along with their families and used the soldiers to move through the rainforest without being seen.'

The major stopped pacing. 'So they're blood traitors.'

The general nodded. 'The colonists threatened to kill their families. They made their choice.'

It wouldn't have surprised Priya if the Freelanders had murdered the families anyway.

'Now we're trying to discover if the Freelanders are preparing for a full-scale attack on Kuwatta,' said the general.

'But if they've found Kuwatta and are on their way here with a large army, then . . .' The major leaned with two hands on the wooden desk, her head hanging. 'That can't be allowed to happen,' she whispered. 'We have thirteen hundred soldiers and cadets. It takes nearly all of them to keep the Dedekedre under control. We won't be able to fight another army at the same time.'

'No,' the general agreed. 'And I've already notified the warrior villages of the threat. They're on the alert.'

'That's not enough.' The major shook her head. 'They can't do it alone. They couldn't even prevent the colonel from almost reaching Kuwatta.'

'That's why it's up to us,' said the general, 'to put a permanent end to the Dedekedre as soon as possible.'

+++

The small room on the ground floor of the Lodge was crammed with soldiers crowding around the central table. The general and the major, directly facing each other, were the only ones on chairs. The floorplans and maps had been taken down from the walls and were spread on the table between them. Priya was at the major's shoulder. Reza stood beside his father.

Priya stared at him. Now that she knew why the general was keeping the Dedekedre hidden, her fury had eased a little, but she still couldn't let go of it completely.

'We have to lure the Dedekedre out. We can't reach her in the sunken hall.' Reza tapped one finger on the map, at the heart of the fortress. 'There are hundreds, if not thousands, of rabidos swarming around here. If you want to reach her, you need to get through that group first.'

'Couldn't we create a way through?' Priya stepped forward. Everyone turned to look at her. 'With a group of deed-speakers.'

'You want to go to the core?' Scholar Afounsowa shook her head. She was the only one in the party without missing limbs or visible scars. 'Getting through to the inner ring is almost impossible. But going to the core is a suicide mission.'

Why had she gone and opened her mouth again? 'If we gather all of the deed-speakers and use gold,' said Priya cautiously, 'isn't it worth a try? I don't see how we're going to get to the Dedekedre otherwise.'

'And what do you intend to do if we lose half of our troops?' asked the general.

'I . . .' began Priya, searching for words.

'Soon there won't be anything left to lose, Father,' said Reza, suddenly backing her up. 'Are you planning to wait until then?'

'Then bring me a good plan,' said the general. 'A plan that will give hope to the soldiers who are fighting. Brute force alone is not enough. We've tried that before.'

Reza nodded, his expression neutral, but Priya could feel his irritation. She hadn't expected Reza and the general to disagree. And she certainly hadn't expected Reza to speak out against his father in public.

'There is a plan.' Major Aïda leaned forward, planting both hands flat on the map. 'My plan.'

'No,' barked the general.

'You wanted a plan that could give the soldiers hope,' said the major. 'This is the plan that can give them hope. There's no point luring the Dedekedre away as long as she's protected by the rabidos. First we have to get them out of the way. Or she won't come out.'

'If we do that, we risk everyone outside Kuwatta finding out what we're holding captive here,' one of the general's advisors objected. He was a chubby Dalinese man with a bald head.

'They already know,' snarled the major. 'The colonists already know. There's no secret left to keep.'

The general rubbed his chin. He didn't seem convinced. 'Even if we succeed in luring out the rabidos, they'll only go and attack the nearest villages.'

'Then we'll have to evacuate the villages and try to limit the damage,' the major said impatiently. 'We don't have much time to think about this. We all know the Freelanders are breathing down our necks and could be standing in front of the fort at any moment. The Dedekedre must be killed at once. No matter what the cost.'

The general pushed himself up out of his chair. The room fell silent. He looked at the map in the middle of the table. Then he turned to the major. 'You're confident this will work?'

'It's the only way, General.'

'Scholar Afounsowa?'

The scholar, who was standing in the corner of the room, stepped forward when her name was spoken. 'I'm inclined to agree with your daughter, General. Unfortunately, we've been unable to find any other way to lure out the Dedekedre.'

'Then we have another issue to consider,' said the general. His sentence was interrupted by a burst of coughing, which made his entire body shake. 'Excuse me. Where was I? Ah, the next issue. Once the Dedekedre is visible, how will she be defeated?'

'That's less simple,' said Scholar Afounsowa. She moved some documents to reveal a sheet of parchment with a drawing of the Dedekedre. 'My probies have not been able to work directly on any samples of the Dedekedre's material, but they *have* dissected rabidos and parasites. Even lesser creatures like the rabidos and parasites are hard to kill, though. A simple stab to the heart is not enough.'

As Priya remembered only too well.

'Cutting their throats works better. Our suspicion is that it's because they don't die until their heads are no longer in contact with their bodies. Then their soul is divided and dissolves. That will be particularly relevant in the case of the Dedekedre. There are a number of souls inside her. But her scales are going to make that hard to accomplish. And then there's the problem of her size.'

'She's in the basement, so she can't be too big,' said an advisor.

'That's because she gets less human flesh down there than she'd like. If she gets out, that will all change. The more human flesh she devours, the larger she'll grow.'

'How do you know that?' one of the major's high-ranking soldiers asked.

'Old writings,' said Scholar Afounsowa. 'How do you think the Dedekedre was imprisoned in the first place? There are tactics from the past that we can learn from, soldier.'

The major pushed Priya forward. 'Fortunately, this time we have powerful deed-speakers,' said the major. 'The Dedekedre's skin is too thick to pierce quickly. We can't dodge her claws while cutting through her neck. She needs to be restrained. To do that, we'll use deed-speakers like Priya. They're the only ones who are strong enough to succeed.'

Priya's skin tingled with the sudden attention of everyone in the room. The major's hand was still pushing her forward, leaving her with no choice but to stay where she was.

The general's stare moved from the major and rested on Priya. Again, she was startled by the sharpness in his dark eyes. His body was frail and sickly, but his gaze was clear. Priya had no doubt that he was aware of everything that was going on at Kuwatta. 'Will it work, soldier?'

Priya gulped. 'Yes, General,' she said. 'As long as I have help, it'll work.'

The general followed her gaze which she'd unwittingly turned on Reza. She quickly looked away, but it was too late. 'What do you mean by that? Why do you need my son?'

Priya felt her face flushing. 'I don't only mean your son. Reza . . . Kapten Reza,' she said, correcting herself, 'is a sense-speaker. He can calm the rabidos and the Dedekedre while I work with the other deed-speakers to keep her under control. Master Yapoma is a sight-speaker. He can distract the Dedekedre if needed.'

'Soldier Priya is one of the strongest deed-speakers of the students who have arrived here in recent lunar cycles. Her strength is exceptional,' the major said. 'But she's still only one person. Getting the soul-singers to work together sounds like a good idea.'

Priya stared at a vague point in front of her, trying not to look at Reza. She couldn't entirely ignore the attraction between them, and that annoyed her beyond measure. She didn't know if she wanted to give him a good shaking or to beg him to help her. For a moment, she thought he wasn't going to react at all, but then he stepped forward. 'I think it's worth a try, General.'

The major smiled her sharp smile of satisfaction. 'Then we shall follow my plan. First the rabidos will be pushed outside and led into the river, so that the path is clear for their mother, and some of them will hopefully break their necks in the plunge down the waterfall. Then we'll lure the Dedekedre out of the safety of her lair. After that, the soul-singers, under Priya's leadership, will keep her under control and we will kill her.'

The general held his daughter's gaze for a moment. The major had taken control of the conversation in an instant and led it as if she were in charge. Yet another violation of the hierarchy. Priya felt the major's soul grow quieter; she was on her guard.

Then the general smiled. 'You heard the major. Now get to work.'

'Yes, General!' shouted the advisors and the soldiers.

39

WITHIN A SHORT SPACE of time, Kuwatta was transformed. The fort was moved to the highest level of military readiness. Lessons at the Academy were discontinued. All the probies and cadets were informed about the rabidos, the Dedekedre and the danger posed by the Freelanders, so that they could fight alongside the rest. As a result, the group of soul-singers that Priya had started with at Kuwatta was reunited for the first time in ages.

'What does it feel like to fight against the rabidos?' asked Makaku, sitting down after a sparring session with Kofi. 'I've heard their souls are more difficult to manipulate.'

'Their souls are mainly just different,' said Kofi, running his fingers over his blade, looking for blunt parts. 'They're jagged and prickly and shoot off all over the place.'

'The trick isn't overpowering them, but giving them a nudge in the right direction.' Paneke sheathed his sword and wiped his hand over his sweaty forehead. 'They're easy to influence once you figure out how to work with them.'

'But whatever you do, do it quickly,' responded Nanu, fiercely lashing out at Kwasi. 'Rabidos come in big groups, and they fight until the bitter end. A wound here or there isn't going to slow them down.'

Priya took Makaku's place as Kofi's sparring partner and assumed a fighting stance.

Makaku sighed and hung his head. 'And there I was, thinking we were fighting the Freelanders.'

'Well, in a way, we are,' said Kwasi, spinning to dodge Nanu's short sword. 'The Freelanders and the Dedekedre: one and the same. Ultimately, their master is the same person.'

The longer the two of them sparred, the clearer it became that their fighting styles were only annoying them both. Nanu was after confrontation, while Kwasi mainly focused on avoiding her attacks and making spiders appear in her field of vision.

Drop your sword, thought Priya. Kofi opened his hand and his sword clattered to the ground. Wearily, she indicated that she was taking a break and dropped down beside Jupta. In front of them, soldiers passed, one after another. Some of them were removing the heavy doors from the Keep, to make it easier for the rabidos to pass through the building. Others were boarding up some of the Keep entrances.

It was only the soul-singers, nearly forty of them, including the ones Priya had studied with at the Academy, who didn't have to help. The general had ordered them to train every day to strengthen their bodies and, above all, their gifts.

'You aren't intruders,' said Jupta suddenly. 'I was wrong.'

'What did you say?' Priya replied, pulling a stray leaf from Jupta's hair.

'When we first met, you asked me if I saw all of you as intruders,' Jupta murmured. 'And I'd like to take back what I said. You belong to Awaran. We all belong to Awaran.'

+++

'There are thirty-eight of you soul-singers, including seven spirit-speakers, who we're going to use to track down the rabidos. They won't be fighting alongside you.' The major paced her room. She'd been wearing her full armour for a few days. The five days that had passed since her plan had been put into action had seemed to last forever. 'Besides you, there are six other deed-speakers, and we have six sense-speakers in addition to Reza. But in the end, it all comes down to the fact that Reza and you are the most powerful and you will therefore be the core of the attack against the Dedekedre.'

'Understood, Major,' said Priya. She felt just as restless as the major. Waiting was not her strong point.

'We also expect you to help lead the rabidos to the river.'

Priya nodded.

'Have I missed anything?'

Priya licked her lips. 'I was wondering if Umed had received his medicine yet.'

'Umed?' The major blinked in surprise. 'Ah, your brother. That's right. Yes, he's received his medication. I'm sure he's fine.' Then the major returned to the strategies for the coming battle.

+++

Kwasi knocked on the door. 'It's time.'

Priya slid the last of the knives into their sheaths and stood up. Her green uniform had been adapted, with extra armour on her chest, arms and legs to prevent the rabidos from tearing through it too easily. Unfortunately, that also made it more difficult for her to move, but that wasn't too much of a problem, as no one was expecting her to fight using a sword. This time she would be protected by other soldiers, so that she could use her gift. It also helped that she was wearing gold bands around her ankles and wrists. The energy of the gold hummed quietly on her skin, leaving a tingling sensation. It was an indescribable, almost imperceptible feeling, and yet it made her feel better, fitter.

Kwasi's green uniform was lighter and more practical. He was carrying a long, broad sword on his back.

'Where's Jupta?' Priya checked that her plait was still firmly in place and tied the end with a piece of string, just to make sure. Then she twisted it up onto her head and secured it.

'Talking to the scouts.'

Priya focused and found Jupta's soul halfway down the corridor. She and Kwasi headed to the meeting point.

At the end of the long corridor, they found Jupta, dressed in a dark green uniform with a bow and quiver of arrows on her back. She was talking to two soldiers in green uniforms and one in black, their leader. Jupta looked painfully small next to them, so slender and young.

'Is Jupta being used as a scout?' Priya asked Kwasi.

Kwasi shrugged. 'I'm sure we'll find out soon enough.'

'Soldiers.' A soldier stopped beside them, pressing his fists together in greeting. Priya and Kwasi responded to the gesture. 'The kapten of Brigade I is expecting you.'

'I'll accompany them.' Ishani appeared next to them, waving the soldier away. She was dressed in a beige tunic with a thick brown belt around her waist, which had a selection of small silver rods and rings hanging from it, along with small jute bags. There were silver rings around her wrists and neck too. She'd pinned her thick black hair in a tight bun on top of her head, revealing her ears, which she normally hid.

'You shouldn't be here,' Priya said with a dry mouth. She hadn't expected Ishani to turn up. It had been enough for Priya that Ishani wasn't fighting and was therefore safe. That was all she needed to know. 'This is dangerous. The sun—'

'Isn't setting yet,' Ishani interrupted her, with a stubborn look on her face. 'And by the time it does, I won't be here. So, will you come with me? You too, Kwasi.'

'Yes, scholar. As you wish, scholar,' Kwasi said, earnestly pressing his fists together before walking along with her. Ishani rolled her eyes at him.

'The Dedekedre's soul is made up of different pieces, fragments that form a chaotic whole,' said Ishani, as they walked past the soldiers who were standing in the corridor in groups of two or three, preparing to take up their positions.

'How do you know all of this?' asked Priya.

'Since my lessons stopped, I've been working under head scholar Afounsowa. Her research focuses on the internal processes of the Dedekedre.' Ishani saw the blank looks on Priya and Kwasi's faces. 'We're researching where her insatiable hunger for human flesh comes from, why her blood, which the rabidos and parasites carry within them, turns us into monsters and exactly how her anatomy works.'

'And you discovered that her soul is made up of different pieces?' Kwasi said with a frown. 'Is that a side-effect of all the people, all the souls, that she "devours"?'

'Well,' said Ishani, sounding a little uncertain for the first time. 'That's a theory. We don't know *why* the souls of the rabidos and the Dedekedre are prickly and chaotic. But those descriptions come up over and over again in the witness statements, particularly about the Dedekedre.'

'Probies!' A soldier in a black uniform was striding towards them. 'I thought I already made it clear that I don't want to see you people here.'

Ishani ducked away and hid behind Priya and Kwasi. 'I've got a quick question, by the way.'

Priya had a bad feeling about the situation. 'So you came here even though you're not supposed to, right?'

Ishani gave her a quick nod. 'Yeah, my mistake. Could I have some of your gold?'

'Probies!' the soldier in the black uniform roared again. He'd almost reached them.

'What do you need it for?' asked Priya, just as Kwasi pulled one of his gold bracelets from his wrist. With an amused smile, he threw it to Ishani.

'Thank you!' Ishani said, pushing the bracelet deep into one of the pockets of her tunic.

'Oh, you're welcome,' said Kwasi. 'I like helping other people to break the rules. It keeps life interesting.'

'I'm not . . .'

The soldier in black had reached them. Priya guessed that he was a kapten, given his attitude. He grabbed hold of Ishani's elbow and pulled her along. 'Now scram, probie, before I decide to investigate which scholar you're working with and have you suspended from your research.'

Ishani looked horrified. 'I just wanted to say goodbye, Kapten.'

She said something else, but the sound was lost in the conversations of others around them. Then she threw her arms around Priya, who froze, not quite sure how to react. She'd expected to chase Ishani away with her words – not *this*.

'Whatever you do,' Ishani said in her ear, 'stay alive. I'll never forgive you if you leave me on my own, didi.'

'The same goes for you, sister,' said Priya quietly. So quietly that she didn't know if she'd said it out loud, or if it had just been a thought.

Sister. Priya's heart swelled until her stomach hurt and her throat felt sore. She swallowed a few times to get rid of the feeling. Then she took a shaky step backwards. It was fine now. Enough.

Ishani let her arms fall to her sides. Kwasi opened his arms wide to her. 'Is it my turn?'

Priya threw him such a venomous look that he crossed his arms protectively over his chest. 'Not even from you?' he asked Priya with an innocent grin.

'In your dreams,' she snapped back.

Kwasi pretended to collapse to the ground.

Ishani was led away by the kapten. The soldier in the brown uniform had returned during their conversation and escorted them to their team.

Priya swallowed the lump in her throat and tried to distract herself by looking at the other soldiers. Here and there, she saw a glint of gold in their ears or around their wrists. She saw the occasional black-uniformed soldier with gold rings around their arms or legs, and a couple with rings around their necks.

Only the Topuans refused to wear gold. Around their necks and arms, they had colourful chains of beads, and they wore bright feathers in their hair.

'This way.' The soldier walked ahead of them.

They didn't have to go far. Priya and Kwasi had been put in Brigade I. Brigades I and II were the last line of defence.

Kwasi whistled approvingly when he saw the huge round hole that had been made in the Keep's outer ring in just a couple of days. The whole wall was more or less a gaping hole.

'Is it big enough for the Dedekedre?'

The soldier looked at him. 'We hope so. She hasn't shown herself for a long time, so we've had to rely on the memories of old survivors.'

The two teams tasked with controlling the huge flow of rabidos and forcing them through the hole lined up on either side of the gap. Priya moved closer to the edge and saw the Cotari glistening. The plan was for the rabidos to disappear into the river. A little rash perhaps, but hopefully most of them would break bones and some of them their necks. Those that survived the waterfall would be cut down by the soldiers positioned at its foot. The Dedekedre was Priya's problem. She licked her chewed-up lips, expectations weighing heavily on her shoulders.

A wonder, she heard Reza saying inside her mind, *that's what they call you*. Subconsciously, she was looking for him, even though she knew he was now on his way to the inner ring.

The soldier pointed at the troops in front of them and pressed his fists together. 'This is Brigade I.'

Priya gave a quick nod and turned to the team in front of her.

Right at the front was Master Yapoma. His long, snow-white hair was in a plait, and he was wearing a black uniform that was very lightly armoured. The long spear that he was holding loosely in his right hand ended in a large, curving blade. The rest of his uniform was covered with small daggers and spearheads. At his waist were two sacks, filled to the brim.

'Kapten.' Priya and Kwasi pressed their fists together.

'Soldiers.' Their former master nodded at them. His eyes were dreamy, his gaze focused on nothing. 'I am glad that you have joined me.'

The rest of their team, most in black or green uniforms, stood close behind their kapten.

The basha who led their brigade stepped forward. He was a broad-shouldered man in a black uniform with a huge axe on his back.

'To the left flank,' said the basha. 'Make sure you don't stand too close at the edge. There are soldiers waiting to protect you and the others, should that prove necessary. I want you further at the back, sight-speaker.'

The 'others' he mentioned must include the deed-speakers who would be working with her to get the rabidos under control. It was a group of around twenty people in total.

As soon as Priya was in position, her gaze went to Master Yapoma. As usual, he seemed to be in a world of his own. Kwasi came to stand beside her. Priya saw him pulling a face at the basha's back, and she gave his shoulder a thump.

'I know that, deep down, you wanted to do that too,' he said to her. 'You really need to work on the way you say thank you to your friends.'

'Be serious for once,' she hissed. Although the sun was already setting and the evening wind was cool, her skin felt clammy.

'And what then?' Kwasi nudged her with his shoulder. 'Would that make it any easier?'

'What?'

'Dying.' He raised his hands dramatically but then lowered them sheepishly after a glance from the basha.

'We are not going to die,' Priya said through gritted teeth. She couldn't even bring herself to kick him in the shins, as she usually did when he was talking nonsense. Even though it wasn't actually nonsense this time, as she knew only too well.

'Eyes forward and mouths shut,' boomed the basha. 'The sun's going down. Prepare to fight.'

Priya felt the last rays of sun that shone in through the hole behind her disappearing one by one, leaving a hollow coolness. She looked over her shoulder.

The sun was sinking behind the tops of the trees, turning the river into an explosion of orange, red and pink. Bows were drawn. Swords were raised. Torches were lit.

Dusk came.

Bare feet slapping on stone. Panting. Screaming. Growling.

A long cry that went through the marrow of her bones.

The monsters were coming.

+++

Time seemed to be moving extremely slowly. Brigade I was still standing motionless in position. Priya heard the clashing of swords and the muffled snarls of the rabidos coming through the walls. Now and then there was a thud and sand came sliding through cracks in the walls.

'Brigade II has fallen,' said the expressionless voice of the spirit-speaker standing beside Master Yapoma. She had pinned up her hair, as had most of the other female soldiers, so her narrow face was clearly visible. Although Priya couldn't read her expression or soul very clearly, she sounded calm. She rattled off the deaths of her brothers and sisters as if she were reading from a textbook.

'How many are left?' asked Master Yapoma. Even now there was a gently lilting tone to the words he spoke.

The spirit-speaker held her head at an angle. 'Three in the first ring. Ah, now there are two and a few scattered soldiers. Ten in the second. Eighteen in the outer ring.'

Several soldiers in Brigade I shuffled back and forth. Priya couldn't read their souls or faces, they were too well trained for that, but their uncertain shuffling told her enough. She stretched her cramped fingers before gripping her swords tightly again. The wait was nerve-racking.

'How long until impact?' asked the basha.

A short silence. 'The rabidos could reach the third ring any moment now.'

'Is everything going according to plan?'

A short nod. 'More or less. In the second ring, the flow has basically stabilised. There are a few blockages here and there. The major is leading the vanguard. Reza and his water panther are chasing down the rabidos from behind.'

At that moment, a loud roar from Kohóna echoed through the walls. The hairs on Priya's arms stood on end. She was close – and that meant the rabidos were too.

Priya licked her bottom lip and tasted salt. Her heartbeat was pounding in her ears, but it couldn't drown out the shrieking of the rabidos. She hoped Reza was safe and prayed silently to her Suryan gods for his protection.

A loud thud sent a ripple through the soldiers. Priya couldn't tell if they screamed, because all she could hear was the shrieks of the rabidos. The wall in front of them was cracking but didn't break. Another roar from Kohóna. Priya heard slapping feet. So close. So terribly close.

Kwasi turned to look at her. His mouth formed words.

The door burst open.

First, soldiers in brown and green came running out, their uniforms torn and bloody. Some of them had lost their weapons and were more stumbling than running.

The second wave was made up of a few rabidos. The major came sprinting after them, swords drawn. She was surrounded by three soldiers in black uniforms – soul-singers, Priya realised – who ensured that no rabidos would so much as touch the major. Behind her came a dozen soldiers – and then an endless stream of rabidos stumbling over one another to get to the soldiers faster. Priya's stomach turned at the sight of their bleeding mouths and unnatural movements. Their jagged souls screamed as loudly inside their bodies as their mouths did outwardly.

'Weapons at the ready,' screamed the basha, almost drowned out by the shrieking of the rabidos. The swords were raised again. 'Brace yourselves.'

Running forward, Master Yapoma let out a roar that, for a moment, rang above everything else. The sound triggered something within the soldiers. No one doubted. They ran after their kapten, storming towards the rabidos. Priya stayed with the other deed-speakers somewhere in the middle, but the clash with the rabidos could be felt even from there. She stood up straight, feeling for the chaotic souls of the rabidos and trying to get a grip on the three at the front.

To the middle, she commanded. It felt easy, almost natural. Even easier when one of them had its throat slit. The gold around her wrists became hot, but not unpleasantly so. The other two rabidos came stumbling to the middle. Kwasi ran past her. As he jumped up, she felt his soul crackling. For a moment, she lowered her shield and saw the big tarantulas running with him. The rabidos in front of him shrank away with raised hands, falling over backwards.

Then he disappeared into the throng of bodies.

Stay in the middle, Priya commanded four more rabidos. Because of the command, she missed the monster behind her. The rabido clawed at her back but was cut in two by the basha's axe. He'd stayed to fight in the middle while Master Yapoma was up front, hacking down one rabido after another. Priya had never seen her master work with such efficiency and power. His white hair was soaked with dark red blood.

More and more rabidos came pouring in. Priya sliced off the arm of one that came too close, while trying to force two others into the long, chaotic procession leading to the hole.

A high-pitched scream made Priya look up. Kohóna had leaped through the doorway, landing in the middle of the last tangle of rabidos. The monsters became frenzied, frantically trying to run in all directions. The water panther swished her massive tail, flooring about five of them and then standing up on her hind legs. On her back was Reza, one hand on the straps that held him in the saddle on Kohóna's back. In his other hand, he gripped a long sword.

A rabido smashed into Priya. With a short scream, she went down.

Immediately, another monster pounced on her. She kicked out as it panted down her neck.

Priya reached out her hand. Placed it on the monster's chest. 'Still.'

It froze, falling stiffly onto her. She almost weakened her grip as she felt its bleeding mouth coming for her throat. Almost. But then she pulled herself together and kicked the monster away. Grabbing her sword off the ground, she slit its throat. 'Stay there,' she snarled at the rabidos nearby. A few parasites came crawling her way, and she slid backwards.

A hand pulled her up. 'I saw you fall,' Kwasi said breathlessly. The right side of his uniform was soaked with blood and grey slime.

'Break your neck,' Priya whispered at the rabido that came running towards Kwasi with clawed hands. The monster grasped its own head and gave it a hard tug. 'I'm fine,' she added in a louder voice to Kwasi. 'But thank you.'

Priya drew her second sword and pushed further forward. A new wave of energy swept through the troops. She peered around to see what had given the soldiers renewed courage. Sweat streamed down her face, but still she pulled her hood further down over her head to protect herself from the maggots crawling all over the ground.

Further on, Master Yapoma on the left flank and Reza on the right were systematically eliminating the rabidos that escaped from the dense, controlled stream, spear and sword flashing so fast that Priya couldn't follow their movements.

Makaku was fighting just behind Reza. He jumped forward. In mid-air, he was pierced in the back by a spear that one of the rabidos had picked up. Priya saw his mouth open in a silent scream. She saw him fall. Saw him disappear under writhing bodies. He did not stand up again.

Her heart thumped painfully.

Then a rabido shrieked right beside her.

Priya hacked at it with her sword. Tried to slit its throat. It didn't work. The rabido had bitten into a soldier and was using the limp body as a shield. She drew her dagger and plunged it into its neck. Out of the corner of her eye, she could see Nanu fighting off three rabidos at once.

Priya pulled back her dagger and threw it at one of Nanu's opponents. The dagger landed between its shoulders and it went crashing to the ground. Nanu glanced up.

'Thanks,' she panted.

'You're wel—'

'I still don't like you, by the way,' said Nanu, before mowing down a rabido in front of Priya.

The thick stream of rabidos was straying from the path. They were beginning to lose control. Priya looked across the way. Reza, on the other side, suddenly turned round. He was standing higher than the rest, presumably on a fallen section of the wall, more and more pieces of which were crumbling away. Outside, night had well and truly fallen. Moonlight shone in, falling on Reza's face.

He looked to one side and for a fraction of a second it felt as if they were looking straight at each other. Not because she could see his eyes, but because she felt his soul brush against hers. It was a brief touch. Nothing more. And yet, in that one moment, she felt his emotions.

He was worried.

Before she could react, he jumped from his vantage point and started running back. She followed him from the other side, because she knew what he was planning. The flow of rabidos had been lingering for some time at the edge of the Keep. They were veering backwards and changing direction at the last minute to avoid falling into the water. They seemed to be afraid of something.

Reza brought the dazed rabidos to a stop at the edge of the building. Priya reached out. The chaos in their souls was lulled by Reza's influence.

Move forward.

They obeyed.

The first of the rabidos plunged into the water.

40

THE PLAN WAS WORKING.

Priya grinned as another group of rabidos disappeared into the river. It was *working*. Reza immobilised the rabidos close to the gaping hole and Priya made sure they disappeared over the edge. Without him, she could manage only five rabidos at a time. Together, they dealt with about twenty monsters at once. The tiny spark of hope that she'd buried deep in her heart flared up inside her. They could do this.

She could do this.

Reza caught her eye over the heads of the rabidos. His face was a small point in the moving mass and yet she felt his eyes burning on her. His energy occasionally merged with hers and kept doing so, until he no longer retreated. They were connected. It wasn't that she heard his thoughts or that she *was* him, but she could feel what he was feeling. Sometimes she couldn't tell if it was her energy or his – or some sort of combination of the two.

Their gifts, working side by side, intertwined in spite of their shields, made her weightless. It felt as if she had wings and was soaring through the air. He was electric. Magnetic. His gift was blazing. And she blazed with him. She smiled in delight. Something flickered in his soul, something she couldn't place. Then it was extinguished.

Priya slid one of her swords back into the sheath. Kwasi ran up and covered her back. In front of her, three soldiers wrestled with the rabidos that had broken through the first line of defence. Instinctively, she reached out her hands and grasped the souls of five rabidos. With a twist of her hands and a clear command in her thoughts, she snapped their spines. A stabbing pain in her head forced her, panting, to one knee. She pushed herself back to her feet.

The other deed-speakers moved closer and closer to her, pushed there by the rabidos, until they stood together in a circle. The soldiers of Brigades I and II fell in line and, led by the bashas, they stood in a protective semi-circle around them. Priya brushed back strands of hair that were stuck to her face. She was so hot inside her uniform.

Together with the other deed-speakers, she made more than forty monsters move at once. Far more than Priya could manage alone, but still fewer than she'd expected. Her enthusiasm waned a little. These were powerful deed-speakers. Why was it going so slowly?

The stream of rabidos was endless. Priya switched off. Without thinking, she pushed monsters over the edge – monsters that had once been people she'd trained and fought with.

Right at the front, Master Yapoma's hair streamed out as he single-handedly kept the vanguard under control. Priya felt the power of his gift rippling from him in waves.

'We can't keep this up all night,' a soldier in a black uniform shouted at the basha. 'Where is she?'

The basha's answer was lost in the commotion.

The Dedekedre. The soldier was right. Priya's arms and legs were getting heavier too. Doing this all night would be too exhausting. Normally they fought in narrow corridors with barricades and the soldiers took it in turns to fight and to rest. This time there was nowhere to hide.

Priya felt the sweat running down her neck and onto her back. Her clothes were soaked with blood and sweat. The uniform was clinging to her body like a second skin. She slammed the hilt of her short sword into the jaw of a rabido and felt herself becoming light-headed before she pulled herself together.

Reza immobilised another group of rabidos on the edge of the abyss. He looked for her with his soul. Priya reacted, driving the monsters over the edge. Their screams disappeared as soon as they hit the water. She tried not to think about what would happen if they survived the fall and climbed out of the water.

There were troops standing down below, waiting for the first rabidos to surface. But would that be enough to prevent an outbreak?

'There's another wave coming.' Kwasi had stayed near Priya and was fending off the rabidos that attacked her from behind.

'More?'

Kwasi grinned and yelled: 'The Dedekedre has been here for a century, Pri. This is nothing yet.'

The new wave of rabidos was closely followed by more soldiers and Reza's water panther, Kohóna, who ran alongside like a dog herding sheep. When it looked as if a rabido might escape, she closed her sharp mouth on its throat and shook it like a ragdoll until its head came off its torso.

Priya felt a strange ripple and looked to one side. If her soul had been a sitar, then it felt as if someone had just plucked one of her strings. She stuck her knife in the neck of a rabido and used it as a shield against another rabido. It struggled as she twisted her dagger. Blood dripped over her hand and clothes.

Again she felt that peculiar tugging. This time she recognised it. Priya widened her range. It was Jupta. She wasn't there yet, but she was about to come running through the stone door, surrounded by other soldiers and rabidos.

Priya turned, quickly wiping a sleeve over her soaking face. She was exhausted. Pushing her way forward, she held out her hands in an attempt to move the rabidos at the entrance to the tunnel even faster, so that Jupta would have more room. With the help of Reza's powers, she didn't even need to express her will in a thought or utterance. She just imagined it happening – and the rabidos obeyed. This time, too, she almost managed to do it.

But then she felt the dark energy.

Her breath caught in her throat. Cold claws raked through her body and clutched her heart.

Priya staggered and fell into a soldier, who almost thrust his sword into her.

From somewhere behind Jupta, an enormous form of energy was steadily approaching. Priya took a step back. The primitive fear she'd briefly felt when Major Aïda told her what sort of monster was hidden deep inside Kuwatta multiplied by ten at that moment. This was not a force she had felt before. The hundreds of rabidos swarming through the corridors paled in comparison.

The rabidos shrieked even louder. Priya clenched her jaw, trying to keep the nearest rabidos under control. Her ears were ringing from the high-pitched, sharp sound they were making. Slowly but surely, she began to make out a bizarre melody in the sound. As if they were calling their mother, as if they were singing to her.

The first heavy thump made her teeth clash painfully together. Stone and rubble slid down the walls.

A tug at her soul left her gasping for breath. She looked up. Reza was pointing at the rabidos between them and then at the river. Priya bit hard on her bottom lip to wake herself up. Tasting blood, she bit harder, so that the pain would keep her head clear and her body would stop shaking. Trembling, she raised her hands again. With desperation, she grabbed as many rabidos as she could.

A second thump made cracks in the wall and in the ground beneath them. Priya strengthened her grip on the souls of the rabidos who were screaming for their mother.

She clenched her jaw, trying to ignore the fierce stabbing pains. With a scream, she pushed the rabidos over the edge. Panting, she doubled over. Kwasi patted her on the shoulder. A moment later, a rabido, mouth gaping, ran straight into his spear.

'Damn it!' she heard him yell. He let go of the spear.

A high-pitched roar made Priya's bones vibrate and her ears whistle. Her heart skipped a beat.

This was a sound she had never heard before. The terror somewhere deep inside – a primal fear not only for her own survival but that of the whole world – rose again within her. She tasted ash and iron.

Master Yapoma drove the soldiers in the vanguard to the rear. The flow of rabidos was interrupted. Together with the kapten of Brigade II, he reorganised their teams to form a shield in front of the doorway.

'Forward.' Reza appeared beside Priya and reached for her hand. His hand was warm and sticky. Hers probably felt the same. Yet still she clung to him.

'She's coming,' Priya croaked. 'She's coming.'

But before the monster broke through the wall, a small group of soldiers came running through the door. Tiny and painfully insignificant, they looked like ants beneath the immense stone wall, which could collapse at any moment. Jupta was one of them.

Reza squeezed her hand. 'You know what you need to do.'

Priya ran forward.

'You lot too!' Reza shouted behind her. 'All of you!'

She didn't know if the others were following or not. She didn't care. All she could see was Jupta. Little Jupta standing between the Dedekedre and the rabidos, with nowhere to go.

Using her gift, Priya pushed aside the rabidos who got in her way. As soon as she was past them, she let go of their souls and grabbed for the next ones.

A third thump sent enormous blocks of stone tumbling down from the wall. The soldiers who were standing too close tried to jump out of the way but not all of them managed to get away in time. Some disappeared beneath the rubble. Jupta's long black plait swished to and fro. Her arms flailed. She fell. Priya darted forward, but Jupta was out of her reach. With outstretched hand, Priya used a rabido to pull her friend to her feet. Then she killed the monster by breaking its neck.

Unfortunately, at the same time, her panic and exhaustion made her lose control of the nearby rabidos' souls. One of them grabbed hold of Priya's arms and pulled her closer, digging its nails painfully into her flesh. Priya tried to snatch the dagger at her waist, but her fingers were slippery with blood and she dropped it. She kicked up her foot, turned halfway round and pulled out the knife hidden in her boot.

Then the wall broke. The rabido disappeared in a tangle of soldiers who were trying to run away. Chunks of stone the size of Reza's water panther flew into the air. Soldiers screamed. The painstakingly maintained line of defence broke. Then a white clawed foot emerged from the cracked walls. With a thump that made the building shake, it landed on the ground. The Dedekedre roared. Priya pressed her hands to her ears and screamed. She couldn't hear her voice, she couldn't hear anything but the howling roar of the Dedekedre. Tears sprang into her eyes. It felt as if her skull were about to split open.

The wall crumbled further, and the Dedekedre stepped forward. It took her a few attempts to get her entire body into the open space. On curved claws and legs, she slowly advanced. Her body was naked and gleamed creamy white in the moonlight. Priya blinked a few times. Scales. She had creamy white scales. Her head looked like a deformed dragon's head, as if parts of it had melted and solidified again, with a mouth full of the sharpest teeth. A long, thick tail with spines dragged behind her. She truly was monstrous. Yet at the same time there was something horrifyingly human about her, which repulsed Priya. The Dedekedre sniffed loudly as she came forward, her milky-white eyes staring into space.

Kwasi crashed into Priya. She looked at him. His eyes were wide open and he was screaming at the top of his voice, but she couldn't hear him. She followed his gaze and her world came to a standstill.

Jupta was lying on the ground in front of the Dedekedre, her leg trapped under a block of stone. The Dedekedre slowly approached her. Her mouth gaped open, revealing rows of razor-sharp teeth.

Priya didn't hesitate for a moment. She held out her hands and made three rabidos run forward. Surprised, the Dedekedre stepped back a little when they collided with her. Priya sent another three. It wasn't enough. They were too small, too insignificant.

Sweat beaded on Priya's forehead. Her ears were still ringing from the Dedekedre's roaring. Then she saw Ishani running to Jupta, followed by Rohan. Priya felt the blood drain from her face.

What were they doing here?

Ishani and Rohan came to a stop and kneeled beside Jupta. They grabbed Jupta's arms and slung them over their shoulders, as Rohan tried to push the heavy block of stone off Jupta's foot.

The kapten of Brigade I screamed orders. Master Yapoma stepped forward. He spread his arms and once again Priya felt the immense power of his gift. Then he brought his hands together and the Dedekedre shook and made a whining sound.

'Come on,' hissed Priya, trying to control the rabidos near Jupta, Ishani and Rohan, as well as the ones around her. The soldiers nearby began to carve out a way through for Priya and the other deed-speakers.

The Dedekedre shook her head wildly, and Master Yapoma went to stand in front of the monster.

'Now!' screamed the kapten of Brigade I. 'Archers! Spears!'

A volley of spears and arrows flew forward. The Dedekedre covered her head with her paws. Priya tried to reach Jupta but was prevented by a line of soldiers with shields.

Master Yapoma lowered his hands in a controlled way, and the Dedekedre bowed along with his movement. He stood motionless in front of her, only his mouth moving. He had her in his power. Priya squeezed out a short laugh.

Then the Dedekedre lashed out, knocking Master Yapoma away like a ragdoll. He smashed into what was left of the wall and slid down it, leaving a red imprint behind.

That was the starting signal for the rabidos, who were still singing to their mother. The Dedekedre ran forward, grabbing soldiers in her mouth. She bit until their bones broke and she tossed their limbs aside.

With Ishani and Rohan's help, Jupta had stood up and was tugging at her leg, which was bent at a strange angle. She took something from Ishani, but Priya couldn't see what it was. It didn't appear to be a weapon. Ishani's mouth moved. Jupta firmly shook her head.

Priya gathered all her energy until her core was glowing and pulsating. The gold bracelets around her wrist became blisteringly hot, burning into her skin. But she barely felt it. The other deed-speakers joined her.

'Stand still,' screamed Priya. *Stand still,* she commanded.

The Dedekedre, drooling, came towards Jupta, who pushed Ishani away. Rohan threw himself in front of a rabido that flew at Ishani and got bitten in the neck. A soldier grabbed Ishani and pulled her aside. Fearlessly, Jupta held out her hand.

No.

Priya did something she'd never done before. She grabbed her friend's soul and she pulled. Jupta moved backwards, narrowly avoiding the Dedekedre's claws. Spears rained down upon the monster. Most of them just clattered off her scales. The Dedekedre opened her mouth wide and lashed out at her unseen enemies. Ishani had disappeared. Where was she? Priya saw a flash of her tall figure and her dark plait. Then she was gone.

'Again,' Priya shouted at the other deed-speakers. 'Stand still,' she screamed, and the others repeated it. 'Stand still!'

Kwasi stood, tense, beside Priya. She felt his gift glowing fiercely.

But it wasn't enough. It was not enough.

The Dedekedre stepped forward and scooped Jupta into her maw.

41

JUPTA DISAPPEARED INTO THE Dedekedre's massive jaws.

Priya couldn't breathe.

Jupta struggled, part of her upper body emerging from the monster's mouth. With a dagger, she hacked at the side of the Dedekedre's head. The Dedekedre clawed at her mouth, hitting Jupta on the head.

Priya clumsily shoved a rabido away. She hit its midriff, and parasites fell from the wound her sword left behind. Stamping on the maggots, she ran forward.

Jupta's dagger carved into the Dedekedre's head, but the monster's jaws closed. Jupta disappeared. Even from a distance, Priya heard the bones breaking. She clapped her hands over her ears. 'No! No! NO!' she screamed frantically.

She tried to get the Dedekedre under control. Tried to force her to open her mouth. Clawed with everything she had at the monster's chaotic, overwhelming soul. She drew on Reza's soul for more power. The monster's soul was a stronghold of loose tangles of energy held together by thin threads. And yet that soul felt like an avalanche crushing her. Priya's vision blurred as she grabbed hold of the red-orange threads glowing brightly within the Dedekedre. For one unbelievable moment, it seemed to be working.

'Let go!' she screamed with so much conviction that she swayed on her legs. 'Let go!'

Then Priya was hurled out of the Dedekedre's soul.

Too late, too late, too late.

More bones cracking. Jupta's dagger fell.

And when it hit the ground, it felt as if Priya's world broke. A piercing sound chilled her to the core. Her body was made of shards, of splinters.

Stumbling, she stepped forward. The world was spinning. The walls were moving. White shadows came towards her. In a reflex, she raised her sword.

Suddenly she was lying on her back.

A rabido was impaled on her sword. The monster's hands had been curled in the air, but now fell limply. Its stinking mouth gaped over her head, blood dripping from it onto her face. She pulled out her sword.

As she looked up at the monster's mouth, all she could think was that maybe it would be better just to disappear into that hole. Then perhaps the pain would disappear.

And then she felt teeth in her right leg. Another rabido was squatting over her.

It bit. Hard.

She let out a cry. Her throat felt raw, as if she'd been screaming and screaming, but no one had been able to hear her. The monster's teeth pressed through her flesh, hit her bone. It hurt. It hurt so much. But not enough to match the pain in her heart. She swung her sword in its direction, but there was no force in the blow. She didn't even know if she managed to hit the monster.

More shadows. And she thought about Jupta. And she thought about Mawar. And she thought: *maybe dying isn't so bad*. So she let the monster have its way while the walls danced and her ears rang.

'Pri! Priya!'

A voice. Priya tasted its fear on her tongue. She began to laugh at the absurdity. At the absurdity of the world.

Someone was moving her. Her fingers slid over the uneven ground. The pressure on her leg was gone. However, the pain still reverberated. The edges of her vision turned red. Fiery and full of pain.

'Her leg! The poison's spreading . . . If we don't . . .'

'We have to get out of here!' someone else yelled.

Other hands on her wounded leg. Softer, kinder.

'I can't hold them off!' said a voice, sharp and urgent, cutting through Priya's giggling.

'No time for . . . The poison . . . Do it! Now!'

Now? What's happening now? Priya wanted to ask, but her mouth couldn't form the words. Her throat was raw and painful. The hands disappeared. Priya tilted her head. For a moment, her vision became sharp again. Reza's face swam above her head. Ishani stood next to him; she was crying. Her beige uniform was covered in blood. Priya was about to reach out her hands to her sister, but then she saw Reza again. Strong Reza raising an axe high above her.

It was coming down.

Straight towards her wounded leg.

Priya shot up in alarm. Hands grabbed hold of her, pushing her back down. And then the axe sliced through her flesh, through her bone. With one single blow. A gasp escaped her lips. Her lower leg lay on the ground. Separated from her body. Useless.

Then the world exploded into white-hot stars.

Priya threw back her head. And howled.

IN THE
CURSED HEART
OF THE WORLD

42

PRIYA'S WORLD CONSISTED ONLY of pain.

Colours exploded behind her eyes, ranging from bright red and orange to whitish yellow. She felt nothing but a white-hot line of fire that began at her right lower leg and moved on to her torso and head. She screamed, shrieking until no more sound came from her mouth.

Every heartbeat pounded painfully in her ears. Every breath scorched her lungs. In the background, she heard voices. Murmuring. Unintelligible. Hands touched her, some softly, others roughly. It hurt. Everything hurt.

'Stay away from me,' she said weakly, but the pain didn't ease.

More voices.

'Leave me alone,' she mumbled. Her body was burning. Her lower leg hurt so much that she was aware of only fragments of her thoughts. Jupta, snatched by the Dedekedre. Reza, looking at her as their souls converged and merged into one. Kwasi, laughing as he ran through the rainforest. Ishani, her eyes wet as her mouth formed the word 'didi'.

It hurt so much.

Why didn't it stop? All she wanted was for it to stop. Somebody, she begged, please make it stop.

So much pain.

The dark spots in the corners of her eyes grew larger. Slowly, everything dulled. Overcome by exhaustion, she sank into a pitch-black warmth.

It swallowed her.

+++

A few times she woke up but soon lost consciousness again. The reality was too bright, too full, too painful to confront. Strange dreams, made up only of colours and shapes, filled her head. Some of them were orange-red, and then they were shattered by splinters of ice blue and black cones. Priya floated back and forth between blissful ignorance and dark depression. Her father, smiling and looking down at her, until she realised that he couldn't see her and he dissolved into clouds of mist. Crying, she called out for him. Jupta was alive, Jupta was not alive. Alive, not alive.

In the end, Priya couldn't escape it any longer.

She woke with a start.

She saw a high black ceiling. She wasn't in her own room. This was somewhere else. She slowly tilted her head, the mist in her mind clearing. Just above the windowsill, she saw the sun shining between thick grey clouds. Some of the tension left Priya's body. It was daytime.

She ran her fingers over the thin sheet that covered her body. Her right leg was throbbing painfully; a nagging thumping sensation that went all the way up. She shifted her position and tried to look down under the sheet, which sent a shot of pain flashing through her leg. She flinched, but that didn't stop her from looking down again.

Her right leg was wrapped in white bandages just below the knee and ended in a rounded stump. Her lower leg and foot were gone.

She breathed in sharply and looked away, feeling light-headed. The bottom of her leg was no longer there. Her head was thumping. She gulped painfully. She heard nothing but her own heavy breathing. She couldn't get any air.

Then she realised there was someone else in the room.

Beside her, on a wooden chair, sat Reza. He was dressed in a simple black tunic and had exchanged his prosthesis for a slimmer black one. It could have passed for a human hand, were it not for the fact that the material had been polished to an unnatural sheen. Despite his light clothing, he was still heavily armed. Around his waist hung several daggers, and the rounded handles of two more knives protruded from his black boots. His left hand rested on the hilt of a long sword, which leaned against his chair.

He was asleep. A small frown line had appeared between his eyebrows, and the corners of his mouth were turned down. Even in his sleep, the general's youngest son could find no rest.

Priya shifted in her bed, so that she could see him better. She tried to do it quietly, but a flash of pain shot through her, making her hiss.

Reza woke immediately, his hand grasping the hilt of his sword more firmly. He blinked a few times and then gave her a slow smile. 'You're awake.'

'So are you,' she croaked. It confused her that his energy glowed warmly as soon as he looked at her.

'How do you feel?' His gaze moved around the room before landing on her again.

She didn't know how to respond. Her head still felt muzzy. There was an emptiness deep inside her; a hollowness she didn't dare to probe. Her fingers dug deeper into the sheet, pulling at it and turning it into a crumpled ball.

'I'm fine,' she said. 'But where am I?'

Reza's eyes moved to her hands, to the bandage, which had pinkish patches on it, and back to her face. He leaned forward, resting his elbows on his knees and clasping his hands together. Priya smelled the wind and rain on his skin and saw that his black curls were damp. His clothes were clean and unwrinkled; the rusty bloodstains on his uniform and face were gone. It was as if the fight had never taken place. But Priya's wounds told a different story.

'We moved you to the Lodge.' A brief pause. 'We didn't know if you were going to make it.'

Priya felt a flicker in his soul, an emotion that was thick and heavy. She didn't react at first. She drew circles on the mattress with her finger, trying to ignore the dull pain in her leg. The sheet was of good quality, and that made her wonder whose bed it was. At first she thought of Reza but no, that was impossible. She'd seen his sleeping quarters; this room was a lot smaller. 'How many days?' she asked finally.

'What?'

'How many days have I been unconscious?'

'Three.'

She stopped drawing circles. Her eyes went to the window. All she could see was an ocean of green trees with a twisting, glistening ribbon running between them. No buildings. She looked out over the waterfall. 'What happened to the Dedekedre?'

'She destroyed half the Keep,' said Reza in an almost matter-of-fact tone, 'and disappeared into the sunken hall as soon as the sun rose. Since then, we've been fighting her from the Academy and the Lodge.'

She had failed. That was as clear to her as a cloudless sky. Kuwatta had been counting on her, and she had failed. A raw sound escaped her throat. It felt as if the walls were closing in on her, crushing her. She should have tried harder, trained longer. So many lives had been lost, just because she hadn't done what was asked of her. And Jupta . . .

Her breath caught in her throat. She couldn't breathe.

Jupta was gone. She was gone. And it was Priya's fault. She hadn't been able to save her friend. Just as she hadn't been able to save Mawar. And she certainly wouldn't be able to save Kuwatta.

'Priya.' That was when she felt Reza's hand on her shoulder. He pulled her a little closer. 'Breathe in for me.'

She *tried* to breathe in.

'Look at me.'

She did as he asked.

His dark eyes were alert, studying every inch of her face. 'Breathe in.'

She breathed in.

'And out.'

She breathed out. And then, following his instructions, she repeated the process again and again until her breathing was back to normal and her heart began to beat more slowly. His hands slid over her throat, holding her head on either side. His prosthesis felt cool and smooth. She vaguely registered the mattress sinking a little and the throbbing in her missing foot intensifying. Reza held her close, and she leaned against him. Her hands clutched his uniform and she howled into his shoulder. He gently stroked her back, her throat and her hair. His touch was tender.

'I'm sorry. I . . .' she said to his shoulder. 'I just don't know how . . .'

'I understand,' he said into her hair. 'You don't need to explain.'

Then she felt his body tense up, and his arms slid from her body. 'I have to go,' he whispered close to her ear, his hand brushing a strand of hair behind her ear before his warmth disappeared. When she opened her eyes, he was no longer in the room.

'Soldier Priya.' A probie in a beige uniform stood in the doorway, holding a bowl of steaming water and clean bandages. 'You're awake.' He looked over his shoulder and shouted, 'Fetch the major!'

+++

After Priya's lower leg – stump, she mentally corrected herself – had been cleaned and the bandages changed, Major Aïda came into the room. She was followed by a female soldier who Priya didn't know and, behind her, Kofi. So, he'd been promoted to the position of the major's confidant.

Priya leaned against the pillows that the probie had arranged behind her back. Her leg was in the worst state, but her whole body felt bruised and fragile. She just wanted to disappear, or – even better – for all the other people in the room to vanish. All she wanted was to be left alone.

'Soldier Priya,' said Major Aïda. She stood at the foot of Priya's bed, looking down at her. Her black uniform was immaculate, and her long plaits were half up in a bun. Long gold earrings glistened by her neck. Kofi stood with the other soldier behind the major, loosely holding a long spear in his hand.

Priya wanted to run away. Away from them, away from Kuwatta, away from the world. But of course, she thought cynically, running away was no longer an option.

'We're all most relieved that we still have you in our midst. I've spoken to my personal healers. So far you've escaped infection. That means that in a few weeks, when the wound is fully healed, we'll attach a prosthesis to your lower leg. With . . .'

Priya stopped listening as soon as she heard the familiar sound of Ishani's footsteps and sensed her sister's soul. She was close, and there was someone with her. Priya's hands became fists. Ishani was the last person who'd been with Jupta before she was taken by the Dedekedre. She'd said something to Jupta, something that had stopped her from trying to escape. Priya racked her brain to remember more, but then Ishani appeared in the doorway and all other thoughts left her mind.

'Soldier!'

Startled, she looked up.

Major Aïda crossed her arms. 'I want your attention here. I hate having to repeat myself.'

Priya nodded weakly.

The major turned to look at the newcomers. 'Scholar Afounsowa, probie Chkadhari. What brings you here?'

Scholar Afounsowa pressed her fists together before pushing Ishani forward. 'The girl has something to say.'

Ishani's bottom lip was trembling slightly. 'Priya,' she began shakily. 'Jupta made her own decision at the last minute. I want you to know that before I tell you the rest.'

Major Aïda narrowed her eyes. 'Where are you going with this?'

Ishani's eyes flashed to the major. For a moment, she looked uncertain, but then a stubborn look appeared on her face and she stood up straight. 'The Dedekedre is made of human souls.'

Priya began drawing circles on the sheet beside her leg again. The Dedekedre looked nothing like a human being, but when Priya thought about it, the chaotic energies shooting in every direction within the monster did indeed feel much the same as the rabidos' restless, jagged souls. The Dedekedre didn't look human as such, but there was something inside her that felt human.

'This is old news,' said the major, unimpressed. 'We know the colonists used souls and put them into a didibri dragon.'

'No, it's different with the Dedekedre,' Ishani insisted. She held out her hand and opened her fingers. In the middle of her palm was a golden ball. 'Only soul-singers can use the magic in the gold. We've studied this. Ordinary people react to gold, but they can't do anything with it. Soul-singers can.'

'What are you trying to say?' The major raised an eyebrow.

Ishani took a deep breath. 'I suggested that, during the attack on the Dedekedre, we should test if she would react to gold.'

'The way the Dedekedre influences the rabidos has long reminded us of the power that soul-singers possess,' said Scholar Afounsowa. 'It's a theory we've often presented to the general.'

'But there was no proof,' Ishani added. 'Until that night.'

Priya's finger slid more slowly across the sheet. Something in Ishani's words made a piece of the puzzle fall into place, but Priya wasn't quite there yet. Ishani and Jupta in front of the Dedekedre. At the mercy of fate. Jupta taking something from Ishani.

Ishani rolled the golden ball in her fingers. 'The plan was to test if the Dedekedre would react to gold in the same way as soul-singers. But it doesn't work at a distance. The gold had to be held to her body for a longer period.'

'And did you manage to do that?' asked the major.

'We were losing.' Ishani's voice became softer. She glanced at Priya. 'I was desperate and tried to get the gold into the Dedekedre's mouth. But the Dedekedre only ate living soldiers. It was impossible to get the gold into her body without sacrificing someone.'

'Did you . . .' began Priya, struggling to sit up. Her leg was throbbing painfully and the sheet beneath her was rubbing against it, causing a burning sensation.

'Then Jupta suggested shooting the gold into the Dedekedre's mouth,' Ishani said quickly. 'I didn't ask her to do it. She wanted to do it herself. And she nearly succeeded, but then . . .' Ishani's voice faded. She hid her face in her hands. 'It went wrong. She made no attempt to run away. I called her name . . .'

'And is the gold now inside the Dedekedre's body?' asked Major Aïda. She strode over to Ishani and grabbed her by the shoulder.

'Yes, Major,' said Scholar Afounsowa.

Priya fell back onto her bed. All the strength had left her body. Jupta had sacrificed herself. Priya had sometimes secretly rolled her eyes at Jupta's strong ideals and her compassion for others. But now, for the first time, she loathed them with all her heart. *Why*, she thought, *why did you always have to do the right thing? Why couldn't you think of yourself for once?*

'Did she react to it?' the major asked sharply.

'Yes,' croaked Ishani. 'Yes, she reacted to it. She reacted in exactly the same way as a soul-singer.'

'So, because of your intervention, half of the Keep has collapsed,' spat the soldier behind the major, crossing her arms. 'So many soldiers lost their lives. What in the name of the Gods was your logic? Was this new knowledge worth paying that price?'

'No!' came Ishani's shocked reaction. 'No, that wasn't my intention. I just wanted proof. Now we know the Dedekedre is made up in exactly the same way as a soul-singer. We can use this to . . .'

'That changes nothing about the case, probie. This knowledge will not bring the dead back to life,' the soldier snapped at her.

'We cannot defeat the monster until we understand her!'

'And what difference has it made? All you did was make her stronger.' The soldier started slow clapping. 'Congratulations!'

Ishani's face reddened. 'It proves that it's no wonder we fought the Dedekedre for decades without succeeding, because we are making her stronger. Everywhere in Kuwatta is gold. Just look around!'

The major held up her hand, and the soldier fell silent. 'We can use this to our advantage,' she said thoughtfully. 'Especially if Priya and Reza join forces again. Does my father know about this?'

Join forces? Priya had failed. She had failed, so why were all these people here?

Ishani nodded cautiously.

'Get out,' said Priya.

She didn't say it loudly, but Ishani tensed up, and the major fell silent.

'Pri, we just wanted to . . .' Ishani began weakly. 'I only wanted to find a way to defeat the monster.'

'Get out,' Priya repeated more loudly. What little control she had over herself disappeared. She sat up, ignoring the pain that shot through her. Eyes flaming, she looked at the people in the room. Her hands were shaking. 'All of you! Get out!'

Major Aïda nodded calmly. 'I understand.'

'I didn't want . . .' began Ishani, warily taking a few steps forward. A lonely tear traced a line down her cheek. 'I didn't want Jupta to . . .'

'You have *no* idea who she was! None of you do,' screamed Priya. 'Don't you dare tell me who she was and what she did. You have no right to speak about her.'

'We'll come back another time,' said Major Aïda. She nodded at the soldier and Kofi, who followed her out of the room.

Ishani hesitated in the doorway.

'Out!' Priya screeched at her. 'I don't want to see any of you. I don't want to see anyone! Leave me alone.'

The bandage around her leg slowly turned red.

43

PRIYA PUSHED HERSELF TO her feet with the help of two crutches. As she fumbled, her stump hit the edge of the bed, making her gasp and double over. She saw stars. But that was nothing. The itching and pain that she'd felt at night in her missing foot were many times worse. Nothing could help to ease a feeling that existed only in her mind.

Hissing, she straightened the crutches. If she wanted, she could make this easier for herself. The major had been encouraging her to leave her room more often for some time now. She could ask for people to support her. But Priya hated support and particularly the dependence it brought.

Slowly, a lot more slowly than she would have liked, she hobbled down the corridor and went down two floors. When she reached the room she'd shared with Jupta, she pushed on the door. It swung open and she peered inside. There was no one there, but the room had changed. There were sleeping tunics folded on the mats and shoes lined up neatly beside them. A small brown comb and a homemade wooden toothbrush lay next to Priya's mat. Priya and Jupta's room had been assigned to other soldiers.

Even so, she pushed the door open wider and limped into the room. She headed straight to the mat that had been Jupta's, where she let go of her crutches. With a clattering sound, they fell to the floor.

Priya kneeled by the mat, excruciatingly painful though it was. She rolled up the edge of the mat. Nothing. Holding her breath, she rolled it further. And there, in the spot where Jupta had always hidden her prized possessions, was a single chain of smooth red-brown stones.

I'm so sorry.

Priya bowed her head – and the tears flowed.

+++

'You look absolutely divine.'

She looked up. Her eyes felt swollen and painful. The crutches wobbled under her weight. Kwasi was standing in the doorway. For a moment, all she could do was gape at him. He was slumped against the doorpost, as if all the strength had gone from his legs, running one hand through his messy black curls. Even from this distance, Priya could see that his eyes were bloodshot.

'And when did you last sleep?' she shot back. Gritting her teeth, she carefully slid forward. It was painful, but not as bad as she'd expected.

He gave her a resigned grin. 'I can't honestly remember.'

She studied him as she tried to move forward. Walking was going frustratingly slowly. 'Took you long enough,' she said finally. This was the fifth day since she'd woken up and he hadn't been to visit her until now.

Kwasi pushed himself away from the door frame and, hands deep in the pockets of his tunic, walked into the room. His back was a little bowed and his step heavier than she was used to. 'I came to see you. You were asleep.'

'I'm pretty sure you could have come when I was awake.' She cursed herself for making it sound like a criticism. Showing her true feelings instead of holding them in felt like a weakness. This reluctance to show her emotions was a feeling that came from her life in Disin, and at certain moments it resurfaced. Sometimes in front of her friends.

Kwasi stood there, wearily rubbing the back of his neck. 'It's not like I didn't want to . . . I couldn't. I'm sorry.'

In a strange way, she understood. Seeing him there in front of her, so broken, it felt as if the wound inside, which she was trying with all her might to ignore, was being ripped open again. Jupta's loss had thrown them both off balance. Priya gave a quick nod. Since the day she'd woken up, her voice had abandoned her when it came to Jupta.

'People are talking about you, you know,' Kwasi continued. He cleared his throat. 'About you and Reza.'

Priya stopped just before she reached the doorway. She'd only come a short way, but her head and neck were damp with sweat. She looked at Kwasi. He'd changed the subject, but she let him get away with it because she needed to talk about something else too. 'Why?'

Kwasi shrugged. His gaze moved down and rested on her right wrist, which she'd wrapped Jupta's beads around. 'Because the two of you did something that no one ever believed possible.'

Priya leaned forward to rest on the doorpost. For a moment, she was back on the battlefield, and she felt Reza's gift merging with hers. Parts of their souls had been intertwined that night. Just the thought of it made her fingertips tingle. The power and energy flowing through her at that moment were indescribable. She had not only been able to bend *more* souls to her will, she'd also done it with more focus. Sometimes she had the feeling that Reza was steering their energy while all she did was fire. And yet it felt right. It even felt good.

'It was incredible,' she said quietly. 'I don't even know how we did it.'

'Well, you'd better find out soon, because they want to use it against the Freelanders.'

Priya pushed his arm away when he reached out to help her. 'I thought they might. I'm trying to regain my strength as quickly as possible. Next time it's going to work.' She *would* succeed in defeating the Dedekedre. Ishani's discovery offered hope. The Dedekedre was made from the souls of different soul-singers. So, it made sense that she was many times stronger than an ordinary human or even a monster.

But she was not untouchable.

Priya had felt that, just before she lost control. Even the Dedekedre could be kept under control. Priya just needed to be stronger.

'Regain your strength?' Kwasi frowned. He moved his fingers and Priya knew that spiders were crawling around them. Only she didn't see the insects anymore; her mental shield was instinctively active these days. 'Didn't they tell you . . .'

'What? What didn't they tell me?' Priya asked sharply.

Kwasi's gaze slid downwards again. To the bandage around her stump, which – Gods! – was turning pale pink again.

'Pri,' he said gently. 'They're not planning to let you fight the Dedekedre again.'

Priya turned round and limped down the corridor.

'The major,' she said, grabbing hold of a green-uniformed soldier who was walking down the corridor. 'I need to know where the major is.'

'Pri,' Kwasi said behind her in a worried voice. 'This isn't a good idea.'

'Tell me where the major is,' Priya hissed at the bewildered soldier. Deep inside, she knew she was being rash, but she didn't care. She had made a mistake. She had failed. She could only live with that as long as she could put it right. She had to defeat the Dedekedre, or she didn't know how she was going to live with the guilt.

The soldier tried to push her off. 'On the top floor.'

His last shove sent Priya stumbling into Kwasi, who pulled her up. Before he could stop her, she had her crutches firmly in her hands again and was shuffling away. Kwasi made several attempts to change her mind, but Priya didn't want to listen. Her heart was pounding, and her arms protested as she climbed the stairs, but it didn't even occur to her to give up.

From the small windows on the staircase, she could see the Keep. The building, once so magnificent, now looked like a ruin. Walls had collapsed, entrances were concealed behind chunks of stone and most of the tall towers were completely demolished. It was a miracle that the Dedekedre had not yet escaped Kuwatta.

As she climbed the final flight of stairs, Priya became light-headed and fell into the wall. She barely managed to keep herself upright.

'What exactly do you hope to achieve?' Kwasi said, sounding pretty irritated. 'You're seriously injured, Priya. What kind of difference do you think you'll make if you join the fight?'

'That's not the point,' she snapped. Her hands trembled slightly as, with Kwasi's help, she stood up straight again. She took a deep breath. 'They can't take this from me. Not when I've already had to sacrifice so much.'

Kwasi grabbed her elbow and stopped her. 'We've all made sacrifices.'

Something in his voice calmed her anger a little. 'So why aren't *you* angry?'

His hand slid from her arm. 'Because I'm tired, Pri.' He closed his eyes for a moment. 'I'm so terribly tired. Aren't you?'

No. She was too full of anger to be tired. It felt as if she might explode with anger any moment, leading the world further along the path to destruction.

'I should never have left my people,' he said, broken. 'I should have stayed with them. You didn't see what happened after Jupta . . . You didn't see how we lost.' Kwasi shook his head. 'You didn't see the Keep collapse in front of your eyes. A quarter of the soldiers died. That's a huge number. Kuwatta can't take the loss of so many soldiers.' His face had turned ash grey. 'I came to Kuwatta to defeat the enemy. But I didn't know anything. And . . .' His voice faltered. 'I don't know if this enemy can even be defeated.'

It hurt to see him like this. Beaten. Extinguished.

'We'll only know that when we've fought to our last breath, Kwasi,' she said, briefly touching his face. Then she turned and continued on her way. Clenching her jaw, she struggled upwards, one step at a time, until she reached the top floor of the Lodge. Kwasi had followed her in silence.

Only one door on this floor was guarded, so Priya headed for that one.

The two guards crossed their spears as she reached out to the stone door.

Priya looked up. Both of them towered above her. 'Let me through,' she rasped.

'We have orders not to allow anyone in.'

'I am the major's protégée.'

'The major is in discussion with the general,' the guard growled. 'Only their confidants are allowed to enter.'

'Then at least tell them I'm here,' said Priya insistently. 'Leave the choice to them.'

'We can't let anyone in,' the guard repeated in a flat voice.

Priya wanted to give him a hard shake and then command him to step aside. But she couldn't do that without being punished. Grudgingly, she stood in front of the guards, trying to find some normal way to get inside. 'Fine. Then I'll wait here until the major finds me. I'm sure she'll really appreciate seeing one of her most valued soul-singers bleed out here in front of the door.'

The guards exchanged an uncomfortable look.

'Let her through,' said Reza, walking towards them. He was wearing his black uniform again. In his ears and his hair, gold ornaments gleamed in the sun. 'She's with me.'

Priya didn't know what had prompted him to give her his protection when he'd never done so in public before. But she decided there was no point dwelling on it. He was helping her – and she needed his help.

'Kwasi too,' Priya said. Kwasi had stepped aside as Reza marched past him.

Reza cast an annoyed glance at Priya.

'The boy too,' he agreed with a sigh.

'Oh, fantastic,' Kwasi mumbled behind them.

'We're out of time! The red moon is close, General. You know what that means . . .'

'If you go on like this, you won't have any troops left. Is that what you want?'

The guards pushed the doors open wider, revealing a small square room. It was simply furnished with a rectangular table in the centre, surrounded by stools. Wooden tables and benches were stacked along the walls – it looked as if it had previously been a classroom.

The general and the major stood facing each other across the table, above a map of Kuwatta that clearly didn't correspond to reality, as the Keep was no longer standing. Behind the general were two advisors and a number of soldiers. The major had brought only two soldiers, who were standing just behind her. One of them was Kofi, whose eyes briefly flashed in Priya's direction.

There was a free stool nearby, and Priya looked at it longingly.

'The lieutenant warned us,' the general said listlessly. His thin, frail body slumped over the table. 'I won't make that mistake again.'

'The girl told us the Dedekedre reacts to gold,' Major Aïda said. Then she realised that Reza had entered the room with Priya and Kwasi. Her eyes narrowed.

'Listen carefully, my daughter.' The general's voice took on a chilly edge. 'I have given you a lot of leeway, because you are a strong leader and the army loves you. But lately you seem to be forgetting that I'm the general and not you.'

'Father . . .'

'That is not how you address me. You persist in making the same mistake, Major.'

The major's face was frozen. For a moment, she did not move or speak. Then she pressed her fists together. 'My apologies, General.'

The general opened his mouth, but before he could say anything, he burst into another of his coughing fits. His advisors, including Scholar Afounsowa, looked at him anxiously. One of his soldiers reached out to him. But before she could touch him, he raised one hand.

'Reza,' the general said after some time, beckoning to his son.

Reza pressed his fists together and went to stand beside his father.

'Ah,' said the general, studying Priya. 'Soldiers Kwasi and Priya. Excellent. Step forward, soldier.'

Priya had a bad feeling. She shuffled forward on her crutches, stopping when she reached the edge of the table. Exhausted, she leaned against it. Luckily, the general did not appear to mind.

'Excellent,' the general repeated, pushing Reza in Priya's direction. 'Demonstrate it. You people.' He snapped his fingers and pointed at the soldiers in the room. 'Go and stand in front of them. Shields up. I want you to disarm them,' he added, looking at Priya and Reza.

Priya cleared her throat. 'General, if I might say something first?'

The general made a gesture with his hands, as if to say: Go ahead.

'I would like to correct my mistake,' Priya said with a dry mouth. 'For you and for all of Kuwatta. Let me fight the Dedekedre. I won't disappoint you again.'

There was a charged silence. 'First let me see how you combine your gifts. Then we can discuss the situation again,' said the general. His dark eyes were cold.

Priya felt Reza's warmth beside her. She became light-headed. One of her crutches slipped from her hands and, a moment later, she felt Reza's arm around her waist. 'Sit down,' he murmured into her ear. With one foot, he pulled a stool behind her, and she sank down onto it with relief. Cautiously, she rested her wounded leg on another stool, which Reza slid towards her. She ran her hand over her head and throat, which felt clammy.

'Those bandages are leaking,' said the major, looking disapprovingly at Priya's stump. 'They need changing.'

'First I want a demonstration,' said the general. His eyes bored into Priya's.

Priya licked her dry lips. She focused on her breathing until she became calmer and regained some of her self-control. Reza pushed at the edges of her mental shield. Focusing, she tried to let him in. But she didn't know how to. A few times she opened herself up and then, startled, raised her shield again.

Reza was doing more or less the same. She could see his growing frustration too.

'Give the command,' he said finally, his jaws clenched. 'I'll follow your lead.'

Priya gave a quick nod. She spread her attention over the ten soldiers in the room, including Kwasi. After some quick consideration, she decided to leave him out. Nine heavily armed soldiers.

Throw your weapons on the floor.

No one moved.

'Throw your weapons on the floor,' she said out loud, with more force. She saw that the soldiers' bodies were tensing up and their eyes were starting to bulge. A few hands went to the hilts of their swords and knives. But none of them threw their weapons onto the floor. Reza reached for her hand. His fingers slid over her palm and closed around hers. He felt warm. She tried not to think about it.

Again, he gently pushed against her shield, as if she were something fragile that he didn't want to break.

Priya didn't know what to do. It wasn't going to work like this. What had they done last time? She felt him – his emotions and feelings. Why wasn't it working?

She heard people murmuring. They were becoming impatient. 'Give them a moment,' the major said.

Control, Master Yapoma whispered inside her head. *You have to stay in control.*

But control was exactly what didn't work for her. Priya hesitated for only a fraction of a second before making her decision. Without warning, she opened up and released her tight hold on her gift. She didn't have control, but she did have strength.

And she unleashed it.

Throw your weapons on the floor.

Her gift flowed out like a roaring waterfall.

Reza flinched. 'Wait,' she heard him say in a hushed voice. His arm disappeared from her waist. There was shouting. Weapons clattered to the floor.

'Stop!' someone cried.

Priya was startled. She let go of the command and looked around. Everyone in the room, including the general and the major, had dropped their weapons. Reza was on his knees beside her and looking up with a pained expression. There were daggers in front of him, and his hand was on the hilt of his long sword. He firmly pushed it back.

'That,' panted the general, 'is not what I asked for.' Two soldiers helped him to his feet.

Outside the room, Priya heard the scraping of metal and brief commands. Her power had reached even beyond the room. Maybe even further than that.

'I'm sorry,' she said. 'I don't know what got into me. If you give me another chance . . .'

'You don't have yourself under control, soldier. You were over-whelmed by your own emotions.'

'I can do this,' she blazed. 'You have to believe me.'

'Apparently not,' the general said coldly. 'Maybe you can do it in the right circumstances, but we have no time to wait for that. Tell me, can you and Reza "merge" with anyone else if the conditions are right?'

'I . . .' Priya bit back her words of protest. She was still just clearheaded enough to know that wouldn't help her. 'I've never tried before.'

'Reza?' asked the general.

'No, General,' he replied.

'I will give you a chance, soldier Priya, but not with my soldiers. I don't want them to be struck down too when you're trying to destroy the enemy. Train with the other soul-singers and maybe we can talk again when you have enough control of your gift to successfully merge with Reza or another soul-singer. At the present moment you are nothing but a danger to the others.'

Priya's breath caught in her throat, and she looked at the major, but she wouldn't meet her eye. 'I want . . .'

'You may leave.'

44

THE MAJOR PACED THE room.

Priya lay dazed against the pillows on her bed, looking out of the window with half-open eyes. The sun was slowly setting. Not long now and night would fall. Not long now and the monsters would come.

'That was not a good idea,' said the major, coming to a stop in front of Priya's bed. 'What exactly did you think you were going to achieve?'

Only Kofi stood guard at the door. Kwasi had been sent back to his own quarters, even though Priya had protested. She had at least made him promise to visit her again when she was awake.

Priya turned her gaze from the sun, which could barely be seen through the heavy rainclouds. The great monsoon season had arrived, and the skies were weeping along with Kuwatta. 'I thought you wanted me to get out and walk around more.'

'I said that you must do your best to get fit again, soldier, not that you should confront the general directly.'

'I didn't confront him,' said Priya. 'He *wanted* me to demonstrate how Reza and I combine our gifts.'

The major didn't react at first. There was a deep frown line between her eyebrows. 'He's tense. His plan is to save our troops for the colonists who are on their way here.'

Priya knew the colonists were coming, but this was the first time the major had confirmed it. 'Aren't the warrior villages dealing with that?'

'They can't handle troops like that on their own. The colonists used to send small legions, but this time . . .' The major cursed. 'Even if they lose a quarter of their people before they reach us, we still don't know if we'll make it. The colonists have changed their strategy. They didn't know before exactly where Kuwatta was. But now they do.'

Priya racked her brains. 'How did they find out? The colonel was our only living prisoner. We killed the rest of the colonists we encountered.'

'Apparently not.' The major sighed. 'Or maybe they sent other soldiers into the rainforest. We were too focused on the Dedekedre to keep a close eye on the situation. Maybe they realised because of the rabidos that survived the plunge down the waterfall,' she mumbled.

'How many of them are heading this way?'

'It's hard to estimate in the rainforest. At least five thousand according to our scouts. Some of them will probably be intercepted by the warrior villages or get lost in the rainforest. They're moving this way very slowly because of their large numbers, but they're coming.'

Five thousand soldiers with weapons that were not used at Kuwatta. Priya's head was spinning. She didn't know exactly how many soldiers Kuwatta had, but it certainly wasn't anything like five thousand anymore. Probably around thirteen hundred, although the last battle against the Dedekedre had reduced that number. Now they were very much in the minority and were closed in by two enemies.

'My father wants to leave the Dedekedre be, as he believes we won't be able to defeat her anyway. His focus is on the colonists. He doesn't want to use you and Reza against the monster. Do you understand?'

'What about you?'

'It doesn't make sense focusing only on the colonists,' the major said angrily. 'The rabidos are causing chaos. If the Dedekedre gets out . . . I don't see how we'll survive that. We have to defeat her before the colonists get here.'

The major gave Priya a piercing stare. 'And that means *you* have to find a way to get your powers under control. Otherwise I'll just have to accept his decision.'

'I can only do that with Reza.'

'Reza obeys only his father,' the major growled. 'We can't count on him. Make sure that you can keep yourself under control, or find another sense-speaker who can help you.'

+++

Large drops of rain fell from heavy dark grey clouds. In the distance, a thick mist hung low over the green forest.

Priya stood with her back to the Academy and sighed. The nightly fights were becoming more ferocious. The cries of the rabidos were sometimes so close that she shot up, startled, and looked for her dagger. But all the other buildings had remained standing, and the Dedekedre had not yet been able to leave Kuwatta.

Here, on the other side of the Academy, where the Keep could not be seen, it even seemed as if nothing had happened. The black training grounds in front of her showed no signs of wear or damage. They looked exactly the same as they had a few weeks ago, when Priya was still unsuspectingly training here. And yet there was a world of difference.

'Again,' she said to the soul-singer in front of her.

She was practising with Paneke, the only other sense-speaker in the group Priya had started with at Kuwatta. He'd put up his sleek black hair, but a few strands had now come loose. He'd recently also become one of the major's confidants, and he was particularly guarded around Priya.

Kwasi was standing between them. Their test subject for today.

Forward, Priya commanded Kwasi. At the same time, she tried to find Paneke's soul and to open herself up to him.

Paneke pressed his lips together until they were a thin line. His mental shield flickered. Down, up, down, up.

'You have to take over my gift,' said Priya, trying to maintain her command. Kwasi obligingly stepped forward. He wasn't even trying to resist. Priya sent him a look of warning.

'Don't take this the wrong way,' he said, 'but I've already obeyed the same command at least a hundred times and I'm starting to get tired.'

Priya narrowed her eyes. 'If you'd prefer me to make you jump off the edge, that's not a problem.'

Kwasi straightened his back and spread his hands, looking at them in mock astonishment. 'That's strange. I can suddenly feel renewed energy flowing through me.'

She rolled her eyes.

Forward, she thought.

This time, Kwasi didn't move. She pushed against his shield while trying to reach out to Paneke. Their clothes were already soaked through, and Priya's leg was throbbing. She'd become good at ignoring the rhythmic pain by now, though. The hardest part was not blasting everyone around her with her command, while also using enough power to make things difficult for Kwasi.

'Come on,' she said to Paneke.

'I'm doing my best,' the soldier responded, unsmiling. 'You need to open up.'

That's what I'm doing, Priya thought irritably. Lowering her mental shield again, she felt Kwasi's presence. Immediately, reality changed. Twisted trees shot up into the sky, creepers hung low above the ground, and a tarantula the size of a parrot came crawling towards her. She pushed Kwasi out and threw up a shield. The image disappeared in a flash.

'I'm just trying to sketch a realistic scenario,' Kwasi said innocently when he saw the look on her face. For the first time in days, Priya felt the corners of her mouth twitch upwards. But then she felt Paneke's frustration coming to a head.

'It's not working,' he exploded. 'No matter what I do, it's not working! I don't even know what exactly you're asking me to do.'

That was because Priya didn't really know either. She didn't know what she and Reza had done that night. It just happened. Their souls had instinctively merged. They didn't need to *do* anything. It didn't feel like a fight with Reza.

A black shadow in the corner of her eye caught her attention. Paneke's frustration disappeared and Priya's eyes widened. The heavy rainclouds made it seem like dusk and, for one terrible moment, Priya thought a rabido was coming towards her, but when she looked again, she saw that it was Kohóna. The water panther reached them in three big jumps and Priya saw that Reza was sitting on her back. Involuntarily, she took a step back. She'd long since forgotten her command, so Kwasi was free to move again.

Reza jumped out of the saddle and crouched in front of Priya. 'So this is what you're up to,' he said, standing up. 'On my sister's orders, I imagine?'

His cutting remark hit home. 'It's not like you're making much time for me,' Priya said irritably.

'I would.' He looked straight at her. 'If you asked me.'

She'd been looking for him for the past few days, but he was nowhere to be found. The soldiers she spoke to said he was out combing the rainforest for traces of the colonists. 'Fine,' she said. 'Then I'm asking you now. Tell the general that, from now on, every morning you'll . . .'

'Every morning sounds like a lot.'

'Every morning,' Priya repeated with more emphasis. 'How long is it going to be before the colonists' troops reach us? A week? Maybe two?'

His mouth twitched. 'Twelve days, if they keep going at the same pace.'

'I need you.' This time she didn't hide her emotions from him. She let him feel her despair, her fear of what was to come. 'You felt it too. You must have done. We almost had the Dedekedre in our power.' With the help of her crutches, she moved closer to him and smelled his scent: grass and rain. 'We can do it again.'

'She tore herself away from us, Priya.'

'Because I couldn't control myself!' Priya said, clutching his black uniform. 'Come on, Reza. You know this is the only way.'

'There's another enemy out there. You're focusing too much on the Dedekedre.' His reply was flat, almost mechanical. As if he was trotting out something he'd been taught. 'The Dedekedre was *made* by the people who are coming for us. I don't have time to focus on her every day when the real enemy is almost here.'

Priya wasn't ready to give up. Her fingers gripped his uniform. 'We can use this against the colonists too. We're so much stronger together than we are alone.'

Drops of rain slid down his forehead and the bridge of his nose, but Reza didn't move. If she hadn't felt his heart thumping under her hand, he could have been a statue.

'The Dedekedre isn't our priority at the moment.'

A red mist descended before her eyes. Disgusted, she pushed him away. 'Those aren't your words,' she spat at him. 'Those are your father's words. The major's right. I can't count on you.'

A muscle in his jaw started twitching. 'I just said that I—'

'No,' she interrupted him. 'I don't want to see you just when it suits you, Reza. That's no good to me.'

+++

Exhausted, Priya let the crutches fall to the floor as she dropped onto a chair. Her leg was in a bad way. The rain had soaked into the thick bandages around her stump and the wound was itching really badly. She'd soon have to go limping to the healers for fresh bandages.

She looked out of the window. She couldn't see the sun because of the grey clouds, but she knew it would be setting soon. That meant she'd spent another whole day trying to merge her gift with Paneke's. And she had failed.

Wearily, she leaned forward, her gaze falling on Kwasi, who was putting on a clean, dry shirt that he'd grabbed from the storeroom on the way. She tilted her head thoughtfully. 'Hey,' she said. 'Why don't we give it a try?'

'What?' He slid his arm into the second sleeve, tugging the shirt down.

'Merging our gifts.' She sat up straighter. 'Maybe our thinking's too narrow. What if it doesn't matter what kind of gift we have as long as we're soul-singers?'

He stared at her for a moment. 'Are you serious? I'm not a sense-speaker. It's not going to work, at least not in the same way. You know that.'

'Gods, Kwasi. Help me out here. We don't have much time left.' Priya reached for her crutches and tried to get up. One of the crutches slid in the puddle of water that had formed beneath her, and she thudded back down onto the chair. Pain shot through her leg like sharp flames. With a hiss, she breathed in.

'If we have so little time,' said Kwasi, 'why haven't you been to see Ishani? Doesn't it matter to you that these could be our final days?'

Priya's face grew warm. 'What does Ishani have to do with this?'

'She visited you several times when you were unconscious.'

Priya shook her head. She knew she was being stubborn. Kwasi was right. How could she keep on ignoring Ishani when their lives were at risk? It was pure selfishness, and she was well aware of that.

It was such a muddle inside her head.

'How's she doing?' she croaked, fiddling with the bandages on her stump.

Kwasi sighed. 'Why don't you ask her that yourself? She's worried about you, you know. How long do you want to keep pushing her away?'

'I can't . . .' But she *could*, and that was the painful thing. She could go to Ishani, just as Ishani had come to her. In her nightmares, she often heard her sister crying in despair, and it seemed as if Priya couldn't move. No matter what she did, the distance between her and Ishani didn't get any smaller. It felt as if there was a physical barrier that she couldn't break through, but Priya knew deep down that she'd created that barrier herself. First out of anger, and now out of habit.

'Wait.' She looked at Kwasi again. 'How do you know she's that worried?'

'Ah.' Kwasi self-consciously ran a hand through his hair. 'I've spoken to her a few times.'

'What? When?' Priya fired her questions at him.

'Well, it got to a point where I kind of had to speak to her, when I ran into her yet again in the corridor outside your room.' Kwasi made a face. 'She was practically sleeping there. Listen,' he added in a more serious tone, 'you're her sister. I understand that the two of you have a complicated history, but right now she's doing her best. Are you sure you're not going to regret it if you carry on like this?'

'Are you really giving serious advice for the first time in your life?' Priya said, raising her eyebrows.

'I have three brothers and a sister, and I left them all behind,' he said in a defensive tone. 'Believe me, I know how it feels.' His dark brown eyes moistened, and his fingers drummed restlessly on his thigh. His dark mood had returned, and her stomach clenched at the sight of it.

'Sometimes you have to show that you're the older one, and take the first step,' said Kwasi. 'Even if you think it's too late.'

'Do you miss them?' Priya said, massaging the area around her wound. Like most of the other soul-singers, Kwasi rarely talked about his life before Kuwatta. In general, they hadn't had great childhoods, so they tried to forget about all that when they came to the fort.

Priya couldn't help thinking about Umed now, who she'd risked her place at Kuwatta for. That all seemed so long ago . . . Her gaze moved to an open window in the Academy, which had a view of the rainforest. Somewhere behind all those trees was Disin. She hoped with all her heart that he was still alive.

She loved her little brother.

She loved Ishani, too.

In a twisted way, she also loved her mother. And at the same time she hated her.

'So very much,' whispered Kwasi, his gaze elsewhere. He sounded tormented.

Priya made a decision. 'Do you know where Ishani is?'

+++

A range of emotions went through Ishani's soul when she opened the door of her room to see Priya standing there. Surprise, sadness, anger, pain and relief. In the end, they all melted together into a pained grimace. Silently, she pushed the door further open. Her room was small, and the furniture was minimal. On the right was her mat, and in the corner on the left was a low table with a stack of paper on it and a pot of ink and a quill.

With the help of her crutches, Priya entered the room. Ishani looked out into the corridor before quickly closing the door.

'How's your leg?' Ishani asked with concern. Her eyes flashed around the small room. 'Sorry I don't have a stool, but you can sit on the mat if that's easier.'

Priya bit her bottom lip. She felt like a terrible person. 'It's fine. I have these things for a reason,' she said, lifting one of her crutches a little.

Ishani nodded. 'Of course.'

A silence fell, weighing heavily on Priya. It was up to her. She had to take the first step, as Kwasi had said. 'I shouldn't have yelled at you.'

'It's not a problem,' Ishani said quickly, picking a bit of fluff off her beige uniform. 'I'm so sorry about Jupta. I hope you know I didn't want it to happen. I never meant for that. If I could turn back time, I'd have stopped her.'

'I know, Ishani. I'm sorry too. I . . .' Priya's voice died away. 'I haven't been honest either. I'm so used to blaming you. To be honest, I was usually jealous when we were growing up. I still am. You were always popular, but most of all . . . you were always more intelligent. Better.'

Ishani gave her a cautious smile. It was gentle, even a little sorry. 'The more I find out, the more doubts I have. Intelligence is almost impossible to measure. We talk about intelligent people when they're quick to absorb and build on information that we as a society consider important. But the problem is that society decides which knowledge or skills are important to possess and which ones aren't. There's nothing objective about it.'

'See,' said Priya, 'that's why the villagers always called you the intelligent sister. As long as you go on speaking in a way that ordinary people don't understand, they'll always be impressed.'

Ishani laughed. 'Whereas I'm impressed by you.'

'By me? I find that hard to believe. You've never acted like it.'

'I couldn't stand not being the best at everything,' Ishani admitted. 'But that's obviously impossible.'

'What are you talking about? You *are* better at everything.'

All her life she'd felt that she was in the shadow of Ishani Chkadhari.

It was only when they got to Kuwatta that things had changed. And yet that feeling of inferiority had resurfaced.

'You've got it wrong. I've never been physically stronger or faster than you. Everyone could see how you flourished in Master Ramsaroup's training sessions. You loved the pressure he applied; you even kept going at night until you dropped. You focused so hard on training that all you could see was who was in front of you. Did you have any idea where I was when we had to go running along the Cotari yet again? How far I was behind you? No, you didn't, because your eyes were always on Reza and Kofi.'

That was because they were the best in the class. 'I . . .'

'You're also better at making choices under pressure. And then there's your gift. It perfectly reflects the core of your personality. You're strong, you're powerful and you kneel to no one. You're right. In Disin, I only paid attention to myself. But that doesn't mean I can't see now how difficult it must have been for you. The whole world was against you, but you never gave up, didi. That's a power that not many people possess.'

Priya had a lump in her throat.

'I just couldn't face it for years because I . . . Well, like I said, I wanted to be the best at everything. I couldn't stand the fact that there were areas where you were better than me. And . . .' Ishani gulped. 'I had the feeling that you didn't like me. I'll admit that I probably played a part in that myself.'

'You were only following our mother's example,' Priya said softly. 'You didn't touch me, just like she didn't. You pushed me aside, just like she did.'

'That shouldn't have been an excuse. Maybe when I was younger, but when I was older, I knew better. I *should* have known better,' Ishani said, correcting herself. 'But I was desperate. Maybe not as bad as you, but enough to be devastated if I didn't win the test and couldn't go to Kuwatta.'

'You didn't want to get married,' Priya recalled.

'That's right,' said Ishani quietly, closing off a little. 'But maybe I should have been more specific. The thought of falling in love, getting married, having children . . .' She shuddered. 'I couldn't do it. Still can't. But I knew what my fate would be if I didn't win the test. And I know that I behaved selfishly because of that.'

'No more than I did,' Priya admitted.

'I don't know how to make it up to you,' Ishani said, looking down at the floor. 'But you're my sister. You'll always be my sister, no matter what the world calls you.'

Priya already knew the hug was coming before she felt Ishani's arms around her, and this time she responded immediately. Warm affection, which she'd been without for so long that it had become a stranger, flowed through her.

'I'm sorry,' said Ishani, leaning her head on Priya's shoulder.

'I'm sorry too,' said Priya in a tearful voice.

45

'NO.'

For a moment, Priya thought she'd heard it wrong. She was standing, supported by her two crutches, in front of the major, who was busily leafing through sheets of parchment. The small room in the Academy that she'd been using as her study since the Keep had become uninhabitable, was in a state of chaos. The small table she was standing at was almost completely buried in maps and notes. Behind her, Priya saw the symbol of Kuwatta – the rising sun – cast in gold on the wall.

Around the symbol, there were several cracks in the wall. Although the Academy had so far remained standing, the Dedekedre advanced a little further out of her prison every night. The rabidos had thrown themselves at the building a number of times, trying to claw their way in. After the first time, the general had ordered that the ground floor should be barricaded. The bottom two floors had been emptied and, except for a small passageway, bricked up. The soldiers who had slept there were moved to higher floors.

'This could be our only chance to defeat the Dedekedre, Major.' Ishani had explained it clearly to Priya once again, so that she would hopefully be able to convince the major. All the gold in the building was just serving to feed the Dedekedre.

The major shook her head. 'Don't get me wrong. I *do* want to defeat the Dedekedre. More than anyone here. That's why I'm so eager to find a way to get your gift to merge with another soul-singer's.' She found the sheet of parchment she'd been looking for and glanced up, distracted. 'But I can't have all the gold removed. Firstly, that will take time – time we don't have – and secondly it's been proved that it makes soul-singers stronger.'

'Hasn't Scholar Afounsowa explained it to all of you?' Priya limped further forward. 'The gold is actually ensuring that we *don't* defeat the Dedekedre. I'm not trying to say we have to remove all the gold, but it must be possible to get rid of some of it. It's in absolutely everything. We don't need that much. The gold in the walls isn't making the soul-singers stronger. It's making the Dedekedre stronger.'

'We don't know if it makes the Dedekedre stronger.' The major sighed. 'It's a theory, nothing more. All we know is that she responds to it, and we don't have time to test the theory. What we do know is that the colonists could be here at any moment. They have rifles, pistols, cannons. Weapons we don't have. But we,' said the major, 'have more gold. And trained soul-singers who can use it.'

'Didn't we agree that the Dedekedre had to be defeated before the colonists get here?'

'That was my plan too, but as you see, we have been unable to do so,' the major snapped. She tapped on the parchment in her hands. 'The warrior villages are falling, one by one. It's just a matter of days before the colonists are here. We have to prepare for a direct confrontation.'

'This isn't the right way . . .'

'There is no right way,' barked the major. She held two fingers to her forehead and waited a moment until she calmed down. 'I understand that you want to make yourself useful, soldier,' she said after some time. 'But the only way you can do that is by merging your gift with that of another soul-singer. And then we can talk again about removing gold. Until that time comes, I have no need for you.'

There was a knock at the door.

'Yes?' said the major.

The door opened. Kofi poked his head around the corner. 'My apologies for the disturbance, Major.'

'Speak, soldier.'

'We found out why the supply of cassava and rice has been cut off.'

'And?'

Kofi pushed the door open a little wider. 'The local villages have been destroyed by rabidos, Major. The plague is spreading faster than we anticipated.' He was silent for a moment. 'Even Bronskondre has fallen.'

Priya knew this news would only reinforce the major's new vision. Even she felt the impact of those words almost physically. Bronskondre was one of the strongest warrior villages in Awaran. Not only that – if the supply of cassava and rice, their primary sources of food, were lost, they would soon be in even worse trouble. Even with the fish they caught from the river, it was unlikely they would survive a siege from the Freelanders for long.

The major nodded. 'Make sure this news reaches the general and Scholar Afounsowa. We will have to introduce rations. You may go.'

'Yes, Major.' The door closed again.

Priya tried to contain her frustration. She understood the major's reasoning. The threat of the advancing Freelanders was palpable in Kuwatta. Particularly combined with the rabidos, which now had free rein in the forest. If Kuwatta fell, what would remain of the resistance?

During the daytime, soldiers with drawn faces and dark rings under their eyes worked at breakneck pace to reinforce the fort, while at night they fought to keep it standing.

The stone that had connected Kuwatta to the bank had been blown up, so the river now formed a natural barrier. Unfortunately, this had also made the fort unstable, but that had been relegated to a problem for later.

On several occasions, during her exercises with Paneke and Kwasi, Priya also saw stones being carted along to make a wall, which was to serve as the first defensive shield against the Freelanders' attacks. The soldiers were irritable, chronically exhausted and increasingly disconnected from one another.

Several times, Priya had caught herself staring out of the window at the rainforest, searching for signs of the enemy soldiers. Sleeping seemed to be an activity that belonged to the past. If she dozed off, she soon woke with a start, afraid of the Dedekedre and the Freelanders closing in on them.

'With all respect, Major,' said Priya through gritted teeth. She *could* make her soul merge with another's person, just not every person. And the person it had worked with rarely showed his face. 'I don't know how to do it. I've been training, but it's not working.'

'Just make sure it does, soldier.' The major was unrelenting. 'If you don't find out how, you can forget about defeating the Dedekedre altogether. Then I'll need you on the front lines against the Freelanders.'

'Really? Because you won't let me do anything now.'

'You have a wound that needs to heal. Or have you forgotten about that?' Major Aïda looked pointedly at Priya's leg.

It was a pragmatic move to have Priya fight on the front lines. But, for one incredible moment, Priya had felt that she'd had the Dedekedre under her control. She knew that it was possible. She was almost there. 'If you give me more freedom, then I'm sure that the Dedekedre—'

'I don't have any choice!' the major shouted. Her composure and her cold, calculating smile were gone. 'I have no choice,' she said more quietly. 'We're short of soldiers. Ultimately, it's most likely a choice between an early demise and a later one. I'm trying to stretch this out for as long as possible. And for the first time in my life, my father agrees with me,' she added wryly. 'So keep your mouth shut, and follow my orders.'

+++

'The wound's looking good.' A healer was studying Priya's lower leg, from which he'd just removed the bandage. About a month had passed since she'd woken up without a lower leg and in spite of the positive responses from the healers – and the reprimands, when she'd overloaded her leg – Priya was still struggling to get used to the sight of it.

The healer was a thin man with a short goatee and a balding head. He was older than most people at Kuwatta but, given his profession, that wasn't surprising. Healers didn't have to fight, so they had a better chance of survival. 'Considering the circumstances . . .' he added thoughtfully. 'The wound has healed over, and I see no signs of infection. In about a week, we can start looking at a prosthesis.'

Priya wondered if this would just be a training prosthesis, or one of Kuwatta's famed masterpieces. That would allow her to run on two legs again, albeit in exchange for a huge amount of energy. She wondered how Reza managed to attach his prosthesis night after night and to keep on fighting while the black stone sucked him dry.

'Isn't that a little soon?' asked Ishani, looking over the healer's shoulder at the wound.

'In normal circumstances, that would indeed be the case, but nothing is normal right now. It's certainly possible. The special prostheses are made from a material that's both strong and pliable. They combine with the skin and respond to signals from the brain.' The healer raised his eyebrows at her. 'What do you specialise in, probie?'

She blushed. 'Minerals, energies and gemstones.'

'Ah.' The healer clicked his tongue. 'Then you should know all this.'

It sounded rather condescending, and Ishani pressed her lips together. Priya felt the shame and resentment rolling off her. Knowing Ishani, she probably wanted to argue with him, but she managed to bite her tongue.

'The major has already had one made for you,' the healer said to Priya, swiftly wrapping clean bandages around her stump. 'Days ago. Even though we didn't know at the time that the Freelanders had almost reached Kuwatta. Maybe we'll even get the prosthesis on in time to . . .' He sounded uncertain and cleared his throat. His hands went on bandaging her leg. 'I've heard they'll be here in two nights.'

With the help of her crutches, Priya began to stand up but stopped when his words fully sank in. 'Where is the prosthesis?'

'Hm? Somewhere in our new storeroom.' The healer pointed casually over his shoulder. 'Two rooms down.'

'No,' said Ishani, seeing the look on Priya's face. 'I might not know as much as a healer,' she said, glancing at him, 'but I do know that a prosthesis is not a good idea right now. You'll probably destroy the rest of your leg, Pri. Don't do it.'

Priya, who was, of course, intending to get hold of the prosthesis as soon as possible, did not reply. She was thinking frantically. Her skin was tingling, and she felt nauseous. Two days. That was hardly anything. Even though the Dedekedre was now frequently hitting the Academy with devastating attacks, the major and the general seemed more concerned about the approaching army. Meanwhile Priya was being kept out of everything because she couldn't merge her gift with those of the other soul-singers.

She was being treated like a failed plan, an abandoned plaything.

+++

The rain streamed down Priya's skin, making puddles under her foot and crutches. She welcomed the cool it brought to the sweltering night.

There were no soldiers on this side of the Academy. Not at the barracks just in front of the newly built black wall and not by the white line. The rain fell and the bright flashes of light that split the sky were followed by booming thunder. Her emotions howled along with the wind. The moon was hidden behind a grey wall, but Priya knew that it shone perfectly round and white behind the clouds.

Priya perched carefully on the edge of the bridge, so that she could look down at the river.

She closed her eyes. And then she tentatively allowed part of her soul to wander. She felt the fish and the reptiles in the Cotari flashing by and skimmed past a flock of birds sheltering in a tree. And there, in the middle of the river, she found the general's son.

She immediately opened her eyes.

In the darkness, her eyes couldn't make out any movement but, to her subconscious, his soul shone as brightly as the stars in the sky.

Kohóna roared above the sound of the Cotari.

Priya pushed herself up with the help of a crutch and then braced herself.

A second later, the water panther emerged from the darkness, landing with a thud on the stone beside Priya.

She felt Reza's soul brush against hers and he came half out of his saddle.

'Fall to one side,' she whispered, and the command slipped through his body. He was already teetering on the edge of his saddle, and her words were no more than a gentle nudge in the right direction. A ripple against the shield around his soul; pinpricks in the spots where his energy was weakest. Maybe that was why it worked and, looking surprised, he leaned to one side.

She moved forward and pulled him closer. He turned during his fall, and she leaned in, landing on top of him, her crutches clattering beside them. Fierce flashes of pain swept through her wound. But she knew pain. Pain was by now a familiar friend.

She raised an elbow, intending to bring it down on his windpipe. He dodged most of her arm, the impact hitting his collarbone.

'What are you doing?' yelled Reza, trying to pin down her hands. Kohóna roared.

'We are all going to die!' she yelled back. The rain washed away the tears that were streaming down her cheeks. 'It's over. Did you know that? And all because *we* aren't working together.'

His soul rippled against hers, becoming entangled with the threads of her existence. In short, jerking moments, she felt his frustration, his despair, but above all his longing.

Priya looked at Reza, once again noticing his eyes, like bottomless pools of water.

'I hate you,' she said.

'I know you do.'

'I hate your position, your rank, your blind obedience. I hate that I can't get you out of my head.' It came out in gasps. 'Why do you keep working against me?'

He tensed at her words.

The pressure placed on her shoulders was too much for her. She was falling apart, becoming hysterical. She'd come to Kuwatta to escape and to prove herself.

But now all she wanted was for the world she knew to survive all of this. But she'd failed and that world would soon be gone. She would probably cease to exist, and so would everyone she loved.

It was too much. It was too painful.

'I've failed,' she sobbed. All the strength had flowed out of her, and she lay limp on top of him. 'I had just one task, and I can't even do that. And because you only follow your father's orders, I can't even put it right! Do you know how it feels to fail when the whole world is watching?'

'Yes,' he said, and she knew he meant it. All that did was make her angrier.

He swallowed. His gaze moved over her face, seeming to see everything. 'Priya.'

Her hand on his chest trembled. 'Shut up.'

'Alright,' he breathed.

She let go of his fingers to take hold of his black shirt and pull him closer. His eyes were a hand's breadth from hers, their noses almost touching. The only sign of time passing was Reza's agitated breath as it stroked her cheek, setting her skin on fire. 'I warned you,' she rasped, her voice thick with emotion. 'I told you to stay away from me and you didn't listen! But now that I need you, you disappear. I hate it.'

He touched her face and she let him. His fingers ran through her black hair. Reza's expression softened. He stroked the side of her face, brushed a strand of hair from her cheek. 'Priya,' he said again, softly.

And then he kissed her.

For a moment, she didn't move. Then she lost her self-control. All by themselves, her hands moved to his hair and she kissed him back. His soul was warm and made sparks that lit her up inside. He gently rolled her off him, kissing her more deeply. She grew weak under his touch, sighed as his fingers stroked her throat and his lips found a place under her ear. She pulled him back to her lips when that lasted too long. He was everywhere. In her thoughts, in her soul, against her body. And it felt so, so good.

Then a boom resounded throughout Kuwatta.

Reza froze, then moved back. 'No,' he said. 'No!' More words followed, but she didn't hear them.

Another thump shook the ground beneath Priya.

Reza's eyes were wide open. His mouth moved again.

They're here.

46

ANOTHER VOLLEY OF CANNONBALLS followed.

The Freelanders – the thought shot through Priya's head.

Reza leaped to his feet, pulling Priya up with him. His hand felt rough but warm. On his middle finger was a gold ring that was cool to the touch. His honey-coloured eyes and skin glowed in a flash of light as another boom shook the stone plates beneath their feet.

'According to the scouts, they weren't supposed to get here until tomorrow,' said Reza.

'Seems they can move through the rainforest faster than we thought.' Priya struggled to stand up on her crutches, as the rain poured down and the wind tugged at her clothes and hair. By the time she was upright, she saw that other soldiers and students had come outside.

Two teams, each under the leadership of a kapten, came running up. The line at the front was armed with spears; the soldiers at the back had bows and arrows. Running with them were a few soldiers with torches that flickered in the rain. Following a brief command, the first spears flew over the wall.

Other soldiers climbed onto small platforms that had recently been built and shot their arrows.

'Get back!'

Reza grabbed Priya around the waist and pulled her back. About fifteen paces away from them, a cannonball hit the black stone. The power it released made Priya and Reza fall to the ground and sent her crutches flying. Kohóna threw herself between them and the cannonball, growling. The stone beneath them groaned. A fracture line appeared under Priya's fingers, running back across the plate until it disappeared into puddles of rain.

Priya scrambled back up. This time it was faster. Adrenaline screamed through her body.

'We have to get away from here.' Reza grabbed her hand, pulling her towards the Academy. She leaned heavily on him as they ran.

'Wait!' Among the soldiers, Priya saw a familiar silhouette running past and disappearing behind a curtain of rain. 'Is that Ishani?'

'Priya!' Kwasi came running towards them. He handed Priya her sword, which she quickly tied onto her back, and then slung Priya's free arm over his shoulder, so that they could move forward faster. 'We have to report to the kapten of Brigade IV. Major's orders,' he yelled in her ear.

A flash of lightning lit up the surroundings: a brief scene of shouting soldiers, drawn swords, burning torches. Then everything was plunged back into darkness and there was another loud clap of thunder.

Together with Kwasi and Reza, Priya reached the Academy. The major, surrounded by a troop of soldiers, came towards them.

'There you are,' she shouted above the thunder and the commotion. She pointed at a platform that appeared to have been hastily assembled. 'Brigade IV's up there. You can see the colonists approaching.'

'What about the Dedekedre?' Priya shouted back.

The major firmly shook her head. 'No time! Brigade IV. Now.' She seized Priya's arm in an iron grip. 'Keep your power under control.'

Priya pressed her lips together and nodded. That apparently satisfied the major because she let go.

Reza pulled on Priya's hand and brought his head close to her ear. 'I have to go. Please stay alive.'

Kwasi helped Priya onto the platform, and part of the Freelanders' army became visible. As the lightning flashed, Priya saw them standing among the twisted trees and the dark bushes, line after line of soldiers in armour that shone in the moonlight, with two heavy cannons among them. It was a mystery to Priya how the colonists had managed to drag such heavy weapons through the rainforest without getting stuck in the undergrowth or a swamp.

Priya saw Kohóna run towards the only wall that separated them from the enemy soldiers.

'Deed-speaker!' With two large steps, the kapten of their group stood beside her. There were ten soldiers on the platform, including Kwasi and Priya.

'Yes, Kapten?' Priya pressed her fists together.

'I want you to get the Freelanders who are operating the cannon on the left under your control. Turn them against their own people.'

'Yes, Kapten!' Priya tasted rainwater and gunpowder on her lips. Reaching out with her gift, she felt three people by the cannon. At that moment, they fired another cannonball at Kuwatta. It slammed into the wall. Priya couldn't tell what damage it had done, as the rain was too heavy and the night was too dark. But she heard the Freelanders' excited shouting.

She tried to concentrate. Three souls. That wasn't an excessive number. Unfortunately, the soldiers were quite far away, which made it harder to get a grip on them. Another bang. She bit her bottom lip. Gods, there wasn't much time. There. One, two, three. There they were. She seized them.

Back, she thought. *Back. Back.*

A terrible roar filled the night, disturbing her focus. She looked over her shoulder. The Dedekedre had smashed a hole in the side of the Academy. The unfortunate people who were inside came tumbling down, crashing to the ground, their screams and shouts lost in another clap of thunder. A flash of light illuminated their pale uniforms. Scholars, or probies.

Priya lost her balance, falling into Kwasi, who was standing beside her. She heard him curse. He was shaking from head to toe.

Trembling, she used her gift to check the dying and to make sure they didn't include Ishani. She didn't find her. But she did feel the souls of the broken scholars and probies slipping away, and their bodies becoming dull and empty. Priya felt bile rising into her mouth.

The eerie shrieking of the rabidos grew steadily louder, chilling Priya to the core. Their bizarre singing was with her day and night, turning all her dreams into nightmares and echoing in her ears even when she looked out across the river in the daytime. She couldn't take it anymore.

'Eyes forward!' shouted the kapten, trying to restore order. 'I want all eyes on the Freelanders! What's happening behind us doesn't matter right now.'

Priya tried. She tried to drive back the soldiers by the cannon on the left. But when she noticed Reza, her focus on the Freelanders disappeared completely. The daring plan that she'd kept hidden from the major fiercely flared up again in all its intensity.

'Kwasi,' she shouted.

He looked up.

'Come with me!'

'What?' he said, surprised.

She pulled her sword from her back and leaned on it as she made her exit. The kapten of their team seemed to realise at the last moment that she was leaving, but by that time she was already gone. With Kwasi's help, she limped as fast as she could towards Reza. As they went, she reached out to him with her gift, lowering her mental shield completely, and slamming her own emotions into him.

It worked. He turned round.

'We have to try again,' she panted as soon as she reached him. Kwasi walked away from her, and she saw him looking for something.

Reza's eyes went straight to the Dedekedre behind her. He knew at once what she meant. 'My father has a different plan.'

The rain was easing. 'What kind of plan? How does he intend to destroy her?'

'No, that's not it.' He avoided her gaze. 'He's planning something else.'

What could the general be planning to do that would help Kuwatta without the Dedekedre being destroyed? Kuwatta was practically a heap of rubble, so it wasn't as if the prison could still hold the monster. Unless . . . 'No,' said Priya, as it began to dawn on her. 'He can't really be planning to release her from Kuwatta deliberately.'

'We can't defeat both the Freelanders and the Dedekedre. We simply don't have enough troops.'

'Releasing her would mean the end of all the settlements in the forest!'

'And if she stays, it means the final downfall of Kuwatta. In which case we'll lose both wars. We have to make sacrifices.'

'That isn't a sacrifice! It's genocide – and you're knowingly participating in it!' screamed Priya. 'You can't be serious, Reza.'

That seemed to hit home. 'Do you want to know what will happen if the Freelanders win?' he asked. 'That, and a lot more. It was them who *made* this monster, Priya.' He grabbed her by the shoulders. 'I *do* want to help you. But not like this.'

The next clap of thunder was just a low rumble. The sky had calmed down, but inside Priya a storm was raging. Giving the colonists free rein was not her intention, but letting a bloodthirsty monster that would never tire and would sweep through their country like a plague was even more dangerous. She couldn't believe Reza was still blindly obeying his father even now. Unable to look at him, she turned round. Then she would just have to get the Dedekedre under control *without* him. She reached out with her gift for Paneke or another sense-speaker who could help her. Reza grabbed her hand before she could walk away.

'Priya, no,' he said, guessing what she was thinking. 'It's suicide.'

She pulled away from him. 'Go on, then,' she spat. Trembling, she leaned on her sword. 'Follow your father's orders. That's all you ever do, isn't it?'

Reza didn't reply.

Kwasi came back and handed her a broom handle, which she took from him. She didn't know where he'd got it from, but she looked at him gratefully. With a walking stick, she could move a lot faster.

'What exactly is your plan?' he yelled. 'Given that we seem to be heading in the wrong direction.'

'We're going over there.' Priya pointed at the Academy.

'Sounds like a terrible plan.'

'And we're going to destroy the Dedekedre.'

Kwasi burst out laughing but fell silent when he saw her face. He took two large steps to walk beside her. 'Are you serious? On our own?'

Priya had meanwhile discovered Paneke, who was with another team near the Academy. They were dealing with the first rabidos that crawled out through the hole the Dedekedre had made in the building.

Kwasi was yelling at her. It was just as well she could hardly hear what he was saying because of the gunshots and the screaming of the rabidos. She was sure that a lot of his words were curses.

'Paneke!' shouted Priya, reaching out with her gift and pressing her energy hard enough against his to make her presence felt. Paneke looked over his shoulder just as two of his teammates slit the throat of a fallen rabido.

'The Dedekedre. We have to give it a try.' Priya gasped for breath.

'You've gone insane,' was Paneke's reply.

'Thank you,' said Kwasi, skidding on the wet stone as he came to a stop.

'We need to give it a try.'

'We've never managed it. If I go with you, I'll be signing my own death warrant.'

'Listen to me. The general is planning to release her into the rain-forest. Do you realise what that means?' Priya wanted to give him a good shake, so that he'd understand what the future would look like if the general's plan was carried out. The Dedekedre would sweep throughout all of Awaran, leaving a blood-red trail in her wake. 'Do you have family in the villages around here? Friends?' They were cruel questions. And they had the desired effect.

Paneke's eyes darted back and forth. Trapped in a dilemma.

'Go.' Scholar Afounsowa, in a military uniform this time instead of her beige robe, appeared beside him. To her surprise, Priya saw that the scholar was leading Paneke's team as a kapten. 'If this is our last and only chance, then go with her, Paneke. At least try it. Kofi!' she called over her shoulder.

Kofi's tall, broad figure appeared behind her.

'Go with them.' The scholar turned to Priya. 'Find a place where you can keep a clear view of the Dedekedre. Then you'll have more control. If you can, push her into the river first. That means she won't be surrounded by gold, but she won't be able to escape into the rainforest either.'

Priya could only stare at her in bewilderment. She hadn't expected Scholar Afounsowa to openly oppose the general's decision. Kofi, who was standing behind the scholar, looked just as confused. But he still nodded.

'I'll clear it with the general,' said the scholar. 'May the blood moon shine long and red upon you.'

Priya smiled a little. She hadn't heard the original expression, 'May the moon shine long and white upon you,' for some time. It was what the free peoples of Awaran said to wish one another happiness and prosperity – and it was a discriminatory expression coined by those who were afraid of the red moon and everything associated with it. The scholar's subtle twist to the old words made Priya feel warm inside.

47

THEY CLIMBED THE STEPS of the Academy. It was a decision they'd made after a brief discussion. Their other option was to go through the tunnel that led beneath the Academy. That route would also take them to the Dedekedre. But they'd also encounter lots of rabidos that way and they would have less protection. On the other hand, there was the fact that the Academy might collapse, as Kwasi, looking a little anxious, had rightly pointed out.

Priya had decided that dying in a collapsing building was preferable to being eaten by the Dedekedre or a rabido. Paneke had agreed. Kofi had asked when they were leaving. Kwasi had given a loud sigh.

Unfortunately, even in the Academy, they weren't entirely rid of the rabidos. The monsters were able to get in through the hole that the Dedekedre had made in the building. Priya heard just a few muffled cries from the monsters at first and didn't think too much of it – until they found the body of a decapitated rabido on the stairs.

'Gods, that's all we need.' Grimacing, Kwasi stepped over it. He had drawn a broad knife, which he held firmly in his hands. 'I can handle rabidos, the Dedekedre if needed, but the sight of detached body parts still turns my stomach.'

Priya was holding her short sword in one hand and her walking stick in the other. Paneke and Kofi were the only ones who were fully equipped with weapons, and they led the way.

The screams and shouts became louder, as did the clashing of weapons. The familiar rotting stench drifted towards them in the darkness. It was more penetrating and sharper than ever, and Priya, constantly stepping in sticky grey slime, struggled to walk fast with her stick.

A rabido appeared behind two running soldiers, a pale patch of white between the dark bodies. Kwasi raised his knife, but Paneke was faster. In one smooth movement, he slit the monster's throat. The rabido slumped, gurgling, to the ground. Priya nimbly dodged its outstretched hands.

Another rabido ran towards them with flailing arms. Priya sliced an arm from its torso. A handful of parasites tumbled out and she shook them off her arm. Kwasi thrust his knife into the rabido's neck. Wiping her hand over her clammy forehead, Priya ran from the nearest parasites, drops of sweat rolling down her back.

On the third floor, Priya heard a stifled cry. Without thinking about it, she deviated from their route and turned the handle of a closed door. It didn't open.

'Pri, what are you doing?' Kwasi sounded agitated. He scanned the corridor for rabidos. 'This isn't the moment to read a good book.'

She realised she was pulling at the door of the small library. 'Someone's in there. It sounded like a human.'

Kofi and Paneke had also come to a stop and were looking in their direction, confused and impatient.

'Kwasi, give me a hand.' Priya leaned her stick on the wall and slammed her shoulder into the door. Kwasi sighed miserably and did the same. On the third attempt, the door burst open as the weight on the other side suddenly disappeared. Someone in a beige uniform rolled across the floor, scrambling to their feet before disappearing behind the bookcases.

Outside, the Dedekedre let out a long cry. Then the Academy shook on its foundations. Priya held on to the doorframe to stay upright.

'The building's collapsing!' screamed Kofi. 'What are you doing?'

Priya had recognised the person who was still hiding behind the bookcases. She braced herself, bridging the distance between them, small chunks of stone and sand falling on her head and shoulders.

Ishani peered out between two books. 'Priya?' she gasped.

'What are you doing here?' asked Priya, just as incredulously. She pulled her sister to her feet.

'I wanted to protect the findings of our research.' She was barely audible and looked bewildered. There was a fine layer of dust on her face. 'There's a safe that's supposed to survive the worst of natural disasters.'

'And you wanted to do that right now?' Priya stared at her, dumbfounded. 'Even though you know the Dedekedre could smash the building to pieces at any moment?'

'It's research into the Dedekedre. It's vitally important.'

And your own life isn't? Priya wanted to yell at her, but that felt kind of weak given that Priya was standing in the collapsing building too. She pulled Ishani into the corridor and grimaced when her leg hurt. She really wanted to get her out of the building. But that meant a risk of running into rabidos.

Another thud went through the Academy. The network of fracture lines in the walls ran into one large crack. Behind them, part of the building collapsed. With Ishani and Kwasi's help, Priya moved out of the way. Kofi blasted through a dozen rabidos that came pouring through the crack and cleared a path for the group. The gaping hole was so big that they didn't need to search any longer. They hadn't found the Dedekedre; the Dedekedre had found them.

Priya felt the rain on her skin again and heard the wind howling.

The monster seemed to have grown bigger. Much bigger. Her white head was at about eye level for Priya and the others. Down below, hundreds of rabidos swarmed, tearing themselves and one another apart to get as close as possible to their mother. It was a tangle of writhing bodies. The Dedekedre lashed out. She was destroying Kuwatta, her prison, piece by piece. Chunks of stone and rubble stuck out here and there above the swarm of rabidos. Even now, Priya could see the gold glinting among them.

Priya saw small groups of soldiers standing near the Keep, towards the Lodge, which was also half demolished. She couldn't clearly see what they were doing.

'Paneke,' called Priya. She didn't know if the sense-speaker actually heard her or had just had the same thought as her and come to join her.

This is the moment, thought Priya. Hand in hand with Ishani, she closed her eyes and gathered all the energy she had in her. It rippled up, warming her. Tingling sensations ran through her arms and legs.

'I'm ready,' Paneke yelled beside her, just audible above the rabidos' screams.

Good, thought Priya. And then she fired everything she had at the Dedekedre. She tried to open herself completely to Paneke and other soul-singers. She pushed down her mental shield. It was dangerous. But she didn't know how else to do this. As soon as she touched the Dedekedre with her gift, a shock went through her. The Dedekedre's chaotic energy made her willpower shake. So much energy. On the second attempt, it overwhelmed her too. She couldn't handle it. It was too much. It sent her own energy shooting off in all directions. With all her might, she tried to regain control of her gift.

Dedekedre, she thought desperately. *Dedekedre. Look at me, Dedekedre.*

The monster slowly looked up, her milky-white eyes gleaming in the light of the moon that appeared from behind the clouds. The shrieking of the rabidos seemed to die down. The Dedekedre and Priya did not move.

'Now!' screamed Kwasi. 'Priya! Do something, before she attacks!'

But Priya was just as trapped within the Dedekedre as the Dedekedre was in her. She had used her gift to penetrate deep into the monster's energy. But it didn't feel as if she was in control. More as if she was stuck fast inside there. Shocked, she tried to pull back. The Dedekedre was still staring at her. In a bizarre way, the expression on her monstrous face seemed almost human.

This was the monster that had had the four free peoples of Awaran in her power for over a century. The symbol of the oppression by the Freelanders, who had made her with the sole purpose of wiping out the rebel movement and all the other people in the rainforest.

At the same time, Priya thought back to what Jupta had once said to her.

We're fighting against ourselves. Against the monsters we can become.

The full meaning of those words was only dawning on Priya now. It wasn't just the soldiers in Kuwatta who were trained as killing machines. It had been a stroke of genius from the Freelanders. They had made a monster that turned humans into monsters. So the rebel movement focused more on killing their own people who had become monsters than they did on the Freelanders. They had made things so easy for themselves.

'Dedekedre,' screamed Priya. *Step aside.*

At that moment, the Dedekedre tore herself away from her grip and charged forward with a deafening roar.

Paneke did his best. Priya felt his terror as he tried to merge his gift with Priya's. Priya's instincts wanted to push him away, but she stood firm. Ishani pressed herself closer to her.

'Stop!' yelled Priya and, at that very moment, Paneke succeeded in partially merging his gift with Priya's.

The Dedekedre stopped.

The rabidos below did not. Scrambling over one another, they quickly used their bodies to build a tower. Kofi and Kwasi stepped forward, knife and axe at the ready. They balanced on the edge, peering down.

Paneke's presence in her soul disappeared.

'Do that again.' Priya glanced at Paneke, whose face was red with exertion.

Her own body felt warm too. The familiar nagging headache was back.

Step aside, she ordered the Dedekedre. *ASIDE. To the river.*

Paneke pushed and pulled at her soul, making her headache worse. This didn't feel like it was with Reza. Paneke felt like an intruder, while Reza had felt like a part of her. Priya had to do everything in her power not to eject the soldier from her soul while also keeping the Dedekedre under her control.

Kwasi drew back his knife and slashed at the first rabido to reach the gaping hole.

The Dedekedre stumbled over her own feet. She fell. Moved a little to the side.

Further, commanded Priya. *To the river. Don't stop until you're in the river.*

The headache was too intense. The Dedekedre pulled herself free. Ishani screamed.

The monster pounced on the Academy, which began to collapse like a house of cards. Then she slipped, as Priya continued to give her command, and fell to one side.

Priya let go when the floor beneath them moved. Kwasi and Kofi ran back to them, Kwasi screaming something. Instinctively, Priya reached out.

No, she thought, trying to steer her gift, which sent more shooting pains through her head. *Not Kwasi. Not Ishani. Not her.*

'Help me!' she shrieked at Paneke.

The Topuan soldier was struggling to stay upright. But she soon felt his presence in her soul.

Priya focused on the nearest rabidos. With Paneke's help, she seized the souls of five of them. She threw them into the air with a short 'jump' command, turning them into a living shield.

The ground under their feet was collapsing. Kwasi threw himself to one side and slid until he was with Priya, Ishani and Paneke. The floor they were on sank a little, was still for a moment, and then sank some more. Large blocks of stone went tumbling down.

The shield of rabidos was complete. They screeched as the chunks of stone came crashing down onto them.

More cracking and rumbling. Priya and the others landed on the ground with a bang. The impact sent pain shooting through every part of Priya's body.

Then it was silent.

Clouds of dust drifted up. The moon shone in – a good thing, as it meant they weren't entirely cut off from the outside world.

Automatically, Priya searched for the souls of Ishani, Kwasi, Kofi and Paneke. They were alive. Gods. They were all still alive.

Somewhere in the back of her mind, she registered that the Dedekedre's chaotic soul was not in the same place as before. She reached out further with her soul as the feeling returned to her body.

Her wound had opened up. She reached down to touch her leg, her fingers becoming slick with blood.

Suddenly she felt it. She opened her eyes wide in surprise.

The Dedekedre was in the river. She was too big for the current to carry her off between the stone pillars, so she lay there, thrashing away. For the first time in a century, she had left Kuwatta.

'I don't know who that is.' Kwasi coughed. 'But please remove your elbow from my stomach.'

Ishani weakly mumbled an apology and Priya felt her move.

'Is everyone in one piece?' came Kofi's voice from somewhere nearby.

Priya rubbed her eyes. It was just as well she still had the five rabidos under her control because other rabidos had appeared behind them and were doing their best to get through the shield, jabbing their bleeding mouths and clawed hands between the stiff bodies of their brothers and sisters. Paneke moved back as one of them almost grabbed hold of his ankle.

'Something's coming,' said Kofi.

Priya concentrated. It wasn't easy, as the nagging headache wouldn't go away. But she soon felt what Kofi meant. It was Reza, whose soul she could probably feel from miles away. Where she had once felt emptiness, she suddenly felt the warmth of his energy seeping through his mental shield. He was sitting on Kohóna and racing towards them. It didn't take the water panther long to reach them.

'Priya!' his voice echoed. The rabidos disappeared. Priya heard their bodies falling and their shrieking fade into the background. Reza called her name again and didn't stop calling until she answered, although she knew he must long since have felt her soul. 'Help me move these stones!' he called to the others. More footsteps. More bodies blocking the light, shrouding the room in darkness.

'I don't know what you've done to him,' Kwasi said quietly before they were freed. 'But I'm glad your boyfriend's helping us.'

'He's not my boyfriend,' she bit back at him, and Kwasi laughed. Then he groaned. 'Think I've bruised a rib.'

'Nice.'

'Sadist.'

She laughed but soon stopped, because that made her head hurt even more.

The stones were eventually moved far enough to create a narrow exit. Paneke was the first to push his body through the crack, followed by Kofi, who cut the throats of two of the rabidos that Priya still had under her control. Their bodies went limp and they fell to the ground. Kwasi and Ishani held Priya between them, so that she could hold on to them. As soon as she was out, Reza came and stood in front of her. She released her control on the last of the rabidos. Their small shelter disappeared with a loud rumbling of rubble.

Reza grasped her arms and looked at her with a mixture of relief and frustration. His fingers slid upwards and he pulled her closer. She fell against him, in a daze. His clothes were wet and, as always, he smelled of grass and rain. Secretly, she breathed in his scent. 'Why do you always have to be so damn stubborn?' he muttered, with his chin on her head.

The Dedekedre roared in the background. She slammed into the side of the fort and because Kuwatta was no longer fully attached to both banks, the building shifted towards the waterfall. The soldiers who had come with Reza let out cries of alarm. Together with Kofi, who had gone to join them, they formed a protective ring around the group to fend off the rabidos.

Priya freed herself from Reza's embrace. 'The Freelanders? Have they broken through yet?' She had to repeat herself to make herself heard above the screams.

'Partly.' Reza's expression was dark. 'Their troops didn't get the better of us, because of our soul-singers, but Kuwatta is too badly damaged to serve as a fort. My father has initiated the evacuation.'

It was just confirmation of what they'd already known. The Dedekedre roared again. 'I have to go to her.'

'Priya.' Reza stopped her.

'I can't let her escape. I managed to do it just now. I can do it again.'

She didn't add that her previous attempts had been mediocre at best. It hadn't been a real success, but she had been able to exert some control over the Dedekedre. And if Kuwatta was lost, then she at least wanted to drag the colonists to destruction along with the fort. She wanted them to come face to face with their own creation.

'You have to help me,' she said frantically to Reza. 'I need more soul-singers. I need you.'

She saw the conflict in his eyes. The battle between obedience and her plea. Time after time, she'd lost to the general, and she felt yet another rejection coming, until to her surprise he nodded. 'What do you want me to do?'

'Take me to the Dedekedre.'

+++

Kohóna tolerated Priya, but not before she'd growled in complaint at Reza and given his shoulder a petulant nudge. Reza tickled her under the chin and then lifted Priya into the saddle. Her leg was thumping painfully. But before she knew it, they were flying through the rabidos to the edge of the fort.

Reza drew his swords, slashing at the arms, legs and throats of the rabidos who dared to approach Kohóna. Priya hacked with her own sword at a rabido that had grabbed on to Kohóna's neck. That earned her a satisfied growl from the water panther.

On their left, they saw the Academy in ruins. Behind it, there was a clear view of the battlefield. Freelanders in white uniforms with dark jackets fought among the soldiers of Kuwatta. Some of them were using swords, but most had rifles. The sound of the gunshots was drowned out by the screams of the rabidos.

They reached the edge and Priya saw the Dedekedre below. With Reza's help, she slid from the water panther's back. The monster was clinging to the pillars, which were crumbling under the weight of her heavy body. Kuwatta was sliding further and further back. Priya glanced over her shoulder, at Kwasi, Ishani and the others, who were fleeing to the land. If the fort crumbled, then everyone who was still there would be swept away by the waterfall.

Priya felt dizzy.

She looked at the bank, where most of the Freeland legion was positioned. The Freelanders had not all advanced into Kuwatta. There was no need to now, as the fort was a sinking ship.

It was now or never.

Dedekedre, she thought. *Stop struggling.*

The Dedekedre merely opened her mouth and roared right into Priya's face. Then she thumped a pillar. Luckily, it didn't give way.

'Your nose is bleeding.' Reza's fingers turned her chin his way. Behind them, Kohóna dealt with the rabidos that came too close.

Priya's headache had got worse. She didn't know how much longer she could keep this up. Mentally, she was already exhausted. 'Try it again,' she said. 'One last time.'

'What?'

'Merge with me.'

He gave her a questioning look. 'What exactly are you planning to do?'

She grinned through the pain. 'You'll see.'

Priya reached once again into the Dedekedre's energy. The monster was even wilder than before. She resisted Priya's gift with all her might. But Priya persevered.

You are mine, she growled in her mind. *Mine. Submit to me.*

Reza's energy swirled around hers. She lowered her shield. Even his gift tasted like rain and grass to her now. He didn't manage to merge with her completely, but his guidance was already better than Paneke's. Priya didn't know why, but her body didn't reject his presence. It was as if he was supposed to be there.

The Dedekedre howled under their combined force. She moved very slowly aside through the stone pillars, towards the Freelanders. Priya's headache was so intense that the world around her was spinning. Blood gushed from her nose. Reza kneeled beside her. She felt his gift drop away and grabbed the front of his uniform. Concern hummed in his energy, engulfing her like a thick blanket. He wanted to give up.

'No,' she said with one hand over her nose. 'Don't you dare. Stay with me.'

'Then do it quickly.'

She nodded.

And then she threw everything open. It wasn't enough to get the Dedekedre fully under control. She still moved only slightly to the side. But Priya kept going, trusting that Reza would ensure her command affected only the Dedekedre. She looked up. Saw the clouds drifting by and the moon changing colour.

It became red.

A blood moon.

A horn sounded. She didn't recognise the sound, so she assumed it must be the Freelanders. An emergency order. They were retreating. The blood moon had come, bringing with it the monsters that the colonists had *not* made themselves. Primeval monsters. Vengeful spirits.

And blood children.

Priya felt fresh energy streaming through her.

'Here they are!' someone shouted. Paneke. Why had he come back?

'The Dedekedre's down there.' That was Kwasi. Gods, no, not Kwasi. 'Help Priya.'

More soul-singers hurried their way, led by Scholar Afounsowa. Priya could feel Nanu, Kofi, Letitia. The major was running somewhere behind the group. The Dedekedre was still tugging to get free. Priya threw her head back.

Everything around her blurred. People became hazy; shouts and screams fell silent. She no longer felt the wind pulling at her. All she saw, heard, felt was the Dedekedre. The monster was being forced to move more slowly. More deed-speakers joined her. They came to stand beside her, pinned in position, their focus only on the Dedekedre.

Blood dripped from the monster's maw as she tried to struggle free from Priya's powers.

She heard thousands of voices, felt thousands of souls whispering, pulling, screaming. Her head was too hot, too full, too heavy. But she would not give up. If she let go, everyone and everything would fall apart and be lost. If she gave up, everyone here was going to die.

The souls thumped into her.

The monster took another step aside.

Priya's body groaned under the weight of the souls. She panted, arched her back and gagged. Adrenaline rushed through her. How long could she do this for? She pushed the Dedekedre a little further. But she didn't know if she could give any more without losing herself.

A pillar came loose and the plate on top sank down. River water gushed over the edge. Priya fell backwards.

The shock of her landing made her lose her grip on the souls for a moment.

It was too long.

The Dedekedre tore herself away and the other soul-singers fell to the ground. Priya moved back, her heart pounding. The Dedekedre roared, coming towards them. The plate would break if she reached them. Priya knew that with all her heart. The plate would break and she, Kwasi, Reza, everyone, would die.

No. No more deaths. No. No.

'Stop!' she yelled. Her voice was lost in the sea of screaming people. The monster rose into a standing position. Reached out one massive claw.

Priya gave even more. Her emotions, her gift, everything. The invisible thread with which she desperately held together her entire existence almost snapped.

It felt as if knives were stabbing into her head. She felt her body being torn apart by the number of souls she held in her grip.

Her mouth opened in a silent scream.

'Priya!'

She didn't know who shouted her name. The headache consumed everything.

Her emotions were pushed into the background. A strange sort of calm came over her. She braced herself and forced the souls of the Dedekedre to obey her. If she was going to leave this world, then she would make sure that the Dedekedre went with her.

Her body was torn asunder by the energy. Skin ripped, organs turned into dust. She ceased to exist.

'Not so fast,' someone whispered in her ear.

She felt arms wrapped tightly around her. She looked down and saw a glove with a gold ring.

'You've not got rid of us yet,' said Reza, his lips touching her ear.

She felt his arms. She felt his energy, warm, crackling and full of fire. He was everywhere. In her arms, legs, torso. In her head and heart. He was an anchor holding her steady and stopping her body from tearing apart. Her emotions melted into his.

His energy calmed her. His regular heartbeat slowed hers down.

'What . . .' was all she could say. She was still holding the Dedekedre's souls, but she couldn't see the monster. Her vision had gone dark.

'Let go,' he whispered. 'And destroy the world for me.'

And so she let go of the last trace of self-control and surrendered to the chaos.

Priya's force hit the monster like a bomb. The Dedekedre stood still. Priya grasped all the souls the monster contained. She let go. She gave everything. Her complete power. Her energy. Her vitality. Her love. Her life.

When she opened her eyes, it was as if she was seeing the world through the Dedekedre's eyes. The strong current pressed her heavy body against the fort. Priya forced the monster – herself – to wade through the water. Towards the colonists' camp. The souls within her swirled restlessly in a spiral. They felt dirty. Echoes of the people they had once been, languishing in sorrow and despair. And no matter where they drifted, they had nowhere to go; they were trapped inside a monster that was consumed by pain. For a moment, she felt Mawar, then Jupta, and she had to force herself to keep going. She had a mission. With a few large steps, she reached the bank and pulled herself up. Above her, the red moon glowed.

Somewhere in the distance, she felt something awaken. A primeval monster. Its shadowy body slipped between the ancient creaking trunks of the jungle. Although the primeval monster had no solid body, Priya could see through the Dedekedre's eyes how it moved through the forest as a dark shadow that caused the river to fade and the trees to groan under an invisible weight.

Primeval monsters are attracted to violence, as the Dedekedre knew. One of the souls inside her had whispered it to her.

Then the words dissolved into the chaos, because the Dedekedre knew only pain and an insatiable longing for human flesh and blood. She wanted to see the world in ruins. Destroyed. In pieces. Just as she was torn into pieces inside.

Priya threw the monster at the tents. The screaming and shouting began. She felt bodies snapping under her massive claws. Scooped some up in her mouth and crushed their bones. The primeval monster reached them, descending upon the soldiers that ran from their hiding places. Wherever it passed, humans fell in droves. It left behind a trail of corpses.

Priya knew she didn't need to fear the monster.

She was a blood child. And all the children of the blood moon left each other alone.

In no time, it was over. The Freelanders' camp had been razed to the ground. Priya screamed at the top of her lungs until she came to her senses.

Enough, she whispered to the souls in the Dedekedre. *Go. Disappear.*

She shot back into her own body and was caught by Reza. The other deed-speakers looked at her, questions on their faces.

'Go,' she cried out loud. Suddenly she knew what she had to do and what the Dedekedre was longing for. She had felt what the monster and all the souls within her felt. 'Free yourselves.'

The deed-speakers repeated her command. Within the Dedekedre, the thousands of souls she had swallowed let go of one another, one by one. The threads connecting them became thinner until they disappeared, along with the constant pain felt by the souls.

They moved out of the Dedekedre and rose slowly, lingering somewhere in the clouds above. Thousands of souls, finally heading for freedom. At their centre circled the souls of the three soul-singers out of whom the monster had initially been created. Priya felt a strange sort of warmth move through her. The souls faded slowly until nothing of them remained. At last they had been able to leave this world to find their peace.

Priya sank to her knees, but luckily Reza was still holding her tight. Her eyes stung with the intense sadness that overcame her.

'The Dedekedre,' Reza said in her ear. 'Look. She's changing.'

With the greatest difficulty, Priya looked up. Her body felt weightless. As if she might dissolve at any moment, like those thousands of souls that had just left them.

In the distance, the Dedekedre had fallen onto her side and was staring, glassy-eyed, up at the cloudy sky from which fat raindrops were falling. Her white skin turned dark grey and deep cracks ran across it. She was falling apart. The moon high above had returned to its usual yellowish white and was shining down on them. After the red glow, its pale white gleam was a relief.

There was a commotion. Rabidos lay motionless on the ground, and the soldiers looked around, disoriented. The major stepped forward.

'We did it!' She was delirious with joy. 'You *did* it, Priya.'

Not only her. Priya couldn't form words with her lips. Black spots danced before her eyes.

'She needs medical treatment.' Priya fell limp in Reza's arms, her knees giving way and her head falling to one side.

She couldn't move. Her body refused to do what she wanted it to. That should have scared her, but it just felt like liberation. All she really wanted to do was to let go completely, so that everything weighing down on her, all the cares and needs and expectations, would fall away. A little voice in the back of her head shouted at her not to do that. But she was so tired. So terribly, intensely tired.

'I can't keep on holding on to her soul.'

Kwasi appeared beside them. 'Why do you need to hold on to her soul? What's wrong with her? Pri? Can you hear me? Priya!'

48

NEXT TO HER MAT was a gold ring.

A simple, narrow band with the emblem of Kuwatta engraved on the inside. A gift. A gift from Reza.

Priya sat up and placed the ring on her palm. She ran her fingers over its smooth edges, trying to ignore the pain in her missing leg. A gecko darted up the wooden post beside her mat.

She was on the mainland and lying in a tent. She ran her fingers through the grass beside her mat. Crickets chirped and a fat bee buzzed around her. Priya smiled. A healer was sitting on a wooden chair in a corner, reading a book by the light of the only kokolampoe in the tent. A quiet snoring came from the only other patient in the tent, three beds along.

The rest of the casualties were in other tents or were already getting up and about. Many people had not survived. She didn't know the numbers, but it wouldn't have surprised her if at least a quarter of their army had been killed.

Priya closed her eyes, gulped.

They had made it. They had defeated the Dedekedre. The army of the Freelanders was destroyed. It was over.

Days had gone by, but her body could not find rest.

Once she had dreaded the moments when she was conscious, fearing what kind of monsters might disturb her days. Now it was the nights that she couldn't escape. Nights when she was paralysed by nightmares that she couldn't wake up from. A nightmare in which Jupta was torn apart before her eyes, over and over again.

She preferred to stay awake.

Outside, it was still dark, but birdsong could already be heard above the roar of the Cotari. Their camp was not far from the river. It wouldn't be long before the sun came up, marking the start of a new day.

She slid the ring onto her ring finger, where it was a little too loose. An indication that she was not its rightful owner. Then she carefully sat up, grabbed the stick that was lying on the ground and limped out of the tent.

The healer glanced up but said nothing.

The nearby tents were silent. There were only a few people wandering about – a stray scholar who smiled at her, a lost soldier who gave her a nod. No screaming, no shouting. Just a little snoring. The silence that filled the air was proof of their salvation.

Priya stopped after a few steps, leaned against a tree. She was already out of breath.

At the edge of her consciousness, she felt the presence of someone she knew.

'You up already?'

She looked up. Ishani came walking towards her. She was wearing a simple beige uniform that left her arms bare. By the light of the torches, the gold studs in her ears glinted. Now that the Dedekedre was no longer alive, she dared to wear it again.

'Couldn't sleep.'

Ishani gave her a gentle smile. 'How's the walking going?'

'Making progress.'

Her sister nodded. She seemed to want to say something, but the words did not leave her lips.

'What is it?' Priya resisted the urge to ask about Reza. The first night after the Dedekedre had been defeated, when the healers were taking care of her, she'd felt the presence of the general's son. But afterwards the healers had denied that he'd been with her. Her only proof was the ring she'd found by her mat upon waking. The days that followed, she'd silently waited for him, but he'd never come. He had survived, she was certain of that. So, where was he?

'The major asked after you, so I came to see how you are.'

'Is that all?' Priya said.

'And Mother sent a letter. Some time ago.'

'Did she say anything about Umed?' Priya looked away, considering herself lucky that at least Ishani couldn't feel her emotions.

The first rays of sunshine were creeping between the branches of the trees. Priya didn't feel their warmth.

'Yes. Umed is back to his old self.'

'Really? Gods be thanked.' Some of the tension slipped from her shoulders. She smiled. 'Oh, I miss him so much.' The only words that felt genuine.

'And she . . .' Ishani's voice faltered. 'She asked after you.'

Priya stiffened. 'Don't lie.'

'I'm telling the truth, didi.'

The undisguised sincerity of her words surprised Priya. 'Good. Let her worry. That's the least she can do as a mother.' Priya could hear herself how exhausted she sounded. When she had just arrived in Kuwatta, it had felt as if it was only a question of time before she exploded. She'd worked hard so that she could hit back at the relentless world, including her mother, just as hard as it had hit her, over and over again. But lately, exhaustion increasingly had the upper hand. Priya was tired of a life full of fighting.

She was tired of the monsters that lived inside her heart.

Ishani appeared to understand. She held out her arm. 'The major's waiting for you.'

For a moment, Priya just stared at her sister's arm. Although her life in Disin had been very different from her current life in Kuwatta, the most surreal difference had been the change in her and Ishani's relationship. Just a few weeks ago, Priya would have flatly refused any offer of help from her family. This warmth, this affection, was strange to her.

It was strange, but it was something that she welcomed.

She slid her fingers into the crook of Ishani's arm.

+++

Major Aïda had the second-largest tent in their camp, although many soldiers felt that she deserved a tent at least as large as the general's. As she entered, Priya saw that the major's new study, in spite of her status, was sparsely furnished. A rickety table served as her desk, and her chair was a simple stool. The rising sun, cast in gold, that had hung in her old room had been replaced by a canvas with the symbol of Kuwatta painted on it in yellow brushstrokes.

Priya saw that they were not the only people in the tent. Several high-ranking soldiers were already present, as were Paneke, Kwasi and Nanu. She exchanged quick glances with them.

'Sit down, soldier,' said the major. Although the battle had been fought, she still wore her black military uniform every day.

Priya let go of Ishani's arm, limped to the only other stool in the tent and sank down onto it. Then she pressed her fists together. 'You wanted to speak to me, Major.'

Major Aïda rubbed her chin, with a slight frown on her face. 'How are you, soldier?'

She sounded tired.

'I'm fine, Major.'

'Are you managing to walk on your training prosthesis?'

'I'm doing my best.'

'That's not an answer.'

'Not really. Just short distances at the moment, but I'm trying to build it up.'

The major nodded. 'Excellent. I shall ask the head healer to take the measurements for your new prosthesis.'

'With all respect, Major,' said Priya. 'Did you really make me come here to ask me questions about my wellbeing?'

An amused glint twinkled in the major's eyes but then disappeared. 'Certainly not, soldier. Although it pleases me to see my troops fit and healthy. Lieutenant Somohardjo, perhaps you could repeat the most important points of our discussion for the newcomers?'

Lieutenant Somohardjo gave a brief nod. 'The number of soldiers remaining in our camp has fallen drastically. We first noticed this just after our victory. Some of the formations shrunk here and there. After the second day, according to our figures, a third of the troops had disappeared, including high-ranking soldiers. Although we didn't notice this until after the victory, we suspect that the desertions were already taking place to a lesser extent before. And that they were getting help from inside.'

A terrible suspicion stirred within Priya. 'You said that high-ranking soldiers have also disappeared. Who are we talking about?'

The major clasped her hands together on the tabletop. 'We're talking about bashas, kaptens, elite soldiers.'

She didn't dare to ask, couldn't get the words out of her mouth.

'Including Reza?' asked Nanu.

'Yes,' said the major, 'including my brother, the general's sharpened weapon.'

The words echoed in Priya's ears, paralysing her. She dug her nails into her palms to keep herself from making a sound, to hold her emotions in check. Had he left her? Without saying a word?

His ring had not simply been a gift. It was a farewell present.

The major spoke again. 'Over time, the underlying pattern became clear to us. The people who had disappeared had made it clear that they sided with the general on political issues. And my father has made it clear that he can no longer work with me as long as I continue to undermine his authority.'

Ishani's hand came down on Priya's shoulder, but she barely felt it. 'What does this mean, Major?'

'That from now on, we will form a separate rebel movement.' The major – or was she now the general? – looked at each of those present in her tent, one by one. She didn't need to fear anyone here in this space contradicting her. After all, this was part of the small army that she had personally assembled. 'My father is a good general, but he is also an anxious man. He refuses to make difficult decisions and he tries to keep all parties happy. He forgets that this strategy does not work in a war.'

A few soldiers murmured in agreement.

'At this moment he is retreating deeper into the rainforest and again refusing to make tough decisions.' The major shook her head. She spoke powerfully and confidently. 'The colonists have lost this battle, but they have not yet lost the war. They have a much larger army ready at the coast and are likely to be preparing to advance into the rainforest as we speak. They could even send another Dedekedre after us.'

'But if they do that . . .' Ishani's voice faded.

'They've already done it once. And I'll bet they can do it again,' said the major. 'Which is why I'd like to strike before they do. I want to wipe them out.'

There was a moment of silence.

Kwasi coughed. 'Um, how exactly are we going to do that?'

The major gave him a sharp smile and leaned over the table, so that she could look directly at Priya. 'By using primeval monsters. Soldier, you've already succeeded in defeating a Dedekedre. I'm sure we can win this battle, too.'

AFTERWORD

Suriname is, along with the Netherlands, the country I know best. Suriname is the land where my parents were born and raised. And Suriname is the country to which my Indian ancestors were taken, under false pretences, by the Dutch. Doubly colonised, first by the British, then by the Dutch, it was where they worked as indentured servants. For that reason, Suriname, like India, occupies an important part in my life. I am Dutch, but my vision of the world, my culture and my beliefs were also shaped by these two countries.

So, soon after writing *De Zwendelprins*, I knew that my next book would contain elements of Suriname. However, this book turned out to be a far greater challenge than I'd imagined. I wanted to incorporate the complexity, the scents and colours, but also the dark days into my book, without delving into subjects that I couldn't give a proper voice to, because of my lack of knowledge.

And that proved difficult, because Suriname is a country with a huge variety of different people, different stories and different voices, all of them intertwined and yet each with a history of their own.

In my book, the largest population groups of Suriname (under different names) work together against their oppressors: the colonists. In the real world, that did not actually happen. Partly because they were too different, partly because the language barrier meant they didn't understand each other, partly because they were oppressed in different ways, and partly because they were kept apart by the Dutch.

And there are probably other reasons that I'm not aware of. So, what I've written in this book is pure fiction. Even the symbolic battle that forms the central thread of my book never took place. The Afro-Surinamese, the indigenous groups (Arawak, Wayana, Tiriyó, and many more), the Indo-Surinamese and the Javanese certainly fought, but for the most part separately.

And those rifts of the past continue to make working together in the present something of a challenge at times. Which is not to say that it's not a beautiful country with a rich culture, nature and history. As Kwasi says in the book, it's 'a mosaic, beautiful and colourful, but the cracks are painfully visible'. I hope that my book, even though it is fantasy, will encourage people to find out more about this beautiful country.

ACKNOWLEDGEMENTS

Phew, writing *Within the Heart of Wicked Creatures* wasn't easy. I've heard that second books are supposed to be horribly difficult, and I can only agree.

Unfortunately, it made no difference that I'd already written various stories in the past. With every book, you have to rediscover how to go about writing another one. There are no shortcuts.

When I look back, there were maybe . . . No, I'm not going to start counting how many deadlines were missed or shifted. In the end, the most important thing is that this book, despite absurdly often seeming impossible, still came into the world. I am absolutely delighted with it. (When I finished the most extreme round of editing at around half past one in the morning in Suriname, I danced around the dark living room in a house where everyone else was asleep.)

As is often the case with such projects, I didn't do this alone. This book would never have seen the light of day if my publisher didn't have one hundred per cent confidence in it. That's why I'd like to start by thanking my Dutch publisher, Luna Wong Lun Hing. Not only for all the feedback and brainstorming sessions about *Within the Heart*, but also for your flexibility and support. This was a huge project that took a lot of time – more than expected – and I'm extremely grateful that you gave me all the time and space I needed so that we could make the best – and most beautiful! – version of the book together. I'm also very happy with the sharp insights and feedback from Nina Schouten and Elke Cremers. Your comments were truly indispensable.

Also, I can't forget my wonderful agent, Margot Belet. Thank you for always believing in *Within the Heart* and for working so hard to help the book reach more readers. Let's hope all our nefarious plans work out!

Many thanks to the whole team of Ink Road for taking a chance on an unknown Dutch writer – it means the world to me. Thank you, especially, Clem Flanagan and Leonie Lock, my amazing editors, for your genuine enthusiasm and insight.

Thank you, Laura Watkinson, my brilliant translator, for the wonderful English translation of *Within the Heart*.

This book would never have been written without the full support of my family at a time when I thought I'd never be able to finish another book. Thank you, Mam and Pap, for doing everything you could to make writing this book easier for me. I could dedicate every book I ever write from now on to you for all that you've done for me. (Sorry that I kept bothering you with questions about Suriname at the most random moments.)

Thank you, Anisha Orie and Rewie Orie – my sister and brother, who insisted on being named with both first and last names, because 'otherwise no one will know it's us!' – for your warmth, love and enthusiasm. Thank you, Reshma and Kaby, for all your great suggestions and ideas for the book.

Noa – you knew it was coming – thank you, as always, for tirelessly reading all the pieces I throw your way and for helping me to think through all the plot holes and inconsistencies that come up when writing. Your built-in spellcheck is worth its weight in gold. In a sense, you were an additional, private editor. And thanks too for your positive mindset, which always pulls me out of the doldrums on those difficult days when I think I've written the worst book in living memory.

And of course I can't forget the greatest, coolest writing group in the world (yes, that's what we are). Thank you, Berith Balfoort, for your careful reading, your sharp analysis and your medical knowledge. Without your help, I'm sure I'd have made a lot of mistakes in that area. The same applies in a different field to Doreen Hendrikx: I don't know what the fight scenes would have looked like without your advice as a judoka, and I also benefitted enormously from your economic and trade knowledge. (Now at least it's clear where the fort gets its food from.) Last in line, but certainly no less important: Merel De Keyzer, thank you for the wonderful conversations about culture, politics and language, and how they all merge and blend together. Oh yes, and our conversations about different types of monsters and horror as a genre were sublime. The discussions within our group always help me to understand our complex world a little better, which comes in handy for my stories.

And a quick thank you for Liselotte Schipper, who helped me with the – ahem – 'romantic' relationship between Reza and Priya.

Finally, I would like to thank you, dear reader, for picking up this book and reading it to the very last page – because why else would you be reading this? I hope with all my heart that you enjoyed it.

GLOSSARY

TITLES

Kapten – Literally: captain. In this book, it's a designation for the leader of a small group of soldiers. In Suriname, the Afro-Surinamese people in the interior and some indigenous groups sometimes refer to the head of a village community as 'kapten'.

Basha – The kapten's assistant, second in command in the group of soldiers led by the kapten.

Koelaman – The person who navigates the boat (the korjaal) with his koela (a stick).

Kantrakti – Contract labourer.

CLOTHING

Angisa – A specially folded headscarf worn by Afro-Surinamese women. In this book, it's worn by the Luanan women.

Kamisa – A long piece of fabric worn between the legs, which hangs over a cord or belt at the front and back. A pangi can be worn over it, a brightly coloured, checked cloth. Worn by Afro-Surinamese people in the interior and some indigenous groups. (In this book, it's worn by Luanans and Topuans.)

OBJECTS

Kokolampoe – A tin lamp filled with coconut oil with a cotton wick that's pulled through the spout.

Korjaal (plural korjalen) – A dugout canoe, made from a hollowed-out tree trunk.

FOOD

Bravoe soup – A hearty Afro-Surinamese soup made from various root vegetables, with okra, meat and/or fish (in this book Luanan).

Sukru bakba – Small, sweet bananas.

Jarabaka – A large river fish.

EXPRESSIONS

Mi no sabi – 'I don't know/no idea' in Sranan Tongo (Luan in this book).

Beti – Daughter in Hindi (Suryan in this book).

Didi – Sister in Hindi (Suryan in this book).

ANIMALS

Tigri kati – An ocelot, a medium-sized wildcat found in Suriname. Resembles a smaller version of a jaguar.

RIMA ORIE

Her friends describe her as 'mom friend', 'pure chaos' and 'pulled-another-all-nighter-to meet-her-deadlines-Riem', but in fact Rima Orie is simply an author who loves taking her readers on fantastic adventures to magical worlds.

During the daytime Rima works as a lawyer for the council because hey, every superhero has an ordinary day job to hide what they're really up to, don't they?

Rima's debut, *De Zwendelprins*, was nominated for the Hebban Debut Prize, the Beste Boek voor Jongeren (Best Book for Young People) and De Kleine Cervantes. *Within the Heart of Wicked Creatures* is her second book and was recommended by the Jonge Jury (Young Jury) and won the prize for the Beste Boek voor Jongeren. In 2023, Rima was invited to write a story for the Book Week Gift for Young Adults: *3PAK*.

THE JOURNEY STARTS HERE

As a Young Adult imprint, Ink Road is passionate about publishing fiction with a contemporary and forward-looking focus. We love working with authors who share our commitment to bold and brilliant stories – and we're always on the lookout for fresh new voices and the readers who will enjoy them.

@inkroadbooks

INK-ROAD.COM